Stormy Whether

Certainism: Reason Over Morality

Dr. Martin H.S. Millette

*This book is dedicated to
Esther, my beloved wife
and best friend*

With special thanks to

Peggy Keeran

Professor of Arts and Humanities and

Reference Librarian of the Penrose Library

at the University of Denver

Also I wish express

immense appreciation to

William R. Massa, Jr.,

Archivist of the Department of Manuscripts and Archives

at the Yale University Library

New Haven, Connecticut

Foreword

    My name is David and I was born on November 6, 1920. At my christening my parents named me David Tolstoy Hugenberg. My mother, Mrs. Helena Hugenberg, told me she always loved the name David, and that was the name she wanted for her first son. However, my father, the Protestant Pope of Springfield, Massachusetts, being an erudite pastor, had chosen the middle name Tolstoy from Count Lev Nikolayevich Tolstoy, the famous Russian novelist and social reformer who took it upon himself to defend the Christian religion in Russia at a time when the government sought to utterly destroy religion in his country, and all that represented the useless ideals of religion. Therefore, Count Tolstoy gained the reputation of being a Christian nihilist and also a nonviolent activist in the golden age of his life. My father, the Reverend Rommel Hugenberg, believed that by naming me after Tolstoy, who used the message of the Gospels to defend the Christian religion thought, I would become a religious man in the end and defend the religious tenets of Christianity. But, my egregious father was mistaken, though, since I learned certain unpleasant facts about his ethical teacher. It appears that Count Lev Nikolayevich Tolstoy was somewhat familiar with the Gospels. Nevertheless, like most religious people, the teachings of the Gospels did little for him in the spectrum of transformation. There are those who claimed that the renowned author found what is known as *universal love* in the Gospels. Consequently, this *universal love* appeared periodically in his writings, but Tolstoy tried to live by this so-called *universal love*. So, in the end, I came to the metaphysical conclusion that he took his theory of *universal love* to the extreme, in a literal sense. For Tolstoy was indeed a religious zealot who never learned to master or temper his insatiable appetite, in view of the fact that he himself dealt with his very own *Kreutzer Sonata* (the social prostitution of marriage and how it's inculcated in the minds of young men and women by religious institutions, and also his sexuality).

Tolstoy believed that the human race could only reach the ultimate enlightenment if mankind learned to overcome the weaknesses and obstacles of human sexuality. Throughout the years Tolstoy longed to be freed from his carnal desires, which he never learned to surmount. The irony is that this religious man's carnal desires mastered him. That's why his marriage with his wife Sophia failed. He considered his marriage to be a constant strain and a burden to him. Tolstoy was a religious womanizer and a victim of a certain suppressed predilection. In addition, because of his self-engendered guilt, he tried for a time to follow the rules of self-denial of the Franciscan Brethren. He always failed as he struggled to live above his human weaknesses that he despised. I think that Count Tolstoy, like most religious people, is a prime example of a failed attempt; in the end, their hypocrisy is always revealed to the masses, since most religious people are the ideal hypocrites who hide behind the façade of religion. Like my father, Tolstoy was a religious man who advocated the doctrines of self-control and self-denial, which he believed would eventually lead to the ultimate enlightenment of the human race, but he himself didn't practice what he believed or wrote about in his books. In the end, what drove this great author overboard? The answer is found in the aspects of religion, that immense nemesis of mankind. But it was the tragic loss of Tolstoy's brothers, whom he loved dearly, that drove this great man into the tenets of religion. Prior to 1941, I had also experienced a dual loss in my life; however, reason showed me the way and how to deal with my dual loss through the philosophy of Certainism. It was not so with Count Tolstoy, who used religion as a crutch in his time of grief. Most people aren't aware of the hidden ironic continuum of *War and Peace*, which portrays the conundrum of the human will, in that mankind's lust can be a destructive force.

In his famous novel *Anna Karenina*, he emphasized the glorious appetite of the human race: its carnality, which can evolve to be a destructive element. The fact of the matter remains that these two passions were constant reminders of his weaknesses, which he believed are prevalent in all men. The count wrestled with these flaws all through his life, especially as he advanced in age. And even though he exploited the tenets of religion as a mechanism of conscious denial, like most religious people, I believe he really tried to transcend his carnal desires. I have to say I admire the man. And I wish he had been more certain about his sexuality, for he was a normal man, and all he had to do was embrace what he called "sin and carnal weakness." Then, by being honest with himself, true emancipation and enlightenment would have liberated him in the midst of religious opaqueness. Instead, religion became his addictive panacea: he experimented with the different facets of asceticism as he buried his true feelings in pious good deeds. In his philosophy and moralistic quest he did not discover a rational answer to logical progressivism that would equal his epicurean investigation, which inevitably did not produce a metaphysical denouement, and at the end of his quest he began to question the authenticity, validity, and integrity of religion and its fatuous tenets.

Count Tolstoy's questions about the Russian Orthodox Church eventually caused the leaders in the church to excommunicate him. He was a Russian aristocrat who dressed like a simple peasant, but was an intellect and a gifted author who despised learning. However, the influential writings of Tolstoy reached all the way to India. Gandhi became an ardent disciple of Tolstoy's phenomenal literary work and an activist of nonviolent opposition against the British Empire.

Tolstoy never agreed with the philosophical views of Nietzsche and his theories of how great men will eventually change and impact the world by their insight into certain intelligent issues. Tolstoy believed that the simplicity of the humble and his unrealistic approach of *universal love* would, in the end, conquer all and make the world a better place. He also advocated that the Christian faith is not just a religion. These views did nothing for him; the Russian government saw Tolstoy as a political revolutionary who was creating social unrest by the power of his pen, while the leaders in the religious arena considered him a vile heretic who held some unorthodox views, as he went directly against the status quo of his day. My father told me some years ago about one of his favorite books by Tolstoy, *What Is Art?* First published in 1898, in this book the great nineteenth-century author condemned the famous authors of the world for not living up to the ideal expectations of their vocation.

As a philosopher, Tolstoy held to the opinion that reason and logic were futile in the spectrum of the human quest for meaning. Despite this, my religious father, the Protestant Pope of Springfield, Massachusetts, loved and admired the writings of the late count. His literary work was certainly not lacking in Father's knowledgeable library; nonetheless, from the age of nine, when I first started reading and studying the writings of Tolstoy, I have to admit that I wasn't pleased or impressed to a great degree with Tolstoy's philosophical ideals. However, Nietzsche's views about the ridiculous notions of religion influenced me greatly. Tolstoy was a humanitarian and a great author; nevertheless, he certainly didn't learn the fundamental lessons about human weaknesses or the principles of self-government as related to man. I guess he was looking for the answers in all the wrong places. After some years of studying his writings I came to the exclusive conclusion that this unique individual, with whom my father was so impressed, was both a genius and a renowned author, but also a man who was never really satisfied with his achievements in life.

The years from 1929 to 1936 were called the era of "Stormy Weather." But something incredible happened to me in the year 1930. I was just a boy at the age of ten when I first had the inspiration of my very own philosophy, known as Certainism. Many people may think that philosophy and the realm of childhood don't blend very well, and that children should pay particular attention to the pedagogic field of learning. But on the other hand, I know that this misinformed opinion is totally wrong, because my new philosophy, in fact, came about while in Father's erudite library, studying the Bill of Rights for a school project. My philosophy of Certainism emerged from the depths of the Ninth Amendment, and even at that tender age I knew that most Americans aren't even aware of the enormous privileges that come from this particular amendment. I gazed at the words of this fascinating amendment, which states: *The enumeration in the Constitution of certain rights shall not be construed to deny or disparage others retained by the people.* That's precisely why I love learning, and especially intelligent reading, since the Certainist is a radical explorer of intellectualism. In addition, according to Greek Mythology, freedom represents the highest form of learning. It was the great Greek philosopher Aristotle who was known as par excellence in learning. Therefore, the Certainist knows that, when approaching any subject, especially in the realm of epistemology, he must always review meticulously the contributions of all men as he respectfully critiques their theories. The Certainist knows that his philosophy takes nothing for granted, particularly in the arena of his academic progression and the observation of epistemological data. However, when approaching any subject the Certainist will always review the contributions of all great scholars, criticizing what he believes to be wrong or misleading, as he seeks to adopt new ideas for the purpose of excelling academically.

Certainism advocates that there's no such thing as a genius, only the masters who have learned the great skills of mastering their minds through the method of vigorous academic discipline. Thomas Edison once said: "*Genius is 1 percent inspiration and 99 percent perspiration.*" There's a vast difference in this ratio in the mind of the genius, because to be a mastermind takes more work. The Certainist chooses to develop himself academically by the methodology of 99 percent perspiration of hard work and the disciplining of the mind. Moreover, that's precisely why the Certainist major axiom is the Latin adage *Vir sapientissimus etiam aliquid discere habet*, which means "*For the wisest man has something yet to learn.*" The Certainist knows that he's never satisfied with his achievements and accolades, since there's always room for improvement and excelling academically in a much greater dimension. That's why I love to learn, because the more I learn, the more I become aware that I know nothing. This is the reason for my insatiable desire of always wanting to learn more and more. Furthermore, those leaders in the religious arena would love to silence the relevant fundamental realities of the Ninth Amendment. In the Ninth Amendment it actually states: *The enumeration in the Constitution of certain rights shall not be construed to deny or disparage others retained by the people.* But what do these words mean in conjunction with relativity of reality, and the freedom of individual choices? The noun *enumeration* is, in fact, the counting or the listing of certain things. To be more explicit, it's the listing or counting of certain definite rights initiated in the historical document the Bill of Rights, that rightly belong to the people.

In fact, it is ascertaining the inalienable rights of the people that the government didn't mention in the Bill of Rights, and because a particular right isn't mentioned in it does not mean that the rights of the citizens should be taken for granted. It is the inalienable rights of the people, particularly in the United States, to live in a certain manner of lifestyle; the right to believe in God or not; the right for women to choose to have an abortion—because if the government and religious institutions expect people to be responsible for their children they must give women the right to decide if they want to have children. My philosophy of Certainism is in fact reason over morality, and there's nothing more dangerous in this world than to behold a fool with a purpose. Now, this is the stand of religion. They cry out murder and immorality when it comes to abortion and the gay community; however, at the same time they're denying others their rights in the name of religion. The noun *reason* in Latin is *rationem*, meaning faculty, sanity, and the ability to argue one's point. Reason in the Latin syntax is the ability to think for oneself. Also it is the capability of asking questions, and being able to intelligently argue a point by explaining the logical deduction in one's choice in conjunction with the Ninth Amendment.

For the philosophy of Certainism and the Ninth Amendment are in fact synonymous to the rights of human choices based upon reason as it overrules morality. The Ninth Amendment gives Americans the right to give their children up for adoption, the right to dress how they see fit based on that freedom of choice, the right for teenage boys to have long hair or to be transsexuals, the rights for American parents to bring up their children as they think best. This also includes even if they choose to inculcate neo-Nazi ideals in their children. (*Mein Kampf* is the most uncontroversial book I've ever read, for it deals primarily with the objective rights of the Aryan people and their struggle for self-preservation.) But the crème de la crème of the Ninth Amendment is the right to have homosexual relationships and the right to maintain the privacy of these particular liaisons. That's why Certainism emphasizes the existential fact that whatever people choose to be and do, according to their ideologies, they must make a decisive decision by allowing their reason (*the ability to think for oneself*) to guide them in their free choices. And from the fruition of their decision that they have made in conjunction with Certainism, they should stand by it and shouldn't apologize to those salacious, fatuous hypocrites in the religious community. These people claim to have the "truth"; however, they themselves aren't truthful to what they preach. For that reason, Certainism is the philosophy that will cause mankind to take decisive actions as it is liberated from the shackles of tradition and religion that seeks to think for the masses. And since we've entered the new era of Mass Markets (this period began in 1953), the leaders in the United States should begin to interpret our historical governmental documents, including the Constitution and the Bill of Rights, from a progressive, modern standard of reason, along with the intelligent views of Joseph Schumpeter.

For example, construction destruction: when industries advance in technology they cannibalize the old. Intellectualism and globalization will cause religion to become tomorrow's literature by making it ineffective in its teachings. Destruction is a form of creation, and it's high time that our leaders on Capitol Hill recognize that the old system must be cannibalized by the new ideologies of Certainism. The government of the United States must examine how religious institutions treat the gay community with the same mind-set as the "Black Codes" of the South. Religious institutions forever seek to impose their very own "Gay Codes" through their doctrines of antipathy as they continue to deny gays the social equalities that the Ninth Amendment provides.

As the United States advances in the twentieth century through the means of Mass Markets, the Certainist knows that Certainism is the ideal approach of implementing and substantiating political correctness in the United States, for Certainism holds to the theory of the social development of nations independent of religion, since the teachings of religion are an enormous hindrance to mankind and its progression.

Religion is an embarrassing blip, and the major deficiency that causes men to become imbalanced. It is also the decadent exploiter of the common man. I was a victim of religious abuse. It was my unfortunate circumstance to have a domineering father who sought daily to control us in the name of religion. But my philosophy of Certainism opened my eyes to reason. I know that in the future the time will come when society will cast off the archaic ways of religion, since religion is indeed the stuffy old formal ceremony ridden with the old corpse hags of an ancient superstitious belief.

Throughout the ages history has proven that religion rejects personal freedom. Religious people are so drenched in their beliefs of ideological purity that they think they know what's best for mankind. The approach of religion is in fact very unrealistic and most incommodious to humankind; however, the fact of the matter about religion and religiosity may be somewhat shocking to some individuals who refuse to accept the truth about these people, and what really goes on within the walls of religion. For example, the reality of their *ménage a trois*, and their *Bacha Bazi* (for the priests love to hide their sausage in the altar boys), as these illicit acts occur within the confinement of religious institutions. So, the wicked trade of religion (*the masters of human exploitation*) will soon hear and feel the living reality of the shifting tectonic plates of *Religenocide*, for Certainism is a new philosophy that seeks to accommodate the existential views of reason. In fact, Certainism endeavors to overrule all religious tenets of constraint, since the Certainist does not believe in the infallibility of religion, which seeks to indoctrinate the masses by telling them what to think rather than how to think. Religion is mainly geared to robbing people of their ability to intelligently think for themselves in the spectrum of reason; therefore, the Certainist is a revisionist of religious tenets in the realm of the Ninth Amendment and the reason of man. Reason is the ruling monarch of intellectualism. Without the logical deduction of reason in an individual's life, *stultitia* (Latin for foolishness, which is a constant companion of religion) will now become the interloper of reason.

If reason is not given the sovereign ruling right in the lives of people, mankind will be hindered from reaching the ultimate goal of being the ideal intellect. If mankind is thus hindered then humanity will be hindered from reaching the superlative state of becoming the ideal *Übermensch*. Reason and logical progression are in fact interrelated to the Certainist, who seeks perfection through the pedagogic analysis of intellectualism. The Certainist knows he's far from perfect; however, through his reason he's striving to reach the apex of excellence by the disciplining of his mind via his academic pertinacity. And by his academic tenacity he's reaching toward maturity or completion through the systematic development of his mind as he strives to cultivate his mental acumen. Albert Einstein once said: *"We are, or become, those things which we repeatedly do. Therefore, excellence can become not just an event, but a habit."* The Certainist knows that religion is the greatest hindrance to mankind, as religion is the catalyst that causes the lack of man's mental acuteness. It's the same with religions all over: they're all slaves of a religious regime, like the Nazis. Religious people in particular do everything their leaders and their holy texts tell them to do. They all have one thing in common: they're brainwashed disciples, as their holy texts think for them. These people are very pretentious and fatuous; they're all disciples of a religious fascist's regime. Their so-called holy texts are no different from *Mein Kampf*, which is very similar to Adolf Hitler's rhetoric. Their holy texts have one thing in common, and that's to preach hostility against others, for religious people are fascist bigots. They're all Falangists who're good at crushing opposition through any means. In fact, there are those who might say that some people ought not to be punished for their faith but only for their deeds.

Sometimes their faith causes these zealots to act irrationally and execute some unorthodox deeds in the name of their God. If the Certainist is to believe in a God there must be an intellectual realization of reason that convinces him of the actualization of this deity, since religion is nothing more than an impractical, unrelenting nuisance that has hindered mankind for too long. Religion has been used throughout the ages as a subtle device to cause the atrophy of civilization. Religion has hindered the progression of intellectualism; the progress of science. Consequently, in the end Certainism will eventually become the centralized philosophy that will transcend into the ideal reality when it's recognized as the cognitive factor for mankind. Knowledge is wholly or chiefly derived from pure reason, and intellectualism advocates that reason is the final principle of reality. And when it comes to the fact of reality, the Certainist knows that life can be a *canis* (Latin for bitch) when it's payback time.

Therefore, in the future Certainism that has already produced its first offspring *Religenocide*, through Bill 67, which will silence religion forever. (This bill will eventually emerge from the theory of Certainism, when it convinces the leaders of the world to control the disincentive rhetorics of religious institutions.) Not only does religion need to be silenced irrevocably, but it also needs to be deprived from every secular influence. So Bill 67 is going to be like the *Verbotsgesetz Law* of 1947, which prohibits the voice of Nazism to be heard in the nation of Austria. Furthermore, just with the *VerbotsG Act* (a synonym of the *Verbotsgesetz Law*), which prohibits the rhetoric and thus the rise of all neo-Nazi activities in Austria, Bill 67 will espouse *Religenocide*, and thus all rhetoric in the religious arena from being spoken against certain citizens. Also, Certainism will demonstrate to humanity that religion is actually a dangerous institution to society, and all those individuals who value the attribute of their very own *Ahura Mazda*, mankind's way of wise reasoning, will prove positively that relevant truth is much more important than the mundane teachings of absolute truth, which religion has taught for too long.

Certainism is a philosophy that will inevitably inspire a new revelatory movement against the bigotry of religion. Religion was in fact the first form of all superstitions, which has blinded the human race to all logical reason, and this is a *nuda veritas* (hard fact) according to historical data.

Chapter One

The Reverend Rommel Hugenberg

My demons of religion haunted me. I saw myself running in a strange forest, when suddenly I realized it was getting dark and the chill of the cold weather felt like daggers through my body.

The fierce wind rustled through the trees like an unrelated phenomena. This scared me, but was a declaration that autumn was here. I stopped and looked at myself, wondering what was happening to me, and what I was doing in these cold woods dressed in my pajamas.

I felt as if I was there and a part of me was not subconsciously there, but I saw myself running as if I had to flee like a bird from a life that's ensnared in a sadistic dilemma. So I continued running like a marathon runner, wishing to escape from a life that could only be described as a nightmare that transcended into a ghastly reality.

I continued with great speed, even though by now I was feeling the exhaustion of my perilous journey; however, I knew I had to escape. At that moment, unexpectedly, I realized I was falling from a steep cliff at a violent speed. I tried to gain control of my helpless body as I screamed out, releasing my frustration, longing to be awakened from an incessant nightmare that had haunted me from the age of nine.

I fell from my bed and my feeble body crashed to the floor of my dark and solitary room. The sound of my scream awakened me and I gasped for breath. It was nothing more than the unremitting nightmare that had come periodically for the past five years.

I lay on the floor for a few minutes trying to collect my thoughts. All I heard was the sound of my heavy breathing in the silence of a cold autumn night. Eventually, the uncontrollable tears came rushing down. The reality of these recurring nightmares was too much for a young boy to deal with, and after a while I said to myself in a discreet voice, "I must suppress this anguish in my heart, for oh, how I wish I had never been born!"

After a couple of minutes I staggered up from the floor. I tried to remember what had happened the previous evening to thrust me once again into these nightmares.

I was able sometime afterward to fully stand upright. I tried to approach my bed but fell on my knees next to it. Weakened by the psychological agony of the nightmare, the lower part of my body remained on the floor, and my torso rested on the bed. Then suddenly I reached for my pillow and plunged my head into it as though wanting to suffocate the life from my mortal body. Then once again I began to cry. I wished I could stop, but the tears came like an uncontrollable reservoir that continued to flow. By now my body ached from the fall, and my head from the mental anguish of this repulsive nightmare.

Shivering from the cold in my room, I said, my jaw quivering as my teeth shook uncontrollably, "W-why am I f-feeling s-so c-cold?" I felt the wet and cold garment, and realized that my pajamas bottoms were wet with my urine. These nightmares always overwhelmed me. I remembered falling from the cliff; it was always incredibly realistic, and the screaming always interrupted my sleep.

The embarrassment was too much for me. It was good that I didn't share my bedroom with my sibling, particularly my brother, Georg.

The first person I thought about was my father. This was not a pleasant thought, and his invidious behavior gave me no pleasure. Throughout the years he had become *persona non grata* to me.

My mother had taught me how to conceal my wet garments, because I knew my father would severely punish me (corporal punishment) if he discovered that I urinated on myself when I had these unpleasant nightmares. I heard the old grandfather clock in the hall ticking away as I stumbled to the lamp on my desk.

I gently turned it on hoping that no one would see the light in my room. Afterward, I went to my closet to get another pair of pajamas, and entered my bathroom to have a hot shower. We live in New England, in Springfield, Massachusetts. Our house is like an English mansion; it's huge, with four stories and seven bedrooms.

It is one of the homes built in the late nineteenth century by my grandfather, just before he died. Grandfather left it for my father as an inheritance. The house is located near the Connecticut River, with a conspicuous view. The fifty-by-fifty house stands upon thirty acres. In addition, every bedroom has its own bathroom. This was quite convenient for me—the privacy, that is. I stood beneath the shower enjoying the hot water and the steam.

It was really soothing, like a therapeutic remedy for these nightmares. Most boys at the age of fourteen are staunch disciples of unhygienic practices, but I'm one of the few who's not like that. At the age of twelve, I really became self-conscious about my personal hygiene.

Consequently, I recognized that squalor was not my cup of tea. Therefore, I cleansed myself to alleviate any unpleasant odors from my body. I came out of the shower, dried myself, put on clean pajamas, and was pleased that I hadn't wet my bed, only the floor, which I cleaned up with paper towels. Afterward I sat on my bed, thinking about my life and the person who was culpable for this problem of mine. "My father, of course, and his monstrous antisocial attitude toward us!" I said, but by now I felt like an individual in one of William Shakespeare's plays, performing a soliloquy.

When these nightmares happened, it would be a while before I fell back to sleep. And so, I would just think about the problems that existed in our home, or I would try to read, for reading is a natural penchant of mine, and then maybe I would fall asleep.

My father, the Reverend Rommel Hugenberg, is like a fiend with a wicked mind filled with fetid darkness. Throughout the years, he taught us that man is a *tripartite* being (in Latin, it is *tripartitus*). For example, a human being consists of spirit, soul, and body, but because of his duplicitous nature I wondered if any of us really know who we are, and what we're capable of doing. There's a famous Latin axiom, *homo homini lupus*, which means "man's inhumanity to man." Mankind is like a rapacious animal that seeks to devour its own. I've learned this from my father the reverend, while observing him throughout the years. Most people live a tripartite lifestyle: a public life, a private life, and—the most intriguing one of all—a secret life. This life is submerged in a clandestine façade, for the person who lives a covert life no one actually knows. This secret life can either expose or define us. Those who don't practice what they preach are the biggest hypocrites, and are fooling no one but themselves.

What most people fail to recognize is that a man's reputation will always precede him. Reputation is what others may think of us as an individual based on our behavior and actions. Somehow most people fail to understand this principle: the people with whom you live will also formulate an exclusive opinion about you.

Character is the real you, and we cannot hide from ourselves. We must be honest with ourselves, and should not live a life that is steeped in contradictions. Because no one incident makes anyone what he or she is; it is a series of events that makes us what we are. We're molded by what we hear and see in the home, especially from our parents, for these are the most impressionable years of our lives: childhood.

My father inadvertently taught me more about people and the duplicitous nature of mankind than anyone else. What we heard and saw in our home was very different from how he acted when he was in church. It's by certain unpleasant experiences that I've learned that Certainism is more important than morality. For example, I'm certain that the day is coming when I'll no longer have to subject myself to my father's religious Draconian code. And when I leave no amount of religious tenets will ever govern me again, because my intention will be to irrevocably sever all ties with him and all religious institutions. However, I could never abandon my mother, brother, and sisters, for I'm aware that one's attitude is primarily judged on the epistemological and psychological observation of others. But there are decisions I'm compelled to make, if I'm going to keep my sanity and better myself in the humanistic sphere of this world. I've had enough of my father and his regimented God. My philosophy as a teenager is that I will not be controlled by any religious institution that preaches morality but has leaders who don't live by what they preach.

Hence, my pragmatic code of certainty will indeed overrule all levels of morality, for this is my choice! Certainty is the quality and the established fact of absolute known truth, but what exactly is truth? Philosophically, it can be described as that thing which pertains to the moment of a relevant truth. Simpletons confuse religion and pragmatism, yet morality and reality are actually philosophically antithetical, and do not go hand in hand. Morality is synonymous to such words as ethics, virtue, rectitude, and chastity. Abortion may be illegal now, but I believe the day is coming when abortion will be made lawful in this land. And I'm fully aware that because something is lawful does not make it morally right, but according to pragmatic common sense, abortion is more certain than morality. Why? Because it solves a self-engendered problem for the moment, existentially speaking; abortion may be morally wrong, but it will correct a momentary dilemma for the mother. There are those in my father's church whom I call *Hugenbergnites* because they're so predictable. I know exactly what they'll say about my noxious views: "Obviously, David can't be so myopic and wicked as to have such an audacious opinion." I know my views are somewhat unorthodox, and are primarily based on a postmodern, epistemological methodology. In spite of this, I've kept these views to myself for the past years, but the day will come when I'll share them with my imperialistic, post-Hegelian, authoritative father. These are not the views of a prepubescent, angst-ridden youth, but my father sees me as nothing more than a sophomoric individual.

Nevertheless, these philosophical beliefs of mine are the result of monumentally bad experiences with him. My father's ancestry is of German origin, but he was born in 1891 in the United States. The president at that time was Benjamin Harrison, our twenty-third president, 1889–1893. In my father's Bavarian lineage, Fritsche Rohm Hugenberg was the first to migrate with his family, in 1801, when America was still a young nation.

Fritsche and his family came from Erfurt, a city in Thuringia, located in central Germany. My father is a very proud and arrogant man—that is, when it comes to his Bavarian blood. And it's an incessant habit of his to make fun of minorities, especially blacks and Jews, whom he considers to be subhuman. One of his major problems is his favorite descriptors and personal remarks about certain people, which my mom finds to be rude.

He's truly a very handsome man, and it's not because he's my father that I have this opinion. It's a factual, positive observation about him, even though I have great antipathy for the man. His stature is six feet five inches, he weighs about 220 pounds, and his eyes are Atlantic deep blue. His eyes are very cold, like a man not in touch with his emotions. His hair is golden blond; his skin is a light pinkish color. His nose is very straight and not aquiline. His lips are thin and his ears match the structure of his face. He came from a family of nine siblings, and he was the second-to-last boy among his brothers. His parents had ten children in all; my dad was number nine. His father was a wealthy architect with his own company, which was very successful. Grandfather Hans and his eldest son designed buildings and homes throughout the country. Grandfather Hans inherited this company from his father, Reinhardt, who inherited it from his father, Rudolf. The tradition of my ancestors has always been that the eldest son would inherit the company, and therefore would carry on the family business and name, for money was never a problem with my father's relatives. And even though Grandfather Hans is dead, my uncle still carries on the family successful business. Dad always spoke about his father, how he was a severe disciplinarian but was a hardworking German American. However, it appears that Grandfather Hans did not abuse his wife or his children.

My dad, the Reverend Hugenberg, decided to become a minister. He told us that he wanted to help people and give back to his community. My father is indeed a collegiate pastor, but before he attended seminary in 1914, he already had acquired a college degree from Stanford University of California, in 1913. Interestingly, Stanford University was founded in 1891, which was the year my father was born. Grandfather Hans would have preferred that my father attend Harvard University.

The agreement in our trust fund is that we (the progeny) can choose a university at our discretion. For some reason Dad did not want to attend any of the universities in the New England region. After Dad graduated from the Lutheran Theological Seminary at Philadelphia in 1918, not only was there a high demand for him to lecture at his former seminary (periodically at certain seminars), for he graduated with honors (majoring in church finances and administration), but he also taught history and politics twice a week at a secular college in New England for several years.

The man is a genius, and I love him, but my love for him is somewhat perplexing. It's like the Oedipal love resulting from an Oedipus complex. This is how I feel about my father: I love him, but I also hate what he does to us, and sometimes I wish I could kill him and liberate my mother from his misogynistic, machismo, tyrannical rule. He's a shrewd, litigious, perspicacious intellect, who exemplifies a controversial misanthropic nature toward his family, and because of this I conclude that my father is a non-theistic Protestant minister. Not that I'm saying that I believe in the God of the Bible.

I feel people like him, who profess that they're God's emissaries, would naturally demonstrate their faith and love to the members of their own family as well, not only those outside the perimeters of the home.

The man is an excellent orator; nevertheless, he lacks diplomacy with his wife and children. Our house has never really been a happy home. My mother is nervous whenever my father is at home. It's really amazing how she's a different person when he's not at home, and on several occasions I knew she was crying.

One Friday evening when I came home from school, Mother was in the kitchen crying. I approached her wondering what was wrong. I thought she was ill. But to my amazement, when I entered the kitchen she was sitting on a stool facing the window and staring at the river, and when I tried to touch her she pulled away, as if she was angry with me or I had some contagious disease. When she pulled away I saw that there were bruises on her wrist. Also, her right eye was discolored, as if she had been slapped in the face. Then, she walked out of the room. I knew she didn't want us to know what had happened.

Eventually, I walked out of the kitchen, went into my bedroom and locked the door behind me. I felt terrible for my mother. I wished there was something I could do to help her in this grave situation. But I knew who was responsible for this: my father.

Sunday church service was always an unpleasant religious experience for us. It was like a long sentence of death as we dealt with these wretched religious people. That following Sunday, somehow, and I don't understand it, Mother looked as if nothing had happened to her eye. When we arrived at the church, Father's topic was "How to live out your Christianity." His sermon, as usual, was the same boring, snoring, and smothering redundant message.

I didn't want to hear the man and his meaningless words, which were totally different from his lifestyle at home. I couldn't wait for the inquisition service to come to an end. Besides, it was all a show as he adorned himself in his religious vestments.

Nothing ever changed at home: my siblings and I, in the earlier years of our lives, when we were naïve, competed for our father's affection and attention. However, all this changed throughout the years. We couldn't tolerate his duplicitous lifestyle anymore, for the man personified a religious devil. And when he's up there on the pulpit, it's as if the devil has transformed himself into a temporary angel.

It was all a pretentious façade then. I muttered gingerly, in the midst of this boring church service, "Why in blazes doesn't one of us just tell

Dad what his duplicitous lifestyle is doing to us? It's as if the man is slowly but surely killing us." But the insufferable message continued to flow as if from the lips of the grand inquisitor general, Tomas de Torquemada, and the meaningless, macabre religious ceremony continued. My mind wandered amusedly and intensively from this abattoir and into the oblivion of the past, as I ruminated about my beloved hero, whom I love to hate: the Reverend Rommel Hugenberg.

When my father graduated in 1913, from Stanford University, he was a young man. And this was the year that Woodrow Wilson became president of the United States. My father was twenty-two years old, to be exact, and it was one year before the outbreak of the Great War. Somehow my father felt robbed of the opportunity of fighting in the Great War of 1914, since he wanted to serve his country.

Ever since that unpleasant moment last Friday, I realized not only was my father verbally abusive to my mother—for he loves to use his favorite descriptors—he's also physically abusive to Mom.

She's always pleasant to him and submits to his authority. The Lutheran Church vehemently preaches about the role of women and how they should be submissive and obedient to their husbands, especially if the man is a clergyman.

Consequently, I thought that the executive and deacon board members were not aware of my father's crude behavior and his livid tongue. Sometime later, I learned that the majority of the leaders in the church are just like the man they called their pastor. They're all the same: abusive like my father; cruel men hiding behind the church in the name of God.

I continued to ruminate about the horrid situation and us. Because of my father, and my Certainist views, I had made a decisive decision last Friday, which I knew would permanently change my life forever.

I decided that I'll never want a relationship with the God of my father and his cruel servants. My mind was made up, that the day I leave my father's house I'll never return, nor serve his oppressive, misogynistic, megalomania God that enjoys taking advantage of women and innocent children in the name of religion.

On Friday evening after we had completed our chores and homework, the entire family, except for my mother, sat in the family dining room for dinner. My father was very quiet during dinner. My eldest sister, Jena, who is seventeen will leave for college next summer, took some hot soup to Mom.

Georg, my brother, is ten years old. He loves spending time by the river and helping me groom the horses. Maria is twelve; she enjoys reading just about anything, especially poetry.

Father ate as if nothing had happened—that is, the unpleasant situation between them on Friday. We retired that evening. The following day, Saturday, consisted mainly of chores and studies. Then came Sunday, which was the same mundane routine and all of us had to attend church. My ruminating led to my uncle, who presently runs Grandfather Hans's architecture business. He fought in the war and came back a hero. I wondered if my father might have been as lucky as Uncle Friedrich, to return from the war with minimal injuries and live to tell the tale of the Great War. And as I continued to ruminate during my father's sermon, my mind also reflected on the historical event; when President Thomas Woodrow Wilson addressed the Senate on April 2, 1917. America declared war on Germany on April 6, but war wasn't declared on the Austria-Hungary Empire until December 7, 1917. And it was only a few weeks after that Congress, declared war on Germany, in the month of May, passed the National Conscription Act, for volunteers to join the military. However, few young men were eager to join the fight in Europe.

Then, on June 5, all men between the ages of twenty-one and thirty had to register for the draft. That was when Uncle Friedrich had no choice but to join the army. Soon after, there was a wave of patriotism throughout the land and more than ten million young men enlisted to fight in the Great War.

What's so amazing to me is how a man who claims to be a clergyman could display such a degree of antipathy toward blacks in this land. It's shameful that those brave young men (descendants of Africans) had to fight in segregated units. In addition, they discovered that Europe was much more tolerant than the United States of their music, jazz.

This is precisely what gets me angry about my father: I just can't stand his racial slurs about blacks and Jews. It's like he's resentful that those minorities fought in the war, and he was hindered because of his minor injury. Most of the members in the Holy Lutheran Church where he preaches were not aware that he's partially deaf in his left ear.

This accident, if I should call the unfortunate event such, came about when Dad was a boy, at the age of nine. His younger brother, Dietrich, who at that time was six, thoughtlessly took a sharp pencil and forced it, for the sake of curiosity, to see how far it would penetrate into his brother's left ear. This inevitably severely damaged Dad's hearing ability, affecting his tympanic membrane; since the accident his left ear has always given him problems, especially when it gets cold in the winter. After a number of years my father learned to live with his partial handicap. But this was the grave obstacle that prevented him from being accepted in the army.

Even though Dad wears spectacles, he's not comfortable with people knowing about his injury. So, throughout the years he has also mastered the skill of reading lips, for this is truly a plus for him being able to competently hear. Now, because of my father's looks and stature he thinks he's perfect, and above all, his great intellect makes him feel superior. Hence, when he sees someone who may not be pleasant to look at, according to his standards, he feels compelled to make his personal remarks about the person. However, Mom finds this very disturbing. She said, "I really don't like your father's negative comments about blacks and Jews. They make me feel uncomfortable. And furthermore, I don't want my children growing up thinking it's okay to make fun of people who may be different from us. I want my children to know that it takes all sorts to make the world complete and whole."

Mother felt that his personal remarks were nothing more than racial expressions and the world didn't need to have another racist, particularly a man who's a Protestant minister. Mother would always try to teach us to look at the person inside, and not at the external aspect.

And because of Mom my siblings and I never agree with Father's personal remarks about people, because we know it's wrong to discriminate.

In spite of his shortcomings, he's an intellectual dilettante who enjoys stimulating debates, with his friends and sometimes with us. There are many topics that my father can intelligently discuss; nonetheless, the topics that intrigue him the most are politics, history, and social issues.

Consequently, without his influence I don't think that my siblings and I would have reached such an echelon of intellectual insight at such an early stage in our lives. On the second floor of our house, Father has an extensive library that's filled with information on every topic in the affairs of world history and civilization. I called it "an intellectual center that is tantamount to education."

Oh yes, now I remember what happened that Sunday evening. I was in my room, which is on the third floor; the time was exactly eight thirty p.m. Father likes us to be in bed by nine o'clock sharp. I had just finished my homework, and decided to venture into the library on the second floor. I entered the room and began reading about Theodore Roosevelt and Woodrow Wilson, because these two former presidents of ours are my favorite intellectual heroes, whom I really admire.

Most people aren't aware that these two presidents were the only two Western leaders in the twentieth century who were awarded the Nobel Peace Prize, for efforts toward humanity. Theodore Roosevelt is my hero because he fought in the Spanish-America War of 1898; he called it a "splendid little war."

In 1906, President Roosevelt was the first beneficiary to receive the Nobel Peace Prize outside the continent of Europe. He was the first president to make conservation a political issue, when he signed the bill creating Crater Lake in Oregon as a national park, in May 1902.

This of course was one of his first humanitarian acts while in office; however, in total, he created five national parks in his tenure as president. He was one of those politicians who understood the science behind politics, and knew that if an individual has a personality problem, such as a low self-esteem, he'll never be an excellent politician. These were simple philosophical principles that Theodore Roosevelt comprehended, because he was one of the most electrifying politicians of the twentieth century.

President Woodrow Wilson was the only president with a PhD, from Johns Hopkins in 1886. I was passionately drawn to these two men of great intellectual minds, but my favorite was President Woodrow Wilson, because somehow I felt I have a lot in common with this great man, on the grounds that Woodrow Wilson's father was also a Protestant minister. Unlike myself, the president was a religious man.

As I continued with this enthralling journey of knowledge I became oblivious to the time, as my journey of reading took me deeper into an expedition of seeking further information about the man that mesmerized me.

I don't enjoy only reading, but I have a natural penchant for learning. The more I learn, the more I become conscious that I know nothing; hence, the insatiable desire for learning and reading. My father's extensive library continues to draw me like a scholar addicted to academics.

That night as I continued with my reading quest for knowledge, I learned certain things that are extremely profound about World War I, Germany, and the United States. I had never heard about the foreign minister, Arthur von Zimmermann, and his role in conjunction with the United States and the Great War.

Most people knew that America entered the war because of the provocation, the sinking of the Cunard liner *Lusitania*, which a German torpedo sank in the month of May 1915. The ship carried on board more than one thousand passengers, 123 of whom were Americans, who lost their lives in the attack. During the months of February and March, before the sinking of the *Lusitania*, the Germans had already, in fact, sunk several American ships as an act of provocation, because the president had said that, "America was too proud to fight." Then, President Woodrow, being a high-minded intellect, decided not to declare war on Germany until the Germans had committed an obvious feat against the American people. But in fact, there were two main events that thrust America into the war of 1917. The first was Germany's decision to deliberately attack and sink merchant ships in international waters, without a word of warning. The second was the "Zimmermann telegram," in which the foreign minister, Arthur von Zimmermann, sent a memo via telegram to the German minister in Mexico, requesting him to work toward an agreement with the Mexican and Japanese governments. On August 23, 1914, Japan had declared war on Germany.

The purpose of Zimmermann's plan was a direct aggression launched against the American people, and his plans were to use Mexico as an enticement, with the offer of returning the states of Texas, Arizona, and New Mexico to the Mexican government. But the British naval intelligence discovered and thwarted his tactics, revealing Germany's machinations against America. The plans of the Germans were published on the front page of newspapers on March 1, 1917. Then, the president addressed the Senate on April 2, 1917.

But there was also another extraordinary historical event that happened with America that changed the course of her history in the early twentieth century. The Jones Act, on March 2, 1917, allowed the island of Puerto Rico to became a territory, but not a state, of the United States. This granted the inhabitants of that country automatic U.S. citizenship and the privileges that came with being a citizen of America.

However, the U.S. government's selective draft was also extended to the new territory, Puerto Rico, and about eighteen thousand men were drafted into the Great War. I said to myself, "Isn't history amazing, how—"

But before I could finish my expression of amazement, Father entered the library with an look on his face that I'll never forget. He shouted at me, saying, "What are you doing in here? And at this late hour!"

At that same moment, I glanced at the clock in the room, not believing what I saw: 12:40 a.m. It was as if I had gotten myself into a quagmire with Father while he continued in his abusive tone.

"I've told you in the past, you're not allowed in this room without my permission, boy!"

"Y-yes, F-Father, but I-I'm sorry."

I stuttered, trying to find the right words to express my apology to him, but it was only a matter of time before he struck me.

"You stupid, insolent boy, what the fuck is wrong with you?" At that moment Father violently snatched the book out of my hands as he said, "There's a certain type of insubordination going on in this house, but I'll not stand for it, David! Do you hear me, boy?"

My legs began to shake as I tried to control my body, standing before my father. With that, he slapped me across my face, and I fell into the chair where I had sat for several congenial hours reading.

It was just like him, because he's frequently discommoding the tranquility in our home. I just sat in the chair, holding my tongue, wishing I could fight back. But I decided to remain quiet, as he quoted from the Bible, "'Honor your father and mother,' for it is the first and only commandment with a promise! Must I remind you of this?"

"N-no, F-Father!"

"Then get to bed, you foolish boy!"

Without hesitation, I ran out of the library, feeling demeaned by my father.

I locked my door behind me, crying silently but with much disappointment, and I said to myself, "I wish I had never been born! How I wish I was a bird and could fly away from this cage of hell!" Once again I began to cry, for this wasn't the familiar behavior pattern of a boy, but the dealings of a hard, religious, regimented father. "I try so hard to win my father's approval, but it's like he resents me!" After a few minutes, I decided I needed to rest, because I had a test Monday morning, during first period, about the Platt Amendment of 1901. "Well, enough of my ruminating about the Reverend Rommel Hugenberg. I need to fall asleep." I slipped into a deep and restful sleep, hoping not to dream again.

Chapter Two

A Congregation of Hypocrites

That night I was fortunate to enjoy three restful hours of sleep, with no interruptions of my chilling nightmare. The following morning I was awakened by several knocks on my door, and as I tried to gain consciousness, I shouted, "Give me minute!" I stumbled to the door and unlocked it, and there was Mother.

She said, "David, you've overslept. Son, you're going to be late if I don't drive you to school."

I responded, "I'm sorry, Mom, but I didn't get back to sleep until four a.m.."

"Never mind, David. Your father was called away early this morning, and your brother and sisters have already left for school. They tried to wake you up because we heard your alarm clock going off for about two minutes. So Jena and Maria knocked on your door several times, but it was bolted tight, and you didn't answer so they thought that maybe you were out of it. So I told them to go on and I would drive you to school today."

"Gee, thanks, Mom! I'll wash up and get ready."

But before Mom could turn away I was compelled to ask her why Dad was called away early that morning. "Is everything all right?"

"No, David, I'm afraid that the Reverend Frank Williams died this morning around four thirty-five, in his sleep, and your father was called away because of this unexpected emergency."

I was stunned into silence for a few seconds, and then I mumbled, "A congregation of hypocrites, minus one."

Mother responded, "Sorry, did you say something, David?"

"No, Mom, just a moment of my *soliloquium*." Then I asked, "How is Mrs. Williams coping with this sudden loss?"

"Well, David, I suppose not well. No one is ever really prepared for the unexpected call of death that comes like a thief."

As I closed the door behind me there was an inundation of the unpleasant memories of what had occurred a few hours prior: Father and the library. I sat at my desk thinking about the previous Friday evening: the bruises on Mother's wrist, her left eye, the weekend, and that particular Sunday, which culminated with Dad.

It was a typical autumn morning in the New England region, gray and cold, and it looked like it was going to rain. I just sat there staring at the trees, remembering the horror of the nightmare that had disturbed my sleep. And the awful reality of the cliff, which always seemed to engulf me. Then I ran my hands through my hair, because I couldn't help but think about my grueling indignant father.

Just then, I became conscious of the time, which compelled me to get ready for school. Eventually, I rose from my desk and headed for the shower, walking with great hesitation to my bathroom. After brushing my teeth, I slowly undressed myself, admiring my nude physique while I climbed into the tub.

I was growing up and becoming a young man, with very fine features just like my father's. However, I hoped I'd never treat my wife and children the way he treated us. The water and the steam were refreshing as I stood beneath the hot water.

It was like a strange occurrence: whenever I closed my eyes when taking a shower I could see myself as though looking down from above, admiring my nude physique as the hot water trickled through the pipeline to my hair while each molecule discovered my body in the hot steam. I love to take hot showers, particularly in autumn and winter. It's so soothing, and it actually alleviates any stress that I'm experiencing.

About seven minutes later I climbed out of the tub and dried myself, gazing into the fogged mirror. I wiped it dry with paper towels so that I could have a better look at myself. My height was approximately five feet nine inches and I weighed exactly 120 pounds. I looked just like my dad, except my hair was a reddish-blond color. And from the early age of eight my body had started to become muscular and very lean.

Before putting on my underwear I took a good look at my body, gazing at my rectus abdominis, the muscle that pulls the torso toward the hips. I loved to do crunches in the privacy of my bedroom.

In fact, at this tender age I could actually see the sculpting of my six-pack as I continued to gaze at my rectus abdominis. I started to admire my stomach and how my abs went all the way down to my genitals, in a V-shape, and my broad shoulders. That complemented my stature, making my waist look even much smaller because of the width of my shoulders.

I stood in a trance. There was a knock of interruption, as if Mother was trying to say, get moving! I heard her say from the other side of the door, "David, your breakfast is getting cold!"

"I'll be ready in five minutes!" Just then, I realized the time. I had to stop this daydreaming and get going, or else I might have to stay for detention. And I knew I couldn't afford that, especially with my tight-ass religious father.

I decided to hustle and was down the stairs and into the corridor in no time. Mother was waiting patiently for me. We headed for the garage and were soon on our way. The atmosphere in the car was one of dignified silence.

My mother is a very private person and I knew she wouldn't want me to worry about Father and her. So I simply went along with the dignified silence in the vehicle. Then Mother initiated a dialogue by saying, "What happened to you this morning? I heard you scream, and about twenty minutes afterward, not wanting to disturb your father, I discreetly left the room for the purpose of checking on you. But when I knocked on your door you didn't respond, so I presumed that maybe you were sound asleep."

"I sorry, Mom, for disturbing you, but I guess that when you came to check on me I was taking a shower."

"Another bad dream?"

"Yes, and it's always the same recurring nightmare."

"So I guess you cleaned up after you urinated on yourself?"

"Yes, Mom, and I placed the wet pajamas in my laundry basket. However, I didn't wet my bed or the bed linen. When I fell from my bed I wet the floor."

Mother continued with her cordial conversation as she drove. The drive is about ten minutes, and Mom said, "You know, it's a plus for you that your father is a heavy sleeper, since you've been having your nightmares since the age of nine. And Rommel's partial deafness is also a good thing. He'll never hear you, considering the size of the house."

"Yes, Mom, I'm sure glad that Dad will never know about my disturbing dreams, which most of the time cause me to wet my bed."

Mother responded, "It's better for the both of us that he never knows about this!"

I turned my face to the window, enjoying the fabulous view of the New England autumn, the color of the trees, and endeavoring to discreetly dissuade any further encouragement of this unpleasant topic. For when I think about wetting my bed, particularly at my age, it really troubles me and causes me to have a low opinion about myself. I'm eternally grateful to Mom that my siblings are not aware of my dilemma, which has plagued me for the past five years.

Finally, we arrived at the front of my school. It was exactly ten minutes before the bell rang.

"Thanks, Mom, I'll see you later."

She responded, "Love you, and have a good day."

My friends were all outside in our special corner of the school ground: Daniel McCrory, Jr., Tobey Scott, Harry Adams, Jack Eden, Ryan Whishaw, James Lear, and Jesse Atwood.

My best friend is the one and only Daniel McCrory, Jr. He lives about three miles from my house, and we have been friends since the age of five. Daniel and I have a lot in common, even though he's Catholic and his ancestors came from Ireland. I guess that would make him an Irish American.

My father didn't like Daniel or his parents, because Dad believed that Protestants and Catholics could not agree on anything, much less be genuine friends. However, my views and philosophical theory of Certainism (the active participation of reason over morality) has always overruled my father and his religiosity, particularly his hypocritical Lutheran tenets.

As I walked to the gang they greeted me with cheerful humor; surprisingly, they had all been informed about the death of the Reverend Williams.

"Hi, David," Daniel said to me, fondling his crotch. "So, we heard that the one second to your father is dead!"

"Yeah, and I can't believe it, hurrah! At least that's one less religious hypocrite I'll have to deal with. That man was so crabby. Either he was one horny bastard, or his hemorrhoids made him the most disagreeable clergyman I've ever met!" The gang all started to laugh simultaneously as we continued to debunk the religious cadaver.

Tobey finally asked a question about the late Reverend Williams. "So, David, how did you cope with him and his grouchiness?"

"I didn't. I simply ignored the self-righteous bastard. And most of the time I would cuss him mentally by saying *futue te ipsum*!" (Latin was the gang's sophisticated way of using profanity in an intellectual style.)

Everyone laughed in a hilarious manner, until some of us fell to the ground, holding our stomachs. By now, the rain was becoming more intense, and it's a good thing that we were all under the school shed. As our intense and humorous conversation continued to escalate, the bell rang. We agreed that we would finish this droll conversation at lunch. As we proceeded to our classes, I was certain that I was prepared for the test dealing with the Platt Amendment of the early twentieth century.

By this time, the sound of the rain on the roof was so deafening that it almost drowned out the voices of the students as they walked and talked about their weekends while headed to their classrooms. When I entered my classroom, I thought, *This should be interesting. I'm competent enough to teach this class and to lead the students in this test, assuring them an excellent grade.*

My teachers could never aptly appreciate my intellectual and oratorical prowess, for most of them thought I was too pugnacious.

When I first learned about their ridiculous opinion, it gnawed at me, but when I discovered my theory of Certainism some years ago, at the age of ten, it simply taught me that people's misinformed opinions must never keep me in bondage, or move me.

(My revelatory theory of Certainism has encouraged me to break the status quo and define myself as I choose; that is, *stare decisis* (stand by my decisions), for it's always better to consider opportunities, existentially speaking. In the future, when I'm older, life may limit my choices. Therefore, I'm ecstatic that I discovered this groundbreaking theory, which I'm certain will one day supplant religion and its superstitious ideals. Certainism will eventually become the centralized philosophy that will transcend into the ideal reality, since religion hinders the progression of intellectualism. But getting back to that morning's test...)

I read and studied the science behind the Platt Amendment for about six weeks, going thoroughly through almost every book in my father's erudite library. I discovered that the Platt Amendment was actually an official document, which Congress passed for the purpose of controlling Cuba's rights from making treaties with other nations, and having monetary gain such as borrowing money from other nations.

America broke away from Great Britain because of colonialism, a menacing giant, and heavy taxation, and because of the unjust rule of King George III; the people of America wanted their independence. The Spanish-American War was fought in the late nineteenth century, and the conflict of this hostility stemmed from the problem between the United States and Spain. The core of this political dilemma was Cuba's plight for independence from the old Spanish Empire of Europe.

And when America got involved in this struggle, the main objective was purely selfish: commerce, and expansionism in the clandestine scheme of imperialistic ambitions. Furthermore, the American government declared war on Spain, using the unexplained alleged reason of a battleship, the *Maine*, which was strangely destroyed in the Havana harbor.

Spain had agreed to consent to the freedom of Cuba. In a turn of events, by the end of the war, Spain decided to give the United States two of its former colonies: Puerto Rico in the Caribbean and Guam in the Pacific.

Therefore, after many negotiations Spain received twenty million dollars from the United States and America received the Philippines in exchange for its monetary contribution. The Senate, however, was not in total agreement about the peace treaty of 1898, and many of the people in the United States vehemently protested about this treaty. The citizens of America held to the opinion that the United States was becoming a menacing colonial bully, just like their former oppressor, Great Britain.

The famous American author Mark Twain disclosed his observation, after carefully studying the document of this subtle and uncertain treaty of 1898, that it was mainly for the conquest of the American government.

There was no intention of granting freedom to the people of the Philippines, rather of subjugation as America flexed its muscles to a weak nation. All this was done in the name of expansionism and in the pretext of the treaty of 1898. And since the expansionists were in favor of the benefits of this treaty, they believed that the American navy had to have its bases in the Pacific and the Caribbean, for its own security: national interest. In the great debate, the expansionists disputed that Puerto Rico (in the Caribbean) and the Philippines (in the Pacific) presented groundbreaking territory for United States entrepreneurs,

President William McKinley's argument to Congress and the citizens was accepted when he told the American people that the United States would "uplift and civilize and Christianize the people of the Philippines." But his argument was primarily based on a phony notion: the majority of the people of the Philippines were already practicing the Christian religion.

Inevitably, the Senate approved the treaty by a small margin early in the year of 1899. The expansionists' dream had become a living reality, and America had finally become an empire in the late nineteenth century. Now, the great quest that emerged in the United States was how would it govern its new regions? And since the Platt Amendment had given the United States the power to adjudicate in Cuba's political and social affairs, the United States finally got what it wanted—colonization in the guise of expansionism.

This is so typical of adults. They're hypocrites, even though they're not aware of it. And what's disappointing about this fact is that the majority simply refuse to acknowledge it.

The leaders of the world, and especially those religious people in their religious institutions who practice their foolish religious tenets, pretend to be holier than everyone else. This really gets to me, for their pretentious attitude is the conspicuous evidence of their fatuous hypocrisy.

When the war with Spain began on April 25, 1898, the government of the United States had promised to allow Cuba to administrate its own internal affairs, but by the end of the four-month war the false notion of liberty had misled the American people and the Cubans as well. Besides, the promise of independence for Cuba was never kept, and at the end of the war the American soldiers didn't leave the island-country of Cuba.

Back home in America on Capitol Hill, Congress continued with the great debate. Many politicians in the White House were convinced that the Cuban people were not capable of governing themselves. Moreover, the United States entrepreneurs strongly opposed the independence of Cuba. They wanted to protect their wealth and investments there. By refusing them their rights for independence, all for the purpose of monetary gain, in the end the sad reality of the Platt Amendment was that the United States did not keep its word to the Cubans.

The plutocratic members of the elite society endeavored to keep the people of Cuba under their rule. And the denouement was that the American government permitted Cuba to write its own constitution; however, the condition behind this political façade was that the United States coerced the Cubans to accept the Platt Amendment before granting them their pseudo-independence.

Now, my four main points which amplify the hypocrisy of the Platt Amendment are:

1. This bill sought to restrict Cuba's autonomy by making it a satellite nation, as the United States controlled and monopolized its agenda in Cuba, all in the name of conquest and subjugation.

2. The bill guaranteed the government of the United States the ability to arbitrarily interfere in the affairs of Cuba in the name of national interest.

3. The bill also gave the American government the prerogative to monopolize the naval base at Guantánamo Bay.

4. The bill was nothing more than a pretentious front that mocked the rights, liberty, and freedom of the Cuban people. In reality, it actually meant that Cuba was not entirely an independent nation.

The Platt Amendment was the pinnacle of hypocrisy in the political arena on Capitol Hill, for it was in reality only the exchange of one master for another. From the European imperialism of Spain, which was the dominant power in the Pacific and the Caribbean, Cuba went to its new master, United States.

I wonder how Cuba felt about these foreign invaders. I'm sure it must have caused great anxiety about their nationality. Discovering these historical facts can make some individuals into an enemy of the state.

Politics and religion can be very hypocritical, and religion especially has brought deplorable degrees of misery upon humanity. In addition, hypocrites are the seedbed of a duplicitous society, for they have become the masters of saying one thing and doing the opposite of their promise.

The teacher admonished us about the rules of the test, and told us that any comments or questions pertaining to the Platt Amendment would be discussed after the test. I'm certain that Mr. Simon Curtis; the teacher of U.S. government, would never agree with my sophistry of Certainism and Manichaean point of views.

But as the exquisite torture extended, I made myself oblivious as I gazed through the window, lost in the adventure of the scarlet leaves being tossed about by the gusts of the capricious autumn wind.

I withdrew myself from the tautological speech of Mr. Curtis, unaware of his annoying voice, which sounded like neither sex. Ignoring the travesty of this intolerable teacher (he figuratively killed us with boredom), my mind was taken back to my father's erudition center: his library.

Knowing full well that this might be an overweening consideration on my part, I thought about the countless hours I spent in his library, and the various volumes of books that inspired my mind as I sought the intellectual satisfaction for which my intellect longed. I pondered what my father would say if he knew that my intention for the future was to reject irrevocably what he believed and held dear to his hypocritical heart. I'm certain it was simply inconceivable to him that I might reject what had become the content of his whole life. My father loves to display his relentless enforcement of his religious authority in the home. Nevertheless, he was not aware that I, David, who he considered to be comparatively young, have certainly danced and made an alliance with the schoolmasters that have taught me to praise the ideals of intellectualism. Certainism has shown me the way to reason myself out of the burdensome dogmatic tenets of religion.

To religious and simpleminded individuals, having an intellectual mind may lead too much to the humanistic path of the sophist. My philosophy of Certainism has become my immutable companion, and my theory is the compass in my life.

Furthermore, my theory has sufficed to give me complete confidence and inner peace. Freedom from religion will bring a definite degree of emancipation, because my theory only reflects my master, and who is my master?

As this may be the question of the religious-minded hypocrites, Zarathustra has spoken! And as I sought the intellectual satisfaction that my mind longed for just then, it dawned on me that Certainism of intellectualism is the primary pursuit for the curious mind. Also, it's the best modus operandi for increasing one's intellectual expertise. As my mind was about to go a bit further, I yearned to communicate with Zarathustra, the lover of my intellect and the instigator of my new philosophy of Certainism.

Simultaneously, from a distance I heard someone calling out to me. As the voice became more familiar, I suddenly knew it was Mr. Curtis.

"David!" he called out, about three times before I became aware of my surroundings.

Precipitously, but warily, I responded, "Yes, Mr. Curtis!"

"David, my dear boy, I presume that you're here with us in person, but not in mind?"

"I'm sorry, sir, but I was thinking about the test, and the integrity of the Platt Amendment."

"Then I guess you're prepared for the test today?"

"As much as I can be, sir!"

"What exactly does that answer mean?"

"If you were to examine the certainty and the syntax of my sentence structure, sir, then I believe that you can decipher exactly what my words mean. And I'm certain you are aware, Mr. Curtis, that I'm not a wordmonger, sir."

At that moment the class went up in a grand uproar, laughing at Mr. Curtis and his comical tendencies.

"Well, David, I hope for your sake that you'll score above average on this test!"

"Don't I always, sir?"

"That's enough! I've had just about enough of you, David Hugenberg, and your smart answers!"

Just then, I realized that the infamous Mr. Simon Curtis was simply trying to bait me, and I would not take his bait. So I decided to let him have the last word, because having my father on my back was too overwhelming, and the last thing I needed right now.

The papers for the test were handed out, and in less than five minutes I had completed mine. It was just ten multiple choice questions. If you're well informed about history and social events, this test was easy; however, I remained quiet and didn't seek to draw any attention to myself, as I waited patiently until the other students had completed their test.

At the end of the test Mr. Curtis had promised that we would discuss the intricacies of the Platt Amendment, but I chose to keep my opinion of Certainism to myself. The students went on and on in a redundant manner about this historical document. Eventually, it was lunchtime; the gang and I could resume our droll conversation about the Reverend Williams. We had greeted one another between classes throughout the morning. On the other hand, it was only at lunch break that we were able to fully complete and discuss our topic, the religious dead minister of the Holy Lutheran Church. The gang and I always enjoyed thorough discussions without any meddling, self-righteous hypocrites, and we spoke about the dead hypocrite once again and the pretentious historical uncertainty of the Platt Amendment.

Most of us agree on the same things: we can't tolerate religious-minded people, for they're so set in their ways, and above all when they're ostentatious hypocrites. In our gang we had taught ourselves Greek and Latin, but the language we speak frequently among ourselves, for the purpose of confusing the simpleminded, is Latin, since it's the language of the scholars and the ancient Roman Empire.

At the end of lunch we once again ventured into the academic arenas, and the gray, wet, and cold day finally came to an end. In the evening I found myself in Father's library, only this time by his consent. Then I went to my private chambers, my bedroom. At my desk, after reading my assignments, I was spellbound by the trees, for they looked like a kaleidoscope of colors: red, yellow, green, and gray.

After I became bored with the repetitive view of the colorful trees, I pulled open the bottom drawer of my desk. In it was a copy of the New Testament, below some books that had been there, I guess, for some time. But when I opened the small book my eyes and fingers discovered an intriguing chapter, Matthew 23, which deals with "a congregation of hypocrites"; for example, the Scribes and Pharisees of Jerusalem at the time of the man *Iesus* (Jesus). The verse that really jumped out at me like a Christophany was verse three: "*Therefore whatever they tell you to observe, that observe and do, but do not do according to their works; for they say, and do not do.*" The essence of this relevant verse deals with the warnings that the Prophet *Iesus* is admonishing the people against the religious leaders of his day, because most of the leaders were hypocrites just like today in the twentieth century. They always know what is fitting and proper, but they themselves don't practice what they teach.

These people are uncertain about their faith. In conjunction with this, there's a famous German saying, "*So faengt es immer an,*" which means "Always begins in the same way." It's the same with everything and everyone in life, especially with those religious people who bear no modicum of honesty when it comes to the genuineness of their confession, since there's nothing new with mankind.

It was the famous French essayist Michel de Montaigne (1533–1592) who wrote: "*It is not inhumane to eat the dead; however, true cruelty is to eat a man alive.*" In his satirical discourse, he dealt with certain problems in the domain of the human race, particularly in conjunction with religion and the prejudices that loom within the realms of religious-minded people. He was the first to actually instigate his new revolutionary literary style of writing. And he was one of the most significant authors at a time when the world was facing the great enlightenment of intellectualism: the French Renaissance. As the world struggled to release itself from the bondage and superstitions of religion, Michel de Montaigne encountered and endured many difficulties with the Roman Catholic Church, which was a force to be reckoned with in the sixteenth century. Although, by his indomitable will he was able to emerge and became famous for his abilities of amalgamating the fundamental aspects of intellectualism in the metaphysical province of the social, political, and religious milieu of his time. He attacked, by the power his pen, the hypocritical sphere of religion and how it actually views individuals who are different from what Christendom teaches.

One of the main reasons I love and admire Michel de Montaigne is that I'm convinced that the great French Renaissance statesman and author was actually a forerunner of my philosophical theory of Certainism, as he held the same values that I hold dear to my intellect.

He would say, in spite of the religious hegemony of the church, "*I'm myself the matter of my book.*" He understood the value and importance of being oneself, no matter what religion might try to coerce one to do.

His persona was evident and prevalent in his astounding essays, which challenged the censors of the church in his day. He was also a man of great courage, for even though he was a Roman Catholic, he wasn't afraid when it came to speaking his thoughts through the power of his pen. He loved knowledge and accepted his destiny willingly, and by his method he was able to establish a permanent change through the methodology of the intellectual enlightenment of his literature in the catalyst of the French Renaissance. He knew that by educating the populace they would, in time, be able to break the tyrannical shackles from a superstitious religion that kept them in darkness. By his immense intellectual prowess, he had the foresight to know that permanent change in an individual life could only come to pass if one wanted to accept that change via intellectualism. He believed that if he could be different in the future, this change could only occur if he had learned some new lessons; then, in the accomplishment of the enlightenment of his intellect, he could be changed. Through his quest for intellectualism, Montaigne discovered that humanity in its totality possessed the same common human qualities and principles. Religious-minded persons may deceive themselves by thinking that their religion has made them different, and even better in comparison to other people.

They hold an erroneous view, and are not living in the *actual*, but are lost in their own ideals. History has shown us that religion has violated time and time again the rights of individuals, and this was always done in the name of religion and God. Moreover, individuals in a religious mind-set are not the children of intellectualism, like Zarathustra; rather, in reality, they're the children of mendacity, a congregation of hypocrites. You may wonder what correlation Michel de Montaigne's essay on the topic of cannibalism—"*It is not inhumane to eat the dead; however, true cruelty is to eat a man alive*"—has to do with religion and the church. In fact, the answer is found in the annals of ancient history, because it all started with the Greeks and their city-states. The Greeks fashioned their communities into regions which were known as city-states. A city-state was actually a city with a territory that encompassed it, and within the city-state there were rulers who ran the state; a ruler with the government. Among these regions there were two major and outstanding city-states: Sparta and Athens, the birthplace of democracy. Sparta was a totalitarian city-state, located in the Peloponnesus (the southern isthmus of Greece, between the Ionian and Aegean Seas), and was the capital of ancient Laconia. Sparta was well-known throughout the ancient world for its warriors' gallantry and proficiency. These skills and qualities were inculcated in the children from an early age, and the government was noted for its brilliant sturdiness and its exceptional constitution. The Spartans' educational system actually evolved from their indomitable ability to maintain their supremacy as an ancient military people.

Discipline was their headmaster, and anyone who would not swear allegiance to the military code was excluded from their society. Training began at an early age, and only the aesthetic and healthy were trained for their citizenship as military warriors.

The unhealthy and unaesthetic were deemed unfit for Sparta's warrior code, and were subject to being made candidates for its eugenics program. And, because of Sparta's military ingenuity, the city-state became a powerful force in ancient Greece. Inevitably, Sparta invaded the Dorian Greeks, and possessed a large slave class among them.

Sparta was the dominant factor in the Greek-Persian wars, but later on fought a civil war with the city-state of Athens in 431 BCE. This became known by historians as the Peloponnesian War. The Athenians, who also were Grecians, were somewhat different from the Spartans.

The Athenians' sports, politics, philosophy, education, and prejudices have most definitely influenced and infiltrated our global neighborhood. The city-states of the Greeks were a force to be reckoned with in the ancient world. There were three major elements that actually governed these ancient people: envy, covetousness, and competitiveness. These qualities were visible in their sports (the Olympic Games), daily lives, and politics. And when Athens shifted from a monarchal to a democratic government in the six century, under Cleisthenes ("the father of Athenian democracy"), the life of this new democratic government and the controlling factor behind it was the popular assembly of young wealthy males. For example, a young man over the age of eighteen had the right to share his opinion about the government, in conjunction with the importance of legislative and political matters, in the elite democratic assembly. On the other hand, it was only applicable to wealthy young Athenians, and depended on the amount of monetary contribution they made to the city's treasury. Then, they would have the right to voice their opinion about a particular bill. So much for democracy in Greece. And their competitive lifestyle in the city-state actually created the prejudicial mind-set of "us versus them"—the wealthy versus the poorer classes.

As a result, the entire social and political system of the Greeks was designed to compete for, envy, and covet what the other individual possessed. But it was also designed to provoke and coerce the less fortunate to achieve greater things; to better themselves by dreaming of becoming the ideal citizen in a democratic society.

Athens is the capital of modern Greece. It was not only the cradle of democracy; the ancient city has also dominated and controlled our educational system because it was the center of intellectualism. The three demagogues who were responsible for influencing the educational system of the world were Socrates, Plato, and Aristotle. The Greeks were trained to believe that their culture was better than others, and if certain people weren't like them, the Greeks saw themselves as superior to those individuals and eventually labeled them with a particular derogatory sobriquet, even though it was the norm for a Grecian male to practice a bisexual relationship with his male lover, especially when off in battle.

The fact of the matter remains the same today, because we live in a hypocritical society that loves to put labels on individuals who may be considered different, and most people like to pretend they're better or don't practice what others do openly.

But I've asked myself a profound question: Is reality socially constructed? Most people in our hypocritical society think they know what *reality* is in our societal structure, but no one knows absolutely how our societal order should correspond with what we consider to be "reality." The truth is, good and bad are not so absolute, and society, especially the religious system, loves to tell others how they should live and behave. However, I guess that will depend on your point of view. Religious institutions cannot impose on others what they consider to be *right*, and how people should live their lives.

But, getting back to my argument and the topic of Michel de Montaigne, the Greeks, and cannibalism. King Pyrrhus of Epirus (a region of northwest Greece on the Ionian Sea), after his invasion of Italy in 280 BCE, made an astounding remark about the people whom the Greeks thought were *barbarians*: "I do not know what barbarians these are." The Greeks called all who were different from them *barbarians*, a derogatory sobriquet for those individuals whom they saw as having a culture different from theirs. They couldn't understand why some people were so different from others. The noun *barbarian* connotes an uncivilized person. It also means an infidel, and was used by the church to describe all Moslems. However, King Pyrrhus referred to the Romans, when he first saw them in 280 BCE, as *barbarians*.

The Romans learned this word from the Greeks, and Julius Caesar in turn called other nations *barbarians*. In addition, the Roman Catholic Church called all unbelievers by this derogatory sobriquet, when they couldn't understand the manners and customs of a peculiar people. There's one trait common to all *barbarians*, and that is that they're considered to be uncivilized. But that's only by the parochial views of those religious-minded people. Most religious people are prejudiced and hold some level of vulgar opinion about others who may not share their code of beliefs.

Religious-minded individuals of the Dark Ages believed that all *barbarians* literally were cannibals. This might have had some degree of credence, but not all nations that were considered to be uncivilized were cannibalistic. Even those who were labeled *barbarians* believed in some form of a god, heaven, and hell. The Scythians never fought in a battle unless they first heard from their prophets. In reality, they were not different from other people. After a war, some primitive tribes would take their captives, dismember them, roast the flesh, and then share it with their companions. The Scythians also practiced these rituals. There were tribal groups that practiced this heinous crime as an extreme measure of retribution against their enemies, and history has proven that in war, most people have practiced some form of crime against humanity.

Some have committed more atrocities than others. I understand that cannibalism is a heinous crime against humanity; however, most individuals have practiced cannibalism in various manners against others, figuratively speaking. For example, when people promise to live or do things based on their religious teachings and don't live up to their religious tenets, isn't that like the odious crime of cannibalism? And when a man cheats on his wife and children, isn't that some form of cannibalism against humanity?

When religious people say one thing and do something totally opposite of their religious teachings, like living a hypocritical lifestyle, isn't that being deceitful and devouring the integrity of the human race? Religious people enjoy criticizing and condemning others; they love to call others "sinners" and declare, "I don't live that way!" When people live a hypocritical life, it's in reality living a lie. They practice in secret what they condemn publicly as they live out their cannibalism against their fellow men.

With my theory of Certainism there's no room for anyone who wants to live a life of double standards, like the hypocrites. On too many occasions religious people, with their pretentious lifestyles, have devoured others alive by way of their duplicitous everyday life and their inhumane acts toward mankind. And then they say all the right things in the public's ears, such as, "Oh, that's so wrong, and it's a sin in the sight of God!" Within the chambers of their hearts they know that they're living a hypocritical life when they themselves practice in secret what they condemn openly. But it's only a matter of time before their cannibalistic misdeeds become known to the general public.

It is the height of wickedness when we lie to ourselves and others. Certainism advocates: decide what you want to do and who you want to be, be the best at what you've chosen to be, and be proud.

"*It is not inhumane to eat the dead; however, true cruelty is to eat a man alive.*" Religious people have not committed the inhumane crime of eating the dead, no, but they have certainly gone much further by eating humanity alive. Religion has slowly but surely torn apart the feeble body of humanity. They have damaged society by torturing the body that still had the breath of life in it when they roasted the flesh of the living; through the slow process of torturing the human race and then casting the remaining flesh to the wild dogs on the streets, while making a public spectacle of those who may not share their same beliefs.

These religious leaders have tried to justify what they did when they condemned the world by declaring, "I'm God's servant, and therefore I can do no wrong!" But there are those who may want to adamantly declare, "How can this be true? This is a lie, and I must protest! We who're righteous have never committed such atrocious acts in the name of God and religion!" They're quick to condemn others before performing a thorough inspection of themselves; however, empirical facts and evidence do not deny the credibility of reason. On the contrary, they'll declare, "We have never been malicious or cruel toward our fellow man." Nevertheless, the pages of history are the ideal source for proving that religion, particularly Christendom, has certainly eaten the flesh of those who were still alive.

Religion has violated the rights of mankind throughout the centuries and committed crimes against humanity. These crimes were committed via the system of injustices when religious institutions controlled and influenced civil authorities and were able to turn their church dogmas into certain laws; hence, the Certainist strongly advocates that the toxic titans of all religious institutions must have their authority divested from all judicial and civil influences. Another crime committed against humanity was those religious wars that were launched in the name of God: the Crusades of the eleventh and fourteenth centuries. It was the first female historian of the Dark Ages, Anna Comnena (1083–1148), who wrote the account of the cannibalistic acts committed by the Crusaders, particularly against the Tafurs in the sieges of Antioch and Maarrat an-Numan. For example, they roasted infants over a slow fire after they were impaled.

The leaders in the church ordered the burning of unbelievers, as well as immoral and amoral individuals of Europe, allowing the fires of the Inquisition to devour the flesh of innocent persons. It's futile to deny the sincerity and authenticity of the words of Michel de Montaigne: "*It is not inhumane to eat the dead; however, true cruelty is to eat a man alive.*"

It's really difficult when you're living with the prince of hypocrites and having to rub shoulders with a congregation of them every week. It's amazing how adults operate; it's as if they assume that once you're a teenager you can't see what's right in front of you.

I've always heard rumors about the leaders in the Holy Lutheran Church. One of the rumors that had credence was the one about the Reverend Williams, who for some years had a mistress besides his lovely wife.

Well, my attitude about this was that I really don't care what other people do. But a few months ago I was on my way to second period when Harry, Tobey, and Daniel met me in the hall with some interesting news about the Reverend Williams.

"David, have you heard the latest about the assistant pastor of the Holy Lutheran Church?"

"No!" I answered. "Well, I guess rumors can become a reality in time, because I'm sure that the leaders in the Holy Lutheran Church aren't that holy after all!"

I started to chuckle because I knew that Daniel can be the ideal clown when he wants to be. But I couldn't believe my ears as Daniel continued. "I heard this from my father while he shared it with my mom." Daniel's father is a medical doctor who works at the general hospital in Springfield. "My dad conveyed the hot news to my mom yesterday in the corridor downstairs. And they didn't see me on the staircase, listening. It was about how the Reverend Williams brought a strange woman with two children to see my dad, and in the process, my dad discovered that this woman was the reverend's mistress, and those two children are his."

"Daniel, I thought the information between a doctor and his patients is supposed to be confidential?"

"Yes, David, that's true, but the information my dad shared with my mom didn't violate his Hippocratic oath. Furthermore, it was about the Reverend Williams and his Mistress, who has borne him two children. And the boy, his eldest, was born mentally challenged! My dad and mom were both shocked, because they thought Protestants were not supposed to practice infidelity."

I couldn't respond, even though I wanted to, because the information was too disgusting. Tobey and Harry were about to add their personal comments, but I said to them, "Hey, guys, we're going to be late. We need to discontinue this discussion and head for our classes."

Then, there's the unpleasant matter of the church's worship leader, the former minister Nathan Carlson: he's serving a five-year prison sentence for involuntary manslaughter.

I guess it's the habit of these men in the Holy Lutheran Church to thrash their wives, since Minister Carlson abused his wife for several years. One night while practicing his religious beating of her, she couldn't take the abuse anymore. She ran out of their apartment and headed straight for the streets as he chased her. The sad fact of the matter is that she was killed on the spot by an automobile and left a ten-month-old baby girl.

The neighbors testified against Minister Nathan Carlson about the regular abuse of his wife, and he was sentenced to serve a five-year prison term. In addition, about eleven months before Minister Carlson's case of manslaughter, there was the unfortunate circumstance of a young man by the name of Freddy Chabon.

He was a young lawyer from the city of New York who had moved to Springfield. Mr. Chabon soon became a prominent member of the Holy Lutheran Church. It seemed that almost everyone loved him, especially the young women, who saw him as an eligible bachelor.

About six months into his membership of the church, the late Reverend Williams and former Minister Carlson brought some accusations against this young lawyer. This offense, as placed before the church's executive board, was the sin of homosexuality.

In 1934, people did not mention that lifestyle because it had a societal stigma, especially in the religious arena, but the accusation against Mr. Chabon was proven two weeks into the investigation. And when the board had confirmed the accusation against Mr. Chabon, he was run out of the church as an abominable sinner and then snubbed by everyone in town. Eventually, he was compelled to leave Springfield, and was never seen or heard of again.

But what I thought so ironic was, just look at these two men who brought the accusation against Attorney Chabon. Honestly, I didn't know him personally, but in the little acquaintance I had with him during those six months, he was always polite, neat, and smart, had a good sense of humor, and was very good-looking.

I'll never know what it's like being a homosexual, and thank goodness I'm not that way, because what I saw, and how those religious people treated Mr. Chabon, wasn't pleasant at all. They made a public spectacle of him, when the church leaders openly humiliated the young lawyer in front of the entire community.

Then, there was the incident involving my dad; however, nothing ever came of this, and I'm not sure if the people of the church ever heard about that unpleasant incident.

My father went to California for two weeks, for his usual annual conference at Stanford University. It wasn't long before news got back to Mom about what had happened to my father, the dean's secretary, and a professor from Stanford University. It appears that they had too much to drink one night after a social function. The driver who was responsible for taking these three to their destinations had relatives in Springfield, and I guess this was the main avenue of how the news got to my mother, Dr. McCrory, and the gang so quickly. My dad was sitting on the left side of the car, the secretary was in the middle, and the professor sat to the right. It wasn't long before the driver saw the objectionable problem in the rear of the vehicle. Both men had put their hands simultaneously in the private place of the dean's secretary, where they shouldn't have been. This inevitably caused the men to become violent and hostile toward each other. Not long afterward, it was understood that this woman was sleeping with both the professor and my father.

These things are not edifying to think of or even talk about, and after that episode our relationship with Father changed considerably. There was also the shame of facing the gang, who heard about it, and Daniel's father, Dr. McCrory, who always heard about these things firsthand.

In addition, Daniel shared with me what his father had said about my dad, and most religious people.

"I thought it was only the Roman Catholic priests who practiced illicit relationships. I presumed that those of a Protestant faith were too holy to live in sin. But it appears that it's the same all over with these religious leaders!"

I only spoke with my father when it was absolutely necessary, and at times to show the respect he's entitled to, in view of the fact that I honor my father. I love my mother; however, throughout the years I've learned how to transform my silent anger into my practical philosophy. I practice and utilize my theory of Certainism, which eventually became my relevant panacea.

My theory of Certainism has taught me to stay the course by being certain with my decisions to be a better man and not be like those religious hypocrites in my father's church. Those hypocrites who always say, but never do, can never be a Certainist, who understands the philosophy of Certainism, which strongly advocates the teachings of reason, because they're uncertain in what they believe and in themselves. They say but they don't do; that's why they're a congregation of hypocrites.

Chapter Three

The Fire in the Stable

I'm in the stable executing my daily chores for my egregious father. Two winters have come and gone since the Reverend Frank Williams passed away. I'm now sixteen, six foot one, and I've gained an additional twenty pounds, which brings me to a weight of 140 pounds.

During the past two years there seems to have been some unsettling turbulence going on in Europe. We have been listening to the broadcast on the radio every night and hearing the words of President Franklin Delano Roosevelt, and the comments of Great Britain. This has forced me to conclude that things do not look good in Europe, especially for the Jews.

The year is 1936. On February 7, 1934, Hitler's defense council declared its purpose to mobilize for another war in Europe.

Besides that, there were rumors of laws passed on September 15, 1935, called the First Nuremberg laws, which took away the civil rights of all German Jews. My dad made some *stultus* (foolish) remarks about the Jews in Europe. He would say things like, "I'm sure glad I'm not a member of the dead Jewish race in Europe! Because I know they don't stand a chance under Hitler's regime." Mother, on the other hand, would always look very disturbed whenever Dad made his racist comments, especially about the Jews. My father has two copies of Hitler's autobiography, *Mein Kampf* (My Struggle), in English and in his native tongue, German. The book was first published in the United States in 1933. Interestingly enough, this was the same year that Hitler became Germany's new chancellor, on January 30. It was also the year that the first concentration camp was set up at Dachau (a city in

South Germany, near Munich), on March 10, for the purpose of dealing with Germany's political enemies.

I read *Mein Kampf*, which is lengthy, when I was fifteen. It took me two whole months to complete the 687 pages. The book is not only the story of Hitler's life; it also displays the ingenuity of a gifted orator rising to power. At the same time, it justifies his peculiar methods of ethnic cleansing.

The book was enlightening to read; it's a literary masterpiece of Hitler's political ideals and the most uncontroversial book I've ever read. And Dad was right; I did enjoy the book, even though the author's rhetoric was somewhat unorthodox for a political leader. However, I saw things in a different light. I said to myself, "I'm so glad that I'm not a Jew, and above all, not living in Germany." My father always said the Jews were the cause of the global problems, and Hitler was the ideal man to deal with "the Jewish Problem" in Europe. Honestly, most of the time I didn't understand the term "the Jewish Problem," though I recognized that Dad knew what he was talking about in conjunction with world Jewry and Adolf Hitler.

But that's enough about Deutschland politics. At this moment it's the middle of summer; July, to be precise, the warmest month of the year. I look forward to this season every year because my friends and I always take advantage of swimming in the Connecticut River, mainly off West Springfield River Road. When my Bavarian ancestor Fritsche Rohm Hugenberg migrated with his family, my relatives had an interim stay in Connecticut and finally settled in Springfield. Since that time the Hugenbergs have always been residents of Massachusetts in the New England region.

Immigration in the United States radically fashioned our multicultural American society. And one of the main causes of this was the government's uncommon constitutional stance on immigration laws. According to our history, the United States did not pass the first American citizenship statute until the year 1790. This constitutional statute passed by Congress actually sanctioned the naturalization of particular individuals, but there were certain preconditions that made the candidates eligible.

Such as, the person had to be a member of the Caucasian race, a free person, and had to have lived in the United States for approximately two years. There were two more preconditions that made the individual eligible for naturalization: the person applying for citizenship had to have lived in the state where he was applying for one year, and had to possess a good moral character.

But when my ancestors came to America in 1801, the laws in this country were relatively different. The laws of 1790 seemed somewhat unfair to certain immigrants and blended with racial prejudice. The history of Massachusetts is very interesting. The English Protestant sect, the Puritans, was the first religious group to impose religious tenets on everyone, and condemned all indulgences in the newly regimented community. Throughout the years of the early seventeenth century, many of the Puritans eventually immigrated to the American colonies and settled in the Massachusetts Bay colony. And 1620, when a group of the Puritan sect came to Massachusetts on the pretext of freedom of religion, eight years later schools were established in the American colonies.

In 1642, the civil war that exploded in England was mainly due to religion, and those members of the English Parliament some years later had their revenge on King Charles I. In 1649, the English Puritans took their king to the chopping block and silenced their sovereign forever. But after the migration of the Puritans, all citizens in the new region of America had to worship in the manner that the Puritans had chosen for them—so much for freedom of religion. The Puritans came to the New World for freedom of religion, but in return, they did not permit others to exercise their freedom. Consequently, the religious government of the Puritans was a hard, self-righteous, and conceited group. They were bent on regimentation and conformity, for they ruled by imposing their religious ideals on other people.

From the nascent establishment of the American colonies, religion sought vehemently to control every sphere of secularism, as the Puritans aggressively endeavored to dominate the lives of all by transmitting their religious tenets to the secular masses.

For this reason, Roger Williams was compelled to leave the Bay of Massachusetts, and he traveled through the woodlands in search of a new district where he could practice what his conscience dictated, and not be controlled by a religious system that attempted to take away the rights of the people. On his journey to escape the religious bondage and severity of the Puritans, he came across some Native Americans, and they were kind enough to assist him through his great peril in a strange land.

With the help of the OPS (Original Peoples: Native Americans), he was able to establish a new city by the name of Providence in 1636, and as time progressed the area became known as the colony of Rhode Island, with the small city of Providence as its capital. In concurrence with the accuracy of American history, it was Rhode Island, not Massachusetts, where freedom of religion was first granted to the people.

Since religious people are so narrow-minded and inept, they can't differentiate between their religious personal faith and the facts in relation to individuals and their constitutional rights. They misconstrue the difference between their religious institution and its dogmas, their personal convictions of what they choose to believe, and the violation of human rights.

In fact, what may be one's conviction may not be the conviction of another; therefore, the faith or teachings of religious institutions shouldn't be made into a regional or universal law. They should not seek to impose their beliefs on others through the means of proselytizing. What religious people may call sharing their message or faith is, in fact, a violation of the rights of individuals who may not want to accept religion and its fatuousness. Such religious measures do not ameliorate the affairs of mankind, but only exacerbate the conditions of all free men.

Springfield is currently the largest city on the Connecticut River, and it's located in Hampden County, in southern Massachusetts. On June 2, 1641, Springfield was incorporated as a town. Massachusetts was the sixth state to obtain statehood, in 1788. But our town became a city on May 25, 1852, by verdict of the elected representatives of Massachusetts. There are six states that make up the New England

Region: Connecticut, Maine, Massachusetts, New Hampshire, Rhode Island, and Vermont.

And Springfield is most definitely not without its fair share of greatness and fame. The city is noted as the birthplace of basketball, which was invented by James Naismith in the year 1891. This year will always be indelibly etched in my mind due to the fact that it was the same year in which both my father was born and the university he attended, Stanford, was founded. The famous American author Theodor Seuss Geisel, known as Dr. Seuss, was born in Springfield, Massachusetts, on March 2, 1904. In March 1936, Springfield was hit with a severe inundation of floods.

Our summers are hot and humid, but I love them beyond the shadow of a doubt, even though Dad always gives us more chores in summer than at any other time throughout the year. Nevertheless, he's fair, as long as I complete my chores on time and they're done methodically according to his standards. And once I've finished my chores for the day, if I'm not studying, Mom can always find me either in the stable, because I love horses, or swimming with my friends in the Connecticut River, but only if my dad consents to this.

One day, after completing my chores, I went into the house and entered my room. The house isn't the same without my eldest sister Jena. She's nineteen now and has been in college for one year. She is attending Wesleyan University in Middleton, Connecticut, majoring in anthropology. Though Jena usually comes home for the holidays, she's spending part of her summer vacation with her roommate from South Carolina. I'm aware this is only a pretext, for she's really avoiding Dad.

Maria is fourteen and Georg is now twelve, and most of the time they're arguing about silly things. So I prefer to stay clear of them, and usually keep to myself when they start on the war zone.

I entered my room, shut the door behind me, and started to undress, but before I could undress myself completely, Georg opened my door and just stood there, staring at me. For a split second I was in shock. Then I shouted at him, "What's wrong with you, Georg? Are you stupid, *stultus puer*? Must you always display such churlishness?"

"Well, you shouldn't have left your door unlocked."

"Get out! Mom!"

Just then, Mom walked in my room. "What's going on?"

"Georg is encroaching on my privacy and my individuality once again!"

"Georg, did you enter your brother's room without knocking and waiting to hear if you could enter?"

"Yes, but I just wanted to talk, Mom. I'm bored."

"Well, Georg, I'm sorry to hear that you're bored, but there are rules in this house. You know that you don't enter a room unless you knock first, and only after you've heard the voice of the person on the other side of the door may you enter."

"Yes, Mom," Georg said, sounding discouraged, "but—"

"No buts. You know the rules. Apologize to your brother. He needs his privacy. Come on, I'll find something that will keep you busy."

But before Georg left my room, he turned to me and said, "I'm sorry, David."

"That's okay, just don't do it again. Do you understand?"

"Yes, David."

Mom and Georg left my room, and I made sure that I locked the door behind them. After showering and putting on clean clothes, I sat on my bed for a while taking in and enjoying the cool, refreshing breeze from my portable fan.

Alone in my room, it wasn't long before I started to ponder on the problems going on in Europe, particularly in Germany, and with the Jews. As I continued to ruminate about these crucial matters, I thought about the Jews in the state of Massachusetts, and a comment my father had made a few days ago about the Jews in New England after listening to the news on the radio. His remark was, "There are approximately two hundred sixty thousand Jews living in the New England region."

His remark caused me to do some serious thinking. While I reflected on the components of Mein Kampf, I asked myself, "What if Congress passed a bill expelling all the Jews in the New England vicinity?" I was only hypothesizing here, but if that were to happen, where would these two hundred sixty thousand Jews go, and what would they do? This figure represented the Jews in the New England region only, not the entire United States.

Just then, I realized something I had failed to comprehend from Mein Kampf—that the content of this fascinating book was not just the theories of a man who was about to take extraordinary measures for solving "the Jewish Problem" in Europe. Because Hitler knew precisely what he was about to do to those Jews in Germany, if he meant what he wrote in Mein Kampf. They would certainly be labeled as criminals and enemies of the Fatherland, simply for being Jews.

The First Nuremberg laws stripped the Jews of their German citizenship, and by this approach the government made these people criminals, enemies of Deutschland, a crime punishable by expulsion or even death. Then I remembered the Jews of Spain in the fifteenth century, and their expulsion.

In theory, Mein Kampf is actually the architectural design of preserving the Aryan race, and at the same time eliminating its enemies for its own protection before it becomes extinct.

These things may be the unnecessary concerns of a situation that may never come to pass, since I'm basing this on mere conjecture. I love reading intelligent literature, especially those books that provoke the mind and reveal new ideas.

In the early history of Massachusetts, the Jews played an integral part in constructing our social mores. The first Jew to be naturalized in our state, in the eighteenth century, was Aaron Lopez from Lisbon, Portugal. His former name was Duarte Lopez. He was born in 1731 and died in

1782, twenty-five years after his naturalization. Aaron Lopez, being a consummate humanitarian, established the first Jewish community in the town of Leicester in Worcester County, Massachusetts, which was founded in 1777. This occurred two years after the commencement of the American Revolutionary War (1775–1783).

Then there was the famous Judah Monis. He was born in 1683 and died in 1764. He was the first Jewish man to receive a college education in the British-American colonies, and also the first Jewish professor to teach at Harvard. His parents were Italians, *conversos*, and when his family first migrated to the American colonies they lived in the city of New York. On February 28, 1716, Judah Monis was declared a freeman of that city. Soon afterward, in the 1720s, he left the Jewish community in the city of New York and settled in Cambridge, Massachusetts.

At that period, few Jews lived in the state, and before Professor Judah Monis started his new career at Harvard University, he was inevitably forced to embrace the monolithic nemesis of the religious system of belligerent Christians and to accept their tenets and faith. These situations have not changed in the world in conjunction with religion. One of the Draconian rules of the university was that all of Harvard's professors had to be at least professing Christians, in order for them to remain on staff.

Therefore, the curse of religion continued to plague the Jew who left Europe for freedom of religion. Monis was once again being forced to accept a religion that his heart did not want or desire. It was happening again, like a recurring malignant cancer, in the form of the dreaded dogma of religion, which continually seeks to conquer the souls of men while trouncing mankind into submission, desiring to control all men in the name of a malevolent religious system.

Judah Monis was being forced to renounce his principles, which meant everything to him. He thought he could practice his ancient faith in the New World; however, he was told that in order to keep his new career, he would have to accept the uncompromising religion that his parents had resisted in Europe.

So Professor Judah Monis had no choice but to accept the universal religion that both he and his parents spurned. And one month before he started his career at Harvard University, he was baptized, but his conversion still wasn't enough for those religious zealots. And both the Jewish and Christian communities criticized his conversion. The Jewish community felt betrayed by those in the colony and the professor, and the Christians eventually questioned the sincerity of Monis's conversion.

I speculate about these religious people; most of the time it's a no-win situation. They are so consumed by and inebriated with control it's as if they're determined to break the will and the spirit of humanity.

Religious institutions have made the un-reached their number-one victims, and for that reason they have mastered the skills of violating the rights of others every time they endeavor to force the "truth"—or, to be more accurate, what they consider to be their relative *truth*. People need to be intelligent and sagacious about the subtlety of religion, because what might have been the religion of the past will be the ancient literature of the next generation.

And from my personal experience, religion always seeks to impose its beliefs on others, like Professor Judah Monis. In the light of all this, religion is truly an expert in presenting its pretentious tenets by declaring free choice, but then it turns around and contradicts its facetious doctrines by imposing its beliefs on others and denying them their human right of free choice.

For this reason, in the perspective of my opinion, religion is nothing more than an impractical and unrelenting nuisance which has hindered humanity for too long. And certain intelligent people can be an asset in the demise of religion. Furthermore, all disciples of religion are nothing more than individuals who have actually been deluded and are drunk on their spurious teachings, whose main objective is to exploit humanity as they seek to triumph over the human will through the device of their cunning message.

Moreover, under the tutelage of Father Grigori Yefimovich Rasputin, religion was the instrument that drove the majority of its followers to insanity. As a result, it was Karl Marx who said that religion is the opium of the people.

But I, David Tolstoy Hugenberg, will add a deeper meaning to this adage: religion is the instigator of all those superstitious individuals who have chosen to bend their knees to folly. And these religious people act as if folly is their next of kin. However, when I say, "*as if folly is their next of kin*," I have chosen to use this phrase in the manner of a hyperbolic statement, which is my euphemistic expression of religious people. The noun *folly* in Latin is *stultitia*, and *dementia*, for it actually describes the condition or state of being foolish, as if people are suffering from a deficiency of understanding and intelligent awareness.

Humanity is no longer a member of the primitive Folsom Culture, and religious people act as if they have eaten, indubitably, the *excretus* of their leaders. Religion throughout the centuries has controlled, dominated, and even extorted money, property, and wealth from simpleminded and superstitious individuals. These people were all looking for some kind of solace that came in the guise of religion. At particular times, religious leaders have also lied to, misled, and taken advantage of people who were vulnerable.

I'm definitely speaking from an experiential concept and not a theoretical perception. I've been in the church from an early age, ever since I can remember, and I can't wait for my deliverance to come from these insane religious Neanderthals.

For example, when religious people go to their particular assembly of worship, I'm convinced that most of these people leave their brains by the door, and after the service they collect them from outside the building.

Furthermore, in conjunction with religion and its members, these people are taught just about anything, and they simply swallow it without questioning the authenticity of what they're being taught. They display such an impeccable degree of credulity, which in fact causes the intellectual community to label them as disciples of folly. Hence, my euphemized phrase, "*as if folly is their next of kin*." It's as if these people refuse to use their intellect or simple common sense in the service.

As for the topic of money, their leaders are always in need of this precious commodity. Religious people must stop being so damn spooky, which is a common trait they misconstrue for spirituality. There should be laws to govern and protect foolish people from the con artist of religion, which seeks to abuse its own people. Their leaders are vultures, feeding on the flesh of their own people.

Sometimes I think religion is the father of all simpletons. The leaders say and the people demonstrate their blind obedience, which they confuse with faith, and they're taught to believe this is the manner of good disciples in conjunction with religious institutions.

It's as if religion is the ultimate mastermind behind all who display such naiveté. In addition, these religious leaders and their members carry on as if they are the arbitrary de facto of the human race.

Religion tells its members anything, and most people will believe just about anything and accept it as the gospel truth. However, those of us who refuse to submit to the inflexible religious system of these wicked, conceited men are the ones who are the lost sinners, all because we will not bow to a system of a man-made, fanatical, dogmatic religion that seeks to control people.

Thinking about religion has forced me to conclude that I hate what this Draconian institution does to humanity. It makes mankind into nothing more than a social religious marionette. Besides, religion is mainly geared at controlling people through the misleading notion of superstitious tenets and fears. Religion is robbing mankind of its reasonable ability when it comes to acting and making intelligent decisions, which are based on intelligence and not platonic myths.

The famous Hannah Adams (1755–1831) was a native of Medfield, Massachusetts, and was the first woman in the American colonies to have a career in the writing profession. She was one of those great authors who wrote about the late Professor Judah Monis, the first Jew in the colonies to receive an honorary master's degree from Harvard University, in 1720. Throughout the years, and after much study in my father's library, I contemplated on these historical facts. I came to the conclusion that in spite of my father's opinion, Jewish people have lived in New England since colonial times and have contributed significantly to this area.

The first Jew ever recorded in the archives of our country was a man by the name Joachim Gans. He was born in Bohemia, the province of Prague, but his family migrated to England when he was young. As time progressed he became a subject of the English Crown and was later known as a metallurgist. Metallurgy is the science that deals with procedures used in extracting metals from their ores, with the main objective of purifying and alloying metals in order to create useful objects from metals. It was the famous Sir Walter Raleigh who encouraged Gans to join an expedition in 1584. They traveled to the New World, to the territory of Virginia, in the hope of founding a new settlement in honor of Queen Elizabeth I. On their journey they were looking for metals such as gold, silver, and copper.

But the Jew, who would go down in our history as an outstanding individual, and also a friend of General Washington before he became the first president of our young nation, was Haym Salomon. He was a financial wizard who worked with another great man by the name Robert Morris, a Gentile. Haym Salomon was a Jewish Polish immigrant who worked with General Washington and was one of the crucial merchant bankers during the turbulent years of the American Revolutionary War (1775–1783).

My father became enraged when Mom shared this historical data about Haym Salomon. It wasn't long before Mom realized that Dad is an American Nazi. This explains everything: his antipathy of blacks, Jews, and Catholics. Then, at times Dad would speak with a fervent passion about post-World War Germany, and the millions that died during the war. Furthermore, he believed that the Communists and the Jews, who were working together for global control of the world, betrayed Germany, and that the German people were in desperate need of a new political *Heiland* (savior) and hope. My father believed that the man to reestablish the Fatherland to its greatness was Adolf Hitler. He kept a copy of *Mein Kampf* by his bedside, along with the Bible, because he was convinced that the Fuhrer wrote this precious book, the Aryan man's bible, to eventually liberate the white race from all mongrelized people.

As I said before, I've read *Mein Kampf*, and in fact I found it to be an extraordinary piece of work, but to declare that it's the Aryan man's bible? Honestly, I think that's going a bit too far, because *Mein Kampf* actually goes against everything that my theory of Certainism stands for, since being a Certainist advocates respect for humanity.

The philosophy of Certainism does not seek to discriminate on race, sex, or sexual orientation, for my theory essentially embraces all peoples and their lifestyles. The only entity that Certainism repudiates is the standard of conservatives, such as hard-line religious people who seek to thwart the intellectualism of intelligent people.

Dad is often expounding on how *Mein Kampf* is the greatest piece of literature ever written by an Aryan man. He's also convinced that *Mein Kampf* is the second greatest best-seller after the Bible.

He would go on and on about the book, and how it made the Fuhrer rich and thrust him into notoriety. I'm fully aware of the contents of *Mein Kampf*; the book is the greatest uncontroversial literary work I've read. In fact, the book has taught me an indelible lesson: no matter how controversial one's theories might be, an individual must never be afraid to share his or her unpopular views, because what's unpopular for some may be accepted and welcome by others. I guess in conjunction with my theory of Certainism, there's even room for Adolf Hitler in my philosophical ideals, as my theory welcomes and supports all ideologies. On the other hand, somehow I can't seem to forget that *Mein Kampf* is Hitler's blueprint that was meticulously written for the purpose of restoring the glory of Deutschland. However, in my broad-mindedness, I'm compelled to ask myself that important question: At what cost? And eventually, I'm fully aware of the answer, and that is through the method of blood!

The blood of civilians, Jews, homosexuals, non-Aryans, the useless eaters of society, and all those who are deemed *Lebensunwertes leben*—"life unworthy of life." In the name of eugenics and in the political guise of ethnic cleansing and *de-lousing*; I ask myself in my soliloquy: How can Father say that he's God's servant, and at the same time advocate Hitler's theory of totalitarianism as the means of controlling racial superiority?

And for Germany to accept Hitler's unorthodox methods, the nation would have to carry out his merciless policies without any degree of nonnegotiable creeds attached to the Fuhrer's will. In Germany, more than seventy million people embraced their new bible, *Mein Kampf*, which vehemently seeks to preserve the Aryan bloodline (in Nazi ideology, a Caucasian Gentile, especially one of Nordic stock).

Hitler's new course of action was being propagating in Deutschland in the middle of the 1930s, and the teachings of Nazism were proliferating in Germany. Nazism had already decided to spread its wings across the Atlantic Ocean. At the same time, the Great Depression was crippling the economy in the United States. In the 1930s, America was experiencing its very own social and political commotion. The financial disaster of the Great Depression ended in 1933, and because the United States is a nation that welcomes all forms of new ideas, in its dilemma it was ready for the ideologies of Nazism. Besides, in the early 1930s, German Americans amounted to one-fourth of the United States population.

Two famous American sportsmen were of German origin. George Herman Ruth, Jr., better known as "The Bambino" and "The Sultan of Swat," played with the famous American Major League baseball players through the years of 1914–1935. The second celebrity of German origin was Lou Gehrig, better known as "The Iron Horse." He was given this name because of his indomitable ability as a hitter. He played American baseball in the 1920s and 1930s. These two great German American baseball players became American icons in the sports arena.

But as Hitler continued to mobilize his Aryan people for battle, the shores of the United States received inundations of new immigrants, particularly from Germany, who brought with them their Aryan ideals of Nazism, for the purpose of supporting their theory of racial superiority in the American culture. These new arrivals from Germany decided to settle on the East Coast and in the Midwest, because thriving, reputable Germanic communities already existed in those regions.

Yorkville had the largest German population in the United States, and these new German immigrants were somewhat different from the German Americans who had already been there for some years. Those new arrivals were adamant Nazi supporters, and politically inclined to the message of *Mein Kampf*, the exposé of the Fuhrer's ideology. The idealistic concept of Nazism had already germinated in the fabric of the United States as early as 1923, and was strengthened by the birth of a new entity, The Friends of the New Germany, which started in 1933.

My religious Aryan father believes just like this Nazi group, that a person of Germanic blood could be a good American and also a good German who supports the Fuhrer's policies. The Friends of the New Germany was an organization that established itself in United States with the goal of promulgating and supporting the ideals of the Nazis in America. In 1933, the Nazi Deputy Fuhrer Rudolf Hess actually endorsed, appointed, and authorized—but only with Hitler's blessings—Heinz Spanknobel, a German citizen living in the United States, to form an organization for the purpose of supporting and encouraging the Fuhrer's message in America. Most people believe the Nazi Party was established by the Fuhrer, but the fact of the matter is that a Munich locksmith named Anton Drexler created this German organization in 1919. However the party was first known as the DAP—*Deutsche Arbeiterpartei*—*German Workers Party*, and from the inception of the DAP the policies of this party was: Nationalistic, Anti-Semitic, and Anti-Marxist (Judeo—Bolshevism).

The idea of the political party was passed on to Hitler in 1921, but not before the new name was accepted officially in 1920, the NSDAP—*Nationalsozialistische Deutsche Arbeiterpartei*, or *National Socialist German Workers' Party*. They believed that their philosophy of racial purity was endorsed by the famous ethnologist, Arthur de Gobineau, the father of modern racial demography, along with the comprehensive devotion of Heinrich Gotthard von Treitschke, and with the nineteenth-century German philosopher Friedrich Wilhelm Nietzsche and his theory of his "superman."

It's difficult dealing with my father and his *"streng verboten"* mentality, because if you don't agree with his ideals you can end up being in big trouble.

"David, Daniel is on the phone for you."

"Thanks, Mom." I went downstairs in the hall to speak with my best friend.

"Tomorrow afternoon the gang is coming over to my house for two days," he said. "And I thought maybe you'd like to join us, because it won't be the same without you, buddy. I would like us to go swimming while the gang is here those two days. So bring your swimming trunks, if you can come. I know how much you enjoy swimming off West Springfield River Road, especially during summer."

"Gee, Daniel, I'm not sure. I'll have to check with my parents, and Dad is not at home right now. But I'll ask my mom to ask him when he comes home tonight."

"Well, ask, okay? And if they agree, call in the morning and let me know. How does that sound?" Daniel asked.

"Sure. By the way, what exactly are we going to do for those two days at your house? And where would we sleep? Because it's the whole gang, isn't it?"

"David, don't worry about that. My mom and dad have everything planned and under control. By the way, have you forgotten four years ago, when the gang spent three days at my house? Man, David, sometimes you can act like an old woman!"

"It was just a legitimate question, Daniel."

"All right, I'm sorry, man, but must everything be so organized and perfect all the time?"

"Yes, I'm sorry, Daniel, but it's a Germanic trait I've learned from my father. *Kleinarbeit*, he calls it, attention to detail. But you can't deny that I'm the most meticulous one in the gang."

"Yep, that's true, and sometimes a real pain!" said Daniel.

"However, I guess it will be fun for us to be together once more Daniel, right?"

"*Sieg Heil, Mein Fuhrer!*"

"Up yours, McCrory!"

"I think it's that Germanic blood in you that compels you to be so organized all the time. You must learn to relax more, David."

"No, it's called *Kleinarbeit*, and that's easy for you to say, man. You don't have to live with a religious fanatic!"

"Okay, I get it, but ask them, all right?" said Daniel.

"Yes, I'll ask my parents and get back to you as soon as possible," I assured Daniel. "Bye, and thanks for calling."

After my conversation with Daniel, I decided to approach Mom about the matter of Daniel's question. She was in the dining room getting things ready for dinner that evening.

"Is everything all right with the McCrorys?"

But before I could answer Mom's question, I was lost once again in my rumination as I gazed at her, admiring her awesome beauty and elegance. She looks so young, with her small waist and diamond-shaped face. She has a voluptuous physique for a woman who has born four children, and her calves looked so perfect in the blue dress she was wearing. Around her neck was a strand of lovely pink pearls, and her smile was so refreshing and gracious, just like the splendor of spring, which brings with it joy and new life after the deadness of winter. Dealing with my father is like dealing with the model man of winter: he's cold and indifferent. But with Mom, no matter what I face with him, she's always there, her smiles uplifting and bringing the newness of life.

My dad is five years her senior, for she was born in 1896. Her eyes are bright green and her hair is blonde, with a touch of red like mine. She's exactly six feet tall and very slim. Strangely enough, I don't know her weight, for she has never discussed such matters with us, not even with Jena. My dad and mom are the ideal Aryan couple.

"David!"

"Yes, Mom."

"Are you all right?"

"Yes, I was just deep in thought."

"For the past few months, it seems that you're always very pensive."

"Yes, that's true, Mom, but I can't help it if I'm the youngest and most gifted philosopher who ever lived!"

"All right, David. I know you're very intelligent for your age, but don't forget that with much knowledge comes much responsibility."

"Don't you think I'm responsible for my age?"

"Of course, David. That's what worries me sometimes about you. From an early age you were too responsible, and always so serious about your studies and life."

"Don't I always get excellent grades?"

"Of course you do, ever since I can remember you have always been an A student. Even though on two separate occasions we were asked to attend a special meeting with the principal and some of your teachers, because they think you're a bit obnoxious and love to display your Athenian inclinations too much."

"Can I help it if some of my teachers don't really know what they're talking about? And furthermore, why must I be moved by their folly?"

"That's enough, David. I'm not raising you to be disrespectful to your teachers."

Frowning at Mom's remark, I said, "By the way, Mom, Daniel is having the gang over at his house for two days. And he would like to know if I can join them tomorrow afternoon. I told him that I would have to ask you. I know Dad is working late tonight, so I was wondering if you'd ask him if I can join the gang for those two days."

"You know it's okay with me. However, I don't know if your father will agree to this. I'm sure you're aware of how he feels about Dr. Daniel McCrory, especially given that they're Catholics."

"Yes, that's true, Mom, but I'd really like to go. In fact, I've been on only one sleepover at Daniel's house, when I was twelve, and since then I haven't spent the night there."

"But aren't you worried that you'll wet yourself while on the sleepover?"

I really loathe dealing with this problem. It's too depressing, it causes me to feel so dirty, and it's embarrassing just thinking about it. "Yes, Mom, but remember when I slept over at Daniel's house I was twelve? I didn't wet myself at that sleepover with the gang."

"Well, seeing that you explained it that way, I'm sure you're right. And furthermore, your father isn't aware of your problem."

"Mom, I wish you would cease discussing this unpleasant topic. For the past year, even though I still experience those horrible nightmares, I haven't wet my bed or myself, because I really want to get over this embarrassing problem."

"Okay, David, I understand the point you're making. However, I don't know if Rommel will agree to this. And it's a sensitive issue."

"Fine. That's all right. What I'll do is, before he leaves for work in the morning I'll just ask him myself!"

"I prefer that you don't do that, David. I'll ask him. Just don't push it, all right? The mood he's in when he comes home tonight will depend upon his answer."

"Thanks, Mom."

"You're welcome. By the way, could you inform Maria and Georg that dinner will be ready in fifteen minutes? Tell them to wash up and be on time for dinner."

"Yes, Mom."

That evening we enjoyed our family time together. I missed Jena, but certainly not Dad. After dinner we helped Mom clean up, and after making sure the house was secure I withdrew to my room, where I read for about one hour and then was fast asleep.

The next morning I was up by seven a.m. because I wanted to get a jump start on my chores. But while I was in the stable, Mom approached me.

"Morning, David, did you sleep well last night?"

"Yes, Mom, and how was your night?"

"It was fine. Your father arrived a bit late, but after his meal we had a good talk. So I felt comfortable enough to ask him about the two days at the McCrorys. You can go, but after your chores are done. And Rommel has given me strict instructions to convey to you that you should ride your bike to the McCrorys', because he feels the exercise is good for you. Make sure that you pack your knapsack, and if there are any thunderstorms while you're riding or swimming, he said that you know what you ought to do in situations like those. Furthermore, you are to keep away from Professor Bechstein's house."

"*Ich verstehe.* (I understand.) Is that it?" I said, annoyed at my father's demands.

"Yes."

"Well, thanks, Mom. When I'm finished, I'll call Daniel and let him know that I'll be there as soon as possible."

"That's fine, David. Did you have anything to eat this morning?"

"Only fruit and a glass of milk, Mom."

"I'm going to make pancakes. Would you like some sausages?"

"Oh yes, please! You know that's my favorite."

"I thought you'd like that. I'll call you when they're finished."

Around one p.m. my chores were all completed, so I headed for my room to wash up, and was soon on my way to meet the gang, but not before saying *auf Wiedersehen* to Mom, Georg, and Maria. It took me about twenty minutes to arrive at Daniel's house. The day was hot and humid, typical of a New England summer.

"Hi, David, thanks for coming! I'm glad you made it," Daniel said.

"I should be thanking you, Daniel. Thanks for inviting me, buddy," I replied.

The first thing Daniel did was offer me some soda pop and a huge slice of watermelon. It wasn't long before the entire gang had me laughing at their silly jokes. I knew it was going to be a two great days.

We ate and listened to music on the radio as we talked and laughed, taking delight in our friendship and company. After our time of fun, we were so satisfied that we lay under a huge oak tree, enjoying the shade from the hot summer sun. It wasn't long before we were fast asleep.

By four p.m. we were up, and decided to go for a ride, with the plans of swimming also. After our brief stop we were on our way once again, and soon at our destination. We parked our bikes under the shade of the trees, and then we undressed, stopping at our swimming trunks, which we had on underneath our jeans. Afterward, we ran violently and with much enthusiasm down to immerse ourselves in the cool, relaxing water of the Connecticut River, off West Springfield River Road. We were not the only ones that day who were riding bikes, and there were others in the river as well, either in boats or swimming. We laughed so much as we exchanged jokes that my mouth felt as if it was about to split. We dived, played, rolled over, and duck-dived. We came out of the water periodically to keep ourselves hydrated, and entered the river again and again, as we endeavored to descend into the depths, trying to get as deep as we could. As we came up for air I felt alive, and for the first time in many years my thoughts were not about Father, his church, religion, *Mein Kampf*, philosophy, and the seeking of his approval.

I'm always trying to prove to him how intelligent I am, and many thoughts are often ruminating in my mind. Thrashing my feet, I headed for the deep. Looking up, I could vaguely see the appearance of the people above me in the water; however, as I came closer to the surface, I could see the images of my friends at a distance. I headed for them and head-butted Daniel.

He shouted, "Hey, I'll get you, man!" I laughed at him. We were racing for the shore, but suddenly I could feel the current tugging at me and pulling me down. I shouted for Tobey and Jesse, who were near, and they came and assisted me out of the water. I was zonked out from all the excitement of the day, but in spite of this, I felt marvelous. The water was exhilarating, even though Tobey and Jesse had to help me out. My legs were cramping up, since certain parts of the river were very cold. But when we came out of the water, I felt completely relaxed and drowsy. Before we lay on the hot rocks, we spread out our towels on them to reduce the intense heat while we enjoyed the sun. My skin is white like paper, so I knew that I shouldn't expose myself to the direct sunlight for too long.

I asked the gang, "What time is it?"

"Almost six o'clock," James answered.

"We should get moving."

"David, would you relax!" said Ryan.

"Okay, but I honestly think that we should get moving."

"Hey, Hugenberg, your old man is not here nagging your ass!" Jack shouted.

"I know, but—"

"No buts, David, just relax!" said James.

"Sometimes I find it difficult to relax, and furthermore, I think I can't relax, because my father is the tight-ass Protestant Pope!"

The gang started to laugh.

"That's a good one, David. Just try to unwind, man, you'll see. It's a good day," said Harry.

"Yes, but I'm coming out of the sun," I said to Harry. "I don't want to get a sunburn, or my father will be all over me."

"Good for you, David, you do that," said Ryan.

About thirty minutes later we left and headed for Daniel's home. On the way we stopped at Professor Bechstein's home, not too far from where the McCrorys live. We all agreed to this, as we were determined to enjoy the cigarettes James had taken from his father's store.

Professor Jeremiah Bechstein is a Jew from Europe, and he had lived in the United States for about thirty years. Before the octogenarian professor retired from Wesleyan University, he taught political science for many years. He's a widower who lives on his own. His home resembles a house that was built in the days of colonialism, for the gray outside of the house looks quaint but neglected. It has a direct view of the Connecticut River.

The gang and I entered the old stable. It's lonely and abandoned, and the absence of animals, particularly horses, makes it a bit creepy. Most people in this region have horses.

We became relaxed and accustomed to the environment of the old stable. We lit our cigarettes and began to talk. The majority of the folks in town believe that Professor Bechstein has horns. This is because he wears a hat at all times, and the religious people, especially the Protestants and Catholics, say that Jews belong to the devil and have horns, and wearing a hat conceals his deviant deformity. I know this is absurd and foolish, but even I've heard my father's personal remarks about Professor Bechstein.

"So, Ryan, what do you think about Peggy?" asked Jesse.

"Peggy who?" Ryan responded with a confused tone.

"Peggy Whittaker. She lives four houses from you and goes to our high school, the school we all attend. You know, it's in the town we live in, which is known by two famous nicknames: *The City of Homes* and *The City of Firsts*," Jesse said, provoking Ryan.

"You dipshit! Fuck you, Jesse Atwood!"

"Hey, guys, please refrain from those negative remarks. I hear things like that from my religious father every day," I said.

"Yeah, cut it out!" said Daniel. Being my best friend, he knows exactly what I encounter every day from my father and his capricious tongue.

Ryan and Jesse continued with their profanity before they calmed down and started talking about Peggy Whittaker in a sensuous manner.

"Man, Ryan, every time I look at Peggy, she always gives me a hard-on! Man, looking at her is sheer voyeurism!" Jesse told Ryan.

"You're lucky that she only gives you a hard-on, Jesse! But with me, I'm frequently having wet dreams about her!"

The gang laughed together as we took great pleasure in our cigarettes, but not before Daniel stepped in and told Ryan and Jesse to stop talking about a young girl like that. He said, "You two have sisters, so cut it out!" However, Ryan and Jesse continued with their inappropriate conversation while the rest of us started a dialogue of intellectualism and stimulating similes, seeing who could get the right answer quickest, followed by a few simile questions and Latin sentences.

"As eloquent as?"

"Cicero!"

"As elusive as?"

"Quicksilver!"

"As empty as?"

"An idiot's mind—as space!"

I concluded our simile questions with a religious joke. "As empty as? A religious dummy, for ignorance can be a curse!"

The gang chuckled hysterically, and someone said, "That's a good one, David!"

"*Aut Caesar aut nihil?*"

"All or nothing!"

"*Aut viam inveniam out faciam?*"

"Where there's a will there's a way!"

"*De asini umbra disceptare?*"

"Little things affect little minds!"

I responded that this Latin axiom was meant primarily for religious fuck-heads. "That's precisely why we can't have any acquaintances with simpleminded teenagers," I expounded to the gang. "For I do not wish to have social acquaintances where I may encounter unequal stations of intellectualism, because I can't deal with simpleminded people!"

Before I could continue, the gang agreed that it has always been this way, and it will never change.

We certainly had a good time in the professor's stable. Either he was not at home, or he was already fast asleep. We were there for more than an hour, and finally we left. As we ventured to Daniel's home, we were not aware that one of us left a burning cigarette in the stable, and that Professor Bechstein was already in a deep sleep. In addition, the old man suffered from a weak heart, and in the evenings, just before he retired for bed, he would take his medication. And one of the side effects of his narcotics was drowsiness.

When we arrived at Daniel's home, the sun was setting, and while we prepared for dinner, the fire had already started in Professor Bechstein's house. That night he would die from asphyxia, before the flames consumed his feeble old body.

Chapter Four

The Secret Unveiled

Secrets are a master disguise for some people: they protect certain individuals and shield them from not allowing others to know the truth. Certainism teaches that a person shouldn't live a double-standard life, because to encourage such a life is to be an activist of secrecy. With the philosophy of Certainism, the Certainist cannot be a disciple of duplicity.

The Certainist should be truthful to his conscience at all times and live in accordance to the germane truth by which he has chosen to live. To have secrets is to actually live in the ideal and deny the actual.

It's foolish to hide the real you from others, and it's a waste of time to conceal the truth. My theory of Certainism says to be certain to oneself. However, there are those who believe that secrets are meant to be concealed. But what exactly is a secret, and should it be revealed?

A secret is the act of deliberately keeping back or removing the essential facts from the conspicuous observation of others. Therefore, in reality a secret is analogous to the lie of omission, since in the end the truth will be known. That's exactly what this chapter is about: the secret unveiled.

That evening when we arrived at the McCrorys', the sun was about to set, and Dr. McCrory and his wife were outside preparing dinner for the gang. After such an adventurous and exhausting day, we were hungry and ready to indulge in the sumptuous feast. Daniel's father greeted us that evening and made us feel at home.

"Hi, guys!" he said, smiling at us.

We responded together to his warm salutation. "Hi, Dr. McCrory!"

"I guess you guys had fun today? All of you, with the exception of David, look tanned. How's that?" asked Mrs. McCrory.

Daniel answered her curious question before I could. "That's true, Mom. However, he has a slight tan. But Mom, the reason for David's light tan is that he exercised much caution and did not lie in the sun, like we did."

At that moment, we were eight hungry young men, yet before we could partake of the banquet, it was mandatory that we wash up first.

"Oh, I see," said Mrs. McCrory. "That's very clever, David. Is it that you preferred not to be exposed to the sunlight? Because you could use some color."

"No, Mrs. McCrory. It's just that I don't want to do anything that might upset my dad."

"Well, I think that's very thoughtful of you, David."

"Thanks, Mrs. McCrory, I try."

Daniel discreetly interjected, "Hey, buddy, I didn't know you could be such a *putain* sycophant!"

Since Daniel was being so sarcastic, I responded to his negative comment with a witty Latin reply. "*Suge meum aquaeductum.*"

"Oh, you want to be a smart-ass, eh, Hugenberg? Well, I too can use the scholastic tongue to insult you. *Linge bacillum glycyrrhizae meum!*"

Then we began to laugh, because generally speaking, the average person, if he or she heard us, wouldn't understand what we're saying. That's precisely why I told the gang that evening in the professor's stable, "I don't wish to have social acquaintances where I may encounter unequal stations of intellectualism, because I can't deal with simpleminded people!" Furthermore, the gang and I understood one another, and spoke the same language.

"Boys, I'm sorry to interrupt your simulating discourse, but my wife thinks you guys should hurry up!" said Dr. McCrory.

Daniel responded to the gang, "My dad's right. We've been idling for too long."

"Okay," said Harry. "But Daniel, you need to tell us what to do."

"Come on, guys, I'll show you where you can clean up before dinner."

We followed Daniel into the house. His house is not as large as mine; however, it's still a considerably large house. It stands upon thirty acres, and the size of the house is about forty by forty. It has four floors, and it's the most recently constructed house in Daniel's neighborhood.

His house has four bathrooms, one on every floor except the basement. So we consecutively shared the bathrooms. Daniel told us that he would use his parents' shower, as he wanted to hasten for dinner.

The McCrorys' house has four bedrooms, and this includes the master bedroom. Daniel is the only child. His parents waited seven long years before they could have their first child, but on the night that Daniel was born the doctors realized that Mrs. McCrory was, in fact, giving birth to twins. Because there were serious complications with the babies, Daniel was the only one that survived; his twin brother lived just a short while. They were born on October 22, 1920. Daniel is my senior by fifteen days. The oldest person in the gang is Harry; he's six months older than the rest of us. In our gang, we're just days apart in conjunction with age, since all of us were born the same year. Moreover, besides the family disaster, Mrs. McCrory was told that it would be too risky for her if she tried to have another child. Daniel's parents love him very much, and have always tried to show it and to take special care of their one and only child. His parents make it their duty to go the extra mile for their son and his friends. That's why the McCrorys are always kind and considerate to us. They know that we in the gang genuinely care for one another.

And throughout the years I've discovered that they're very genuine people, and the most unpretentious couple I've ever met. Dr. McCrory is the only genteel man I've even known. He's nothing like my cold religious father.

Nurse Estella Bradley (Daniel's mom's maiden name) and Dr. Daniel McCrory are in fact childhood sweethearts, and both natives of Massachusetts. They decided to get married when Nurse Bradley was fresh out of nursing school.

After our cleaning up, we went outside to partake of the sumptuous feast. There was a permanent large table on the lawn not too far from the kitchen entrance. We sat down to eat and the food looked great: corn, corn bread, barbecued beef ribs, chicken, mashed potatoes, carrots, and pies. I noticed two large apple pies, my favorite. As usual, Dr. and Mrs. McCrory were the perfect host and hostess, and because of their kindness, we had a grand time. And as we got to dessert, Dr. McCrory noticed a bright light in the distance that looked like a fire.

"Oh my God! What's that? It looks as if there's a fire some distance from here."

At that moment, the gang and I didn't think much about it, because we were oblivious to everything and wanted to continue our meal. Dr. McCrory eventually decided to call the sheriff's office to make sure they were aware of the fire in the area. The sheriff told him that everything was under control and his family should keep clear of that area, considering that it was still an uncertain situation. The light from that particular area got brighter and brighter as the darkness of the night came to Springfield. We were enjoying our dessert and had our pie with milk. Soon after, the McCrorys' phone began to ring, and Dr. McCrory went in to answer it. Surprisingly, it was my dad, the Reverend Rommel Hugenberg.

"David."

Oh boy, what does this grump want with me now? I wish this man would just disappear from the face of the earth, I thought. "Hello."

"David, how are you?"

"I'm fine, Dad. We're having dinner."

"That's fine, I'm sorry to interrupt. I'll not keep you long from your friends. I just wanted to make sure that you're okay. And Dr. McCrory assured me of that."

"By the way, Dad, thanks for allowing me to spend these two days with the gang."

"You're welcome, David, but I'm afraid it's your mother you should thank."

"But just the same, thanks, Dad. By the way, what's the latest with Germany? And the Fuhrer? Have you listened to the radio this evening?"

"Yes, I did, but nothing has changed in Europe. However, I'm sure this is going to escalate into another world war. By the way, I got two new books today. They're about two great German philosophers. I think you're familiar with their writings."

"Who are they, Dad?"

"They're Johann Wolfgang von Goethe and Johann Christoph Friedrich von Schiller."

"Oh yes, I'm familiar with their writings."

"You know that I enjoy reading stimulating topics."

"I'm aware of that, Dad. Who do you think I got that from?"

"What the fuck do you mean by that remark?"

"I'm sorry. I was just trying to show you how much I'm like you in certain things."

"Well, that's enough, you stupid fuck! Stop trying to flatter me!"

There was silence for a few seconds, because I knew it was hopeless trying to please my father. *Here he goes again with his religious capricious tongue. So much for his messages of self-control, the hypocrite!*

"Would you like to say good night to your mother?"

"Y-yes, D-Dad," I said, sounding discouraged as I began to stutter.

"David."

"Y-yes, M-Mom."

"How was your day, son? Are you okay?"

"I-I'm—"

"You don't sound all right."

"I-I w-was f-fine u-until I-I sp-spoke w-with D-Dad." I tried to keep my serenity.

"What did Rommel say to you?"

"N-never m-mind, M-Mom. I-I'll b-be f-fine. I-I'm s-sorry, M-Mom, I-I d-don't f-feel l-like t-talking m-much r-right n-now."

I was still standing by the phone, trying not to become emotional about Dad's insensitive disposition. I knew what might transpire if I allowed myself to become perturbed. I didn't want to mortify myself by having the dreadful nightmares, and to make matters much worse, by wetting myself at Daniel's house.

Dr. McCrory came into the kitchen to see if I was okay. "David, what's wrong?"

He saw the color of my cheeks and the redness of my eyes. Tears trickled from them as I tried my best to control my emotions.

"N-nothing, D-Dr. M-McCrory."

"Now, David, it's okay. I'm fully aware of your circumstance, because before you spoke with your father, you were terrific. Now, after your conversation with him, here you are stuttering. I can see you're emotionally upset and are trying your best not to break down."

"I-I s-sorry f-for u-ups-setting y-you, s-sir."

"Nonsense, David, you haven't upset me! Please try to understand my intentions. Remember that I'm also a father, and a physician, and my purpose is to help you."

"I-I r-really d-don't w-want t-to d-discuss t-the m-matter, p-please! A-and t-this, D-Dr. M-McCrory, i-is o-of m-my o-own v-volition."

"Fine, if that's what you want, David. But please know this: if you need help with anything, son, and I mean it, or if you ever need to talk, I'm here for you! Now, please go to the bathroom, blow your nose, and wash your face. Then go to the sitting room and stay there and I'll get Danny boy for you. Maybe if you open up to him, he can help you."

Mrs. McCrory saw her husband's expression and asked him, "What's wrong?"

"It appears that bastard, the most Reverend Rommel, has verbally abused and upset his son once more! I went in the kitchen to get some paper plates, and I overheard their conversation from the other room. I couldn't believe how David's father was yelling at and cussing him. I don't understand it. How can a man who claims to be God's mouthpiece be so cruel to his own flesh and blood? Really, Estella, I don't understand. How can Helena stay with that invidious righteous bastard? And to think, for all those years most of the people in town knew of his illicit affairs, not just in Springfield, but also in California."

At that moment, Daniel, suspecting something was wrong, came in and asked, "Mom, Dad, where's David? Is everything all right?"

"No, Daniel. I think you need to be with your best friend," said Dr. McCrory to his son.

"Okay, but where's David?"

"He's in the bathroom, but I told him when he's finished, you'll be waiting for him in the sitting room," said Dr. McCrory.

Daniel went to the sitting room to wait on me. Meanwhile, Dr. and Mrs. McCrory continued with their conversation.

"I hope he'll open up to Danny, Estella, because I sense that David is building some impenetrable walls around him. Furthermore, he doesn't need insularity at this moment in his life, for if David turns away from God and the church it will be an irrevocable choice that will turn his mind against all types of religion."

"What do you mean, Daniel?"

"Estella, I'm aware how the home—and especially a father—can impact children, particularly a boy. And the Reverend Rommel appears to be a saint, but at the same time, he has the temperament of a devil! I know about these religious people, especially those blasted Protestants. They're so self-righteous, and always criticizing us Catholics, and saying that anyone who doesn't believe like them is doomed to hell. And I certainly don't agree with those perverted priests that molest young boys, because men like that who do such dreadful things need psychiatric help. But those Protestants condemn such acts, but they, in turn, sleep with their members and have illicit relationships outside their marriage," said Dr. McCrory.

"That's just terrible, Daniel. But what can we do to help David?"

"Well, if you had seen and heard him when I approached him, I know your heart would have reached out to him. As a parent, I don't ever want to do anything that will cause our son to feel like fucking shit! Please excuse my language, Estella, it's just I'm so upset by all this."

"Honey, you know that I love you very much, and thank you for being a good father to our only son, and for loving me. Are you aware this is the first time in almost twenty-four years that I've heard profanity from those tender lips of yours?"

"You know I don't like using profanity. My opinion about such words is that they're only for empty-headed wantons, and religious deviants like the Reverend Rommel."

"Look, the fire seems to be dying out," said Mrs. McCrory.

"Do you know what David's father told me?" said Dr. McCrory.

"No, what?"

"He said that he thinks it's Professor Bechstein's house that's on fire, and he said, 'I'm not sure, but it appears that the fire is coming from that old Jew.' One of the deacons informed him about that. And as he continued with his diatribe, he said, 'But I don't know if that story has any credence to it.' He was talking about the fire. Then he said, 'God knows we can do without the Jews, for they're the nemesis of the human race.' I felt led to interject about such a sensitive issue by letting him know that I really don't appreciate such comments. But I knew he became annoyed with me. However, I really don't care what the Reverend Rommel thinks or says about me. He's certainly not God. And the Protestant Church cannot condemn me through any form of its foolish anathemas! But Estella, before I could end my conversation with the Reverend Rommel, I was so annoyed with that self-righteous bastard. David overheard my conversation when he came in to use the bathroom."

"Oh no," said Mrs. McCrory.

"I can assure you, there's no need to take to heart what David heard, Estella, because I'm sure he's fully aware of his father's tongue."

As Dr. and Mrs. McCrory continued with their conversation, they decided to venture out for their walk. As I came out of the bathroom Daniel was waiting to speak with me. The rest of the gang—James, Ryan, Jack, Jesse, Harry, and Tobey—did an excellent job as they completed their chores of their own volition that evening and entered the house. But prior to that, Daniel came to me, as Dr. McCrory had said he would, and came to my aid as the ideal concerned friend.

"David, what's wrong, man?"

"I-It's m-my d-dad. H-he m-makes m-me t-feel I-like sh-shit."

"Do you want to talk about it?"

"N-no, n-not r-right n-now."

"I'm here for you, David, and you know the gang is also here for you."

"Y-yes, b-but m-my p-problem i-is m-my o-own."

"That may be so, David, but you need to look at things from a different angle."

"W-hat d-do y-you m-mean?"

"If it was the other way around, and it was me, or one of the gang, wouldn't you want to help us? Because to deal with this on your own isn't right, David."

"I-I guess s-so."

"Well, allow me to help, buddy, because that sort of an attitude is one of insularism, and is certainly *contra bonos mores*!"

"Okay, I get the point, Danny boy!"

"Hey, your stuttering has stopped. And how did you know about my parents' sobriquet of endearment?"

"Your dad used that term when he was talking to me."

"Oh, I see. Well, what the heck, friends shouldn't hide things from one another, right?"

With that remark from Daniel, I looked at him in amazement, and with some degree of envy. However, the envy I felt toward my best friend that evening had a positive result to it, and not a negative effect. I admired the relationship Daniel has with his father, and I longed for that relationship with my dad.

"David!" said Daniel.

"Yes, I'm sorry. I was just thinking how lucky I am to have you and your parents in my life. You remember when we first met, that day in elementary school?"

"Yes, we were five, and how could I forget? All the girls were busy looking at you, and they forgot all about me. Because, man, your hair is that reddish-blond color, and your blue eyes are so bright. Those girls couldn't stop looking at you, and they ignored me. And because of that, I was pissed at you."

"And remember that time when we were eight and got into a fight? And Tobey and Harry came to our rescue. We would have killed each other."

Daniel and I were laughing once again, as we reflected on those early days of our lives. I knew that, as my best friend, he was trying to help me forget my abusive father, at least for the moment. "You know, Daniel, I'm really glad you invited me to spend these two days with you and the gang."

"Hey, buddy, as I told you on the phone, it wouldn't be the same without you. In this gang we complete one another. And furthermore, wasn't it Robert Hall who said, 'A friend should be one in whose understanding—'"

"'And virtue we can equally confide.'!" I ended the wise literary writing of Hall.

"So, David, please try to understand. Remember some years ago, when I told you about my twin brother, and how disappointed my parents were when they realized they could never have any more children?"

"Yes, I remember, how could I forget that, Daniel? You trusted me with that piece of information. I've never shared it with anyone."

"I'm aware of that, David, but what I'm trying to say is you're my best friend. And I love the gang very much. But if there's something my dad or I can do, we would like to help."

"I appreciate your concern, Daniel. However, I must deal with this on my own. You know that my father is nothing more than a religious hypocrite. And I must surmount these problems which he has engendered for us at home. Remember, Daniel, becoming a man means we must prevail over those things that trouble us. When I was a child, and now that I'm a teenager, my father has always been abusive. And what I'm about to share with you, please don't ever share with anyone, except your parents, if you feel comfortable about it. My father is not only verbally abusive, he's also physically abusive to us. And that means my mother as well."

"That fucking bastard!" said Daniel.

"And this has been going on for some time. Please, Daniel, this isn't easy for me. And now I'm wondering if I did the right thing by sharing this with you. No, I'm sorry, Daniel. I shouldn't have shared this with you. Please forgive me, and forget about it!"

At this time, about ten minutes into our conversation, the rest of the gang came in.

"Hey, guys! What's up?"

"Hey, David, we missed you, buddy. You didn't finish your dessert, so we placed it in the refrigerator for you."

"Thanks. I'll finish it later," I said.

James then asked me, "Are you all right, David? We missed you at the table, and I know I speak for the entire gang."

"Is everything all right at your home, David?" Ryan asked.

"Yes. My dad just wanted to make sure we're okay, and that's only because of the fire."

Then Tobey asked, "Yeah, what's that all about, and whose house is on fire?"

"We're not sure," said Daniel. "But I heard my dad telling my mom that they think it's Professor Bechstein's house."

"Get out of here!" Tobey responded with much surprise.

"But we were there, just a couple of hours ago," Jack commented.

"Well, I would suggest that we keep this to ourselves, and take it to our graves, if it comes to that!" Daniel replied. "And no matter what happens we should swear to secrecy, and keep to the same story: we were at the river, and left there around six thirty p.m. However, we were so exhausted from the time we spent swimming that it took us much longer to arrive at my house, since we were simply cruising along the way. And furthermore, no one can prove or disprove our story. We left Professor Bechstein's stable around eight ten p.m."

"But why should we prevaricate? As far as I can remember we did nothing wrong."

"And you can't arrest someone for smoking a cigarette in the old man's stable," Harry interjected.

"That may have a strong element of credence to it, Harry! But I'm not going to break my parents' hearts because all of a sudden you decided to have an awakening of conscience. You know, really, Harry, it's better to be without wits than to apply them as you do! Sometimes, you can act like a genuine simpleton! And you must really try, Harry, to extricate yourself from the presence of folly, since those of us in this gang will not tolerate an ignorant person! Because ignorance can be a formidable image! Besides, you all know how my dad feels about cigarettes and one's health. Furthermore, I'm not prepared to tell them that I was smoking with my buddies in Professor Bechstein's stable, so I suggest that we all swear to secrecy and never talk about this again! Is that clear, gang?"

"Yes, we agree. Let's swear our secrecy as brothers to never mention this again."

"Okay, Danny boy!"

"Cut It out. Oh, well, what the fuck. And frankly, I don't give a shit!" said Daniel.

But the gang all started laughing simultaneously, including Daniel and Harry, in spite of their disagreement.

"All right. Seeing that's all over with now, I think we need to help our friend. If I may, David?"

"Of course, Daniel."

"His father, the self-righteous bastard, called him tonight, but it ended with the Reverend Hugenberg making David feel like dirt. Well, the gang knows what he's like anyway."

"A man who loves to put his hand in women's underwear while they're being driven home," Tobey said sarcastically.

"That's enough, Tobey! No genitive declensions, please! And furthermore, I don't think David needs to be reminded of that macabre incident that happened some time ago. He's our friend and in this gang. We protect our own, right, gang?"

"That's absolutely right, Daniel!" the gang shouted.

"I recommend that we have a group hug in a circle as we renew our allegiance to this gang. And to the power of higher learning," said Daniel.

"It has been a long time since we've done that," said Ryan.

"That's true," said Daniel.

So the gang gathered in a circle, our heads touching, and we encouraged one another by swearing allegiance to our friendship forever. "*Perfer et obdura iuvenis!*" Daniel told me, meaning "hang in there, young man." He inaugurated the Latin chant, and the rest of the gang repetitiously chanted our Latin axiom glorifying intellectualism and the bond of our friendship. This was also done with the purpose of encouraging me to hang in there, and overcome the rigors of religion, which is *stultitia*.

Before we concluded our brief meeting, Daniel's parents returned from their walk. We ended with our fraternity pledge to higher learning: "*Nos honos Ahura Mazda et Zoroaster as nos cantare Gathas ad vos!*" (This is a mixture of Persian and Latin words, glorifying reason, wisdom, and intellect). It was an enlightening gathering; even though it was short, we were able to reach out to one another and receive the strength that was needed at that particular moment, especially me. As we exchanged greetings with our secret handshake, Dr. and Mrs. McCrory entered through the kitchen door.

"Hi, guys, what's up?"

"We're fine, Dad," Daniel said to his father.

"The kitchen looks great, boys. I can't thank you enough for your effort."

"You're welcome, Mrs. McCrory!" the gang responded, except me, because I couldn't take any credit for this.

"No, Mrs. McCrory, it's we who're indebted to you and Dr. McCrory, because we were able to spend one of the finest days in our summer vacation with our buddy, Daniel," Tobey said.

At this, Mrs. McCrory became emotional. She expressed circumspect tears of joy, as she took great delight in their kind words. "We consider ourselves lucky, boys, that Danny has such genuine friends."

At that moment, Dr. McCrory asked his son, "What were you doing?"

"We were just having a meeting about our education and grades, and also exchanging and renewing our fraternity pledge to one another."

"That sounds great, guys. Your mom and I met the sheriff while we were walking and he told us the fire was in fact at Professor Bechstein's house. It's out now, but not before consuming the entire place, which included his house and the stable. The sheriff is not sure, but when I spoke with a fellow colleague of mine, he told me it looks like Professor Bechstein died of asphyxia before the fire reached him. But no one knows for sure how the fire started. They think it may have started because the house was so old, although there's going to be an investigation into this unfortunate incident."

"We're sorry to hear about Professor Bechstein, even though we didn't know him," said Harry, but not before Daniel and I gave him a sudden glance.

"Well, I'm sorry to hear about the old man, boys. All the same, please excuse me. I must say good night now. I have a long day tomorrow and must rise early. But please, continue with your precious moment, guys."

Daniel told his parents good night, and they responded with the same phrase to us. Then we all sang a harmonious chorus to Daniel's parents: "Good night, Dr. and Mrs. McCrory! Sleep well!"

That night I felt such relief, because I knew with all certainty what I must do. My father will never again cause me to feel like shit. Yes, those haunting nightmares and my bed-wetting were a thing of the past.

Between us, we shared three bedrooms, and had already decided who would sleep where. Tobey and I would sleep in Daniel's room; Harry, Jack, and Ryan shared the second bedroom; and Jesse and James slept in the third bedroom. That night we spoke for some hours before deciding it was time to end the long day, since tomorrow was another big day: our final day.

Daniel slept in his bed and Tobey on the other side of the room. I made my bed next to Daniel's bookshelf, which was opposite to where Tobey was sleeping. I had chosen that particular side because it was next to Daniel's bookshelves. Because of my nocturnal predilection, reading always helps me fall asleep, but that depends on if my mind doesn't start to do some serious thinking as I read.

The windows in Daniel's room were open, and the night was still, humid, and muggy. It felt like eighty degrees and there was no breeze, only the intense heat of the hot summer. The fans in the bedroom alleviated the heat to some degree. I lay on the sleeping bag trying to relax; it was just too hot to cover up with or get into my sleeping bag, so I tossed and turned.

I gazed for a few minutes at the ceiling, thinking about the fabulous day and my conversation with Dr. McCrory, but I felt so thirsty and a bit dehydrated. As a result, I had to get some water. Coming back to Daniel's room, I noticed that those in the other rooms were already fast asleep, and some of them snored so loudly I thought they would disturb Daniel's parents. I returned to Daniel's room and watched my friends sleeping, looking so peaceful even in the heat of the night. Just then, it dawned on me: *why am I wearing this thick jersey?* Daniel and Tobey were sleeping in shorts, their chests bare; therefore, I took off my jersey. I looked through Daniel's bookshelves for something interesting and noticed a book about the state of Wyoming and women's rights. I took the book from the shelf and started to read.

I learned that the state of Wyoming is in fact a place of firsts. Wyoming was the first state to have a national monument in 1906, President Theodore Roosevelt proclaimed Devils Tower to be the nation's first national monument. Wyoming inaugurated women's suffrage in 1869 on a territory level, and fifty-one years later, in 1920, was the first state to give women the right to vote. It was also the first state to have a female judge.

I was about twenty minutes into the book when Daniel woke up, looked at me, and said, "Hey, David, you're reading?"

"Yes. I guess I'm addicted to the written word."

But before I could complete my sentence, he was again fast asleep. Not long afterward I closed the book and set it on the floor next to me, because I was now thinking about this country and the Nineteenth Amendment, which was passed by Congress on June 4, 1919.

When I thought about the fact that it was just sixteen years ago that women were granted their civil rights to vote, I couldn't help but realize that political reformation did occur in the early twentieth century. The winds of change brought radical and permanent changes across the earth as women cried out against their misogynistic masters.

In the end, they finally succeeded in breaking free from the shackles of a patriarchal society. Nevertheless, changes for most women didn't occur until after the end of World War I, in 1918, when women were granted the right to vote.

Religion loves to oppress women, which it considers to be the weaker sex. The women suffragists were fighting for the rights of women in this country, not only to vote, but also to have equal rights with men.

The British writer and feminist Mary Wollstonecraft promoted the first women's suffrage in 1792. Soon after, a blaze was inexorably ignited that eventually ended with the liberation of women in the early twentieth century.

Prior to the historic political change of August 18, 1920, the shackles on women in the United States and other nations around the world began to experience a universal atrophy. Then came the breakthrough for women in New Zealand in 1893. Finland followed in 1906, and then Norway in 1913. Great Britain granted the right for women to vote in 1918, but according to Parliament, a woman had to be over the age of thirty in order to vote. However, in 1928, this preposterous law was changed to the age of twenty-one.

When America granted women the right to vote with the Nineteenth Amendment, the eligible age was over twenty-one, not the ridiculous age of over thirty like Great Britain. And in the arena of religion, the Roman Catholic Church didn't support any level of women's suffrage in most Catholic countries. I guess that's the sad reality with religion: it will suppress you, and will never seek to liberate you as an oppressed minority.

I was listening to the silence of the night, and even though I was thinking, I was starting to get a bit sleepy. I couldn't help but think that the world we live in is indeed imperfect. Men are certainly far from saints, and that goes particularly for religious people, and also politicians. Nevertheless, if we were living in a world where men were considered to be virtuous, I'm certain that common sense would benefit us little.

When I look at the system our nation was founded upon, I'm left breathless. The leaders of this great nation have betrayed our county's ideals, and what freedom actually means for the people in the United States. For example, can you fathom a constitution that denies the basic civil rights of citizenship to women and minorities?

Congress passed the Fifteenth Amendment on February 26, 1869, and it was ratified on February 3, 1870, granting former slaves the right to vote. I question certain things about the ideals in our country, such as the basic concept of human rights within our sacred document, the Declaration of Independence. It was the Father of Virginia, Thomas Jefferson, who wrote it, although he got advice from other wise men while writing it. This document was in fact written to legitimatize and justify the raison d'être for independence. The Declaration of Independence was actually presented to Congress on July 2, and in the meeting the members in Congress made a few changes that would strengthen their grounds against King George III. The document was not accepted until the Fourth of July. The question that causes me to be ambiguous about these men is, what exactly did the framers of the Declaration of Independence have in mind when Thomas Jefferson used the adjective *all* in it? For example: "*We hold these truths to be self-evident, that all men are created equal; that they are endowed by their Creator with certain unalienable rights; that among these are life, liberty, and the pursuit of happiness.*"

The adjective *all,* depending on what the author had in mind, can be extremely equivocal. I'm obligated to conclude that in the Fifteenth and Nineteenth Amendments, the adjective *all* did not include women and minorities, who also were created by their Creator with certain unalienable rights. And for that particular reason, I'm forced to formulate a logical deduction that the author of the Declaration of Independence, when he used the adjective *all,* used it in the indefinite sense, meaning some but not literally *all* individuals. Furthermore, I think he meant only white Christian men who owned land. I wondered if these so-called religious men really understood and studied their Bible. Thomas Jefferson was not a religious man, and never revealed his religious affiliation because he was a deist. Science was actually his higher power of intellectualism. Most people who aren't properly informed about the events of our history presupposed that the framers were, as some religious groups have called them, "born-again believers, or Christians." However, if that pseudo-statement has any credence to it, then they have failed to recognize that the majority of the Founding Fathers were in fact idealists and deist philosophers. The majority of them might have been God-fearing men, but certainly not religious fanatics like the majority of Christendom has claimed, because if these men were truly "Christians," as Christendom has labeled them, they most certainly would have been mindful of Genesis 5:2, which reads: *He created them male and female, and blessed them and called them Mankind in the day they were created.*

The English translation of the Bible does not establish the true meaning of the word *mankind* like the Hebrew syntax does, which gives a much clearer definition of the Hebrew word. In the original Hebrew of the Old Covenant literature, the word that is used for mankind is literally אדם, *man*, meaning Adam.

This definition causes me to ask myself: Does that mean these men deliberately overruled the rights of the female sex and others because they were not white "Christian" men? The framers of the Declaration of Independence and our Constitution began this nation by denying certain individuals their constitutional rights. Furthermore, to be more specific, by their actions, what they failed to do was the crucial paradigm of those leaders who had betrayed our country's ideals, by failing to procure equal rights for all individuals.

I'm aware that most people will not agree with my Certainist views on the contents of *Mein Kampf* and our governmental documents, which have certain similarities in their constitutional elements. *Mein Kampf* led to the First Nuremberg laws of 1935, which stripped the Deutschland *Juden* (Jews) of their civil rights. The framers of our young nation did not care to extend the rights and security to women and other minorities in the Constitution, which is the supreme law of the United States. The Declaration of Independence inadvertently denied some citizens their basic human rights.

This is a cardinal sin against humanity, for these rights and privileges naturally belong to all citizens of America. Women and certain minorities were not considered to be free men created by their Creator, with the same measure of unalienable rights.

However, I have learned that the framers of the Constitution were indeed great men, and they knew one thing that all great men should know: that they certainly didn't know everything. I believe that they, like David Hume, repudiated the potentiality on the certainty of knowledge; therefore, I'm sure the framers of the Constitution had this in mind when it was written. In fact, they wrote it in such a manner that future generations could have the opportunity to correct what they failed to secure in the Constitution of the United States of America.

The method by which these wise men wrote it epitomized their impeccable wisdom, for the Constitution of the United States is a living entity, not a stagnant, lifeless document. The eminent genius of the Constitution comes from the will of the American people, for this living document can always be changed by the faith and wisdom of the people; that's precisely what the word *amendment* means. It describes a change for better, the removal of what is faulty. It connotes correction, such as the changing of a law or bill. The legislative branch of government can be used as a positive and permanent vehicle for change.

The people who were robbed of their constitutional rights and treated like pariahs of society were Native Americans, women, and individuals of African descent.

When the War of the Rebellion broke out in 1861, no one knew it would last four long years. One of the major causes of this war was the question of slavery. This was the result of the economic discrepancy between the industrial Northern states (the Union), and the slave-based mentality of the Southern states (the Confederacy). The war ended on April 8, 1865. It cost the nation its sixteenth president, who was assassinated one week later on April 14, and died the next day on April 15, 1865. In addition, more than six hundred thousand soldiers died in the Civil War, when the United States came so close to becoming the Divided States of America.

As far I can see, and in conjunction with my philosophy of Certainism, slavery was an unfathomable crime against humanity. It was a wicked act against others, since it violated the essence of human rights.

The Certainist theory advocates that all human beings are born free, with the dignity of human rights, and are equal to all, in spite of color, gender, or sexual orientation. But it's 1936, and I'm fully aware of how society and those religious-minded people view homosexuals. I'm also conscious of the fact that homosexuals are human beings, and being gay most definitely isn't by choice. In fact, they should be respected and free from all levels of discrimination and persecution.

However, getting back to the topic of slavery: "Boy, I'm so glad that my father's ancestors were not involved in the slave industry," I said to myself discreetly, not wanting to disturb Daniel or Tobey.

All of a sudden, a strong wind began to blow, and it looked like it was going to rain. "Oh, I think I should close Daniel's windows, and do the same for the gang in the other rooms who are sound asleep," I muttered. When I entered the room with Jesse and James, Jesse had gotten up because he was awakened by the sound of the thunder. While he was making an effort to shut the windows, James headed for the bathroom.

"David, haven't you gone to sleep for the night?" asked Jesse.

"No. I'm reading an interesting book about Wyoming and women's rights. And it just ignited my ruminating temperament."

At that moment, James came back from the bathroom. "Hey, David and Jesse, if you want to talk, I suggest you get the hell of out here!"

"Take it easy, James. There's absolutely no need to become vociferous. And furthermore, do you want to wake Daniel's parents?" I said to him, like a good gentleman. On that note, I vacated the room and got myself comfortable once more in my sleeping bag, forgetting about the other room with Harry, Jack, and Ryan. "Gosh, I didn't know that James is so sensitive about his sleep," I said. Nevertheless, I decided to resume my reading and ruminating about slavery.

I thought about all the families who suffered the injustices of slavery, when their loved ones were taken from them against their will and transported to a foreign land in the name of human exploitation.

The Certainist knows that life can be a *canis* (again, Latin for bitch) when it's payback time. Therefore, the Certainist endeavors to be an excellent humanitarian. Certainism knows that humanity is the only and ultimate reality, and that's why the happiness of others is very important to the Certainist. Reason over morality is the philosophy of Certainism.

Consequently, the main reason the Certainist strives to be an excellent humanitarian is because he believes what you do to others is exactly what you'll reap in the end. What goes around comes around. This is not based on religious teachings; this is a natural universal law, which has absolutely nothing to do with the superstitious teachings of religion. The slave-owning individuals in America, who claimed to be Christians, murdered and committed many atrocities in the name of human exploitation. The people in that period believed that slaves were not human beings with human rights. Rather, they were viewed as nothing more than the property of a free man. Then again, as time progressed the nation became very unsettled. The North and South shared different values and opinions about the slave trade. And when the Civil War broke out in 1861, the people of America became their own enemies. The United States was in tatters as its citizen's waged war against each other.

In the Civil War, neighbors, families, brothers, and citizens all fought against one another. The ground of America was stained with the blood of its own people. Prior to the Civil War, the slave masters had caused the blood of many innocent victims to stain the ground of our nation.

Retribution finally came to the American people in the guise of the Civil War, and by the end of the war blood had met blood in vengeance and justice, as the balanced scales of Themis were satisfied according to the laws of nature. The Thirteenth Amendment was finally ratified on December 6, 1865.

In the following year, 1866, there was a major disagreement between the new president, Andrew Johnson, and Congress. In the early spring, Congress had passed the Civil Rights Act, which granted U.S. citizenship to blacks. This was the first Civil Rights Act, which was passed to rescind the Dred Scott verdict of 1857. In this case, the Supreme Court had ruled that those of African descent were not citizens of the United States. It was hoped that the sagacious steps of Congress, with the act of 1866, would solve the problems in the South. For example, there were black codes in the South, and African people living in the United States were being denied their constitutional rights even after the war.

President Johnson's intention was to veto the new bill; however, the sagacity of those members in Congress outwitted the old fox and the bill was passed. Nevertheless, Congress feared that the judicial branch of government might declare the Civil Rights Act unconstitutional.

Not wanting to encounter a condition similar to the Dred Scott policy of 1857, the Republican Party made reference to the Fourteenth Amendment, for the purpose of legalizing the Civil Rights Act of 1866. The Supreme Court overruled the bill, and blacks in the South were still being persecuted, as they were considered second-class citizens.

Furthermore, in 1920, women were granted the right to vote. It's hard to accept that this happened only sixteen years ago. Our social milieu is still one of a patriarchal society. This erroneous view came about from those dominant men—and it's still prevalent in the twenty century—but before 1920, most men believed that women were not entirely human, like them.

The third and last group of people denied their constitutional rights were the Native Americans. In 1924, they were granted citizenship. Before then, they were considered nothing more than aliens, and some Americans thought they had absolutely no right to be here. I was four years old when the American Indians were finally recognized as citizens.

These people were actually here long before the first group of English people came in 1585, and had lived on this continent for centuries. The fact that almost four hundred years later they were granted their citizenship is indeed ludicrous. In the Constitution of the United States, Native Americans are mentioned twice. The first reference to these ancient people is found in Article 1, Section 2: *"for a Term of Years, and excluding Indians not taxed."* The second reference is found in Article 1, Section 8: *"To regulate Commerce with foreign Nations, and among the several States, and with the Indian Tribes."*

The first major attempt that the American government made to establish a relationship with the Native Americans was the decree of 1790. This was the Trade and Intercourse Act, which legitimized the licensing of trading with Native Americans. In reviewing all three major documents that formed our country—the Declaration of Independence, the Constitution, and the Bill of Rights—as great as these documents are to this nation and its citizens, they never applied to the female sex or minorities in the United States of America.

And furthermore, there was never any universal protection for these three groups of people. The framers of the Declaration of Independence and the Constitution knew exactly what they meant when they wrote: "We hold these truths to be self-evident, that all men are created equal; that they are endowed by their Creator with certain unalienable rights; that among these are life, liberty, and the pursuit of happiness." The preamble of the Constitution begins with the words "We the people." The pronoun we, in grammar, is the nominative of the first plural in this sentence structure. However, even though the pronoun we may support the plural definition of the people in the Constitution, the framers deliberately excluded women and minorities from this universal protection. Their intentions were not to include all the people in this great privilege. The nominative we, was literally meant only for those of a particular group and not the general public. Also, the adjective all was not used in a generalized sense, but in the indefinite expression, because the framers were not making a reference to the entire population of the United States. In fact, people need to be in touch with the fabric of historical events and how they have fashioned our society. In addition, the general public has neglected to thoroughly comprehend the historical and philosophical background of these governmental documents and how they have intrinsically molded the American psyche and its milieu.

These are my diagnostic observations, being a young Certainist. These were influenced by my philosophy of Certainism, and this is the domino effect of the continuity of my scholastic pursuits, which have resulted in this tenacious conclusion.

The conclusion of my thoughts is not meant to embellish an argument of flippancy. The main objective is to establish and substantiate my relevant views that are based primarily on historical facts, and not what I may have presumed to be the truth.

The Founding Fathers propagated their patriarchal demographic ideals in the nascent stage of the United States, and by that endeavor they were able to separate certain groups in our society. Given that, what is the difference between *Mein Kampf* and our governmental documents? The only difference is that *Mein Kampf* was very conspicuously the Fuhrer's answer to Germany's problems. In looking at the theoretical and philosophical aspect of *Mein Kampf* and our governmental documents, there's no difference in the constitutional elements of these. In our documents the framers were very subtle and inconspicuous about the ideals of demography, while simultaneously promoting, discreetly, a society of ethnology (the science of subdivisions and the families of the human race). If people would hold these truths to be self-evident—that the Founding Fathers were indeed great men, which cannot be disputed—the truth of the matter will remain the same: they were only men, and men will make mistakes.

"Gee, I think that's enough of my philosophical ruminating, because the time is two fifty a.m. I need to get some sleep," I said to myself, and finally I fell fast asleep.

I slept for about eleven hours. My eyes didn't see the light of day until two o'clock that afternoon. While I slept, the gang was up by ten a.m.

Mrs. McCrory had told Daniel, "Make sure you shut your windows, close the curtains, and leave the fans on for David." Daniel is truly a good friend, and as such, he followed his mother's instructions to the letter. Daniel made sure his room was conducive to my sleep, by making it dark and cool. And because of his effort, I slept for more than ten hours.

The gang had breakfast, and then swam for a while, and by the time they were coming back into the house, I was just getting up. As I regained consciousness from my long rest, I felt a great relief, since I had had no nightmares, nor did I wet myself.

Coming out of Daniel's room, I stepped into the hall. Daniel was waiting for Tobey to come out of the bathroom.

"Hey, Mr. Sleepyhead! David, do you always sleep so late during summer vacation?"

"No. I didn't fall asleep until two fifty this morning."

"Yeah, I remember seeing you reading. And I thought I spoke to you. Or was that all a dream?"

"No, you're correct. You spoke to me, but were soon fast asleep again."

"What were you doing all those hours?"

"I was reading about and ruminating on our Constitution and the Declaration of Independence."

"What were you reading?"

"A book I took from your bookshelf."

"Knowing you, David, I guess that's why you wanted the spot close to the bookshelf."

"Exactly, Daniel. You know me, buddy."

"What was the book about?"

"Wyoming and the civil rights of women."

"But David, isn't that a bit peculiar, to be reading while you're on vacation?"

"Nope, not for me. I wasn't sleepy, and I wanted to read."

At the moment, Mrs. McCrory came up to the third floor. "Good afternoon, David. And how are you this fine day?"

"Fine, thanks, Mrs. McCrory."

"And how was your night?"

"Oh, I slept like a baby." *But with no nightmares,* I thought.

"I was up by eight o'clock, because I thought that maybe the gang would be up by that hour, and furthermore, I wanted to have breakfast ready for you young men."

"I'm sorry for getting up so late."

"Nonsense, David, you're Daniel's guest. By the way, what would you like for breakfast, or brunch?"

"I'm not fussy. Whatever the gang had, I guess I'll have."

"All right. Would eggs and pancakes be okay with you?"

"Of course. Thank you, that's great. As soon as I'm finished washing up, I'll be down."

"All right, take your time."

By now Tobey was out, and Daniel went in. The rest of the gang was already upstairs and packing.

"David, I'm sorry we went swimming without you."

"That's fine, James. Man, I didn't know you could get so crabby."

"What do you mean?" asked James.

"Don't you remember? I came into the room this morning because it started to rain, and you went to the bathroom. But Jesse had already gotten up to close the windows, and by the time you came back from the bathroom, man, you were annoyed with me. I was talking with Jesse, and you recommended that if Jesse and I wanted to talk...let me see, your exact words were, 'Hey, David and Jesse! If you want to talk, I suggest you get the hell of out here!'"

"I'm sorry," said James, "and I'm glad you told me about this. I'll have to apologize to Jesse about my irrational behavior. But it's true. I'm very grouchy when it comes to my sleep."

"That's okay. Now that I know, I'll keep clear."

After my breakfast, we said good-bye to Mrs. McCrory and thanked her for her hospitality. Daniel followed us outside, and we said good-bye and went our separate ways.

On my way home it was a pleasant ride, and when I arrived at my house, Mother and Georg were outside, as if they were waiting for me with much anticipation.

"Welcome home, big brother," Georg said, and ran to me with a gleam of excitement in his deep blue eyes.

"Hi, Georg. How are you?"

"I'm fine. Is there anything I can help you with?"

"No thanks, Georg. That's very generous of you, but I can handle it."

"David, we missed you."

"I missed you too, Mom. Where's Maria?"

"She's in the kitchen."

"David!" Maria shouted. "I missed you. Did you enjoy those two days with the gang?"

"Yes, except I got up so late today that I missed out on going swimming with the gang."

"It's good having you home," said Maria.

"How's Father?" I asked Mother. I don't know why, because I didn't miss his vicious tongue.

"He's fine, but he leaves in the first week of September for a convention in Dallas, Texas, for two weeks."

That's the same week school starts, I thought, with much pleasure. Imagine, two whole weeks without the Protestant Pope.

"David, are you listening?"

"Oh, yes, Mom. I'm sorry, I was just—"

"Don't tell me, thinking?"

"Yeah. How did you know?"

"David, I'm your mother, and I should know you by now. You're daydreaming most of the time."

"Well, Mom, it isn't exactly daydreaming."

"Well, what would you call it?"

"I guess I'm always thinking."

"Just don't lose yourself in that philosophical mind of yours, okay?"

I laughed at Mom's comment and said, "No, Mom, I won't. Let me put my things in my room, and I'll be back to start my chores."

"There's no need for that, David."

"What do you mean?"

"Georg and I completed them for you."

"B-but why? Oh, that's stupid of me. I'm sorry, Mom. I should be thanking you and Georg for your kind gesture."

"You're welcome, David. We just wanted to show you our appreciation."

"Yes, I'm aware of that."

"David!"

"Oh, I'm sorry—"

"Don't tell me, ruminating."

"Yes."

"What were you thinking about this time?"

"Dad. I'm sorry, Mom. Could we change the topic?"

"Sure."

"Have you heard anything about the fire?"

"No. The last I heard, they were still investigating the cause. And the whole town is aware that not only did young people frequently spend time in Professor Bechstein's stable, but hobos occupy it as well, especially in the fall and winter. So, anyone could have started that fire. Furthermore, I'm sure it was an accident."

"Why do say that, Mom?"

"Because it was the ideal place for teenagers, and the homeless used it periodically, so why should someone deliberately set fire to a place that was used by so many people?"

"I don't know," I said, as I tried to hide my feelings.

"Anyway, do you want something to eat, David? I'm sure you're hungry."

"No thanks, Mom. I had a late, and also huge, breakfast this afternoon."

"Well, just in case, when you're ready let me know, okay?"

"Yes, Mom."

I headed for my bedroom. Surprisingly, I slept another two hours that afternoon, and Mom woke me in the evening, just before dinner. Dad was home, and was his usual critical self as he spoke in the most negative manner about the late professor, cutting his meat and belittling the deceased with his anti-Semitic remarks.

"Well, the town is finally rid of that cutthroat-dog Shylock, that dead-dog Jew!"

I thought, *He hasn't even asked me about my two days at the McCrorys', and here he goes again with his self-righteous attitude, condemning everyone who doesn't believe like him—but that's just like him. He ignores us, and the only time he talks with us is when he wants us to do something, or if he's in the mood, which isn't very often. Imagine, comparing Professor Bechstein to the character in William Shakespeare's play,* The Merchant of Venice. Mother simply excused herself, heading for the kitchen. Dinner that evening was one of the most unpleasant experiences for us.

It was agonizing and excruciating to hear Dad malign an old man who wasn't alive to defend himself. And furthermore, we never knew the man. How can you have an opinion about someone you never knew?

And what hurt the most was that it could have been our fault. The gang and I were in his stable smoking for over an hour. If Dad knew that I had blatantly disobeyed his orders, I would be in grave trouble, and I guess Mom would too. I was certain the gang and I did the right thing by swearing each other to secrecy about the stable that evening in July. Besides, I didn't want my parents to know I had been smoking for almost one year.

However, as I continued to listen to Dad's unwarranted remarks, I thought I would get a severe case of indigestion from his negative words about Professor Bechstein.

"You know he's in hell, because that's where all those Jews go! In the afterlife, that is. And do you know that, according to the traditions of the church, certain Jews were in fact born with worms in their mouth?"

That's when I really began to feel nauseous. I wished Dad would just stop, but he went on an on with his negative comments.

"Because the locksmith who actually made the nails to crucify the Son of God made sure the points of those nails were specifically blunt, with the cruel intention of increasing the suffering of the Christ. I tell you, these people, they're a perfidious nation. Liars, these Jews are. They're the deicide race, for they have killed God. These Jews are nothing more than niggers wrapped in white sheets!" Dad said to us, as he continued his diatribe. "Do you know that the founder of the Lutheran church, Martin Luther, cursed the Jews even on his deathbed? And what's so

114

ironic is that Bechstein was consumed in a fire. It's as if the fires of hell came for him, even before he was dead!"

"I thought Dr. McCrory said that he died from asphyxia, so he was already dead before the fire consumed his body."

"What the devil are you talking about, David? Why don't you just shut your fucking mouth?"

I kept my head down, staring at the food on my plate, because by now I couldn't finish my dinner. Then I became introverted as I found solace, and safety, in my philosophy of Certainism, for my theory establishes the satisfaction of assurance and peace that is needed in these trying moments. If I wasn't a Certainist, I'm sure that after all these years religion would have brought about my mental instability, or my cessation of life.

After dinner, I said good night to my mother and paid homage to the "Divine Augustus," my father, the *putain* Protestant Pope of Springfield, Massachusetts.

I entered my room and locked the door behind me, which gave a certain comfort of security and separation from that evil religious man who dwells on the other side of my door.

The first week of September was soon upon us and summer for that year was officially over. I was glad that Dad was not going to be home for the next two weeks. I could spend some quality time with the gang, and also invite them to my house. It was the only time I could invite them: when Dad was away.

It's amazing how the weather in New England changes suddenly. There's a saying: "*If you don't like the weather, stick around. It will change.*" The first day of school wasn't a cold day, however; it was pleasant, and the change felt terrific in comparison to the heart of the hot, humid summer in Massachusetts.

The gang and I met before the bell rang, and we spoke about many things, except the late Professor Bechstein. Afterward we headed for our class with Mrs. McKellen. The first day of school was the usual routine of getting back into a new semester.

The fall of 1936 would begin a year I would never forget, which would leave an indelible mark on me. In addition, 1936 brought about the end of my parents and their pretentious relationship as man and wife.

In fact, it all began when I entered the classroom for human and social biology. The teacher, Mrs. Beatrice McKellen, had organized a special assignment for us that fall: to trace our family genealogy on the mother's side, not the father's lineage. We were told that we had to go back at least two hundred and fifty years, with the goal of discovering our matrilineal ancestors and where they originally came from. The gang and I thought this should be interesting. However, there were a few students who didn't know what the adjective *matrilineal* meant.

"Class, for those of you who may not know what the word *matrilineal* means—" But before Mrs. McKellen could finish her explanation, I put my hand up, hoping to get her attention. "Yes, David."

"May I explain to these fellow students of mine what the adjective means?"

"Yes, of course, David."

"It has to do with your lineage on your mother's side; hence, matrilineal, and not patrilineal, which has to do with your lineage from your father."

"That's very good, David. Thanks for your clear explanation."

"You're welcome, Mrs. McKellen." I gazed in amazement at those who didn't understand this simple word. *How stupid can you be?* I thought. *Some of these students are so unintelligent.*

Daniel said, "Suppose that some of us already know about our matrilineal lineage?"

"That's a good question, Daniel. Those of you acquainted with your mother's lineage only need to write a three-page essay about your matrilineal lineage, thoroughly describing the impact of your mother's ancestors and the contributions they made to the social structure of the United States.

"But the ancestors of both my parents came from Dublin, Ireland," Daniel replied, "from the region on the Liffey River at Dublin Bay, more than two hundred years ago. Must I still do this assignment, even though I'm aware that some of my relatives are still living in Dublin?"

"No, Daniel, but please allow me to explain. For those of you who may not know about your matrilineal ancestors, I suggest that you seek out the necessary information to complete your assignment. For those students like Daniel, all you have to do is write an essay about your mother's family, given that you're fully aware of your matrilineal ancestors, and the influence, in Daniel's case, of Irish Americans. Your assignment must be handed in on September the twenty-seventh. So that gives you three weeks to complete your matrilineal project. And please remember, no later than that date."

"Mrs. McKellen?"

"Yes, David."

"I think this should be interesting, because honestly, I haven't the slightest notion whatsoever as to my mother's ancestors and where they came from."

"That's the whole purpose of this assignment, class. It's meant to build and establish a social pride in you as you discover your unique social contribution to this diverse country of ours. It's only when you examine your matrilineal lineage that you'll know they, too, played an integral part in what you are today."

The school day came to an end, and I couldn't wait to get home to start my matrilineal assignment. That afternoon I asked Mom about her ancestors, but she was reluctant to share any information with me. It was very peculiar; somehow I felt that Mom didn't want me to know anything about them. I couldn't understand her attitude. Mom never spoke about her ancestors. Both her parents died in an automobile accident when she was five, and Mom was the only child.

Her response was the same as always. "I'm sorry, David, but I don't know anything about my ancestors. I think they were English. If you want, you can check in the attic. You may find something there to assist you in your school assignment."

That, to me, was even more intriguing. The mystery of the unknown drove me to seek out the truth about Mom's ancestors. I entered my room and began a soliloquy of questions. "Where were my mother's ancestors originally from? Who were they? And why doesn't Mom care to know anything about them? Father knows a lot about his Germanic ancestors, and he's not ashamed of his Aryan lineage."

I decided that before three weeks came to an end, I was going to have the relative information about Mom's ancestors. So I said, "The ideal place to begin, according to Mom's words, is the attic. Yeah, that's an excellent place to begin this quest."

After dinner, I informed Mom that I was going to be in the attic for the rest of the evening. However, she really didn't pay much attention.

I headed for the top story, hoping to discover something that would lead me to my matrilineal relatives. The attic looked so inaccessible and scary; the last time I had been up there was maybe about seven years before. I turned on the lights. There were so many boxes and other items stored in this forgotten room. I thought, *Can I find anything of value in here?*

I contemplated where to begin while I took a deep breath, trying to keep my composure. However, with my theory of Certainism, I decided to take it one step at a time and not get overwhelmed by this quest of mine. Two hours into my investigation, I finally found something that would help me: two separate documents that had some information about Mother's relatives, who, it appears, were English jewelers. The second document was written in a foreign language; I couldn't understand the writing. It certainly wasn't Latin, German, or Greek, for these languages I understand quite well. I had never seen this language before that moment.

The first document, which was written in English, dated back to 1712, and the second one had the date 1648. Both documents had a word on them that I will never forget.

The document dated in 1712 had the word Khmelnitzki. The foreign document had a similar word, which gave me chills: Chmielnicki. Somehow, I felt there was a connection between these two words, because even though they were spelled differently, something told me there was a connection. This, I knew, would give me a comprehensive explanation of my matrilineal lineage.

After some time went by in the attic, it was time for me to stop and return to my room. Georg and Maria were not in their rooms; the house was very quiet, for Mother had retired for the evening. Georg and Maria were miraculously not arguing; this was unusual, because most of the time these two are at loggerheads and arguing about stupid things. But to my surprise, they were playing chess in the most civil manner in Father's library. I spoke with them briefly, and then took those important documents with me into my room, where I hid them in a safe place.

I thought, *Who can help me with these documents?* Just then, I remembered what Dr. McCrory had told me that night, when he comforted and encouraged me. He had said that if there was anything I needed he would help me. I thought of calling Daniel, but realized it was ten thirty and it would be inappropriate to call him at that late hour. So I decided to wait till the following day, and share my particular dilemma with him.

During the day at school I was able to converse with Daniel about these documents, particularly the one written in a foreign language. He told me he would have to speak with his dad and get back to me the following day. I waited patiently for his response. Daniel conveyed to me that his dad would like very much to assist me in this matter, but because of the long hours he was working that week, he would not be able to meet with me until the following Monday. I was glad that

Dr. McCrory would make the effort to meet with me, in spite of his long hours at the hospital, but I didn't want this to coincide with Dad's return from Dallas. I tried my best to prevent this from happening, so as not to create a problem with my dad.

Eventually I knew what I had to do, and I met with Daniel's dad the following Monday after school. I shared with him the intricacies of my assignment, and also expressed to him the confidentially of these particular documents.

He told me that he had a friend in Cambridge whose majors had been history and philology, and if I could wait till Friday he'd take me to meet him. I decided to wait, even though I knew Dad was returning that same day.

The day finally came to unfold the mystery of the document written in a foreign language. That Friday morning before I left for school, I told Mom that I had to be at Daniel's house for a school project that afternoon, and that Dr. McCrory was helping me with the information. She didn't seem to give much thought to what I was saying to her.

Finally, after waiting for two weeks, I met Dr. Mark Herbert, a professor at Harvard University. "Hello, Dr. Herbert. It's an honor to meet you, sir."

"The honor is all mine. Your name is David, right?"

"Yes, that's correct."

"Now, what is this about these mysterious documents of yours?"

"Well, Dr. Herbert, my teacher gave us an assignment a few weeks ago, and it led me to our attic, which my mother advised me to look in. While looking for any information that might lead to my matrilineal ancestors, I found these documents in a particular box. What caught my attention were these two words: Chmielnicki and Khmelnitzki. Even though I'm aware that these words are not spelled the same, somehow I have a strong feeling they're actually connected."

"May I see the documents, please?"

"Oh, I'm sorry. Yes, of course."

About five minutes into Dr. Herbert's scrupulous examination of the documents, he paused and stared at me. In those few seconds, it was as if his eyes were scrutinizing my soul. He took off his glasses and gently pressed his fingers at his temples, as if to indicate a coming question. Then, he got up from his desk and excused himself from the room. He was out of the room for more than five minutes.

When he returned, he said, "Now, David, do you realize what you've actually brought to me?"

"No, sir. That's why I'm here. I hope that your expertise will answer my questions once and for all."

"These documents are genuine, but what they say will change your life. If you want, you can forget that you ever met me and continue your life as normal. However, if you wish for the interpretation, this document written in English is the key for understanding the other document, which is written in Polish."

"Polish!"

"Yes, David, Polish. The question is, how do these documents actually tie in with your matrilineal ancestors?"

"Well, as I said before, it all started with the assignment at school. My mother directed me to our attic, and I found these documents."

"Well, the document written in Polish is about two hundred and eighty-eight years old. I'm not an expert in dealing with valuable historical articles like these, but I can assure you that if you decide to go public with these documents, especially the one written in Polish, I'm certain there are museums that may be willing to buy these for a reasonable price."

"Well, that depends on what they say."

"Okay, the document in English is approximately two hundred and twenty-four years old. The document from Poland is from 1648, and it's actually a description of a family who lost the majority of their relatives and possessions in a pogrom, or I think the accurate word to use would be holocaust. This holocaust, which occurred in 1648, was meant mainly for Jews in Poland. It appears that only six people out of the entire family by the name of Sklodowska escaped the wrath of the Cossack thugs. This document is actually an account of those individuals, and the unfortunate incident that forced them to flee Poland and immigrate to England. As they weren't able to communicate in the native language of England, the individual handling the case of your matrilineal ancestors was responsible for seeking out someone versed in the Polish language to explain to the authorities what had happened in the spring of 1648. They were admonished to write down the events of the Chmielnicki massacre, for the purpose of legitimizing their stay in England."

As Dr. Herbert advanced in his thorough exegesis, my mind inevitably began to ruminate. *So what does this mean? Is my mother part Jewish? Or were her relatives Jewish? What would Dad say if he were to know about this? Does that mean I'm not of the pure Aryan stock? Oh my God, does that mean my siblings and I are half-breeds? Does that mean we're niggers wrapped in white sheets, according to Father's racist remarks? What does all this really mean? Mother doesn't look anything like a Jewess; she looks pure Aryan.*

"David, are you all right? Would you like to go outside, or do you need some water?"

"I think I need some fresh air."

"Okay, you can go on outside, and I'll finish translating this for you."

"All right."

I don't understand. How could a simple assignment lead to all this? It's like an anomaly that has given birth to a nemesis. As I left Dr. Herbert's office and stepped onto his porch, Dr. McCrory was there, sitting in a chair.

"David, is everything all right? You look a bit flustered."

"I'm sorry, but I don't feel like talking at the moment."

"If you need to talk, son, I'm here."

As I left the porch, I muttered to myself, "Why would I ever want to talk to you about anything? You have done enough already." I walked a few steps from the porch and sat beneath a tree, thinking, *What should I do about this information that for so many years was lingering in the attic? Why did Mom keep these lethal documents all these years? Wasn't she aware of the complications these documents could bring to us?*

Then I said to myself, "Father must never know about these documents. I'm sure he wouldn't take this with good grace. He already acts like the prime jackass with us. Just think, my brother and sisters and I, we're all mongrels, and Father has helped breed the things he hates. Honestly, I don't know what it's like being a half-breed, much less a Jew. How can I live with myself? But am I not the same person who entered Dr. Herbert's house? Nothing has changed since I received the information about the documents."

"David, Dr. Herbert needs you."

"Thank you, Dr. McCrory."

As I was passing him, I felt led to apologize for my irrational behavior toward this kind man, for I knew that Dr. McCrory was not only a gentleman, but also a mature one.

"Dr. McCrory, I'm very sorry for my negative and rude behavior, sir."

"Oh, David, think nothing of it."

"No, please allow me to finish."

"If it would make you feel better."

"Yes, it would, and also it's the right thing to do. I'm certain about that. You're my best friend's father, and I could never hurt Daniel, much less his parents, whom he loves very much. Furthermore, you were kind enough to take time out of your busy schedule to assist me in this most important matter. I just wanted to thank you, and please accept my apologies!"

"I do, David. And to ease your mind, know that I have the greatest respect for you, son, because you and the gang are a great influence on Danny. I know you're maturing into a fine young man. And after this, I have an even greater understanding of what you sometimes go through. So please, remember that I'm here to help in any way. Okay?"

I spoke with Professor Herbert, and he explained certain things to me before I left his office. Dr. McCrory drove me home that evening, and as he drove toward Springfield, I decided to examine the translated document that Dr. Herbert had written for me. The history of my matrilineal ancestors started to unfold with much understanding.

The Jews of Polish nationality are, in reality, Ashkenazi Jews. These are Hebrews of northern and central European descendants, and the name Ashkenazi is first mentioned in the book of Genesis 10:3. Therefore, in conjunction with the teachings of ethnology, Ashkenazi Jews are not Caucasian Gentiles; of Nordic stock. (In the study of demography, the Nordic people were those individuals of the blond-haired subdivision of the Caucasian ethnic stock inhabiting Scandinavia, Scotland, and England, and other Germanic peoples of northwestern Europe.) The Hebrews, however, are indigenous to Southwestern Asia, not Europe.

The Jews who settled in Poland were in fact driven out of the Rhineland. In addition, the Jews in Poland had lived in that part of north central Europe since 936 CE. According to historical archives, Poland had the largest percentage of Jews throughout the whole of Europe. In the beginning Poland was a haven for the Jews and a utopia when it came to religious tolerance. This lasted for more than seven centuries, but changed by the middle of the seventeenth century.

The catalyst that brought about this sudden change was the political, religious, and social unrest among certain religious groups. This social unrest was the main cause of the Chmielnicki holocaust of 1648. By then, the economy of Poland was experiencing some severe changes, and these problems lingered on until 1795. Throughout the centuries, the Jews were always the perfect scapegoats for an angry and discontented people. (For example: deicide, the killing of the Son of God.) In the everyday routine of Poland, religion dominated every sphere. In the end, the religious sects had their way in the social order. Religion controlled and divided the ethnic groups: Catholics, Greek Orthodox, Lutherans, Muslims, and Jews. These factions seriously affected the economy of Poland. The civil unrest between these religious groups only made matters worse with Poland's economic problems.

It all started in the spring of that year. There was a man by the name of Bogdan Zenobi Khmelnitzki who was a hetman of the Zaporozhian Cossacks, from the town of Chigirin. His town was situated in the district of Kiev. The atrocities of the Polish-Lithuanian moguls had angered Bogdan Khmelnitzki, and he launched his Cossack rebellion against them.

In the heat of this revolt, the Jews were caught in the middle of the massacre. Meanwhile, the Polish authorities, wanting to make a prime example of Bogdan Khmelnitzki, plundered his home, arrested his wife, and publicly whipped his son to death.

The Jewish communities, however, would feel the wrath of Bogdan Khmelnitzki due to these actions of the Polish authorities. This was one of the most monstrous events in Jewish history. Some historians believe that the holocaust, in fact, began in 1647 and lasted until 1651, when King John defeated Khmelnitzki at Berestczko. Babies and children were not spared in the atrocities of Bogdan Khmelnitzki's Cossacks.

Children were thrown into wells, and there were those who were cut into pieces like wild animals. Mothers and young women had their stomachs cut open and live cats placed in them. Their enemies then stitched up their stomachs, for the purpose of seeing them tortured by these creatures clawing from within. Jews were burnt alive by the thousands, and in the midst of this, they had nowhere to run.

However, those of your matrilineal ancestors that survived were lucky enough to escape the holocaust of that year and made it to England. But just as they thought they had seen enough blood, they arrived on an ominous day in English history: January 30, 1649. This was the day when Parliament executed King Charles I. The English had killed their king and abolished the monarchy. At that time in history England was no longer the United Kingdom; for a time England became the United Republic. In 1653, Oliver Cromwell became the lord protector and constitutional sovereign of Great Britain. This was the turning point in Anglo-Jewish history, and when your matrilineal ancestors arrived in England.

That day was a depressing moment in English's history for some, but according to the words of the first-century Roman poet and philosopher, Titus Lucretius Carus, "*quod ali cibus est aliis fuat acre venenum.*" David, you know this Latin adage means: what may be good for one man might be harmful for someone else. For those like your matrilineal ancestors, this was truly a fortuitous course in the events of Jewish history.

The king had lost his head; they in turn would keep their lives, and a door was now open to invite the Jewish people back into the English realm. Their name was changed to Knightley, in the hope of anglicizing them.

The lord protector of Britain first welcomed the Jews back to England after their expulsion in 1290 by King Edward I. This was a favorable and gracious moment for your ancestors. It was by the protection of Oliver Cromwell that the Jews were allowed to practice Judaism openly and freely, without fear of being persecuted. By his benevolent act, the Jews were able to live in a multicultural society. A religious man, Cromwell believed the conversion of the Jews would usher in the coming of the Messiah. Cromwell, being a sagacious politician, also knew that the Jewish business networking would make them a priceless commodity to the British economy, and they would eventually improve commerce in Britain. Thus, your ancestors were able to prosper freely in all their enterprises.

Also, this historical event, fashioned by the lord protector, actually helped salvage the condition of your matrilineal ancestors and worked to their advantage. They prospered in England while keeping their Jewish identity as they lived there for the next sixty-three years. Then, by 1712, some of your matrilineal ancestors wanted to immigrate to the New World. The rest of your ancestors chose to remain in England, for they had become wealthy English jewelers and artisans.

It was almost nine p.m. when we arrived from Cambridge. Before I exited the car, I thanked and said good-bye to Dr. McCrory. I had mixed feelings about this new information.

Because of the overwhelming facts from Professor Herbert, when I entered the house I suffered from galloping amnesia. Mixed feelings and excitement came over me. I was not mindful that Father might be home. So, I hastened to the kitchen, since I knew Mom was there, and started to share with her all that had happened that evening. Mom kept trying to indicate to me, but it was too late. When I turned around, Dad was standing behind me and staring at me with his cold blue eyes, which dramatized his vindictive wrath. At that moment, I knew the family secret had been unveiled, and it was like opening Pandora's Box.

Chapter Five

Intellectualism

We stood in the kitchen, frozen by fear for a few seconds. The unexpected vicissitudes of this ephemeral life kept knocking, reminding us of the present danger. I knew Pandora's Box was already open, which spoke of human misery for Mother and the rest of us.

All I could do at this moment was anticipate that *hope* would be at the bottom of the box, and this *hope* I knew was found in my philosophy of Certainism.

"What's all the secrecy about? David, what's that I heard you say? Just because I'm partially deaf doesn't mean I'm stupid."

As I gazed at Dad, I couldn't help but think, *Well, you said it. I think you're certainly stupid to be acting so irrationally with us.*

"David, I'm asking you a question!"

"I'm sorry, Dad."

"You're always sorry, and forever fucking daydreaming. What are those?" Father snatched the documents out of my hands.

A few minutes into his examination of the papers from the attic, and Dr. Herbert's translation, his response was not good. He looked at me, and then walked to the stove, lit the papers, and placed all the documents in the burning fire.

"Please, Dad, don't! I need those for a school a project!"

"Why, you little dumb fuck! You actually went to someone with these? And they actually traced your mother's lineage? I can't believe it. I thought that's what I heard from the other room."

"Dad, don't expect me to feign incompetence for the purpose of inflaming your pride!"

"You impolite little bastard!" Dad began to use his favorite insults, but in German.

"Dad, please calm down," I told my father.

"Shut your fucking pie hole, boy!"

"Rommel, please, take it easy," my mother begged.

"Why don't you just shut your fucking mouth, you Jewish whore!" With his callous remark, he slapped Mom across her face and she fell to the floor.

Mom responded to his violence in German. "*Du kannst nicht tun!*" (You can't do that!)

"Shut up, you lying Jewish whore!" Dad said. "You knew you were Jewish!"

"For Christ's sake, Rommel, please don't!"

Dad raised his leg to kick Mom, but so help me, I wasn't about to simply stand there and see that religious bastard abuse my mother. Therefore, I rushed him. "Nein! You fucking religious dog!" I grabbed his leg. We struggled and then fell to the floor.

Suddenly, I could feel the intensity of his strength as my body tried to withstand his violent punches to my face and stomach. Meanwhile, Georg and Maria kept begging Dad to stop, but I knew from Greek mythology that his fury was like the tale of Pandora.

Just when I thought I was going to pass out, someone pulled Dad off me. After that I heard a voice, the voice of Daniel's dad.

"Reverend Rommel, what in God's name are you doing?"

"Get your fucking hands off me, you fucking Catholic!"

"Now calm down, okay? Haven't you done enough? Do you want to destroy your family?"

"*VerpiB dich!*" (Fuck off!)

"Now, you listen to me, Rommel Hugenberg. I'm going to tend to your family, and when I'm finished, we're going to talk, for I'm about to call the sheriff! Do you understand me?"

"What are you talking about, you fucking prick?" my father replied. "You came into my house and attacked me, you fucking Catholic!"

"As I said, I'm going to tend to your family."

Dr. McCrory told Maria that he would need some clean towels. He tended to me first. I felt like I had been hit by a truck. He helped me into the sitting room and I sat on the couch, where he examined me. There were no broken bones, but my face and stomach were badly bruised. Soon afterward Mom came into the sitting room with me. He took care of Mom, who had only minor injuries. Dad remained in the kitchen. Dr. McCrory made sure I was fine, and then he spoke with Mom about pressing charges against Dad.

Mom, however, didn't want to do that. Dad started to shout at Dr. McCrory, commanding him to get out of his house. Nonetheless, Dr. McCrory ignored Dad's unreasonable behavior since he wanted to talk with Mom privately.

"Helena, why do you put your children through this hell? I think the man needs help."

"I'm sorry, but I don't want to discuss this right now. Furthermore, why did you take David to see this professor?"

"Helena, you're acting like this is my fault."

"I'm sorry. I'm just so confused."

"There's no need to apologize. You've just experienced a terrible trauma. What you need is to press charges against this man."

"No, I told you I don't want to do that!"

"Would you at least consider it? Look, Helena, David needs to rest for a couple of days. Would you and the children like to spend some time with my family?"

"Why would I do that?"

"Because it appears that something has released an uncontrollable rage in Rommel, and it's better for you and the children to be away from him. If you don't press charges against him, he might do something worse next time."

At this time Dad started to accuse Dr. McCrory of attacking him in his house.

"By the way, Dr. McCrory, what brought you back here this evening?" Mom asked.

"Helena, David forgot his books in my car, so I simply came back with the intention of returning them. But as I approached the door I could hear Rommel shouting and swearing. I rang the doorbell repeatedly and then I started to knock. But by then it was obvious—after those unpleasant sounds, I knew what was happening, or about to occur."

"I'm—no, we're forever grateful for your heroic attempt. You saved our lives. And David already thinks the world of you."

While Mom and Daniel's dad spoke, Dad left the kitchen and started to attack Dr. McCrory verbally. "I told you to get the hell out of my house!"

"Look, Rommel, I'm not going to waste my time arguing with you. You want to call the sheriff, go right ahead!"

But as Dad was about to speak with the operator, Mom interjected, "Rommel, if you call the sheriff, I will press charges against you! Just look at David!"

At that moment Dad knew that Mom was serious, and he put the phone down and went upstairs. My head was throbbing, because by now I had a severe headache. So Dr. McCrory gave me something to help me relax and to ease the pain.

Meanwhile, Mom had decided it would be better for us to get away for a few days. Before we left, Mom spoke with Dad, and Dr. McCrory also had a serious talk with him. Then he called his wife, briefly explained the unpleasant events, and asked her to prepare the guest bedrooms.

We stayed with the McCrorys for exactly seven days. Words cannot describe how it felt being away from my abusive father for an entire week. Mother really enjoyed herself, too, as she became better acquainted with the McCrorys and my best friend Daniel. It was impossible for me to attend school that week; however, Mom and Dr. McCrory helped in this particular matter so that my academic progress would not be affected. For two whole days I stayed in bed. I felt terrible, as the intensity of the pain consumed my body. My face was swollen for at least three days. Nevertheless, it was fun spending all that time with Daniel.

We had absolutely no contact with Dad during that week. When the time came for us to return home, Mom told Dr. McCrory that she wasn't going to press charges against her husband, the father of her children.

The McCrorys assured Mom that we could stay as long as she wanted, but Mom thought it was best for us to return home. She never shared with them the fundamental nature of what had caused the problem that Friday evening. Then again, she expressed her deepest gratitude for their kindness and concern.

That evening Dr. McCrory accompanied us into the house. Dad was still at work. The house looked neglected, and when Mom entered the master bedroom, there were signs that Dad had moved out her things and placed them in one of the guest bedrooms. Therefore, Mom knew she would never share a bedroom again with the only man she had ever loved, nor would she ever have conjugal relationship with him.

After a couple of hours Dad came from work, and spoke not a word to any of us.

That night Mom spoke to me about her relatives. "David, it's only fair that you should know the whole truth about your ancestors who left England. However, you will have to make some choices on your own." Furthermore, Mom believed that my siblings must never know about what I discovered. After I had agreed to Mom's conditions, she told me the following.

Those Jews who left for America wanted to separate themselves from their Jewish identity and the relatives living in England. They were fully aware of the holocaust of 1648, and even though the Jews were granted religious tolerance for almost eight hundred years in Poland, they certainly didn't want to encounter anything like the massacre in Eastern Europe.

They came to the New World for the purpose of starting a new life as Gentiles. Before they left England they converted to Christianity, with the intention of permanently concealing their true identity. Before leaving in the spring of that year, they were given certain documents, which they never revealed to anyone.

The inhabitants in the colonies naturally assumed they were of English origin. When Mom's parents died, she was adopted by her aunt and uncle, who were also Lutherans. It appears that they were the ones who had these documents. Mom had an idea what the documents contained, but she had no way of knowing that Dad would change as the years went by. Dad was not aware of her true nationality when they met.

Then she informed me that an individual is only a Jew if the mother is a Jewess. She had never been in a synagogue nor had ever cared to practice the religion of the Jews. It also depends on if the child wants to be recognized as a Jew.

Sometime afterward I found out that Jewish law teaches that if the mother of a child is a Jewess, the child is a Jew, and that fact is substantiated with future generations. It was the fifteenth-century rabbi, Solomon Ben Simon Duran, who unconditionally advocated that with the children of a Jewess woman, the nationality of the father bears no validity. The child of a Jewish mother and a Gentile father, according to the words of the sage, is "for all time" a Jew. It does not matter if the child is brought up as a Christian; the child is still a Jew.

After obtaining this relevant information, I was able to empathize with my matrilineal ancestors and my mother. I understood their reasons for choosing not to be Jewish.

When the time came for my assignment, I had decided not to include that ignominious information about my true identity. I simply stated that my matrilineal lineage originally came from England. I knew the history of Europe and the Jews is a forlorn episode, for the people of Europe caused the soils in their land to be stained red with the blood of many Jews.

As the months went by we kept to ourselves, and Father ate alone most of the time. He hadn't spoken to us in months, and this eventually began to affect Georg. As a result, Mom spoke with Dad and he agreed to keep up his relationship with Maria and Georg. However, he wanted absolutely nothing to do with me. So Mom agreed to his unreasonable request and played along with their pretentious marriage. They accompanied Dad to church regularly. His exact words to Mom were: "I would prefer to die than to know the truth about you and your fucking Jewish swine!"

This was Mom's decision, and I respected her choice with all certainty, even though after their agreement they still slept in separate bedrooms.

The year 1938 was soon upon us, and the problems in Europe lingered on. There was one particular incident that occurred in 1936 that I will never forget. It has been etched in my mind: the matter of England and her former king.

It was some years later when I realized the tectonic reality that this event played in World War II. I was certain this seismic event was going to change the course of the imminent war in Europe. The boy, called David by his royal family, certainly had no deficiency of anything that would equal earthly happiness. When Prince David's father, George V, died, the prince became king on January 20, 1936, with the regal title of Edward VIII. I heard his voice on the radio—I was sixteen when it happened—the king announced to his people, and the world, the reason for his abdication. He was king for only eleven months, and on December 10, 1936, he abdicated for the woman his heart could not live without. Her name was Mrs. Wallis Warfield Simpson. He said, "*You must believe me when I tell you that I have found it impossible to carry the heavy burden of responsibility and to discharge my duties as king as I would wish to do without the help and support of the woman I love.*"

I knew with all certainty the world would not understand the purpose of this seismic shifting with the changing of the monarchs. Yet, I was certain that history in the future would eventually reveal the reason for this earth-shattering episode.

The gang described it as outrageously macabre. I was seventeen and would turn eighteen in six months. Graduation was scheduled for May 15; we were the class of 1938. By this time I weighed 165 pounds and was six foot two. My hair was no longer a reddish-blond color like Mom's. It was now the identical color of my dad's hair, golden blond.

Our graduation was a landmark for us as young adults. The entire family was present at my graduation—that is, except for the Protestant Pope of Springfield.

The greatest gift I got was his absence. I was very pleased that my big sister Jena was there; by the end of that year she would be graduating from college. During her four years in college, Jena came home only twice. She never really cared about Dad and his religion, since he felt it was his paternal duty to force his religious beliefs on her. Furthermore, he never practiced what he preached.

In the fall I was to leave for Yale University. I'd been preparing for that college since I started high school four years before.

Since I started listening to the radio in 1934, a lot had happened in Germany. Hitler had made himself both president and chancellor of Germany. The Nazi Party announced that their new definition of a Jew was anyone who had two or three Jewish grandparents, and anyone who claimed to be a Jew. On July 2, 1937, by the decree of the Nazi regime, all Jewish students were ordered by the law of the land to leave schools and places of higher education. It was now against the law in Deutschland for Jews to pursue any level of education. On July 19, another concentration camp was set up in Buchenwald; this prison camp was located in central Germany, near Weimar. I assumed that most people thought these concentration camps were just for housing prisoners. In America, we call them penitentiaries. In Germany, maybe the synonym is concentration camps.

After the information that Professor Herbert had shared with me almost two years ago about the holocaust of 1648 in Poland, and with the experience of Dad's reaction to our true identity, and Hitler's plans to solve "the Jewish problem" meticulously outlined in his political exposé, *Mein Kampf*, it makes me wonder where all this might be leading. Because it appears that the Germans hate the Jewish race.

It's like the leaders of the world were not perspicacious enough to see the handwriting on the wall. By the end of 1937, all Jewish passports were declared by the German government to be invalid and not fit for traveling. This reminded me again of the holocaust of 1648, where most Jews had nowhere to run. On March 12, 1938, Germany finally took control of Austria; the *Anschluss* (the annexation of Austria into Nazi Germany). The people of Austria wanted this, and as one foreign newspaper printed. *"If Hitler was raping Austria, then the Austrians liked getting raped."* In addition, it also strategically implemented anti-Jewish laws, prohibiting the basic civil rights of European Jews.

After the graduation ceremony, the moment came for congratulations from friends and family. My fraternity brothers and I enjoyed ourselves, for this was a momentous occasion for us. Mom and my siblings decided they should return home and leave us young men to enjoy ourselves. And after a few hours of celebrating with my friends, I arrived home around two a.m.

I didn't wake up until one in the afternoon. I was glad that Mom and my siblings didn't disturb me and allowed me to rest. However, when I got out of bed, I asked myself, "What day is today?" After collecting my thoughts, I remembered that it was Sunday afternoon; therefore, when I came out of my room, there was no one in the house. I realized that everyone was still in church, and I remembered that Jena had told me that she was staying with her friend and would be leaving the following day.

I washed up and had something to eat. Dad and everyone arrived home around two p.m., but as usual, he never said a word to me. I decided to honor him with his same code of silence in return.

"David, have you eaten anything today?"

"Yes, Mom."

"We left around eight thirty this morning. I knew you'd return late from your celebration."

"That's true, Mom. I came in around two this morning. The gang and I went to the movies and then we spent some time at Daniel's home. Dr. and Mrs. McCrory—honestly, I didn't expect this—they had gifts for all eight of us! Can you imagine that?"

"Yes, David, but why should that surprise you? When I spoke with them at the graduation ceremony, I suspected they had a nice surprise for the gang. What did you get from them?" Mom asked.

"We all got the same thing: silver pens."

"Oh, that's very sweet of them."

"By the way, Mom, I'm sorry that I didn't thank you for my watch last night."

"You're welcome, David. I'm so proud of you."

"Mom, what's wrong with Dad? I noticed that he looks a bit yellow."

"Yes, I know. During the service he looked almost jaundiced, and for the past few days he's been complaining of pains in his upper abdomen—severe pains. After the service he told me that for the past week he has had no appetite. And—please David, this is highly confidential—your father informed me last week that six months ago he was diagnosed as a diabetic."

"What? Mom, how can that be? Dad has always been a man of exceptional health. He meticulously watches what he eats. So what's going on?"

"David, I was shocked when he shared that with me. I'm going to make an appointment for him to see the doctor on Tuesday evening."

"Why so late, Mom?"

"Because he wants to see Dr. Simon Harrison, since it was he who detected your father's diabetes. He's out of town and returns on Monday."

"I see. By the way, Mom, on Monday the gang and I are going swimming."

"But won't that be a bit dangerous?"

"Oh, Mom, you worry too much. Remember, we'll just be swimming off West Springfield River Road."

"Well, I'm just concerned, son."

"I know, Mom, but remember, in the fall we're all leaving to begin our new lives at different universities, and we don't know when we'll see one another again. Therefore, we're trying to spend as much time together as we can."

"All right, that sounds fair, David."

"Mom, you know that these guys are like my brothers. We even have our own fraternity."

"I'm aware of that, David, but please be careful. I can't bear the thought of something happening to any of you."

"I appreciate that, Mom."

In my room, I couldn't explain it, but my heart began to experience a deep heaviness about Dad's alleged condition. And I knew without a doubt that I could never hate my father. So I decided to go to him and try to mend our relationship.

However, as I drew closer to his bedroom door my heart started to race. It was pounding so fast and loudly that I could hear the amplified sounds of every heartbeat in those few seconds, and at a certain point I felt like I couldn't breathe. It was tormenting and excruciating. I felt like a condemned man walking to his execution.

Nevertheless, I knew I couldn't give in to my fears. At his door I closed my eyes and took a deep breath, trying to stay focused, but before I could open my eyes and collect my thoughts, Dad unexpectedly opened his bedroom door. I was now facing my father.

The look I saw in his eyes was not one of paternal care. I could see that he was still angry with me. In addition, his eyes told me that he was my archenemy, given what I'd done almost two years ago, in the discovery of my matrilineal lineage during the school assignment. Dad had grown to have a greater level of antipathy toward me, and not simply for being Jewish, but because I had inadvertently revealed the family secret.

"What the devil do you want?"

"I just wanted to see how you're doing."

"What the fuck does my life have to do with you? Listen, you dumb fuck, haven't I given you your emancipation?"

"Yes, but—"

"There are no buts! Look, David, get the hell away from me!"

"I'm sorry, Dad."

As Dad passed me, I turned around and looked at him with tears in my eyes. I knew he was on his way to the usual fortnight meeting with the executive board. I felt hurt, since I really wanted to mend our relationship, but after his response, I knew Dad hadn't and wouldn't ever forgive me, and allow our relationship to have a second chance.

Eventually, I went into my room. As I sat in my favorite spot at my desk, I saw his vehicle in the distance between the trees, and I knew this was hopeless. I felt extremely sad, because the fact remains that no matter if he's an American Nazi, an Aryan, or a Jew hater, he's still my father. I later recognized that at that particular moment when I tried to communicate with him, even though I was nervous, I didn't stutter. And I knew I had overcome the two oddities in my life—bed-wetting and stuttering—because of my philosophy of Certainism.

Moreover, even in the aftermath of Dad's rage with Mom and me that Friday evening, I knew I couldn't hate anyone, especially my father. I decided that people's misinformed opinions and religious institutions would never control me again. As a Certainist, I know that my conscience is clear, because with my philosophy I strive always to be an excellent humanitarian.

The Certainist believes that he should be an excellent humanitarian as he endeavors to promulgate his philanthropic responsibilities through his actions and random acts of kindness to the human race.

The philosophy of Certainism believes that humanity is the ultimate reality. But although I've tried to live out my ideals in a practical manner, when I attempted to reach out to my father, my emotions and feelings fought it all the way. Notwithstanding the negative and apprehensive struggles, in the end my Certainist philosophy overruled my emotions. The fact of the matter is that what the Certainist may feel really bears no validity when it comes to doing the right thing, and how to respond in reality.

The Certainist can never be a centrist, because he is absolutely confident in what he wants and knows what he must do. He understands how his certain choices should apply to reality and humanity, since mankind is the only ultimate certainty in this philosophy. That's Dad's final decision, and I must get on with my life as I embrace my philosophy of Certainism, which advocates reason over morality.

Monday came and it was time for the gang to be at Daniel's house, and then we would venture to the river for our time of fun. That Monday morning began like every second day of the week, but Monday, May 17, 1938, turned out to be an ominous day for the entire gang. Besides, after that day our lives were changed forever, and it was years before any of us returned to that part of the river.

The gang was at my house by eleven o'clock. They spoke with Mom and my siblings for about twenty minutes, and then we got into the cars and headed for the McCrorys'. We had lunch with Mrs. McCrory and hung around their house for about two hours. Afterward, we headed for West Springfield River Road. This is indeed a safer part of the Connecticut River. We were not drinking (as the sheriff later accused us of), since we're all under the drinking age, but we were smoking by the river.

There was hardly anyone at this site in comparison to summertime, for it was remote. When we arrived, the first thing we did was take off our outer clothing, but we kept on our swimming trunks. We lay on the rocks for some time. The day was not hot; on the contrary, it was a very pleasant day. Soon afterward we launched into the deep.

We were laughing and having a grand time, for we felt like young men who were enjoying life and didn't have a care in the world. After four years of arduous study, we wanted to break away from the mundane scholastic custom and enjoy that moment. It wasn't long afterward that we became oblivious to everything around us.

About thirty minutes after we came out of the water, it was Ryan who drew it to our attention, by asking a question we would never forget: "Where's Tobey?" We became alert and began to call out for him, hoping he would answer us. After a few minutes of calling out and looking for him, we saw what looked like something or, regrettably, someone, about sixty feet from where we standing. We ran into water, hoping it was not what it looked like.

As we got closer to what we thought might be Tobey, I couldn't help but wish that this was a big joke. But when we reached the figure, without a doubt it was him. I couldn't believe my friend who had so much life in him was there, floating, with his face downward.

This was truly a dark moment for the gang. Jesse and Harry became almost panic-stricken, and the rest of us tried to calm them down. Then we gently and respectfully, and with heavy hearts, escorted our beloved fraternity brother Tobey out of the cold water that had brought about his youthful demise.

It wasn't long afterward that a few spectators came to us asking certain questions. Daniel told us that he was going to call his dad and the sheriff. I gazed at Tobey's lifeless body; it was difficult to accept that it had been less than thirty-five minutes when we last saw him alive. He was gone forever, and we never had the opportunity to say good-bye.

His death was a ghastly, tragic event that had grave import for the gang to deal with, for it was always Tobey who came to our rescue when we needed it the most. Mom's words echoed in my mind: "*I can't bear the thought of something happening to any of you.*" Nevertheless, the reality of this sad occurrence could never be altered, for he was gone. All we wanted as young men was to take pleasure in and fully enjoy these precious moments in our lives, together as close friends, before the new semester began in the fall and we ventured off to college.

Tobey was gone. We gathered around him in morbid solemnity; some of us cried for our friend in grief-stricken silence. Jesse and Harry, however, found it difficult to accept the fact that he was gone, and they broke down and wept.

"Harry and Jesse, please try to calm down," said Jack.

"What do you mean? One of our best friends is dead!" Jesse replied.

"I know!" said Jack. "However, we must try to stay calm because the sheriff and Daniel's dad are going to be here soon! Acting hysterical will surely cause them to think that we were drinking or doing something out of the ordinary."

"Guys, please stop! We need to keep a clear head," said Ryan.

The sheriff and the ambulance arrived, with Daniel and his father in the vehicle behind the sheriff's car. The men in the ambulance got out. After examining Tobey's body, they placed him in the ambulance and took him away.

The sheriff decided it was time to notify Tobey's parents of his accident, but he wanted to speak with all of us first. Dr. McCrory was very supportive, as usual, and tried to assist Harry and Jesse, since they were struggling with the reality of Tobey's death. After the sheriff had spoken with us, Dr. McCrory assured him that there was no evidence of alcohol in our systems or signs of it in our midst, and that further medical investigation would prove Tobey's death was an unfortunate event of drowning. Dr. McCrory and Daniel thought it best to take Harry and Jesse home. The rest of the gang—Jack, Ryan, and James—took me home.

They explained the unfortunate outcome to Mom, and she was shocked and grieved at the loss of Tobey Scott. Mom tried to console me at that time of despair, because she was fully aware of the fraternity bond that we shared. As far as I can recollect, we started our pack when we were eight. Somehow I felt culpable for Tobey's death, and that I had inadvertently committed fratricide. Mom had known that I would blame myself to some degree, so she tried to calm and comfort me in this grim moment.

Still, I became taciturn and withdrawn, and headed for my room without hesitation. I locked my door behind me to moan about my friend Tobey in solitude. When my seclusion was completed I finally broke down and wept for Tobey. The intense emotions of sorrow and self-reproach, which I had never experienced before in my life, overwhelmed me in a heavy, forlorn inundation of sorrow.

It felt as if someone was reaching deep into my chest and wrenching out my heart. The pain was really existential. I felt the enormity of it and couldn't fathom the reality, or decide how to deal with it in that particular moment of my life.

This pain was real, and I knew it was in the realm of the abstractions of my sorrow, which corresponds to the essential nature of reality was far beyond the physical, but it was real to me since I was having a taste of it experientially. This was totally new to me, and I wanted a release and to relieve myself of this metaphysical burden.

The more I cried, the more unbearable this burden became, and the pain developed into an imperceptibly heavy load. Once I began to weep, it was hard to stop after my emotions were unleashed. Just then, Mom knocked on my door.

"David, dear, do you want to talk?"

In the long run it was futile, but I tried to respond to her question. "Mom, please, I want to be left alone!"

"Okay, David, but we're here for you."

As Mom turned away from my door I had hoped to stop, but on the contrary, my tears returned once more, this time to an even greater degree.

I walked to my bathroom, washed my face, and tried to gain control of my emotions. The death of my friend Tobey certainly coerced me to be acquainted with the moment of sorrow. His inexorable death forced me to experience the greatest inner struggle. After two hours of trying to find a logical conclusion, there was still a great deficiency of intellectual answers. Furthermore, the ontological argument was pointless. According to Anselm in *Proslogion*, chapter two states that the ontological argument is supposed to be one of *priori*, the attempt to prove indubitably the existence of God, and that means not using the contingent proposition that seems to speculate the existence of God. For example, the Latin phrase *id quo maius cogitare nequit*, which means 'something than which nothing greater can be conceived.'

Therefore, this tells us if God can exist in the understanding of the human race and if man can identify with this thought, which eventually will transcend his mental faculties, then anything is possible with the human race in conjunction with the nemesis of creating its own religion, for the purpose of trying to assuage the throes of inconsolable grief.

In reference to the ontological argument, the metaphysical priori argument is that the real objective existence of God is necessarily involved in the existence of the very idea of God. So if an individual was to imagine an imaginary friend, does that mean the idea of the make-believe person will someday transcend into the metaphysical reality?

If God exists—and that depends upon proving the presupposition, which in fact might substantiate the notion of a God—then that means that mankind is bamboozled to believe in the existence of a non-existent God. Therefore, the ontological argument that has transcended into the metaphysical reality via religion has deluded many.

The logical philosophical argument says if man can conceive in his psyche of the existence of God, he can also impugn the existence of God. In underlying principle I'm an agnostic and not an atheist. The atheist has made a conscious decision not to believe in God. The agnostic, however, according to the definition of the word, frankly does not know if God in reality actually exists. The noun comes from the Greek word □□□□□□□ (gnostos), which means knowledge, and the prefix of the letter A provides a negative to create agnostic, an awe-inspiring word. I'm compelled once again to put on the mantle of the sophist. Because of my innate predilection I don't know if God exists, because if I'm to believe in God, there must be an intellectual realization of reason that convinces me of the actualization of this so-called deity.

I'm an agnostic Certainist, and after Tobey's death I speculated about many things, such as when something beyond human reason happens like this, it can turn cynics into religious-minded fanatics. When Tolstoy lost his two brothers he turned to the useless ritualistic regression of religion, but must I do likewise? My father named me after this religious Russian author, hoping that I would in due course become a religious man.

I'm fully aware that religion was in fact the first form of superstition, which has blinded the human race to all logical reason. This is a *nuda veritas* according to historical data. Nevertheless, Certainism is a philosophy that will inevitably inspire a new revelatory movement against the bigotry of religion. Because I'm grieving doesn't necessarily mean that I'll turn to religion for some sort of consolation.

Some individuals hold to the misinformed opinion that if human existence is based primarily on reason, then human life would cease to exist, but this is the way of the religious-minded sects, and how they believe and think. They choose to see divine providence in everything. To me, as a young man endeavoring to be an intellectual, this is very spooky and the way of simpletons. They have neglected to see the facts of pragmatism and how these actually interrelate with life and reason. In addition, they choose to rely entirely on their superstitious beliefs, and neglect the more profound matters: the relativity of knowledge.

With the sudden death of Tobey, should we in our fraternity suddenly decide to believe in a higher power? Absolutely not! Was his death the result of divine intervention, or divine retribution? Was it the result of spontaneous neglect? Or was it accidental? Did we fail to look after our fraternity brother? Honestly, I don't know. In conjunction with religion, a fool can ask more questions than a wise man can answer.

There are those religious people who believe in a God that creates miracles. Then there are those individuals who believe in a devil that can create miracles, or disasters. But if these assumptions have any credence to them, this means that God and the devil without a doubt have a few tricks up their sleeves that they love to play on humanity. As a Certainist, and also an intellectual, who do I blame for the loss of one of my best friends, in view of the fact that I don't believe in anything except my profound theory of Certainism? I know this theory will offer me the right answer, and the solace needed to deal with the loss of my friend.

For some time a battle was waged between reason and my emotions, and reason emerged victoriously. It came to me in the form of intellectualism, which reminded me that time is the only panacea to heal such wounds and that death comes to all men, both young and old. It was Michel de Montaigne who once said: *"It is not death, it is dying that alarms me."* So, the tragic death of Tobey has occurred, but he will never die to me, and his memory will forever be my monument.

But even my Certainist theory certainly didn't eradicate the present emotional pain. Tobey's death was like the besmirching enemy of our fraternity, and we wouldn't be the same without him. My friend was robbed of a long and productive life. Tobey's death caused me to view this ephemeral life in a totally new and different perspective in conjunction with my philosophy of Certainism.

The question therefore looms on the cognizance of life, and how ephemeral it is in relation to mankind. In my room, I sat at my desk looking out the window. I couldn't help but examine the metaphysics of death, and the philosophical impact of this formidable enemy. Then I began with my *soliloquium* as I mourned my friend:

"Oh, lamentable moment; you have stricken me with the first fruits of inconsolable grief, and this grief has pierced my heart.

"You're like a sword, a dagger that has two edges: one side has taken away a loved one, and the other side has left us with great sorrow.

"Oh, death, you have brought forth and sung your dirge, for it's a melancholy requiem.

"The cessation of Tobey Scott has truly brought me into a twilight of an opaque hour.

"Death speaks, and has spoken as it robbed us of our fraternity brother.

"Death has come like an unexpected guest.

"Oh, depart, depart, depart from me, death, for you are the unwelcome foe, and I wish you had never come.

"Oh, death, your mere presence has brought forth a colossal woe. When death rides in it never leaves empty-handed, and it has a lingering effect on unhappy hearts.

"Yes, death, death, you're the lamentable host that sings the dirge.

"Oh, incommodious death, you're now singing, singing, singing the dirge of Tobey Scott, for he's gone, gone, forever!

"For death is the formidable enemy of youth!"

Just after my requiem dirge for Tobey ended, Georg came knocking at my door. He came to inform me that Daniel was in the sitting room, waiting to see me.

But when I went downstairs it was the whole gang. They were all waiting for me. They wanted to include me in their plan to visit Dr. Rupert and Mrs. Imelda Scott that evening. I told them, "Do you think it's proper for us to visit his parents so soon?" Daniel assured me that they would appreciate this, seeing that we were all very close to Tobey. The plan, therefore, sounded good, so I told them I'd get ready.

In about five minutes, I was ready and on my way with the gang to offer our condolences to Tobey's parents. When we arrived at their home, Jonathan and Peggy, Tobey's siblings, were outside. They looked very distraught about the loss of their brother, and when Peggy saw us she came with tears in her eyes. When we saw Peggy approaching us, we thought she was going to accuse us of causing her brother's death, but she came to us and started to weep in a greater degree, and thanked us for coming so soon.

We gathered around her and all of us began to cry as we tried to comfort her. Then Jonathan joined in while we shared the loss of Tobey. It wasn't long before Jonathan broke down. Crying, we soon began to talk about the good times we had with Tobey throughout the years. Tobey's parents had three children: Jonathan, the firstborn, was nineteen going on twenty; Tobey, the second child, would have been eighteen on October 2; and Peggy was fifteen going on sixteen.

Their house is located on the other side of town, about twenty minutes from where Daniel and I live. Dr. Rupert Scott was a dentist by profession, and his wife taught in an elementary school. Tobey's father's ancestors came from Scone, a village in southeast Perthshire in Scotland, and his mother is of Grecian stock. Dr. Rupert Scott was the first generation to be born in the United States. Malcolm Scott, Tobey's grandfather, came to America in the late nineteenth century with his wife and other relatives. I think that would make Tobey a Scottish American.

Tobey was born at Massachusetts General Hospital on October 2, 1920. He was the tallest member of our fraternity at six foot three. His personality was one of the most amiable in the gang. Sometimes I thought he liked to joke around too much. I would miss that about him. Tobey had sandy blond hair that was completely straight. It came down on his forehead, and sometimes when it grew too long it would cover his green eyes. We would make fun of his very straight hair, heckling him because there was absolutely no wave in it, and there was no other way he could comb or cut it. His nose was straight with a slight turn upward.

As we spoke with Tobey's siblings, Dr. and Mrs. Scott heard the commotion and came out. They were very pleased that we had come, even though I thought it was a bit late to call on the Scotts. However, in spite of this, they told us they were just waiting to hear from the doctor about Tobey's autopsy, and his funeral should be in few days.

We discussed the funeral arrangements with his parents, and it was decided that Jonathan and the gang would share the responsibilities of the service and the bearing of Tobey's casket. It was difficult for Mrs. Scott to deal with the loss of her youngest son in the prime of his life, and only two days after his graduation.

We prepared for Tobey's funeral, our moment of saying farewell to our fraternity brother. The funeral was on a rainy Thursday morning. None of the gang had ever attended a funeral service. We never thought we would be attending the funeral service of one of our best friends.

Dr. and Mrs. Rupert Scott are not religious people, nor had they any religious affiliation, so there was nothing remotely religious about Tobey's funeral service. His father opened the service with a reading from his favorite nineteenth-century poet, Walt Whitman, while Jonathan and the gang handled the eulogy and the rest of the service. The building was packed. A large percentage was students, and Samantha, his steady girlfriend, was there. This wasn't easy for her to cope with, for they had been a couple since the seventh grade, and had planned to attend the same college in the fall. Their intention was to get married after their graduation, but all their plans came to sudden end.

This was the saddest moment in our lives. It was especially hard when it came to eulogizing Tobey. It was not difficult to speak the truth about our brother; however, it was a struggle to express our appreciation of him throughout the years.

Trying to control our emotions, eventually all of us broke down as we and Jonathan carried the white casket along to its final resting place. The most heartrending moment of Tobey's funeral was when we viewed his body for the last time before our friend and fraternity brother was laid to rest in that cold, wet grave.

Samantha screamed until she fainted. Her father had to carry her unconscious body away. The sound of the wet dirt hitting the coffin resounded in our ears, reminding us of the macabre sting of death and the reality that we wouldn't see Tobey again.

It was some time before the gang and I left Tobey's grave. We watched the caretakers as they were about to place his tombstone on his fresh grave. We wanted to assist in this, and to our surprise, before we could ask the workers had already decided to let us do so, under their supervision. The gang and I encouraged one another after his tombstone was erected.

A short time afterward we left and headed for Tobey's house in the rain. We wanted to mourn for him by ourselves, since he was part of our fraternity. When we arrived at Tobey's home we were wet, and his parents wanted to get us out of those wet clothes. We were the last guests to arrive at their home. That evening the rain continued to fall. We wanted to support Tobey's parents, and told them if there was anything they needed we would be more than happy to help. The gang and I didn't want to encroach on the Scotts, so after a while we said good-bye to everyone and went to our separate homes. It was still a grave and morbid struggle to cope with the aftermath of Tobey's death.

When I entered our home, my black suit was wet and stained with mud, but the condition of my suit was the last thing that concerned me. Surprisingly, Mom made no comments about the state of my suit. She told me that it was of the utmost importance that she speak with me as soon as possible.

Mom couldn't attend Tobey's funeral, but she paid her respects by viewing his body and visiting his parents. The day of the funeral, Mom had to be with Dad when Dr. Harrison got his results from the lab. I headed for my room, had a shower, changed, and went to speak with her.

"David, I have some unpleasant news to share with you," she said when I returned. "I'm aware of what you have been going through for the past few days."

"What is it, Mom?"

"I'm sorry, there's no other way to say this. David, your father has pancreatic cancer, and has three or maybe four weeks to live."

After hearing this disturbing piece of information I thought, *What the hell is happening in the year of 1938? It is only a few days after Tobey's drowning, and now I must deal with my father's death. In a month he's going to die. I haven't recuperated from Tobey's death, and the sting of death is already knocking at my door once again.*

"Mom, I don't understand. What's going on?"

"I'm sorry, David. I wanted to share this news with you before I tell your brother and sisters."

"Mom, is Dr. Harrison absolutely sure?"

"Yes, David, he had the test run twice, and three other doctors also examined your father's results. Because of the severity of his cancer, he has been given a short duration."

"Look, Mom, I'm sorry to hear this, but is there anything I can do for you?"

"I just need your support, son."

"Mom, you have always been here for us, and I'm here for you now."

"I know, David, and I appreciate that."

"Mom, I don't want to come across as if I'm drowning a dying man, but some days ago I went to Dad, for the purpose of making peace with him. However, I got a taste of his serpent tongue."

"I'm sorry that happened, David, but you did the right thing. His response wasn't your fault and I don't want you to feel guilty about that."

"I won't, Mom, those days are long gone. Anyway, Mom, I think I need to be with the gang. So if you need me, I'm going to be at the McCrorys' for at least two hours."

"Okay, dear."

I went into my room and thought, *The circumstantial events of life can be challenging as they bring with them much vicissitude.*

The gang was very supportive that evening.

Dad suffered as the weeks went by. As he came down to the last days of his life, he was taken to the hospital. The third week of June, the gang and I were visiting various universities. I went with them to visit the college where Daniel would be starting in fall. When I got home that night Mom was in tears, and I knew that Dad had passed away.

Strangely enough, even though I knew that Dad had never wanted to see me again, Mom said that he had asked for me before he died.

Dad had resigned from his vocation in the church, and Mom had cared for him until it became very complicated. He was taken and admitted into the general hospital for special care in his last days. Four days after passing away he was buried.

Jena took his death hard, because she had severed her relationship with him a few weeks before he was diagnosed with pancreatic cancer. I was surprised that Marie and Georg handled his death quite well. They were grieving, but those two are extremely resilient.

Mom informed me that Dad had been suffering from his affliction long before he was diagnosed. He had asked Dr. Harrison not to share his problem with his wife. Dad had aged considerably, and it was hard to believe he was only forty-seven when he died. On his deathbed, he told Mom that he'd known about his medical condition for a while.

As I thought about his confession, I couldn't fathom the level of Dad's hypocrisy. He never apologized to Mom for the way he had treated her all those years. He abused us for years, and then he tried to spare us from the inevitable, but to me that was the height of his *putain* pride.

One day, I sat at the back of our home gazing at the river, trying to make sense of Tobey's and Dad's unforeseen deaths.

I realized that life isn't as simple as some may think it to be. It's complicated, for we're all just thrown into this world at random, with little or no meaning in life. We live, and die, and that's the end of us all.

We live in a world full of chaos and so much confusion, and along with the injustices of malevolent men, this world is full of questions. There are actually no answers, and the so-called profound questions of life are in fact redundant.

There's that forlorn enemy, death, which is always lingering and imminent in our ephemeral life. It's even closer than we think, always around the corner. The religious experts have never defined what the purpose of life is, nor have they presented an intelligent answer to the intricacies of life in conjunction with intellectualism.

The only thing we can do, according to the teachings of philosophy, is strive to be our best, and to do our best.

I had no intention of becoming idle or torpid during the next three months. I would spend most of my time getting ready for college by the necessary means of useful employment. There is a wise and famous aphorism that says: "*a rose is a rose is a rose.*" The exegesis of this proverb is simply that people are what they are, and it makes no sense trying to give them another name.

Simply reading a few good books certainly doesn't mitigate the simpleminded and their oafishness, because these are natural qualities to the simpleton and their pseudo-fecundity, which are prevalent in the sphere of religion and its followers.

For example, from the very beginning of time primitive men invented the idea of gods and religion to account for unexplained natural phenomena. But superstitious beliefs and religion are a major hindrance to intellectual and scientific progress, since no one can prove or disprove the existence of God. Trying to prove the existence of God is futile. It's like trying to legitimize the negative of an irrational theory, which logically is impossible to prove unless a positive concept is first recognized and verified, for a negative concept cannot be defined.

The negative concept, according to intelligent logical reasoning, cannot be subjected to any degree of analysis for the primary purpose of authentication. And it is for this precise reason that religious people have an idealistic concept of life: they fantasize and romanticize about the aspects of life, religion, and God.

These religious people are like the amazing theory of the bumblebee, which is an irrational theory. According to the laws of aerodynamics a bumblebee shouldn't be able to fly, given the ratio of body weight to wingspan. However, the bumblebee doesn't know that. There are various theories to explain why it can indeed fly, but the idea according to *episteme* (knowledge, science, or to know) is mind over matter. What the bumblebee doesn't know won't kill it. This theory can be compared to: what is impossible becomes possible. The bumblebee is doing what's actually impossible in reality. The mind is a powerful tool, and people can believe anything they want to concoct or fantasize about. On many occasions things happen that can't be explained. Superstitious individuals will always equate these anomalies to some "*higher power*"; hence, religion and all its superstitious beliefs. Religion is an irrational theory, just like the bumblebee. All religious people believe in something that isn't really there, and those religious fanatics have always accused the intellects of sullying themselves in the pointless exercise of narcissism.

The intellects seek their answers through academic means. However, to the academic geniuses this is only advancing themselves as intellectual dilettantes, for the purpose of exercising their reason. The noun *intellectualism* denotes the guiding principle that teaches the ultimate code that all reality is intellect or reason.

Religious individuals and their doctrine of faith are, in fact, antithetical to the teachings of intellectualism, which are built entirely upon reason. Religion and its doctrine of faith cannot be proven based on verifiable epistemological evidence.

In reality, epistemology literally presents the concept of knowing, and smart people will know that you cannot understand anything without first reaching a level of certain knowledge that can only be transcended through the methodology of teaching and learning. Therefore, the epistemological concept can only be obtained through the natural process of knowing. Faith and the intellect are actually enemies, and will never walk in perfect harmony; faith and intellect are like night and day.

In the realm of intelligence, if an individual dialectical point cannot be intelligently substantiated, then it must be dismissed as the pure folly of the puerile and the simpleton. Intellectualism is actually the development of the intellect through the practice of academic reason. Intellectualism can also be defined as an attitude of devotion to higher education. Therefore, the word *intellectualism* can be seen as specifying an avenue of philosophy, often referred to as *rationalism*. This intelligent approach of perfecting one's ability of excelling in knowledge can only be attained by the rational exploitation of reason, as one seeks by reasoning all things through the epistemological process, in conjunction with the relationship between intellectualism and philosophy.

It was Socrates who said: *"One will do what is right or best just as soon as one truly understands what is right or best."* Intelligent people honestly cannot make any decisions until they have accumulated the necessary relevant information, which will inevitably empower them to be competent enough to make an intelligent decision.

The word *intellect* comes from the Old French word *intellecte*, and it was also borrowed from the Latin word *intellectus*. These archaic words connote reason, perspicuity, understanding, and intelligence. Intellect was used by Geoffrey Chaucer in his *The Canterbury Tales* in the fourteenth century. There are some people who might presume that intellectualism is in fact related to the creed, the Cult of Reason. This, of course, may have certain credence to it, but reason is an integral existential commodity in the area of intellectualism, and to pursue intellectualism without fully utilizing one's reason is like seeking higher learning without taking into consideration the cost of academic goals, and not understanding the importance of perfecting the psychology of reason, which is paramount for the growth and maturity of the intellect. The Cult of Reason was instigated in the uncertain years between 1792 and 1794, and was meant to irrevocably obliterate the ideals of religion.

The philosophy of Certainism is the ideal concept of being certain of what individuals will want out of life. This can only be accomplished by competently using one's reason.

The reason of man is germane in the thought and alleged core, and is necessary for the rational scrupulous grounds of formulating objective intelligent decisions. Those who are true intellects are in fact the connoisseurs of reason. Religion is geared to hinder humanity from fully developing and exploiting reason. Man's reason is the only moral compass needed when it comes to love and deciding what is best for the individual.

Certainism is a philosophy that vehemently advocates the principle of reason over morality. The Certainist is a revisionist of religious tenets in relation to the Ninth Amendment and the reason of man. Reason is the ruling monarch of intellectualism, and without the logical deduction of reason in an individual's life, *stultitia* will become the interloper of reason. History has in fact proven that religion is the major interloper of mankind's reason. And since religion can be compared to the amazing theory of the bumblebee, religion is indeed the misleading theory.

Chapter Six

Sacrament or Weapon

The season of fall was soon upon us, and it was an arduous test of my character when the moment came to leave home. The day I left for college I felt like I was abandoning my mother, and the melancholy I saw in her eyes caused me to experience a deep sorrow that words can't explain. It had been only three months since Father's sudden death.

It was extremely sad when the time came to depart from my fraternity brothers. We were all leaving our parents to begin this new chapter of higher learning in our lives. The severe pain in my heart was very present as my emotions struggled with the reality of accepting the closure of Tobey's death.

In spite of these feelings, I continued with my journey to New Haven. I drove in my new luxurious car, which offered me some degree of hope and renewed my self-esteem for a brighter future. I felt like an accomplished young man. Here I was, a seventeen-year-old about to turn eighteen in a couple of weeks, and on my way to Yale University, enjoying the pleasures of my new 1931 Chrysler Imperial Custom Roadster. "Gee, life is good in spite of the traumas!" I shouted as I drove, lifting my hands in amazement. I have a natural affinity for the finer things in life, especially exquisite cars. My mother now had two fine Chrysler models in the garage, for before Dad's death, my parents had promised to purchase a model similar to theirs after my graduation. As I stayed the course on my journey heading for New Haven, my mind began to ruminate about my late father.

I couldn't believe he was gone and no longer a part of our lives. I thought about the first college he attended, Stanford, and when he graduated in 1913.

Ever since I could remember I had longed for this auspicious day, when it finally came to leave my father's house. But now that I had left for Yale University, my father was dead. Thus, the reason for my sadness: I would have preferred to stay and help my mom in this time of bereavement. However, I must pursue my new life of higher learning, for this is what Grandfather Hans had prepared for his progenies.

As I came closer to New Haven and thought about my father, two words kept coming back to my mind: sacrament, and weapon. Most people aren't aware that religion has come to humanity in the concealing pretext of a sacrament. In fact, religion is a deadly weapon that has been used throughout the centuries by religious leaders for the purpose of exploiting the people. Religion has endeavored to divide mankind through the machinations of denominationalism. Religion is the most perfidious weapon known to the human race, because most individuals hold to the opinion that religion is harmless. In reality, it is a pernicious and malignant disease that must be dealt with, because the doctrines of religion are not benign; they're malignant, just like my father's pancreatic cancer. If the human race wants to survive the onslaught of religion and its flummery, it must first comprehend the cunning devices of religion. The word *sacrament* is actually a term that religious leaders use as they seek to establish a formal dogmatic institution on earth for their main objective of monetary gain. Dad, as a Lutheran minister, preferred to call sacraments ordinances. However, they're all deadly weapons that must be avoided at all costs.

The day was somewhat overcast but very pleasant, and I was enjoying my drive. I started to miss home, Mom, Georg, Maria, and most of all the gang. I arrived at Yale University after driving for one hour. I decided to make myself accessible for the purpose of ingratiating myself into my new life of higher learning.

My home for the next few years would be a double suite in the male dormitory, and I had one roommate. I met him when the gang and I were visiting our prospective colleges some weeks ago, and he seemed to be a cool guy. However, I'm sure he thought I was a member of the Aryan race, and I was content to let him believe that, because I had decided never to reveal to anyone that I'm a Jew.

I hoped to make psychology my major, for this field of science primarily deals with the knowledge of the human mind; with consciousness, behavior, and the problems of adjustment to the environment. One of the main reasons I was drawn to this field of science was the ambition to posthumously understand my father and his invidious behavior. I was certain that what I would discover in this great field of science would answer the particular questions that I have about life, science, and the human mind.

Psychology is one of the remarkable weapons that will be used in the near future, along with the intelligent spectrum of the philosophy of Certainism, to inevitably explain away religion and at last liberate mankind from it. Sigmund Freud labeled psychology "*the wellsprings of the human personality*"! I was pleased to learn that Dr. Freud is a Jewish-Austrian neurologist who created the psychoanalytic school of psychiatry.

I was amazed by Dr. Freud when I read his insightful book *Moses and Monotheism*. This was the tectonic moment when I started to view religion as a deadly weapon against humanity, and began to question its purpose and integrity. His book actually brought about the fundamental question: is religion a sacrament, or is it in fact a weapon?

Dr. Freud's theories are extraordinary, and those on religion outlined in *Moses and Monotheism* indeed caused my intellectual illumination. They shed new light on the aspects of religion and reason. Religion has always used the guilt trip when it comes to mankind. His book totally revolutionized my entire concept of religion, guilt, and both as malignant weapons against humanity.

I parked my car and began to unload my things. Daniel and the gang had already helped me some days before with most of my heavy items. Everyone was busy getting settled in as I began to unpack my car. Some of the guys in my building came to introduce themselves to me. They couldn't help but make some positive comments about my new Chrysler, which I'm sure they knew had cost about three thousand dollars.

"Hi, I'm Christopher Arne."

"Nice to meet you. My name is David Hugenberg."

"I am William Bray, but all my friends called me Billy."

"I'm Samuel Whitefield, and this is Tommy Saunders."

"Pleased to meet you," I replied.

"Are you from out of state, David?"

"Yes, but I don't live too far from here."

"What state are you from?" asked Christopher.

"Born and raised in Springfield, Massachusetts."

"Oh, you're a New England boy."

"Yep, I suppose that's the truth. And where are the rest of you from?" I asked my new neighbors politely.

"Washington," answered Christopher.

"Is that Washington, DC, or Washington the state?"

"Washington the state."

"Whoa, you're from all the way across the country."

"Yes," said Christopher.

"What part of Washington?" I asked.

"Olympia." Before I could ask the other guys what states they were from, Christopher said, "William is from North Dakota, Samuel is from Arizona, and Tommy is from California."

These guys were my next-door neighbors, for their suites were just opposite ours.

I thought, *So we just met, and that makes us friends? Okay, I guess they're just being polite and friendly.* They offered to assist me, but I thanked my new neighbors for their kind offer and told them I was doing quite well. They told me if I needed anything I shouldn't hesitate to call upon them. Then they were on their way and I went back to unloading my car.

But my mind, as usual, was soon back on track with my ruminating about the facts of religion and higher learning. Religion is the most lethal weapon on the planet. It can be used as a means of placing and keeping laypeople in the bondage of ignorance and superstition. Religion lacks genteel competency when it comes to reason and common sense, because the devotees of religion are in fact the scapegraces of higher learning, and religion has a habit of always trouncing secularism and anyone with a higher level of education. Furthermore, religion has never sought to attune to the times or the existential needs of others. The religious are so wrapped up in their archaic ways that they're impervious to all levels of reason. Higher learning is the great emancipator of the human race.

Most parents aren't aware of the psychological and sociological impact they're going to have on their children. I'm familiar with such things, since I'm fully aware of how my religious invidious father affected me.

If there was ever a man who was the ideal paradigm of higher learning and religion, it would John Dewey. He was born on October 20, 1859. Dr. John Dewey was a renowned American author, philosopher, and psychologist. He is highly praised for his brilliant ingenuity of radically changing for the better and turning around our educational system in the United States during the twentieth century.

His new ideas have certainly revolutionized the educational system in America through social reform. He's the most highly acclaimed educator in this century, and is most definitely not religious in the least. His philosophical theories can be identified as those of a Western philosopher, and he emphasizes his theory of pragmatism in the epistemological progressivism method in education. Dr. Dewey's concept of pragmatism, which has absolutely no room for the erroneous teachings of absolute truth, has proliferated in the educational system. His understanding of truth is largely based on the principle of extreme relativism, because truth must be considered temporary and conditional, and the misconception of absolute truth has no place in the educational arena, especially in higher learning.

His philosophical views of progressivism naturally substantiated the scientific fact that advocates the notion that the future is, in fact, improving from earlier periods in history. However, his childhood days were not pleasurable, since his mother was a religious woman who constantly nagged him about the Bible, God, and sin. As the result of this, he grew into adulthood naturally harboring an immeasurable antipathy for religion.

And this is precisely what religion and those fanatical parents do to their children. Religion has done nothing for humanity except bring burgeoning sorrows upon the world. The only good thing religion ever did in the annals of history was the event of the Crusaders, who turned the course of history in Europe in the Dark Ages, when they brought back from the East a wealth of knowledge: books on almost every topic, such as medicine, language, science, and Aristotelian philosophy.

Finally I arrived in our suite located on the second floor. My roommate should have been there. When I opened the door, some of the guys from the other suites were sitting in the front room having a discussion about something, maybe about classes, which start on Monday.

"Hello."

"Hi, it's David, right?"

"Yes, that's correct."

"Do you need help?" asked one young man.

"No thanks."

"Well, my name is Jim Maitland, and my roommate and I live next door."

"Oh, that's great."

"As you know, the suites come with single or double rooms. However, I think it's only the lucky ones who get the single suites," said Jim.

I thought, *That's a stupid remark.* I had applied for a single suite, but too late.

"David, I don't know if you remember my name. I'm Edward Dryden, your roommate."

"Hi, Edward. No, I didn't forget your name."

"By the way, David, I'm Percy Ireton, Jim's roommate. Are you sure you don't need help unloading your things?"

"Yes, but thanks for offering. There's only a box and two bags left in my car. Besides, I need the exercise."

"Yes, I couldn't help noticing your lean muscles. Do you exercise regularly, David?" asked Jim.

"Yes, at least four times a week, and I enjoy swimming."

After their brief interrogation, I headed to my car for the rest of my things. *Gosh, they can ask a lot of questions. And furthermore, I don't like Jim. I think his father is some kind of a chaplain in Congress. He likes to hug. I don't think he's a homosexual, but he wears his Christianity on his sleeve. I don't care if Jim Maitland is a homosexual or not, because my philosophy of Certainism accepts all people and doesn't judge anyone. However, having any dealings with religion or a religious person is something I don't care for.*

After a few minutes, I returned to the suite and started to unpack, but while I was putting away my things and trying to settle in, Edward opened my door.

"Hey, David, are you hungry?"

"No, not really, I had something to eat on my way here."

"Okay. We're just heading out to get something to eat."

"That's fine. Right now all I want to do is settle in and take a warm shower."

"Sure, but the guys wanted me to ask you."

I walked to the kitchen where they were. "Hey, guys, thanks, but as I told Edward, I had something to eat on my journey."

"Would you like us to get you something?" asked Edward.

"No thanks, it's okay," I said.

"All right," said Edward.

As they were leaving, Edward turned around and said, "By the way, we heard about your dad. We're sorry to hear about his death."

I didn't want to encourage any further discussion about my father, so I became somewhat abrupt with them. "Thanks, but I'm fine."

About fifteen minutes after the guys left, I wanted to take a shower. I then realized that in our suite the bathroom was a shared facility. I'd had my own room and bathroom ever since I could remember, but right now I didn't have much choice. I took my shower and was soon back in my room. I started to feel tired, for it had been a long day, not to mention the emotional anguish of leaving home, the gang, and Tobey's and Dad's deaths. I placed most of my books on the bookshelf and some on my desk, and then I lay on my bed.

Even though I was exhausted I had difficulty dropping off to sleep, especially in a strange place. I missed my room, but this is what college is all about: accepting changes and learning to get alone with new people. The last thing I remembered was thinking about my late dad, before I fell into a deep sleep.

The next day I was awakened by loud music. Surprisingly, it was one of my new neighbors in the kitchen, cooking lunch and listening to the radio. I got out of bed and dashed for the bathroom, because I had slept for almost fourteen hours and had not used the bathroom during my long rest. Thank goodness it's in our suite.

When I entered the kitchen, my neighbor, Percy Ireton, greeted me.

"Good afternoon, David. Man, you can sleep like the dead."

"What do you mean?"

"Well, when Edward arrived last night, it was around ten forty p.m. and he told us you were sound asleep. And even when he checked on you later, and this morning, he said you didn't move an inch."

"I think I was simply worn out from my journey, and a multitude of other things."

"Do you always sleep that heavy?"

"Honestly, Percy, I have no idea, because I've never shared a room with anyone."

"You're kidding, right?"

"No. this is the first time that I'm sharing living accommodations with a roommate."

"Do you have any brothers or sisters?"

"Yes, I have two sisters and one brother."

"And all of you had your own rooms?"

"Yes, we all had our own room, and our bedrooms have private bathrooms. There's also an extra bathroom in the corridor."

"Gee, David, I wish I was one of your siblings."

"By the way, what time is it?"

"I believe it's eleven fifty-five."

"Gosh, I can't believe I slept for nearly fourteen hours. Where are Edward and Jim?"

"Edward took Jim to get some stationery items."

"Doesn't Jim have a car?"

"Yes, he drove from Michigan. But on his way into Connecticut his engine began to smoke, so after he arrived on campus later that day, the mechanics came to take his car to the repair shop. David, not everyone can afford a new Chrysler like yours."

"By the way, what's for lunch? I'm starving."

"Hot dogs."

"That's fine. I'm going to wash up. Then I'll be back to eat."

"Okay, but I won't be here when you return."

"Where are you going?"

"I have to get some things from the grocery store for our suite. Edward was kind enough to allow Jim and me to eat here, until we could get our own groceries."

"All right, I guess I'll see you later."

"Sure."

Even though it was Saturday afternoon, the campus was quite busy. Yale University has been around for exactly 237 years. Its motto is ותמים אורים in Hebrew, *Urim V'Tumim*; in the scholarly language it is *Lux et veritas*; it means Light and Truth.

By the late 1930s, Yale University, like most institutions of higher education in America, was in fact a gentlemen's club. There were few blacks, Jews, women, or other minorities at these prestigious colleges in the United States. For a private college that was named after a wealthy

Jew there's absolutely nothing Jewish about this university, except for a few Hebrew inscriptions located in certain places.

The next few weeks went by fast, and I got better about the living arrangements with my new roommate. But to me, my neighbors were all humdrums. After a few weeks of Jim, Edward, and Percy, it wasn't that bad after all. However, I wouldn't want to remain around these guys for the rest of my life.

Jim the hugger likes to express his affections too much, with both sexes. Why do we have to feel anything? I never knew that men could be so in touch with their feelings, especially when it comes to complete strangers and expressing one's private emotions to just anyone. He's always touching, and he can't talk without moving his hands simultaneously. I don't deny that I too have emotions; nevertheless, I have learned to keep my feelings in hand and not to let people read me that easily. I wished that Jim the hugger had the chance to meet my father before he passed away. I'm sure Dad wouldn't have cared to have an acquaintance with a young man who wears his emotions on his sleeve. I know what eventually would have happened between Dad and Jim the hugger: my father would have put his big German-American foot up Jim's "fucking ass!"—figuratively, of course. That self-righteous bastard wouldn't tolerate someone like Jim the hugger. These are crucial lessons I've learned from my hard-ass father, and these difficult lessons of his made me into the young man I am.

Edward the sponger is an incommodious human parasite. He's always in need of stationery items, or help with Latin, Greek, or some particular subject, and most of the time he's in need of money. In fact, it has caused me to wonder about his family's financial status. Don't his parents send him a weekly allowance?

My tuition fees were paid directly via Grandfather's lawyers, and I'll never get involved in such frivolous matters as fees. Our trust funds are set up in such a way that the lawyers handle our education, because they're responsible for the financial transactions. Every month a check will be in the mail, to keep me going and make sure I lack for nothing while in college.

The last of the three stooges is Percy the freer; he's one of those religious Christians who think that because salvation is "free," everything in life ought to be. He was the ideal antinomian who thinks that he should be given a break in everything.

I'm fully aware that, due to the kindness of Grandfather Hans, my trust fund makes it so that I will never suffer the lack of obtaining a higher education, nor will my children, not to mention the inheritance we're going to receive if we complete our higher education according to Grandfather Hans's legal agreement. The privilege of my education is not a perquisite based on being a Hugenberg. If my GPA had not been above 4.2, as much I desired to go to Yale University, that dream would have never become a living reality.

The weeks went by and the holidays were once again upon us. We were all at home for Christmas, and the new year of 1939 eventually came. Nineteen thirty-nine was another period of greater political and social unrest throughout Europe, which continued to escalate as the world turned its eyes toward that continent. Meanwhile, the German *Wehrmacht* implemented Hitler's policies of Germany's expansionism *Lebensraum*—"living space in the East," and in early October 1938, Hitler's army, which had been planning for some time to invade the Sudetenland, finally executed the Fuhrer's wish and annexed it to Germany.

Nineteen thirty-eight was the year of the Jewish nadir in Europe, which came to be known as *Kristallnacht*. This unfortunate incident occurred on November 9, and it all began with a young Jew by the name of Herschel Feibel Grynszpan, sometimes called "Grunspan." He was born on March 28, 1921, and was a Polish Jew. At the age of seventeen this young *Jude* committed a crime that brought the wrath of the Nazi Party upon his people, the Jews.

Even though Herschel was actually born in Hanover, his parents were Polish Jews, and Herschel's relatives were not exempt from the continuous problems that European *Juden* were experiencing. Herschel became extremely troubled and went to the German Embassy in Paris, with the hope of seeing the ambassador. When he arrived, Herschel asked to see the German ambassador, but the ambassador was not available at that particular moment.

However, the young man was escorted into the office of the third secretary, who at that time was Ernst Vom Rath. The secretary was opening the day's mail, and he asked Herschel, "Why are you here?"

The young Herschel spoke not a word, but took a pistol out his coat and fired five bullets into the head of Vom Rath. This was the spark that ignited the flames of the ghastly event of *Kristallnacht*, and also began the moment of *Welt-schmerz* (sorrow, world-pain) for the Jews.

Herschel Grynszpan was arrested and handed over to the German authorities, but his last words to the public were: "*It is not a crime to be a Jew. I am not a dog. I have a right to live. The Jewish people have a right to some part of the earth.*" On the contrary, the irrevocable damage was already done, and the fate of the Jewish people rested in the hands of Hitler's regime.

On that dreadful night of November 9, throughout Berlin, Stuttgart, Vienna, and other parts of Germany, angry mobs shattered the windows of Jewish businesses, synagogues, and homes. Crowds of angry Germans broke into Jewish homes for the purpose of robbing them and causing grievous bodily harm, and even death.

It was a night of murder, pilfering, rape, and destroying valuable property and items that belonged to Jewish families. It was estimated that 111 Jews were murdered on that cold night of November 1938, and more than a thousand synagogues were set ablaze. That woeful night became to be known as *Kristallnacht*, which in German mean "the night of broken glass." After that night, thirty thousand Jews were sent off to those concentration camps that were built to confine Germany's number-one enemy, the Jews.

The threatening incident cast a dark cloud over the head of Britain's prime minister, Neville Chamberlain, and his image. When he heard the sad news, his exact words were: "*Oh, what tedious people these Germans can be!*"

The government in the United States called for tougher sanctions against Germany, and Congress wanted to loosen certain immigration laws for the purpose of accommodating German Jewish refugees so the Jews in Europe wouldn't have to deal with the nightmares of "the Jewish Problem" in Germany. However, there was another side of this coin: there were those individuals in government whose attitude was somewhat cold and indifferent to the Jews in Europe, for they had great resentment for all foreigners, not only the Jews.

There were those citizens who saw the acceptance of additional foreigners from Europe as a negative approach against America's progression, and advocated that this was not an act of compassion but an act of weakness. Besides, the United States believed that Europe's problems should remain on the shores of Europe, and Congress certainly didn't need to get involved in the affairs across the Atlantic Ocean. But this was just a pretext to preserve the Caucasian Protestant in the United States. Then again, this was the right of the politicians in Washington and the American people, because the generation of the 1920s and 1930s had labored extremely hard and vigorously to protect what was rightfully theirs.

That generation had passed particular laws that were meant to keep all immigrants out of the United States. Many Americans were not willing to open their arms to receive more German refugees. On the other hand, America is not only the land of the free and the home of the brave, but in spite of our history and problems, Americans are also very kindhearted people. There were those who I believe meant well and wanted to protect our liberty in this country.

Nevertheless, in 1939, New York Senator Robert Wagner presented a bill to Congress, for the purpose of allowing ten thousand German Jewish children into the United States. There were thousands of well-meaning American families willing to adopt these children into their families and take them into their homes. Even so, enthusiasm and pure motives are not the right prerequisites for a bill to be passed in the legislative branch of government. Senator Wagner, and the families who wanted to assist those German children, were stupendously mistaken. The bill failed to pass, in spite of the animated support of respected Democrats and Republicans on Capitol Hill. As one lobbyist who was against the bill vehemently said, "*If we are going to keep this country as it is and not lose our liberty, we have got to keep not only these children out of it, but the whole damned Europe.*" After this unfortunate defeat, not only the children but their families had nowhere to run.

During the year of 1939, I continued with my life of higher learning at Yale University, excelling academically in the field of science, but I kept a close watch on the newspaper, newsreel, and also kept my ears close to the radio. After Adolf Hitler's inauguration on January 30, 1933, I had begun to keep a scrapbook of news clippings of the geopolitics in Europe, and I meticulously followed the social unrest in Germany. I wondered about the children who could have been given the opportunity of coming to America, and realized I could have been one of them.

Toward the end of my first summer vacation, on August 23, 1939, Russia and Germany entered into a non-aggression pact known as the Molotov/Ribbentrop Pact.

The world would never be the same again, after World War I began with a single bullet from the pistol of a nineteen-year-old by the name of Gavrilo Princip. He and six others who were members of a Serbian nationalist terrorist group known as the Black Hand had planned to assassinate the heir of the Austro-Hungarian throne, Archduke Franz Ferdinand, and his wife Sophie. Since they were visiting Sarajevo, Princip, along with his associates, took the opportunity to plan and carry out their infamous act that plunged the world into the First World War on June 28, 1914.

World War II commenced after Hitler broke the hated Treaty of Versailles, when Germany invaded Poland on September 1, 1939. The first shots that began the Second World War were heard from a naval base in Poland, when the German defense ship *Schleswig-Holstein* fired at the base in the early morning.

Not long afterward France and Britain took decisive actions against Germany by giving it the final warning, demanding the immediate withdrawal from the borders of Poland. However, when Berlin didn't respond to France and Britain's demands, they declared war on Germany on September 3, and this was the official beginning of World War II.

I never thought I would live to see a world war in my lifetime, because I was born two years after the Great War ended, and I was told that it was supposed to end all wars. Throughout the day at Yale University, I thought about Mom, my siblings, and the war in Europe.

My roommate was surprised about the outbreak of the war. However, my late father and I always followed current events and the news, particularly after Hitler became Germany's new chancellor. After classes I called Mom, because I wanted to talk to her about the war in Europe.

One of my professors shared some useful information with us about a Swiss scientist by the name of Albert Hofmann, and a new drug he was working on, which was first synthesized in the laboratories of Basel, Switzerland, in 1938. This mysterious new drug was called lysergic acid diethylamide, or LSD.

I'm fully aware that drugs and religion have similar properties in common: for example, both can be used as a sacrament or a weapon against humanity, for the main purpose of manipulating and controlling others. Drugs can be used as a panacea to alleviate pain, if they're regulated and not abused. But people can become addicted to their own medication, and also to religion.

Moreover, when this occurs they will eventually lose their natural and rational reason, and when religious institutions gain the upper hand over their minds, religion becomes the controlling factor in their lives. Religion can become an opiate to those who are emotionally hurting, but both drugs and religion, if not properly regulated, can go awry and hurt many people to an enormous degree, which in the end can be a dreadful imposition.

Drugs and religion have one main objective in common, and that's to take control of humanity's mental ability of thinking. Drugs and religion can dull and stupefy one's mental faculties, even though they can be seen as a sacrament. The simpleminded are controlled either by drugs or religion; however, they haven't realized that they have become dependent and are being manipulated by a deadly weapon. On the other hand, the ability and prerogative of mankind is to rationally use its reason in all capacities, especially when it comes to making practical decisions.

Chapter Seven

The War and 1942

Two years had passed since the outbreak of the war in Europe.

The month of December had come, and I was eager for the holidays to commence so that I could see my relatives once again, particularly Jena and the gang.

Weekends were the only time that most of us slept in, and we took advantage of this mainly on Sundays, when the majority of the guys in our dormitory usually woke up very late, sometimes far into the evening.

One Sunday we were awakened by an uproar in the dormitory around two p.m. There was shouting in the hall and a loud banging on our door. When we opened the door, Christopher and Samuel were standing there, looking like they had seen a ghost. The first thing Christopher said to us was, "Haven't you heard the news?"

"What news? I'm sorry, Chris, but we were sleeping. What's all the racket about?"

"Guys, some hours ago Japan attacked Pearl Harbor in Hawaii! And it appears that thousands are dead!"

"What?"

"Yes! I can't believe it!" said Sam.

"You should turn on your radio!" Christopher said.

Before I could turn on the radio Edward had already done so, and the news was just as Chris and Sam had said. The next thing we did, after listening to the news, was to call our relatives. It was a challenge to use the phones in the corridor as we took turns calling our homes.

On Monday morning, December 8, 1941, President Franklin D. Roosevelt addressed the U.S. House and Senate in a joint meeting. The president asked Congress to declare war on Japan. The Senate unanimously agreed with President Roosevelt's request. As long as I live I'll never forget the words of the president about that dreadful day of December 7, 1941: *"There is no blinking at the fact that our people, our territory, and our interests are in grave danger. December 7, 1941: a date which will live in infamy."* As I heard these historic words they resounded in my ears and mind, and were etched into my consciousness.

The United States has officially declared war five times in history: the War of 1812, the Mexican War, the Spanish-American War, World War I, and now World War II. This time I heard it for myself on the radio, and didn't read about it in a textbook.

I couldn't help but remember the words of our president in his national debate in October 1940, when he told the American people explicitly, *"I shall say it again and again and again: your boys are not going to be sent into any foreign wars."*

I believe the president meant what he said, but there was no way he could have known of the event of December 7, 1941. The twentieth century is in fact the bloodiest century of all. More lives were lost in the First World War than in any other war, and twenty-one years after its end, Europe was plunged into another world war. The United States of America had been attacked and was now forced into this war.

According to my journal of geopolitics that I began keeping in 1933, on September 27, 1940, three nations—Italy, Germany, and Japan—signed a pact in Berlin, known as the German-Italian-Japanese Pact. The pact was meant to last ten years, and was based mainly on an economic and military alliance. These three nations agreed to assist one another if they became involved in a war with other nations during the duration of their agreement.

The Kwantung Army of Japan attacked China and annexed Manchuria on September 19, 1931. The Japanese became increasingly belligerent and committed atrocities against the Chinese people. On November 26, 1941, the United States told the Japanese Empire that the time had come to withdraw its troops from China.

However, Japan ignored the continuous warnings from America. In the midst of 1941, Japan had sufficient oil to last for only the next eighteen months, but in spite of the warnings from Britain and the United States, the Japanese government refused to heed their admonitions. As a result, President Roosevelt had no choice but to freeze Japan's assets in the United States, and this included Japan's oil supply, which came from America. After that, the inevitable was December 7, 1941, when Japan attacked Pearl Harbor on the island of Oahu, Hawaii. The ships and servicemen were sitting targets for those Japanese bombers early that Sunday morning. Also, when the Empire of Japan attacked Hawaii, it wasn't a war the United States was trained for, but a war that came to America's shores.

The attack on that dreadful morning lasted less than two hours, but most of the damage was actually inflicted in the first thirty minutes. The sneak attack on Pearl Harbor struck an indelible blow to the United States that will never be forgotten.

Twenty-three hundred thirty-seven military men were killed in the attack. One thousand one hundred fifty-three were wounded. One hundred eighty-three airplanes were destroyed before leaving their posts. Three light cruisers and three destroyers were destroyed in the attack. Eight battleships were also destroyed: the *Arizona*, the *California*, the *Maryland*, the *Nevada*, the *Oklahoma*, the *Pennsylvania*, the *Tennessee*, and the *West Virginia*.

The Empire of Japan had been planning an attack on the U.S. Pacific Fleet since December 1940, and the mastermind behind this strategic military plan was Admiral Isoroku Yamamoto, commander of the Japanese combined fleet. In fact, Yamamoto spent two years at Harvard University, studying the design and execution of Western naval warfare. He would use these lessons against Japan's enemy, America.

Japan came with six aircraft carriers, two battleships, three cruisers, eleven destroyers, and about 430 attack aircraft.

This was a man who in his early years had learned English from an American missionary sent to Japan, but Yamamoto recognized that America was a dangerous enemy. And furthermore, he knew the industrial base of the United States would give America a powerful edge and the upper hand in any war. By crippling the U.S. Pacific Fleet, Admiral Yamamoto thought it would take America at least six months or perhaps one year to rebuild it. By that time, Japan would have already established and consolidated its new empire across the Pacific.

Consequently, Yamamoto thought the United States would then find the cost of driving the Japanese out of their new consolidated empire too risky. Four days after the attack on Pearl Harbor, on December 11, 1941, according to the agreement of the German-Italian-Japanese Pact, the Axis nations of Italy and Germany made a public declaration of war on the United States.

Germany made a terrible mistake when it declared war on America. The moment it did so, it lost the war.

The year of 1941 was one of enormous atrocities, globally speaking. For example, in the month of March, Adolf Eichmann was made head of the Gestapo, particularly of Jewish affairs. In April the Nazis invaded Greece and Yugoslavia, and then in June they invaded Russia.

The *Einsatzgruppen* started their mass murder of the Jews in the east, and by September 1, all Jews in Germany were ordered to wear the *Magain David* (the Star of David). September 28 and 29 were the days of the *Babi Yar* Massacre in Kiev of thirty-five thousand Jews. Also, it was on December 25, 1941, that K. L. Auschwitz executed the planned first gassing of nine hundred POW's with Zyklon B.

As the United States prepared for war, I continued pursuing my bachelor's degree in psychology.

My brother Georg was seventeen, and in less than one year he would graduate from high school. Mom called and was very concerned

THE WAR AND 1942

about Georg. Since Congress declared war on Japan on December 8, 1941, all Georg had talked about was enlisting to fight against the tyranny of fascism.

So I called my "little" brother (the boy was now over six feet two inches tall).

"Hello."

"Mom, it's me."

"Oh, hi, David, thanks for calling. Do you want to talk with your brother?"

"Yes, Mom, but please, I don't want him to suspect that I'm calling because you asked me to talk to him. Mom, before I speak with Georg, I was just wondering, how's Jena?"

"She's fine. However, your sister is engaged, and she's getting married in less than two months."

"Gee, Mom, when did all this happen?"

"Two days ago, David, and she asked me to inform you of the good news when you called," said Mom.

"But why so soon, Mom?"

"Honestly, David, the way things are going in the world right now and with the war, your sister and Andreas believe that it's the best thing for them. Because remember, David, Andreas is a young surgeon, fresh out of medical school. And your sister doesn't want him to be drafted, if it comes to that, before they're actually married."

"Gee, that makes sense, Mom, but now you've got me thinking."

"About what, dear?"

"Well, I guess the government will be issuing another draft pretty soon."

"Well, I don't know, but I wish your brother would keep quiet, and wait and see what the government is going to do next."

"I think that's very obvious, Mom, because we're at war."

"Oh, David, don't remind me. And furthermore, I can't bear the thought of my two boys, especially Georg, going off to fight in a war."

"Mom, honestly, I hope it doesn't come to that. However, I wish I could at least finish my bachelor's degree. Anyway, Mom, would you ask Jena to call me?"

"Yes, David."

"Thanks, Mom. Now I'd like to talk with the little big boy."

Before Georg came to the phone I thought about Jena and Andreas Hansel getting married. Jena is twenty-four, and I think Andreas is thirty. I met him at Thanksgiving and he seemed to be a really decent guy.

"Hey, big brother!"

"Hi, Georg, how are you?"

"I'm fine."

"So, what do you think about America being in this war now?"

"I think it's about time!"

"What do you mean, Georg?"

"David, you of all people don't need a synopsis from me of the historical and current outline of our politics and history."

"Well, Georg—"

"Hey, David, I love you, and I'll always have respect for you as my big brother, but please allow me to finish."

"Okay, Georg."

"Thank you. Remember the year I was born?"

"Yeah, 1924."

"Yes, that's correct, David. Bear in mind that the 1920s were known as the Boom to Bust era. And during that period, America was the first nation in the world. Its citizens drove automobiles, enjoyed new movies, and had the awesome privilege of listening to the radio."

"Yes, Georg, I'm fully aware of theses historical facts about the early part of the twentieth century."

"Yes, David, but allow me to express myself. Allow me to demonstrate my intellectual prowess to you, big brother."

As Georg said that, I realized that it was as if somehow I had become Dad and Georg had become me. I knew how I had felt when I tried to show Dad how intelligent I was, but he never encouraged me. Therefore, I decided to listen to my brother's point of view and respect what he was saying. I knew that since Georg was very perceptive he knew that Mom was in on this.

"Georg, I apologize. Please continue. I'm listening to you."

"Gosh, thanks, David. For a second I thought you were going to cut me off, for who am I to tell you anything, seeing that you're a student of Yale University."

"Georg, before I'm a student—and kid, it doesn't matter what university I attend—the fact remains that I'm your brother, kiddo, and I love you."

"Gee, thanks, David, but could I please finish?"

"Sure, kiddo."

"The 1920s were a time when the arts flourished in our country. Hollywood was making movies at an astronomical rate. And in New York, the skyline was changing rapidly as new buildings were popping up all around the city. But in the late twenties, and to be precise by 1929, the era that was known as the Roaring Twenties and the good old Jazz Age suddenly, without warning, came to an abrupt end, in a complete economic disaster that affected most people."

"Yes, Georg, you're talking about the Great Depression of 1929 to 1933."

"Yes, David."

"But Georg, how does that affect us? We were never affected by the worldwide economic crisis that began on October 29, 1929. Do you know what's really ironic?"

"No, what?" said Georg.

"It wasn't until my first year in college that I learned about the magnitude of the Great Depression. I was amazed at what some families went through."

"You're absolutely correct, David. Thanks to Grandfather Hans, his money and our trust funds were not in the New York Stock Exchange. But David, as long as people aren't affected by something, they honestly don't care unless it comes and knocks at their doors. And that's precisely what happened to us on that early morning of December seventh David?"

"Yes, Georg."

"I hope I'm not boring you."

"No, not at all, I'm glad that you're reminding me of these things."

"Thanks. After the economic collapse, Franklin Delano Roosevelt, the new president of that hour, by his ingenuity and skills rebuilt our great nation once again, and also restored the American people's faith. And this was done by reminding them of what this country believes in and what it stands for. Even though the president meant well, that certainly didn't change the people's views on isolationism, nor did it change our serendipitous future. In the end we were still attacked. And what's so intriguing is that both President Roosevelt and Adolf Hitler became leaders of their countries in the same year of 1933."

"Yes, I remember that, Georg. I was just thirteen at the time."

"That's true, and I was nine. Even though I was nine, I remember Dad and us listening intently to these seismic monumental events of 1933. The United States continued with its views on isolationism. Despite what had happened with the annexation of Manchuria in 1931, and the outbreak of the war in 1939, the president persisted with the country's isolationist policies, because that's what the people wanted. However, David, I'm getting to my point."

"I'm listening, Georg, take your time."

"But those idealistic views ended immediately when Japan made its sneak attack on Pearl Harbor a few days ago. And that's my point, David. It's that in spite of the tragedies in China, and the situation in Europe, the United States thought that having an isolationist policy would keep us safe and out of the war. On the contrary, it certainly didn't work for the Great War, nor did it work for this generation. And David, I know you mean well, but as soon as my high school years come to an end, I'm going to put off college for the interim and my intention is to join the Marines."

"Georg, please, no!"

"David, please try to understand. A world war is being waged in the Pacific and in Europe, and unless it comes to an end no one is safe. David, don't you understand? I'm not going to wait and hide behind my academic ambitions while freedom is gradually taken away from us. Just look at the quagmire in Europe, and the Jews. Do you know what will happen if Germany wins this war?"

"Georg, I really think you need to think this through thoroughly."

"I've thought about this for some time. I know Mom won't be pleased with my decision. However, David, don't you think I'd rather stay in my own country where I feel safe? Go off to college, and meet that special person and settle down? But as long as the freedom of other people is being undermined, it's only a matter of time before that same problem comes knocking at our doors. And then what?"

"Yes, but Georg, the problems in Germany and of the Jews don't concern us."

"David, how can you say that? Suppose we were Jews in Germany, and our freedom was being threatened? Wouldn't you want other neighboring countries to come and rescue us?"

"How does that apply to us? First, we're not Germans, and second, we're not Jew!"

"Yes, but David, just supposing we were European Jews."

"But we're not!" I said.

"Look, David, I don't fully know why I have such a strong certainty about this. All I know is that freedom in the world is in grave danger, and I'm willing to be expendable for the freedom of others. David, I would love to have a family in a few years, but how can I sit back and want this for my progeny? No, my brother, this is a time that our generation must be a selfless one, because the freedom of the world is at stake."

"Well, Georg, my little and wise brother, you have caused me to feel convinced about my duty not only to my country, but also freedom in the world. How did you get to be so mature in such a short span of time?"

"I don't know, David, but I certainly don't see myself as some hero. All I know is that fascism is taking advantage of citizens in the world and I must do something to help humanity. And David, please know that my attitude isn't one of a martyr, but I know the right thing to do when the time comes."

"Georg, I respect your strong certainty. After our discussion, I'm now having some serious thoughts about my motives, and this war."

Gosh, Georg is certainly acting like a true Certainist, and to think I've never shared my philosophy with anyone. He knows what he wants and what he must do.

"David, we need to understand that if this war should take a turn against the United States, I foresee a hopeless America and a global bloodbath much more severe than the Civil War. This war could turn out to be a bloodbath of region against region and brother against brother, just like the Civil War, because this war is a battle between tyranny and freedom."

"Yes, Georg, that's a valid point. But don't you think this war is mainly about who will rule next?"

"Yes, exactly, David. This is a war of who will rule next, and who fixes the currency in the future, and who will control the market. For whoever wins this war will seize the hegemony after the war, because the British Empire has lost it. David, I'm sure that most of the wars throughout the ages had some kind of religious connection. If people were to meticulously examine the main causes of these conflicts, I'm certain they would see the connections. Moreover, I'm sure they'd find some religious basis to those wars."

"You know, Georg, that statement is true."

"I'm sure, David, that you know my views and opinions about religion."

"Oh yes, and our views are exactly the same, Georg."

"It amazes me, David, how most people are totally ignorant of history and current events."

"That's because most people, Georg, just don't want to search out and study anything for themselves."

"I don't understand it. How stupid can you be?"

"That's true, Georg, but that's how the majority of people want to be."

"David, wasn't it in the early fourth century, in the Edict of Milan, when the Christian religion was granted acceptance and tolerance by Rome in the year 313? However, that *stultus* leader Constantine didn't realize he was setting up his Western Empire for an imminent demise. And it was exactly ninety-seven years after the Edict of Milan that the

Western Empire fell to barbarians in 410. Now, correct me if I'm wrong, David, but wasn't it the Goths who were responsible for the fall of the Western Empire? However, it was religion that had weakened it."

"Yes, I believe that's correct, Georg, according to history. Then again, not everyone, my brother, will agree about the subtlety of religion, and how religion can be used as a device that actually causes the atrophy of civilizations."

"Yes, David, I'm in total agreement about that. Nevertheless, wasn't it after the fall of Rome, in 410, that the power of the Western Empire was literally transferred to the religious institution? Spain became the hegemony of the world, because of the Roman Catholic Church and its domineering beliefs. They promulgated their religious doctrines throughout the world. But all that changed in the late sixteenth century, in 1588, when the British Empire defeated King Philip II of Spain. And now here we are in 1941, and the British Empire has lost the hegemony. If this generation just sits back and waits, I believe there'll be a bloodbath for the entire human race, and especially for all those who don't measure up to the racial ideals of the Third Reich and its master race."

"Well, Georg, I can certainly see that not only have you been spending time in Dad's library, you've also been studying intensely about the international perspectives of the war. And I have to admit that you do have some interesting theories about this war."

"David, these views are more than just theories, big brother. Nonetheless, they're based on epistemic observance of current events. I too have been following the problems in Europe and the Pacific that have eventually led our country into World War Two. That's why I have such a strong certainty about my duty in this war. And David, I'll say it again: the nation that wins this war will surely become the dominating factor in the world."

"Okay, Georg, I've listened to your views for almost an hour, and I must say that at first I was somewhat hesitant."

"But now?" asked Georg.

"Well, allow me to finish, kiddo."

"Oh, sorry, David."

"No, Georg, there's no need to apologize. I must say that after listening to your stimulating views, I didn't realize you have grown up and know some germane facts about the war. My intentions were to try to discourage you from joining the Marines. I'm not going to lie to you, Georg. I certainly of my own volition will not be joining any military department, but if our government drafts me, I'll have no choice but to respond to my country's call. But what you're about to do is admirable, and I respect you for your high ideals if that's what you want, then I'll support and encourage you to do what you feel led to do. As your older brother, I don't want you to get hurt in this war. Georg, when young boys go off to fight in a war two things can happen: they can return home with serious injuries, or they may never return home."

"Yes, David, I've considered the cost, and I've realized that chances are I may not live to become an old man."

"Well, Georg, I'm glad you have considered the price of this freedom you've shared with me, and that you're willing to die for it, because I'm fully aware this is a just cause. However, let's hope for the best, and that if the Marines accept you, you'll return to us safe and in one piece. Well, it's getting late, Georg. Let me say good night to Mom."

"Sure, and thanks, David. Love you."

"You're welcome, Georg. I love you too, kiddo."

While Georg went to fetch Mom, I thought about how I knew she wouldn't be pleased with the nature of my conversation with her baby boy. On the other hand, I could only hope to persuade her that we couldn't hold him back, for he's growing up and has become a young man with a mind of his own.

"Hello, David, how did your conversation with Georg go?"

"Mom, I don't want to upset you, but I'm in agreement with Georg and I believe we should support him in this."

"What? David, I can't believe what you're telling me. I came to you because I know you're a great influence on your baby brother, and now you're telling me that I should support my last child in joining this global mêlée!"

"Mom, please allow me to explain."

"Explain what, David? Maria is nineteen and has been in college for almost one year. It's only Georg and I who now live in this big house. What am I to do when your brother joins the Marines?"

"Mom, even if the Marines refuse Georg, he'll have to go off to college anyway."

"Yes, that's true, David, but if he's here I can still see him periodically, like I see the rest of my children."

"Mom, I really think you need to listen to what I have to say."

"I don't want to hear what you have to say! I asked you to dissuade your brother from joining the Marine Corps, and now, after your long discussion with him, you're telling me that we should support him!" With that, Mom began to cry.

"Oh, Mom, please don't cry."

"I don't want to discuss this any further, David."

"Mom, please let me talk to Georg."

"No. You certainly haven't helped, and you've done enough. Good-bye, David."

"Mom! Mom!"

She hung up.

I thought it best to let time take its course, for I was truly sorry about how Mom felt at that moment. I'd talk to her another time, and could only hope that she would understand.

Nineteen forty-one came to an end, and the new year of 1942 commenced in spite of the war that was being waged in the Pacific and Europe. Several Nazis leaders met for a ghastly meeting on January 20, 1942, during which plans were discussed and finalized to deal with the problem of the European Jewish population. Hence, the answer to this problem came about when these high-ranking Nazi officers came to the ultimate agreement and decided how they were going to execute the "Final Solution" of the Jews. This meeting came to be known as the infamous Wannsee Conference. The district of Wannsee is located between two lakes in the southwestern borough of Steglitz-Zehlendorf, Germany, the larger *GroBer* Wannsee and the lesser *Kleiner* Wannsee. It's on the river *Havel* and is separated by the famous Wannsee Bridge.

The Wannsee Conference was in fact appointed by Reinhard Heydrich. He had planned this meeting since the month of July 1941. The whole purpose of the Wannsee Conference was to plan the mechanized approach of implementing the Fuhrer's "Final Solution" to the Jewish question in Europe. For example, what method of industrialization the Third Reich would be using for the systematic extermination of the Jews.

In the Wannsee Conference these Nazi leaders came up with the brilliant plans of carrying out Hitler's "Final Solution." The reality of the "Final Solution" was the gathering of all European Jews into a centralized location, such as ghettos, and then their deportation to concentration camps that would culminate in the Fuhrer's euphemistic term.

This meant the literal annihilation of the Hebrew race: eleven million men, women, and children who were presently living in Europe. The extermination camp in Sobibor, on March 1, officially began its program of gassing a fraction of the European Jews.

Reports were published as early as 1942 in the American press about the systematic extermination of Jews throughout Europe in concentration camps such as Auschwitz, Buchenwald, Dachau, and Treblinka, but the ghastly presupposed information about these stories only created mixed reactions from the people: either doubts or a lack of concern about this unfathomable dilemma of genocide.

On February 14, 1942, my eldest sister, Jena, married Dr. Andreas Hansel. They made a very handsome couple, and Jena looked so beautiful in her bridal dress. Andreas was very slim and tall; he looked like he weighed around 190 pounds at six foot three. His ancestors are from Sweden, so he looked like the typical Swedish guy. The color of his hair was a bright golden blond and his eyes were blue green. Jena was only five foot eleven and weighed 130 pounds. Even though she was somewhat tall for a woman, she looked very short standing next to Andreas, Georg, and I. When they got married, Jena was six years younger than her husband, twenty-four. Andreas was thirty. It was nice to get away from the reality of the war and just enjoy the day.

As the war went on in the Pacific and Europe, the United States government continued with its Selective Training and Service Act of 1940. At first, Congress passed, on September 14, 1940, the first conscription in the United States during a time of peace.

The Selective Training and Service Act of 1940 requested that all men between the ages of twenty-one and thirty-five living in the United States must register with their local draft boards. Once those men were registered, the government would then select those servicemen that were needed through a lottery system.

The law at first required that if a man was selected he would serve in the military for only twelve months. However, this changed when America entered the war on December 8, 1941. At that time, the STSA required that all men in the United States between the ages of eighteen and forty-five register with the draft boards in their area.

In the summer of 1941, the president asked the U.S. Congress to lengthen the tenure of draftees in the military service. By this time the U.S. Congress had already extended the duration from twelve months to twenty-four months, and with the passing of the Selective Training and Service Act of 1940, the U.S. government proposed to set a cap on the military draftees of nine hundred thousand trained men. This changed dramatically after December 7, 1941. As the demand for military servicemen increased after Pearl Harbor, there was a great need of new draftees for the U.S. Marine Corps.

As I read this new piece of information in the newspaper, I couldn't help but think about my brother, Georg Alfred Hugenberg, and his passionate desire to enlist in the U.S. Marine Corps as soon as he turned eighteen.

After December 7, 1941, thousands of men and women rushed to the United States' military bases and volunteered their service to the U.S. military. By the end February 1942, it was estimated that more than five million young Americans had willingly offered their service to the U.S. military force.

By the end of 1942, the U.S. government was drafting up to two hundred thousand men a month, and it wasn't long before the number had reached almost ten million men in the armed forces who were ready to do battle.

That also was the year when the Chrysler plant in Detroit began mass production of M3 tanks. In that same year the United States government resettled almost all Japanese who were living along the West Cast. They were transported to several unpleasant detention camps, where they were kept until the end of 1944.

Nineteen forty-two was also the year of the Allies' triumphant turning point in World War II, with three major battles that impacted the outcome of the war. The first was the Battle of Midway, which was fought on June 4. The Allies were suffering great losses, as the German U-boats were sinking the Allies' ships faster than they could manufacture them. The tide turned on June 4, 1942, when the Allies sank four Japanese aircraft carriers in the Battle of Midway. This halted Japan's offensive progress in the Pacific Ocean. The second decisive victory came in October, when the British won the Battle at El Alamein in Egypt, driving General Erwin Rommel and the Italian forces into Tunisia. The final victory came in November 1942, at the Battle of Stalingrad. The Russian Army launched a secret surprise counterattack on the German armed forces as they attacked the city. The German forces had no choice but to retreat, even though Hitler believed that whoever controlled Russia would control the world.

The Fuhrer had an obsession with Stalingrad, but when General Friedrich von Paulus and his surviving eighty thousand men of the 6th

Army surrendered in the winter of 1942, the Axis lost over three hundred thousand men in the cold weather of Stalingrad. The harsh Soviet winter caught the German Army off guard, for it was not prepared for the deadly winter. Many German soldiers suffered the penalty of frostbite in Stalingrad.

Those soldiers who survived at Stalingrad said the winter in Russia was the coldest they ever encountered. It felt like the temperature was minus fifty-four degrees. It was so cold that the soldiers had to refrain from directly touching any metal object. If they did, it would take their skin right off, as it would stick to the metal. Some of the soldiers remembered that it became so cold that they didn't really care if they lived or died.

A large number of German soldiers froze to death, but as the Third Reich Army continued to endure the harsh Soviet Union winter of 1942, some men were suffering from sheer weakness due to lack of food and the cold weather. Their bodies collapsed into the snow, and their comrades would kick them, because if they lay for too long in that freezing temperature it would surely kill them.

It's really sad when humanity refuses to learn from the lessons of history. One hundred thirty years before this, the French Army, under the leadership of Napoleon Bonaparte I, went into Russia in the year of 1812. The United States was still a young country in 1812; the fledging nation consisted of only eighteen states. However, the War of 1812 brought the young nation of the United States of America into the age of a mature nation.

It was the first time in American history that the U.S. Congress declared war on Britain, in the War of 1812. In that same year, Napoleon and his forces marched into Russia with an army of six hundred seventy thousand men. Less than one year later only a fraction of his troops retuned to Paris. Only a few thousand men survived the harsh winter of Russia. Napoleon's unfortunate and miscalculated tactics during Russia's severe winter bore the fruits that led to his demise in 1814.

In 1942, history would repeat itself, when the German Army underestimated Russia's severe weather, and over three hundred thousand soldiers died mainly due to the harsh winter.

After the burgeoning accomplishment of the three major battles in 1942, the tide was turning against the Axis in World War II.

My baby brother Georg enlisted in the Marine Corps soon after his graduation, which was a few days after his eighteen birthday on May 10. At eighteen, Georg was almost six foot four and very thin, but a fire of patriotism burned within him. This really amazed me about my brother: he had the strongest certainty about his obligation to his country, and little or no concern whatsoever about his own safety. Mom finally accepted what Georg wanted to do. It was hard for Mom to accept the day he went to his training, but we did our best to comfort our mother in that dreadful hour. The reality of war is that it's always so uncertain, and I didn't know if we would ever see Georg again.

As I said good-bye to my only brother, somehow I knew that soon after my graduation in May 1942, the U.S. military would summon me to serve my country in this war. I decided that after my graduation from Yale University, I was going to enlist. The day after graduation I enlisted and was on my way to begin my military training. When I enlisted in the U.S. Army as a young college graduate, I did not expect to begin immediately at the rank of second lieutenant. However, I had to undergo several months of vigorous military training before my deployment.

It was hard for Mom to accept what I did, but I felt somewhat ashamed of myself because my baby brother had enlisted in the Marine Corps before me, and most of the guys from my dormitory volunteered their service before they were drafted.

I was surprised when guys like Jim Maitland, Percy Ireton, and my former roommate, Edward Dryden, enlisted soon after graduation, but they did not want to volunteer their service without matriculation. The gang also enlisted after their graduation in 1942: Daniel, Jack, Ryan, Harry, James, and Jesse.

My life took a total drastic turn at this moment, as I had a job to do for my commander in chief and the American people. Therefore, as a Certainist I committed myself to accomplish my task, hoping not to fail my superiors and country. If I were to die, I could only hope that I'd be ready to face death head-on as an ideal philosopher, and a second lieutenant in the U.S. Army. On the contrary, I had to do some serious adjusting because I was among strange young men, of whom I knew absolutely nothing except that they were not part of my fraternity, the gang, or equal to my station. In spite of our differences, we had one thing in common: to win this war.

As early as 1942, the American government had pressed for the invasion of Northern Europe, and as our superiors told us, the invasion of Northern Europe was an arduous military task that would take two years of training before any major results could be seen. We were told that the casualties would be high.

The invasion of Europe was a great challenge of World War II between two prominent titans, General Rommel and General Eisenhower; however, due to the immense risk of Operation Overlord, the outcome of this mission depended on the effective military tactics of the Allies, who would defeat the Nazis on Normandy.

According to the words of General Eisenhower: "*The mighty expedition is tense as a great human spring, coiled for the moment, but its energy will be released, and it will bump the English Channel in the greatest amphibious assault ever attempted.*"

We were also told that the invasion would be the most ambitious military operation ever planned in the war. This invasion, as far as I understood, would be a high-risk plan to obtain entrance for the Allied powers to Europe, and to force the Third Reich to fight the war on two fronts. Also, if the operation was successful, Germany would be defeated and its forces would be driven back.

Operation Overlord was in fact an enormous united maneuvering of air, naval, and ground forces. The success of the invasion of Normandy would demand impeccable military tactics, dedication, and vigorous training.

Most of the soldiers didn't really know what they'd gotten themselves into. Many of them thought they were just going across into Europe to help and protect the British Isles from German invaders.

But as Operation Overlord continued to build momentum, Hitler was planning to oppose the coming assault on his impenetrable Atlantic wall. Throughout 1942 and 1943, German U-boats continued to sink ships that were taking supplies to Britain. In 1943, the United States and Britain began to bomb the industrialized Axis cities as the Allied forces continued to invade certain parts of Europe. By the month of September they had landed in Sicily and invaded Italy, which led to the downfall of fascism there, and the dictator Benito Mussolini was finally toppled.

As I heard this astounding news I couldn't help but think about my brother Georg, and wondered where he was, and what he was doing at that moment. I hoped that he had heard the good news of the Allied invasion of Sicily and Italy.

Prior to this invasion, and after my training in the summer 1942, I was shipped across the Atlantic Ocean to the British Isles, to Liverpool, for an additional ten weeks of training before the invasion of Northwest Africa, Operation Torch, on November 7, 1942. After my first baptism of fire, and several other combats, we were sent back to England in January 1944, in preparation for the invasion of Normandy.

The United States shipped to England a staggering 1.5 million servicemen for D-Day. Along with the incredible number of men, the military also shipped five million tons of supplies and equipment that would be needed for the invasion on June 6, 1944.

There were also three hundred twenty thousand different kinds of items such as guns, ammunition, cigarettes, gum, and along with these items came the ghastly reality of the countless coffins that would be needed for those who might be killed in battle. In the words of General Dwight D. Eisenhower: "England has been transformed into *the greatest operating military base of all time."* But in the opinion of the British people, the American GI *"is overpaid, oversexed, and over here!"* And as I became more familiar with certain soldiers, eventually a close friendship began to grow, and I discovered that some of the guys had fought, like me, in our debut combat in North Africa. Their units had gone all the way into Sicily and Italy. Surprisingly, I learned that my brother Georg, for a short time, was in Sicily with other Marines from his division.

As the day of the invasion approached, our training became more intense, and longer, but in spite of the difficulties, given my theory of Certainism, I knew what I had to do. I continued to submit myself to the vigorous training for the day of Operation Overlord. Sometimes I felt like my system was being overloaded, but as the weeks went by my body became attuned to the vigorous military training.

One night on the radio I heard that five million Jews already had been murdered by Hitler's regime, and one hundred twenty million people were living under the tyranny of Nazi Germany.

Now the only hope of liberation was the Allied invasion of Europe. The leaders of the Allied powers had planned for the Russian Army to invade Germany from the east, and the invaders from Normandy to invade Germany from the west. As I pondered about these vital matters, given my tendency of intellectual spontaneity, I began to ruminate about the conversation I had with Georg before his enlistment in the Marine Corps.

"My intention is to join the Marines," he had told me. "David, please try to understand. A world war is being waged in the Pacific and Europe, and unless this war comes to an end no one is safe. David, don't you understand? I am not going to wait and hide behind my academic ambitions while freedom is gradually taken away from us. Just look at the quagmire in Europe and the Jews. Do you know what will happen if Germany wins this war?"

I muttered to myself, "Yes, Georg, my young and brave brother, I understand!"

After several months of training, D-Day was just two days away, but the inclement weather might create problems for our landing, and any further delay could mean great risk. Our delay would only give General Rommel more time to secure the beaches with more mines. In the region of West Paris, General Rommel's headquarters in *La Roche Guyon Oberbefehlshaber* received a weather report on the inclement conditions over the English Channel. After reading the report, he recognized that an imminent invasion was out of the question.

Therefore, Field Marshal Erwin presumed that this was a favorable report. The Allies had postponed their invasion until June 15. Being a clever tactician, he saw this opportunity as more time to further mine the beaches of Normandy. Consequently, after speaking with his superior, he saw this as a pretext to get away from Paris for a few days to spend some time with his wife for her birthday, and met with the Fuhrer in Berlin.

However, Field Marshal Erwin thought General Eisenhower wasn't a gambler, but what the Axis didn't realize was that the unpredictable weather was, in fact, working in the Allies' favor. On the early morning of June 6, the orders were given by the supreme commander, General Eisenhower, to launch Operation Overlord. With those orders the launch began, with more than five thousand ships of every description that carried on them one hundred seventy-five thousand men in the first wave.

This was the greatest invasion fleet ever to sail the world. I have never witnessed nor read about anything like it in the archives of history. My stomach was churning, either from excitement or fear; however, I was actually witnessing history in the making, and I was a part of this great amphibious assault. I sat frozen in the boat as we were taken to the shores of Normandy. As part of the U.S. VII Corps, our launch was the first to arrive at Utah Beach, at exactly 0630 hours. Most of us were either worn out from the months of vigorous training, scared, or seasick from crossing the English Channel. As the door opened we were greeted with a volley of countless bullets from the enemy; a reign of terror. Men began to be cut down like flies as they tried to make their way onto the beach. Confronting us were the waters of death, and in the distance was the hope of finishing the race from this rain of bullets, and the beach that was covered in miles of mines.

Some of the young soldiers never had the chance to engage in the Battle of Normandy; they were stuck down by the rain of bullets that first greeted them on the boats. Many of these young men were just teenagers, going into their first time in battle under the leadership of General Dwight David Eisenhower. As we endeavored to disembark from the boats, many of us had to dodge those bullets that were aiming for our demise.

But in the intense battle I was honored—even though I was scared—to fight in the midst of such brave young men, who were marching to their deaths with such honor and alacrity that it actually encouraged me to march onward in the name of freedom. I don't believe in hell, nor do I know if such a place actually exists, but I thought, *If there's really a hell, I'm certainly in it right now, for war is hell!*

This was not a battle for conquest; rather, it was being fought against the unjust conquest of malevolent dictators. I felt so sick because of all the carnage, and the potent smell of death all around us as the beach was being drenched and stained with the blood. This was the signature of these valiant young men who became the ideal martyrs of freedom, for they're the icons of the bravest and greatest generation, who lay down their lives willingly on the altar of freedom that morning of June 6, 1944.

I did not enlist in the military service just to kill, although I knew I would have to do this eventually in the war. I was certain about my duties, and not willing to repudiate them under any circumstances. Even in the midst of many battles I tried to fight with honor, and to show dignity toward the enemy. As of Operation Overlord, it had been two years since I joined the army. Killing men is never an easy task. So, on this dreadful but necessary day I had to deal with the vast carnage of those whom I became acquainted with during my training. There were also brave young Germans who fought for what they believed, and the honor of their Fatherland, who died on this appalling but necessary day.

It was difficult to kill young German soldiers, who were the age of my brother; some of these young men even resembled Georg. It was difficult to repeat the same procedure over and over again on that day. At one particular moment I actually thought I was about to lose my sanity. However, my philosophy of Certainism has taught me from an early age that once I've made my choice I must never look for an easy way out. On the other hand, I felt like running and abandoning my men and duty that day, but that's only if I had chosen to yield to my irrational emotions. I was never a person who submitted entirely to them, and since I didn't permit my emotions to control me, or even let them get the better side of me, I resisted those negative and cowardly emotions and decided to stay the course with my unit, and not to lose my objectivity in this grave battle.

The fact of the matter was that I had job to do, though I didn't enjoy killing in the slightest degree. Nevertheless, it was my duty to do as the U.S. Army commanded me. I couldn't let my men, country, and unit in the U.S. Army, with whom I'd lived and trained for two full years, down. Nor could I let my brother Georg, whom I love, down, because I would rather die in battle with honor than abandon my duty as a second lieutenant in the U.S. Army for temporary safety, and live in disgrace for the rest of my life.

My uniform was wet from the waters of the ocean, my sweat, the blood of my fallen men, and my person. I had no major injuries from the engaged combat up to now, only minor ones. I had never seen the inside of a human being before, or smelled the unpleasant odor of burnt flesh, and particularly the smell of warm blood in battle.

This battle was like a continuous stage of horror and death; the horror was the war. It was the longest day of my life, very similar to a ghoulish nightmare, and how I wished it would end. The reality and continuum of the battle lingered on with intense fighting, which was terrifying as we engaged ourselves in the battle on Normandy beach. The British 3rd Infantry of the 27th Armored Brigade landed on Sword Beach at 0725 hours. The natural colors of that summer day seemed to disappear all around us as the battle waged on, since the carnage and blood of those who were wounded and fell in the battle brought about a certain macabre and unnatural color that covered the beach.

It was as if death had taken on a special color in this battle, epitomizing the event of the day. That particular grayish color eventually became very depressing, and I longed for the day to end, but as more soldiers approached the beaches, the enemy was prepared for them as they landed, greeting them with a special terror. They were cut down by multiple ammunition that never seemed to run out while their bullets kissed them good-bye.

There was much blood and carnage all around us, and this battle would be won or lost in the first few hours. It was difficult running with a volley of bullets coming at you, and at the same time trying to dodge four million land mines buried on the beaches.

If there was ever a time I wished I wasn't so tall, it was then, because being six foot five only made me a more conspicuous target for the enemy. At 0745 hours the 3rd Canadian Infantry of the 2nd Armored Brigade force-landed on Juno Beach. Suddenly, in the midst of the ubiquitous discouragement of terror, death, and hell that was all around us, I remembered a song my brother Georg loved to sing, particularly when he was a boy: the famous song "America."

And as I began to sing this famous patriotic song, a strange but sudden urge came over me, and I knew I didn't want to die on this battlefield of Normandy. This song Georg loved had a peculiar stoic effect on me, and it kept overflowing in me as I continued to sing it while I ran and engaged in battle: *"My country! 'tis of thee, sweet land of liberty, of thee I sing: Land where my fathers died! Land of the pilgrims' pride! From every mountain side let freedom ring!"*

Eventually, I thought I had, at least for the moment, arrived at a safe spot. There were parts of entrails, legs, and pieces of the remains of some young soldiers who had been blown up as they engaged in battle, or tried like myself to arrive at a safe spot.

There it was again: that smell of burnt flesh, the taste of hot blood. By now I could taste the fresh salt of the blood and death that were so potent and prevalent in this place. I could literally taste the unpleasant odor of death and the blood in my throat. I began to feel nauseous as my stomach started to convulse against the smell of death, in the form of burnt flesh and the hot blood of these brave victims of war.

But then, after a brief moment of sickness, for a few seconds I thought I was on a farm; all around me was a rain of feathers. I collected my thoughts and realized that the life jackets were lined with feathers. As the feathers began to settle I could see the stained blood on them that came from the poor soldiers who were blown to pieces.

By 0753 hours, on Gold Beach, there was another landing of the British 50th Infantry of the 8th Armored Brigade, and by 0758 hours, on Omaha Beach, the U.S. 5th Corps landed. All around me were the bodies of men; these were some of the finest and most courageous young men I've ever known from my country. By the afternoon, the U.S. military and Allied forces had seized control of Normandy Beach.

On the first day of Operation Overlord, it was estimated that the Allied casualties reached ten thousand, and many more were killed in this battle of the summer of 1944. When we disembarked from the landing boats, four German infantry divisions and one Panzer division were ready and waiting to challenge us from the moment we set foot on the beach.

Though the beaches of Normandy were now in the hands of the Allied powers, it took us about two long months of continuous and arduous battles before we could break away from the confinements of the Normandy landing zones. The next step was the liberation of France. It was a slow process, as the Germans fought us all the way, but our main goal was the defeat of the Nazi regime in Berlin.

Nineteen forty-two was the year I enlisted in the U.S. Army, and honestly, after several combats I had no notion that I would be part of Operation Torch, much less Operation Overlord, and would live to tell of the events.

Germany's defeat finally came ten months after the Normandy invasion. The horrors of the war were finally revealed; a nation had implemented, through its judicial system, the *Reichstag*, the extermination of more than twelve million people. I guess Georg was right: all we had to do was enlist, and then win the war, and let freedom ring!

Chapter Eight

The Problem with Religion

I'd lost most of my friends, whom I'd known from my pristine childhood days in Springfield, Massachusetts, in WWII. Daniel, Harry, Ryan, and James are all gone. In fact, I also lost certain relatives in this global conflict. The day soon after our graduation from university in 1942, the moment the gang and I enlisted in the military service, I knew we were walking with and holding the hand of death; hence, the reason some of us never saw our homeland again. Those of us in the gang who survived the ordeal of WWII do not have the opportunity of paying our respects to our brave young friends who died in the war, because the majority of our friends were either buried in a foreign land or their bodies were never recovered. At least with Tobey, we could still visit his grave periodically. The forlorn fact of the matter is that four out of seven of the gang died in the war. Those alive have to live and deal with this permanent pain for the rest of our lives. Besides, there's actually no closure for those of us who survived this madness. The war is over and I've returned home, but it's difficult, picking up the pieces and continuing with my life as if nothing ever happened. What am I to do when only two of my fraternity brothers returned home from this ghastly global conflict? The fraternity always had eight members, ever since I can remember.

When Tobey died in the spring of 1938, it was difficult dealing with the reality of his unexpected death. Then seven of us were alive, but now it was only Jack, Jesse, and me.

Furthermore, while I was stationed in Germany, my sister Maria wrote and informed me about the untimely death of Mom, and then some time afterward she wrote again, about the accidental death of our sister, Jena Hansel.

My mom passed away on the day of the Normandy invasion in the summer of 1944. In Maria's letter, she said that Mom was fine on the night of June 5. She retired for the evening as usual, but just slipped away into the oblivion of death, never waking up on June 6.

Also, Jena's husband, Dr. Andreas Hansel, was killed by a bomb in Oran, Algeria, which struck the tent where he was performing surgery, trying to save the life of a young soldier in the summer of 1943.

As a result, my sister, the young widow, was left to raise their baby boy all by herself, without her husband. In the fall of 1944, Jena was killed in an automobile accident, leaving her baby boy, Andreas Jr., without a mother or a father.

I came home to an empty house. Maria no longer lived there after she got married in the fall of 1945. It was a real challenge to deal with these tragedies. Mom and Jena died, and I never had the chance to tell them good-bye.

As for the gang: Daniel, my best friend, was dead. I wasn't aware that Daniel had volunteered his service to the U.S. Army's 507th Parachute Infantry Regiment. The first to see action on the invasion of Normandy was the U.S. 82nd Airborne Division. These brave young paratroopers were dropped by airplanes into Normandy around one a.m., and their main goal was to block the German counterattacks against the Allied invaders coming ashore on the beaches that morning of June 6. Among the thirteen thousand four hundred paratroopers and glider-riders was Daniel McCrory, Jr., my best friend. He was killed in action. Of the one hundred seventy-five thousand Allied troops who landed on that fifty-mile-wide beachhead in upper Normandy, 70 percent were wounded, and another 30 percent were either killed, captured, or their bodies were never recovered.

It never dawned on me that day we met in school at the age of five, in the spring of 1925, that nineteen years later, at the age of twenty-four, we would be engaged in a battle on the beaches of Normandy for the liberation of Europe.

While I was stationed in England, just before D-Day I heard on the radio one of the most penetrating speeches by the prime minister of Great Britain, Winston Churchill, which moved me: *"This is not the end, no, it is not even the beginning of the end. But it is perhaps the end of the beginning."* After the war, I found it extremely difficult to accept the fact that Daniel was killed in battle, and I would return home without my best childhood friend. Philosophically speaking, I understood what the British prime minister meant that day.

His speech symbolized the end of tyranny in Continental Europe, the beginning of freedom for humanity there, and the end of Hitler's despotism. But his speech also contained the elements of human sacrifice. After the war, with the loss of my friends, I comprehended the end of the beginning. In addition, even though I survived June 6 with minimal injuries, how was I to start a life with a new beginning after this horrible war, when my friends' lives had come to the beginning of their end?

It was the beginning of freedom in Continental Europe for its citizens; however, it was the end for many young men who gave their lives for the freedom of the world.

I can't help but think about my best friend, Daniel, and Peggy Whittaker, when they attended the same university. They were married about two weeks before their graduation in 1942. I was very pleased when Daniel called me and asked if I would do him the honor of being his best man. The day Daniel and Peggy got married was indeed a day of great joy, for all of us in the gang. We were all at their private wedding; it was only Daniel's closest friends, his parents, Peggy's parents, and Peggy's closest girlfriends from Massachusetts. That was the happiest moment for the gang, just before our enlistment.

After my arrival back home, in February 1946, I met with Mrs. Peggy McCrory. I was very pleased to see Peggy, and it was delightful to meet Daniel's twins for the first time. They were almost four years old when I returned from the war. The boy and girl look just like their father, especially the boy, Daniel McCrory III. I brought my German wife, Olga, to meet them.

As we spoke with Peggy it was a time of much sorrow and joy. Daniel's wife was glad to see that I had returned from the war with no major injuries, but it caused her to remember her beloved husband, Daniel.

He was my best friend for almost twenty years, and now he was gone.

As Olga became more acquainted with Peggy, and as I became familiar with Daniel's twins, my mind began to ruminate about the summer of 1936, when the gang and I were smoking cigarettes in Professor Bechstein's stable. Ryan and Jesse were having a sensuous discussion about Peggy, and boy, that really pissed off Daniel.

"Honey, are you all right?"

"Yes, Olga, I'm sorry. I was just thinking about when Daniel and Peggy became man and wife, and also when we were fifteen and didn't have a care in the world."

After spending a few hours with Peggy, Olga and I headed for our home. As I drove my wife to the house I grew up in, I couldn't help but think about my friends who died in the war.

My second friend to die in the war was James Lear. He died in the invasion of Iwo Jima, which occurred on February 19, 1945. James and my baby brother Georg were both involved in this invasion, a great sacrifice during which more than twenty-five thousand young Marines died or were wounded. They were two of the soldiers of the 4th and 5th U.S. Marine Division. The Battle of Iwo Jima lasted for thirty-six days. By the fifth day of the invasion, five thousand Marines had fallen in combat; three men for every two minutes. Both James and Georg were among those soldiers killed in that battle, but were killed on separate dates. Both were buried on the island.

My baby brother Georg was just twenty. He would have turned twenty-one on May 10, 1945, if he had lived to see his birthday. Sometimes

I wish I had been killed in battle like my friends and my brother Georg, who died in the prime of their lives.

James would have turned twenty-five on October 13, if he had survived the invasion. He was a young man with the coolest disposition. He was six feet three inches tall, and, like most us in the gang, he was lean and very athletic. The guys in the gang would give him a hard time about the way he looked, because even though James had the body and mind of a young man, his face never really changed. He still looked like an innocent kid when he went off to war. He would have been, if he had lived, the only member of our fraternity who would have looked very young for his age. James never got upset with us; he would say that we were brothers, and if he didn't get annoyed with his younger brothers, why should he get annoyed with his fraternity brothers? I know James did well in the war, since he was a young man that didn't wear his emotions on his sleeve. It was difficult to read James's emotions. He was the ideal phlegmatic, a very covert young man. He looked like a Tudor, just like the young Prince Edward VI, with milk-white skin, green eyes, and fiery red hair.

But now he's gone, and I will miss him. I will also miss the cigarettes he would take from his father's shop for the gang.

The little island of Iwo Jima is only six hundred miles from the mainland of Japan. In the war of the Pacific, it was the first time in United States history that the American flag flew in all its glory over Japan's territory.

Out of all the members in our fraternity gang, only James Lear received a posthumous Medal of Honor. One-third of the Marines who perished in World War II died in this ghastly invasion as they fought to take the island of Iwo Jima. More soldiers in this invasion received Medals of Honor than in any other battle of World War II.

Georg also received the Medal of Honor. I had to accept it on his behalf. I felt very proud about Georg's medal; however, I would have preferred to have my brother here with me rather than some inanimate medal.

The third member of the gang who died in World War II was Harry Adams. He was also twenty-four, and if he had survived the war he would have turned twenty-five on April 7. Harry was the eldest member in our gang, six months older than all of us. However, he was actually the shortest one, only six foot one. We all loved Harry very much. He was an Italian American who loved to sing. He came from a family of corporate lawyers, but somehow I always suspected that if Harry had returned from the war he would have pursued a singing career. But he was killed in the fall of 1944, in the battle of the Mariana Islands in the Pacific.

The last member of the fraternity to be killed in the war was Ryan Whishaw. After his graduation he enlisted in the U.S. Army Air Force. Ryan signed up hoping to become a fighter pilot, but instead was assigned as a co-pilot on a B17 bomber. He was with the 8th Air Force 91st Bomber group. In the spring of 1944, he was shipped off to Bassingbourn, England. By that time fighter pilots' jobs had become very dangerous; in 1943, two out of three fighter pilots did not survive their first twenty-five missions.

If the Western Allies were to have any chance of successfully landing safely on the beaches of Normandy on June 6, 1944, the Allied Air Force had to first dominate the skies over the English Channel and France. Before this could happen they had to strike Germany's Air Force with all aggression, and that meant B17 fighter pilots had to fly over Germany, and even into the heart of Berlin.

Ryan did this for several weeks, even two or three times a week, until his plane was shot down over Germany in the early summer of 1944. At the time of his death, Ryan and other B17 fighter pilots had to bomb factories in which Germany's fighter aircraft were being made. His mission in the end was successful, but his plane was shot down by the German Luftwaffe.

Ryan Whishaw was six foot four and we had the same body structure. His ancestors were from Norway; his hair was a light sandy blond color and his eyes were bright blue.

Sometimes, it's very difficult to deal with the reality of the loss of my friends.

Olga and I arrived at our home. I looked at my wife in amazement, with the strongest feeling of lust. I gazed at the perfect structure of her breasts and her provocative lips. At that moment I felt like a young buck, trying to lead his fallow ewe (seeing that Olga was only eighteen, and just in the past few months had been exposed to sex) into marital copulation.

I said to her, in the most romantic and loving voice, "Do you know, Olga, how beautiful you are?"

"David, my husband, where did that come from?"

"I said that because I'm so desperately and hopelessly in love with you. And Olga, for the rest of your life that's all you're going to hear from these lips of mine." Then I took her soft hands in mine. "Olga, my sweet, I swear to you, you'll never hear from these lips any abusive words, because when my lips are not praying the unceasing interlude of steadfast love, all you'll hear from my lips when I'm not making passionate love to you will be the sweet melodies of praise. My intentions are very selfish, because I'm going to woo you so you'll always want to give yourself willingly and freely to me in the art of lovemaking. Olga, my sweet, from an early age I realized that poetry is the language of love."

Olga was amazed by what I had just said to her. She placed her arms around my neck as she tried desperately to reach my lips, hoping to speak the language of love, which is the union and the prayer of the lips when they're joined together for that special moment of pleasure in the gratification of sexual intimacy.

"Oh, David, I love you so much. Kiss me, my love. I'm yours completely, now and forever. Take me. I've never wanted you more than right here, right now, at this moment."

It's hard for her to reach my lips if we're standing, since she's only five foot eleven and I'm six foot five. Olga speaks perfect English, but with a strong German accent. Honestly, I really don't care. I fell in love with her while stationed in Germany and find her accent quite appealing.

Our journey from Normandy was a long and arduous one. For the first few weeks our division had gone only ten miles from the beaches of Normandy where we'd first landed on June 6. Yet, after a few weeks we were lucky enough to reach our destination. I will never forget the stench of the first death camp we encountered.

Oh no! I don't want to think about that grim incident, because it was hard enough thinking about the loss of my friends as I drove home. I dismissed those thoughts and focused on my beautiful wife.

"Olga, I'm so attracted to you. I have never felt like this before."

"I love you, David, and thank you for taking me away from that terrible place. All that was left of Germany was only rubble, destruction, and chaos."

"I will do anything for you, Olga. Are you aware of that?"

"Yes, David, and I'll do anything for you. When you're in love with that special someone it's not difficult to do anything for that person. So I hope our marriage will have no secrets. Is that okay with you, David?"

"Of course, Olga, and I have no desire to hide anything from you, my sweet."

Then we embraced. I held her so close to me and didn't want to let her go. All I could feel was her soft and voluptuous young body. As we kissed I closed my eyes, because all I wanted at that moment was to enjoy her to the fullest of our intimacy, which for the past few months I'd grown to enjoy. Then I lifted her face close to mine. I felt like a totally different man with Olga, and honestly, I didn't know how I would cope with all the grief in my life if I wasn't married to her.

"I'm yours, completely and forever," she whispered to me.

Our lovemaking in the dining room was a moment in my life as a married man I would never forget. Throughout the years there had never been a moment of pleasant memories while growing up. The memories of my religious father and the years we spent listening to his negative remarks about certain people were indeed tormenting. But everything had changed, and it was certainly for the better. Our dining room was huge and very private since it's on the second floor. I never thought, in all those years of unhappy memories in this house, particularly in the dining room, that life would grant me the favor of creating new and happy memories of my marriage in this room; that one day I would actually be living here and enjoying the art of lovemaking with my German wife.

I couldn't help but think about why some husbands would want to treat their wives badly, whether verbally or physically, and hinder their relationship with their spouses. I had no intention of having an indifferent relationship with my precious wife.

I love everything about my wife. It had been only four months since Olga and I decided to get married. It was at this moment that I made a certain decision: as long as I live, in my marriage I will forever pursue my wife, and never seek to conquer her with any level of control.

After our special moment of intimacy in the dining room, I lay next to my wife as our silence said how much we truly loved spending time together. It wasn't long before we were both asleep.

About two hours later we woke from our pleasant sleep and headed to the master bedroom for a shower together. It was strange using my parents' bedroom. Even though my father is dead, I sometimes still feel his presence. I know that's silly, but I had to accept as actual fact that he's no longer here with me.

We completed the evening with a nice romantic dinner, and after we listened to the radio, we retired for the night. The next morning I was awakened by the smell of hot coffee and bacon coming from the kitchen.

I got out of bed and headed downstairs to the kitchen. As I entered it, I had a flashback to when I was a boy, because Olga was sitting on the stool in the same position, facing the window and looking at the river, as my mom did when she was in the kitchen. My precious wife looks similar to my mom; the same build, almost the same height, and that ideal Aryan look. I'm certain they're not related, though, because I know that my wife is a pure-blooded Aryan woman.

I approached my wife and said to her, "Morning, Olga." I couldn't keep my hands off her, kissing her and finding delight in the memories of last night's intimacy.

"Good morning, David. Did you sleep well?"

"What do you think, my precious molecule? You gave me a good workout and brought me to great heights of enormous pleasure. I feel like a man who's standing on top of the world."

"Well, I'm glad to hear that. You certainly weren't lacking in the art of sexual arousal, since you have brought me into the new chapter of womanhood."

We held each other for a few minutes as she placed her tender arms around my chest, but Olga had to tiptoe, for she wanted to feel and taste the pleasures of my lips. Then I looked at this gorgeous woman I had fallen in love with and said to her, "Olga I'm hopelessly, irrevocably, and eternally in love with you."

"I feel the same way about you, David, for you're the only man I've known and you're the only man I want to spend the rest of my life with as we grow old together."

I gazed into her beautiful blue eyes and saw my reflection there. Then I said, "You know, when I attended Yale University between the years of 1938 and 1942, my major was science. Psychology, to be more precise. And one semester I read that a molecule that interacts with other molecules has a much greater potential to shine. Olga, my sweet, you're my ideal molecule that has caused me to shine, and to find such happiness after these dreadful disasters. You have made me so happy."

"Oh, that's so sweet, David, but it works both ways. Because, David, if it wasn't for you, I might have been killed."

Placing my arms around her, I whispered in her ear, "I love you."

We had the perfect breakfast that morning, and my two and only remaining friends from our fraternity, Jack Eden and Jesse Atwood, were joining us for lunch that afternoon. At twelve thirty p.m. my friends were on the porch. After I opened the door to greet them, we couldn't help it; the three of us embraced and began to weep. My childhood friends met Olga, and she was the perfect hostess as she made Jack and Jesse feel at home.

After lunch, the guys and I headed for my father's library. I kept forgetting it was no longer Father's library; it's now David and Olga's library. We spoke about the loss of our friends and loved ones, and the terrible reality of the war. I found that Jack wasn't his usual self; he was quiet, withdrawn, and looked very distraught.

Nevertheless, I encouraged Jack to engage in the discussion about the war. Finally, he started to share with us; he began with a speech the late President Franklin D. Roosevelt had made before his death in the spring of 1945:

"I think that from the standpoint of our enemy, we have achieved the impossible. We have broken through their supposedly impregnable wall in Northern France. We have established a firm foothold. True, we still have a long way to go to Tokyo, the carrying out of our original strategy of eliminating our European enemy first, and then turning all our strength to the Pacific. We can cause the Japanese to unconditionally surrender, or to a national suicide, much more rapidly that has been thought possible."

That Jack was able to remember this speech from the autumn of 1944, two years before, wasn't a big deal, because the guys in our fraternity were all brilliant young men. Jack could hear a speech once and it was etched in his mind for all time. This wasn't something that was new to us, but Jesse and I wanted to listen to our friend, so we kept quiet as he expounded. Jack told us that after his enlistment in the U.S. Marine Corps, his first battle was the invasion of Guadalcanal on August 7, 1942.

From the invasion of Guadalcanal, he was sent to the invasion of Tarawa on November 20, 1943. This invasion was indeed a baptism of fire, given that the Japanese had boasted that a million Americans couldn't take the island in a hundred years. The Japs, therefore, were determined to safeguard their fortified island; hence, the great slaughter was nothing short of a bloodbath. However, it was our duty to stand up and fight against the Axis.

"The battle was the usual. You guys would know what I'm talking about." By now the tears had begun to roll down Jack's face.

"Hey, buddy, we understand. But if you want to stop, that's fine with us," said Jesse.

"No, I'm sorry, guys."

"Eden, you're our brother, and we made a promise to one another in this fraternity, remember: *esprit de corps*—pride and mutual loyalty in a group. Listen," Jesse continued, "the three of us, we're lucky enough to be alive, and live to tell the tale of this global conflict. And maybe it was lady luck or something else that kept us alive, seeing that five of our brothers are dead. Jack, no matter what happens, buddy, you can rest assured that the three of us are going to be like the *Second Triumvirate* of the twentieth century. We feel your pain, and whatever you need, you know that David and I will give our all for you."

"I agree completely with what Jesse just said," I added.

"I'm sorry, guys, it's just I felt so useless, especially at the Eniwetok Atoll of the Mariana Islands."

"Jack, it's fine. Do you want to change the subject, or have Jesse take you home?"

"No, that's fine, but thanks, David."

"Because if you want you can stay the night, or as long as you wish."

"That's awfully nice of you, David. I've been spending some time with Jesse. And I have to take my medication before I retire for the night."

"What medication?" I asked Jesse.

"Well, David, I think only Jack can share that information with you."

"It's okay, Jesse, you can tell David."

"Well, it's like this. Jack had an excellent record of combat in the U.S. Marine Corps. On his last battle, the invasion of Saipan on June 15, 1944, it appears that Jack just snapped."

"What do you mean, 'It appears that Jack just snapped'? Are you forgetting that we know Jack Eden?"

"Yes, David, I'm aware of that, but it appears that the war was too much for him to cope with. The entire invasion, the blood, the carnage, and all the corpses of his comrades and the enemy."

"But all of us experienced the same thing, Jesse—oh goodness, I'm sorry. I'm sorry, Jesse, I just realized that the same thing almost happened to me."

"What? How?" asked Jesse.

"It was on D-Day. I felt like I couldn't take the reality of the battle. So many were dying, and there was the smell of blood all around me, and the wounded bodies. Honestly, I felt like a man who was about to lose it, and I'm surprised I didn't turn my machine gun on those from my division, or myself. Please forgive me, Jesse, and especially you, Jack."

"That's okay, David," Jack said. "If there's one thing I've learned from the war, it's that it can do strange things to a man, particularly his mind. I've recognized that the real battle begins after the war ends. David, I know I'm not crazy but honestly, I don't really know what happened to me that day. Speaking frankly, I can't explain it. The last thing I remember was watching the bodies of the civilians going over the cliff. It's like I passed out."

"But how do you feel, Jack?"

"Right now, or in general?"

"In general, Jack."

"Most of the time, I wish I had died in the war. Why did so many have to die? And the loss of our five fraternity brothers…it's hard to deal with all this right now. It's difficult to accept the loss of our friends, and the lives of so many innocent civilians who died in this war."

"Yes, but Jack, please remember that your parents care about you, and at least there are still two of your fraternity brothers who survived the war," I said.

"David, the doctors didn't know exactly what was wrong with me. They said perhaps it was the trauma of the battle. However, while I was on that island that day, there was so much suffering that I asked myself, 'Damn, does war have to come to this?' Because it was no longer the Japs I was fighting. I was witnessing the suffering of innocent civilians. And the children, David, they were being slaughtered by their parents. Hey, guys, parents aren't supposed to do such things to their children! It's enough to make a man weep. And witnessing those civilians committing suicide at Marpi Point...it was too much. Do you know, David, on that day one thousand men, women, and children jumped off the cliff?"

"But Jack, what happened to you that day?"

"I turned on my comrades and started to attack them."

"Why?"

"David, as Jesse told you, I just snapped. And those Marines I shot... two died because of me. So for almost one year I was hospitalized, until the end of the war, and then I was released."

"Do you think it might have been a nervous breakdown, Jack?"

"I wish I knew. Maybe it was buck fever, or may be the battle was just too much. I'm still on medication, and I don't like how the drugs make me feel. Anyway, David, I think we should go," said Jack.

"No, not so soon."

"Yes. It was nice, David, but I think you need to spend time with your new bride."

Olga and I said good-bye to Jesse and Jack. I watched the car as it drove off into the sunset. As they left, I couldn't help but think about the sad tragedy that had taken over Jack on the island of Saipan. Whatever it might take, I knew that Jesse and I would do everything in our power to help Jack get over this unfortunate event. It was great to see the guys. Jesse had served in the navy during the war, and I was glad that he returned home safely.

That night while Olga and I were in bed I spoke to her about my education. I had to resume my studies at Yale University and get my PhD in psychology, if I was to be eligible for my inheritance at the age of thirty, which was only five years away. She had no idea what I would be worth when I came into my inheritance, Olga couldn't believe the amount.

Just then, she looked into my eyes and said, "It's a good thing, David, that you know the only reason I married you is because I'm madly in love with you, and not the millions you're about to inherit." Olga kissed me good night and was soon fast asleep.

But as I lay there I thought of what Jack had told us in reference to President Franklin D. Roosevelt's speech. Then I comprehended what Jack was actually trying to say; that if President Harry S. Truman, who carried out the late president's policies in an attempt to win and end the war, had not dropped those two atomic bombs, the nation of Japan would have committed national suicide if the United States had invaded.

The official name of this invasion was Operation Downfall. The U.S. military tacticians had been planning the invasion of Japan for years. On June 18, 1945, President Truman called a meeting of his closest political and military advisers at the White House. The purpose of this top-secret meeting was to consider the question of invading Japan. The meeting lasted about one hour, and afterward President Truman inserted into the minutes a statement that read: *"The joint chiefs of staff, having carefully considered all possible options, unanimously recommend that the proper course of action is an invasion of the Japanese home island."*

The president was fully aware that the obvious unanimity concealed crucial differences between the U.S. Army and Navy. The crucial question that loomed over Capitol Hill was: how many soldiers would have to die in the invasion of Japan for the purpose of establishing peace in the Pacific? The sensitive issue that would inevitably divide politicians and military leaders would be the invasion of Japan.

The navy had been fighting Japan in the Pacific for some years. An invasion would only lead to casualties on a cataclysmic scale, both for the Allies and particularly the natives of homeland Japan, which would have made the casualties of Iwo Jima and the civilian suicides of Marpi Point look like child's play.

I got out of bed and headed to my former bedroom. It looked just the same as when I left for college in the autumn of 1938. As I sat on my old bed, I couldn't help but continue my rumination of the war. I thought of what Jack had said about war and your mind: the real battle begins after the war ends, and some memories aren't easy to erase. Some memories leave an indelible mark that will never go away.

I guess Georg was right. Hitler lost the war the moment he declared war on the United States on December 11, 1941. The wars in Asia and Europe merged into a single gigantic war that became World War II, and this global conflict became the largest war in world history.

I will never forget the speech that President Roosevelt made in the midst of this global mêlée, after America declared war on Japan, and his views on isolationism. "*In time of crisis, when the future is in the balance we come to understand with full recognition and devotion what this nation is. The task that we Americans now face will test us to the uttermost. Never before have we been called upon, for such a prodigious effort. Never before have we had so little time in which to do so much. Those Americans who believed that we could live under the illusions of isolationism wanted the American Eagle to imitate the tactics of the Ostrich. But we prefer to retain the eagle as it is: Flying high and striking hard. We, not they, will win the final battle, and we, not they, will make the final peace. The harder the sacrifice, the more glorious the price.*"

It was only a matter of time before the United States was eventually pulled into that ghastly war in Asia and Continental Europe, and when I felt that strong desire, after speaking with my brother Georg. My friends and I decided to join the baptism of fire and ventured into battle. I never realized what I was getting into, and the price that was required of us as young men just out of college. The United States in fact wanted isolationism, because in the end, the politicians knew the price was going to be very high, for it meant the cost of America's youth.

As I sat on my bed, and while my mind remembered, verbatim, the words of the late President Roosevelt, I began to cry, moved by the depth of my emotions. The reality of Georg's death struck me again, and the loss of my mother, Georg, Jena, and her husband, Andreas Hansel, not to mention the majority of my fraternity brothers.

After some time I pulled myself together and resumed my rumination. Since my first battle was the invasion of Northwest Africa, Operation Torch, on November 7, 1942, the words of President Roosevelt were amplified in my mind again: "*The harder the sacrifice, the more glorious the price.*" Yes, I must admit, the harder the sacrifice, the more glorious the price, and the price was the loss of so many, for I'm aware that I'm certainly not the only one grieving over the loss of loved ones and friends.

I will have to live with the memories of the war each day for the rest of my life; they are etched into my mind. I'll never forget, after our long journey through Europe, when we entered those death camps. The stench of death was ubiquitous, that sickly sweet, unpleasant odor of decaying human flesh, and also the smell of burnt flesh that came from the crematoriums. It was so overwhelming to the human mind and stomach. Many soldiers, including myself, tried to maintain our composure, but after a while of breathing the potent stench we became disoriented, which eventually led to a degree of nausea and vomiting. I never thought people could commit such atrocities to other people in the name of conquest. What I saw made me understand why my mother never spoke about her ancestors.

The fact of the matter about the Holocaust is that it actually stemmed from the teachings of religion—Christianity, to be precise. I'm aware that many religious people have a natural affinity to live in conscious denial of these epistemological facts. Based on the evidence of history, it was religion that first began social discrimination against the Jewish people.

Christians were the main perpetrators of hatred toward the Hebrew race, for religion throughout the centuries has influenced and dominated the secular realm, and the religious leaders were successful in their mass promulgation of anti-Semitism throughout Europe. And it's religion that can propagate such religious medieval hatred of other people. Hitler was not a monster; he was only the by-product of corrupt religious systems that had influenced the world. The historical and epistemological facts are found in the Latin *Codex Theodosianus* of 438 CE. The word *codex* means a medieval manuscript in leaf form, as distinguished from a scroll. It is a collection of canon or of formulas: a code of laws. The adjective *Theodosian* is the anglicized version of Theodosius II, the Roman emperor who issued the earliest collection of Rome's imperial laws; hence, the *code* of *Theodosian*. The secular atrocities of the Jews had their beginning in the chambers of religion, because religion views people who will not submit to its tenets as potential and eventual threats to its dogmatic doctrines. That's precisely what happened with Constantine the Great in the early fourth century, and then religion continued with its segregation of certain people, and not only the Jews.

But within the Latin *Codex Theodosianus* of 438 CE, this in fact was the beginning. When religion dominated secular laws, this was the start of limiting the Jewish people's civil rights throughout Europe and Asia.

Hitler knew that the First Nuremberg laws of 1935 were actually nothing new in Europe. They were already practiced in early Christendom. Religion will endeavor to annihilate those who may not want to convert to the beliefs of a particular religious system.

Furthermore, when the Jews in Europe were forced to wear a yellow badge, this was the Star of David. This was not some new device that the Third Reich invented; it existed long before the birth of Adolf Hitler. The situation of Jews wearing the yellow badge first began in the Middle Ages with Pope Innocent III, who in 1215 ordered that all Jews should wear the "badge of shame," with the main intention of differentiating the Jews from Christians, since they were Christ's killers.

Honestly, how can people believe such nonsense? This is pure horse shit! But religion can concoct such superstitious *Nugas*. No intelligent person would ever give the slightest inclination to such foolish gullibility. The problem with religion is that it has always sought to invent nocuous tales of superstitious doctrines for the purpose establishing lies. And it makes no difference what sect of religion it might be; they're all the same.

They're in fact the perfect Svengalis, whose one mission is the irrevocable control of the masses. In addition, they're just like the evil hypnotist in the novel *Trilby* by George du Maurier, whose main objective is to hinder the ability of mankind's objective reasoning. Religion seeks to hypnotize the populace through fear. Religion will always attempt to convert and will forever try to infiltrate the secular realm, for the purpose of getting its dogmatic tenets to the masses.

In the sixteenth century, there was the dilemma of Martin Luther, the father of the Lutheran religion. When he first left the Roman Catholic Church, his intentions were to convert the Jews in Germany, but he realized the Jews were not that gullible. Then he turned on them and advocated their annihilation in the Fatherland. Isn't this the height of ignorance and folly?

Religion forever seeks to make disciples of or proselytize others. And by this method, these people honestly believe that they're saving your soul. However, there are so many different religious institutions, which can you believe? If you don't belong to their particular little cult you're doomed forever.

When Hitler came on the scene on January 30, 1933, all he was trying to do was to restore Germany's glory, save the Aryan race, and deliver Deutschland from the tyranny of social democracy. The rhetoric of Germany's new chancellor was no different from that of the father of the Reformation, Martin Luther. He was simply repeating what he had heard for years and what the religious system had advocated for centuries—the Jews should be *deloused*.

Hitler knew the Aryan race was in danger of eventually becoming extinct through the means of miscegenation. The Holocaust was a method of practicing eugenics and endorsing the theory of Darwinism. There were those who believed that the most disturbing idea ever published in the nineteenth century came from the British naturalist Charles Darwin, when he published *On the Origin of Species* in 1859. Its prodigious topic was one of his most challenging theories. His fascinating theory actually legitimized and supported the idea of natural selection. Charles Darwin had in fact adopted the famous theory of Thomas Robert Malthus (1766-1834), the English political economist and founder of Malthusianism. Malthus's theory held to the assumption that the population of the world increases much faster than agricultural means can support it. If the population of mankind is not controlled, through the methodology of birth control or by other means, in the end the ratio of people increases too fast or suddenly becomes overpopulated. The elements of natural forces such as famines, pestilence, wars, and natural disasters will keep the population of mankind in check by creating a perfect balance. The population will not be able to survive if it continues to produce offspring in a careless manner.

The food chain cannot produce the source of a food supply fast enough in order to feed everyone. The only logical conclusion for this earthly dilemma: each race would have to constantly compete for its survival. Hence, the essence of the theory that only the strong will survive: "survival of the fittest." According to this theory, natural selection was born: those with excellent physical traits will best adapt to their environment.

Darwinism was accepted into the social milieu, and eventually evolved into the concept of *Social Darwinism*. Darwin himself never sought to promote any social ideas; however, certain theorists promulgated his theories, for the main purpose of supporting their own presuppositions by making their theories much more acceptable. In the early twentieth century, this new theory, which began with Thomas Malthus in the nineteenth century, became the ideal and advocated the survival of the fittest in relation to war, disasters, and global economic competitions.

By the Roaring Twenties, many entrepreneurs, and especially industrial tycoons, held the opinion that the idealistic theory of Social Darwinism had earned them their vast wealth and success. They were the "strong ones" who were able to surpass those who were considered to be "unfit." However, as Social Darwinism continued to be promulgated and accepted, not only by industrial tycoons but also by leaders of the world, the mentality of war brought with it much glory in blood and carnage. Weaker nations were perfect targets for stronger nations to conquer. In addition, nations, and certain races, were now considered not only to be weak but also inferior, and less human. Victory in war was viewed as the tangible evidence that the victor was the stronger and more superior.

Social Darwinism gradually evolved into the ideal pretext for racism, and the belief that some races are better than and superior to other inferior races. The father of modern racial demography, Joseph Arthur Comte de Gobineau (July 14, 1816 to October 13, 1882), was a French aristocrat who developed his racial theory of the Aryan master race in his book *An Essay on the Inequality of the Human Races*. The Third Reich adopted his ideals, and the Nazi Party declared that its views were supported by the French racist Comte de Gobineau. Therefore, with these theories that took root in Europe, the stage was set for the ethnic cleansing of Jews and other minorities.

But not before religion laid the foundation and the groundwork necessary for the Holocaust to come to full fruition, for religion is the spurting laceration that hinders mankind. The official leaders of the world must neuter the belligerent doctrines, influences, and effects of religion globally. Religion has set the global stage for discrimination against innocent victims, as it seeks to promulgate its message of folly, while at the same time condemning others with its inept, wicked religious clichés, such as "you are going to hell" or "you will burn in hell."

These phrases, of course, are laced with venomous hatred toward certain people, and this kind of hatred is the major problem with all religions. What these fatuous hypocrites fail to recognize is that "*God is a comedian playing to an audience too afraid to laugh.*" But the joke is on all those religious fanatics with their *schmozzle* tenets. In fact, religion has brought on mankind the problem of the Medusa touch, which actually turns sensible men into stones.

Men become the stones of religion when they're transformed into PK disciples of their particular religion. For example, the thing that religion is noted most for is that its disciples will pray for you. However, if you refuse to believe what they believe, they will eventually kill you—either literally or figuratively. Throughout the centuries the biased influences of religion have had a negative impact on our social milieu. For that reason, religion is the great divider of humanity; in fact, it is the instigator of all levels of hatred against law-abiding citizens.

Chapter Nine

The Solution for Religion

Religion is a social system that believes it is the only binding element to connect the natural man with the spiritual nature of man and his deity. It is also an institution of endless rules and fabricated tenets. According to the Certainist and the philosophical views of David Hume, certainty of knowledge must be rejected irrevocably, since no single individual can possess the capability of having absolute knowledge.

In addition, the same approach must be used when it comes to religion. No single religious institution can be so absurd as to claim that its denomination alone holds the absolute truth. To make such an incoherent statement is to display the highest level of folly and conceitedness. This, in fact, is having an overweening self-esteem for one's religious institution and its dogmatic tenets.

Certainism advocates making choices based on one's intellectual persuasion. The Certainist gathers the appropriate information needed for making an objective decision and the reason of man is given total and complete preeminence. The Certainist knows that progressivism is the logical methodology for the individual who depends on reason, such as relativity of knowledge. There are no inherent ideas, only those of the biased consciousness of life and its metaphysical experiences, which is the relevant catalyst of the necessary data of one's reason. This is the only method for the pedant, as the Certainist relies entirely upon his reason: *Ahura Mazda*, or *"Wise Lord."* These remarks are not the philosophical statement of profanation. They're primarily based on the epistemological observance of social events in conjunction with religion.

So, to claim that any religious institution holds the absolute truth is in fact patently untrue, and furthermore, it denies the credibility of the progressionist. Humanity's progression does not depend on the social gathering of religious institutions, with their teachings of superstitious beliefs. Mankind's progression depends entirely upon the ability of using reason to the fullest capacity, since all reason burgeons from life's experiences.

History has proven incessantly that religious people who claim to be "spiritual" can truly display a carnal nature, engage in sexual debauchery, and execute grotesque crimes against humanity. Throughout the ages, religious institutions have rejected the personal freedom of humanity.

Science and facts do not lie, nor can they fabricate reasonable evidence against the reality of religion. Religion and its members have become masters at the charade of expressing their disincentive rhetoric about sin, while at the same time practicing those same acts in secret. The profound evidence is concluded in the epistemological and historical data of exploitation. The church exploited children in the name of religion, which eventually led to the deaths of thousands. It seems to me that religion has an incessant tendency to produce hallucinative disciples, and a good example is the episode of the Children's Crusade of 1212.

The Children's Crusade was a sad chapter in history and epitomizes religious deception. It all started with a fifteen-year-old boy by the name of Stephen in the village of Cloyes, France. While attending his sheep, the young boy claimed that he had a Theophany—to be more explicit, a "Christophany," a literal manifestation of Jesus Christ. (I think he stayed out in the sun a bit too long.) Stephen's apparition finally declared that it was the Son of God and gave the young boy a letter to take to the king of France.

Before the apparition departed from the young shepherd, he commissioned Stephen to lead the Children's Crusade, and also guaranteed the success of its mission. The alleged "Son of God" told him that the other male warrior Crusades in the past had failed miserably.

The church soon sanctioned Stephen's mission, saying he was "the Prophet" and his followers were "minor prophets."

As the Children's Crusade left Paris, the ceremonies of the Roman Catholic Church accompanied its members on their "holy mission." The Children went on their "holy journey" without weapons; they believed that the apparition had assured "the Prophet" Stephen that his mission would not fail, so there would be no need to defend themselves and disobey the "Son of God." However, not long after the seven ships that sailed for the Holy Land departed, a storm arose in the sea and two ships were blown into the region of the island of Recluse. The children on board those two ships drowned.

The five ships left were taken to Africa by the men who had been commissioned to take the children on their "holy mission," where the remaining children were sold into slavery. They never made it to the Holy Land, and the words of the apparition that claimed to be Jesus Christ had no credence, for the Children's Crusade was an even bigger disaster than the male warrior Crusades had been.

With religion, these people are always seeing or hearing some hallucination. Most of the time, it's some figment of the imagination. People will eventually believe whatever they want to believe, even if there's nothing factual about what they claim to be seeing or hearing. The apparition usually ends in some unfortunate disaster, murder, or mass suicide. The existential nightmare of religion has brought an inundation of human misery to the world.

It's the same with religion all over; they're all slaves of a regime, like the Nazis. Religious people in particular do everything their leaders and their *holy texts* tell them to do. They all have one thing in common: they're brainwashed disciples, as their *holy texts* think for them. These religious people are narrow-minded, just like the *Sturmabteilung*—stormtroopers of Nazi Germany.

They're extremely pretentious and inane disciples of a religious fascist regime. They have killed in the past, and I believe these people may willingly kill again for what they believe. In addition, their so-called *holy texts* are no different from *Mein Kampf*, which preaches hatred toward the Jews, the gay community, or anyone who doesn't believe what a particular religious group teaches and adheres to. Religion's main objective is the segregation of certain people, those whom they call sinners or unbelievers, or who won't permit religion to brainwash them in the name of its God. These *holy texts* all have one thing in common, and that's to preach antipathy against others.

Religious people are fascist bigots. They're all Falangists who're good at crushing opposition through any means. There are those who may say that people ought not to be punished for their faith, but only for their deeds. In contrast, sometimes faith causes these zealots to act irrationally and execute some unorthodox deeds in the name of their God.

As long as I live, I'll never forget the unpleasant incident of the young gay attorney, Freddy Chabon, from New York City, which I mentioned earlier. The gay community, I hope, someday will find its place in this religious world, and at the same time not lose its unique identity. Religious institutions believe that they have the power to change people, even those individuals with unique, innate traits. Freddy Chabon was born like that, and his lifestyle stemmed from his reason, and from what he knew and had experienced about his human nature.

Therefore, the fact of the matter is that religion is a canker on the body social, and cankers are meant to be cut out from the body social. How can this canker known as religion be dealt with once and for all? It can be accomplished; however, it must be done through the irrevocable metaphysical scalpel of a global judicial system. And according to the words of George Orwell, *"Big Brother Is Watching You."* (A new world order is coming, and it will deal with religion once and for all.)

Religion and its social system are nothing more than one enormous hallucination, like social democracy. The aid to mankind of religion is indeed paltry when it comes to the reason of man. The political science behind the theory of social democracy is the principles and policies of a social democratic ideology.

This political principle was an entity in Germany that advocated the policies of social organization. This was based primarily on the economic and political ideology of Karl Marx. The term *social democracy* was first used in Germany by Wilhelm Liebknecht and Ferdinand August Babel. They used this term to describe the inauguration of the German Social Democratic Labor Party in 1869. This, however, most definitely wasn't a good state of affairs, because in the years that followed it was used to harm the Jews in Europe, especially those in Germany. As time progressed, in 1875, the political ideal of social democracy was interwoven with the German Workers' Association, which was founded by Ferdinand Lasalle (a German-Jew), who formed the Social Democratic Party (SPD) of Germany. These ideals were entrenched in the Weimar Constitution that ruled Germany from 1918 to 1933.

By the early twentieth century, many European political parties were advocating a gradual and slow transition to socialism or a modified form of socialism by and under the democratic process. In Russia there was a division between the parties of the Bolsheviks and the Mensheviks in 1903.

The Bolsheviks were the radical political party in Russia. They were the extremists and dominant hard-line members of the Russian Social Democratic Party. After 1918, they were the ones who were called the Communist Party, because the word *Bolshevik* comes from the word *bolshe*, which means the greater, referring to the majority of the members. The Bolshevik Revolution had indelible repercussions on Russia and the entire Western hemisphere. The famous American journalist John Reed, who wrote about the event from New York City after his return from Russia, titled his report *Ten Days that Shook the World*, the revolution came to be known as that. (Incidentally, Reed died in 1920, the year I was born, and is buried in the Kremlin.)

The report is still a phenomenal force to be reckoned with. The headline refers to the end of the Romanov Dynasty, which came to power in 1613 and to an abrupt end on November 7, 1917. Not only did the Bolsheviks supplant the last czar of Russia, Nicholas II, they annihilated the entire Romanov family in the form of a summary execution on July

17, 1918. In that same year the Bolsheviks defeated all anti-Communist opponents and became the single autonomous ruling party in Russia.

I wonder if Karl Marx ever thought that his little book of only 120 pages, *The Communist Manifesto*, which was first published in London in 1848, would have such a tremendous impact, particularly on Europe.

I must say that the twentieth century is indeed a century that has witnessed phenomenal and cataclysmic global vicissitudes. It is an era when the world was actually plunged into a baptism of blood. It's as if the entire world suffered simultaneously from the mental disorder of lycanthropy. Certain leaders in Europe and Eastern Asia acted as if they drank from a cistern of blood, for the beginning of the twentieth century was a period when men praised the carnage of war, bloodshed, and iron.

It was only in the art of war and subjugation that those who considered themselves to be superior to inferior nations and races, by the process of natural selection, could prove their superior abilities, and be able to fully emerge in the midst of the battle as the victors and the stronger ones. I know from experience that this century has seen more blood than any other period in world history.

In Germany, the SPD was in fact the largest political party at the time of the Weimar Republic. This political party governed Germany until January 30, 1933, when the Fuhrer became Germany's chancellor, and then everything changed in the course of the nation's history.

Soon after 1933, social democracy was banned in Deutschland, and the SPD was now considered an enemy of the Aryan race. There were several reasons social democracy was outlawed in Germany.

In the fall of 1918, a parliamentary (*Reichstag*) republic became the governing body in Germany. This republic was better known as the Weimar Republic, as the new constitution was written in Weimar, a city in southwest East Germany. Weimar, not Berlin, was the new capital where the government was ruled by the Social Democratic Party of Germany. After his humiliating defeat, Kaiser Wilhelm II had fled his country and settled in the Netherlands. Soon after the abdication of the Kaiser, Germany became a republic.

The political party of the Weimar Republic had strong beliefs, which included a political policy of a progressive system for the German people. In addition, the Weimar Republic was certainly not lacking in the basic governmental assistance of social welfare. The Weimar Republic was born out of a defeated Germany and the severe peace settlements of the hated Treaty of Versailles after the Great War.

From 1919 to 1933, Germany was known as the Weimar Republic. Nevertheless, the sad mistake that its first socialist president, Friedrich Ebert, made was to accept the unreasonable terms of the Treaty of Versailles. The hated Treaty of Versailles was meant to keep Germany down; this treaty had 440 clauses and 414 were devoted to punishing Germany's role in the war. Also, there was a war guilt clause, which stated that Germany alone was responsible for the outbreak of the war in 1914, hence Germany's harsh reparation. As time progressed, the Weimar Republic encountered some challenging confrontations from the communists and the Nazi Party. In 1926, Germany became a member of the League of Nations, but because of civil unrest within its borders, in 1933 the nation withdrew from the League of Nations.

It was at this particular moment when Adolf Hitler became the appointed chancellor of Germany, and this was the irrefutable end of a republic government. Hitler's first ambition after coming to power was to unite Austria and Germany into one sovereign nation. On the other hand, with the unjust stipulations of the Treaty of Versailles, the Allied powers had strongly forbidden such ambitious attempts. The main reason France and other countries had prohibited any expansionist policies with Germany was that they thought this attempt would most definitely make Germany too powerful. However, the people of Austria and Germany wanted their two countries to unite as one nation. Hitler's new government now wanted to reclaim the territories it had lost in 1919.

The Treaty of Versailles actually assisted in the economic demise of Germany. The harsh settlements of the treaty made very unfair peace terms for the nation. The terms of agreement offered by the Central Powers by the end of the war in fact offered little hope to a defeated Germany. But not only did Germany have to sign the peace agreement, but there were absolutely no terms of negotiation for a nation that had been ravished by the carnage of the Great War. Furthermore, the Allied powers showed little mercy to a defeated nation in the unreasonable terms of the treaty. Not only was Germany forced to bend to its knees in mud of defeat and humiliation in front of the Allied powers, but the conquerors of Germany took the nation's face and rubbed it in that mud when they placed such harsh reparations on Germany's economy. The Treaty of Versailles forced the German people to pay a huge sum to the Allies. And by this act, many Germans lost their life savings when the value of the currency plunged. Consequently, the people eventually rejected the Weimar Republic, because they did not want a government of social democracy and soon realized that the Weimar democratic administration, as a political party, in fact had nothing to offer the German people except extreme national humiliation, social and political conflict, and economic disaster.

But in spite of the inadequacies of the Weimar Republic, this policy lasted for fifteen years, before it was supplanted by the National Socialist German Workers Party in 1933. Germany's only hope was Adolf Hitler, who promised to restore Deutschland with his new expansionism policy, which promised Germany *Volksgemeinschaft*—a people's community of a classless society, and this meant taking back those territories Germany had to relinquish under the demands of the hated treaty. Hitler took territories such as the Sudetenland and Czechoslovakia, in direct violation of the terms of agreement. Therefore, the quandary of social democracy gave birth to the Holocaust in due time, as Hitler blamed the Jews and the labor unions for Germany's problems.

By the time Hitler came to power, the hour had come for the bourgeoning of a national holocaust of certain minorities in Europe. The time had come for Nietzsche's *master race* to begin its promulgation through the theory of the *Übermensch*. Most people aren't aware that certain Jews themselves actually helped to instigate the methodology of the "Final Solution;" the reality of the Holocaust.

For example, some of the philosophical hypotheses of the well-known German philosopher Friedrich Wilhelm Nietzsche (1844–1900) were embraced and accepted by the Nazi Party. Most intellectuals, philosophers, and historians would agree that the German Jewish philosopher Nietzsche was paradigmatically a Nazi. There's no doubt about this: the man was a proto-Nazi who advocated the theory of a *master race*. He was one of the greatest thinkers of the nineteenth century and greatly influenced the intellectual method of thinking. In fact, he was a gifted philosopher-poet who sagaciously mastered the art of skillfully employing the techniques of using idioms that were somewhat mesmerizing to those who read and studied his literature.

Friedrich Nietzsche's literature is not only thought-provoking, but it can actually awaken certain scopes in one's intellectual ability of thinking like a sophist. The first book I read by Nietzsche was *The Antichrist*. I was nine, but that's when I started questioning every aspect of religion, and one year after reading that book I created my new philosophy, of Certainism. Nietzsche's *The Antichrist* actually opened my eyes and showed me how inept and oafish religion can be, particularly in the sphere of reason.

Religion, as Nietzsche pointed out in his breathtaking philosophical discourse, *The Antichrist*, leads many of its members into a stage of hallucination, like when "*Paul desired the end, and therefore he willed the means.*" Nietzsche went on to explain how the Christian religion actually grew in a soil of downright prevarications; of nothing more than mere fancies and hallucinations of its members, who will imagine just about anything for the purpose of fulfilling or meeting the needs of their particular religious institution. Furthermore, in *The Antichrist* Nietzsche presents himself as the perfect Hercules of intellectualism, the man who's competent enough to debunk the hallucination of the religious system which has stupefied mankind for too long. According to the words of the father of Intellectualism, "*The Christian is only a nonconformist Jew.*" It was amazing how a little book of only sixty pages had such an extraordinary and profound impact on my life as a young sophist and Certainist in the twentieth century.

The awe-inspiring book *Thus Spoke Zarathustra* is absolutely amazing. In this philosophical treatise, Nietzsche, through the power of the pen and his brilliant mind, insults the censors of his age as he presents a radical psychological outlook about mankind and religion. For example, how the main goal of mankind ought to rest entirely in the ability of individuals to excel academically, which is the highest achievement of humanity, and not the superstitious tenets of religion; hence, his theory about the *Übermensch*.

Nietzsche wrote about the coming of the *Übermensch* in *Thus Spoke Zarathustra*. In the Nazi Party, Hitler used Nietzsche's theory for the sake of transcending his ideal and making it into an actual reality, for the purpose of substantiating the dream of the Third Reich.

The Fuhrer's dream was to produce a *master race*, and at the same time eliminate from the earth's population all those "useless eaters" and the unaesthetic of society; those undesired individuals who didn't measure up to the ideals of the *master race*. It all started as a philosophical presupposition; however, the evidence was seen in the reality of the Holocaust. It's mind-boggling that a man's literary work can influence an entire nation, or even the world. The epistemological and historical evidence found in Nietzsche's inspirational work took root in various different milieus: the devotees of physical culture, the feminist movement, the socialist party, the Nazis, and the archconservative sects.

It's as if Nietzsche, as the ideal intellect, had such perspicacity that he was able, by the power of his pen, to look into the future and see exactly what his country, Germany, would need. For those who may be perturbed by my views, I wish them *requiescant in pace*.

Most people usually presume that the origin of the Holocaust was the meeting of the Lake Wannsee Conference on January 20, 1942, which initiated the decisions of certain nihilistic leaders in the Nazi Party to annihilate the eleven million Jews living in Europe. The evidence will speak for itself: it was Friedrich Wilhelm Nietzsche who first began the theory of a *master race*. The reality of his theory is that there cannot be a *master race* without first obliterating all minorities. The Nazi Party's mechanized method of the Holocaust was the only way, in the minds of its members, of securing their own race.

According to Sigmund Freud's *Moses and Monotheism*, just as the Jews began the idea of a monotheistic religion, they in fact ignited the fire of their religion. But in the twentieth century the fire of their religion turned around and burned them in the reality of the Holocaust, since Jewish survival means Jewish intellectualism.

Just as Nietzsche's father was a pastor and he grew to hate all forms of religion, the same happened to me. Yes, the fires and the useless ideals of religion manifested into the metaphysical reality of the Holocaust and eventually consumed six million Jews. The Certainist adheres to the premise that reason is the final principle of reality, and when it comes to the fact of reality, the Certainist knows that life can be a *canis* (bitch) when it's payback time. As difficult as this may be for some to grasp, the reason of this reality is that if the stories in the Old Testament writings have any element of credence to them, this will explain many things to the Certainist. Adolf Hitler believed he was doing the will of God when he implemented his harsh policies of ethnic cleansing throughout Deutschland.

The Old Testament gives the historical details of the Hebrew people practicing a form of ethnic cleansing in the land of Palestine under the leadership of Moses and Joshua. So, if this is a definite part of the Hebrew people's history, which most people seem to conveniently forget, then the Holocaust, according to the Certainist, was grand payback time for the Jews of Europe, who in the past had slaughtered many innocent civilians in the name of their religion.

However, in conjunction with my nihilistic philosophy of Certainism, are the Jews a destructive race? The answer would be most definitely no! I firmly believe that it is religion, in any form, that is the destructive factor to human existence, unity, and progression. The Lutheran religion loathes the Jews, and my mother repudiated the fact that she was a Jewess. Furthermore, my very own experience of the Holocaust compelled me to wonder about my own people and the negative influence of religion, which forever seeks to marginalize certain people.

The idea of a *master race* was birthed in the mind of a Germanic Jew, and the metaphysical dimension of the Holocaust was, in fact, executed by another Germanic Jew.

The fate of the Jewish people was placed in the hands of Reinhard Heydrich in 1939. He was a brilliant intellect, and without his ingenious contribution the reality of the Holocaust wouldn't have materialized. Hitler called Heydrich "the man with the iron heart." There were rumors in the Nazi Party that the man who was to implement the Holocaust was in fact a Jew.

Then there were those Jews who worked in the concentration camps, assisting with the systematic killing of their own people: the *Sonderkommando*. These were Jewish prisoners who specifically were selected to work for an interim in the crematoriums. Their ghastly job was to dispose of the bodies of those Jews who were gassed. These concentration camps literally epitomized death in every sphere. Once a prisoner was taken to one of those camps, there was no hope of ever leaving that place alive.

When we crossed the Rhine, months after the Normandy invasion, our division, along with the Allied forces, began our campaign of heading eastward toward Nazi Germany. The destination of the forces was the Elbe River in central Europe. This was our last natural barrier before the city of Berlin, Hitler's headquarters. A few days before we reached the Elbe River, the Soviet Army had already arrived in Berlin, encircled the city, and launched devastating attacks against the Germans.

The Fuhrer's days were about to come to a catastrophic end. When we began our journey toward Nazi Germany, some days we could only travel ten miles a day. However, after our progressive victories over the Germans, as we got farther into Germany, our division would sometimes travel as far as sixty miles a day.

Germany was devastated; everything looked ruined, as the Allies had bombed most of the country. One day, as we continued with our advancement into Germany, our convoy stopped suddenly outside a small town. After a few minutes of waiting, my men and I got out to see what was happening. As we looked around, I thought, *There is something oddly quiet and strange about this particular town.* To our surprise, there were people behind barbed-wire fences.

These people looked like walking corpses, and I knew then that what I had heard on the radio and read in the newspaper for years back home was true. I remembered what Hitler wrote in *Mein Kampf*, about his methods of dealing with the Jews in Europe. But when I read *Mein Kampf*, I was just a boy, and I thought his rhetoric was nothing more than just conjecture about a particular race. But I guess I had been wrong to think that, given what my eyes now beheld. I couldn't fathom the magnitude of the atrocities done to these human beings.

I said to myself, "Is this what certain people will do to the Jewish race?"

Then one of my men asked, "You said something, Lieutenant?"

I responded, "No, soldier!"

As we looked at these people, they seemed overly subdued, like they were in a daze. Their rights had been taken away from them, and they looked as if they themselves couldn't fathom the horrible crimes done against them in the name of a *master race*. I realized why we were here in Europe. As we moved a bit farther into the camps, there was that smell again; that stomach-turning, nauseating smell of human carnage.

The people were staring at us, as if they were trying to communicate to us with their eyes, because these poor souls had no strength to articulate their circumstance to these strangers in their midst. Tears flowed down my face as I looked at them. I tried to control myself while I wept discreetly, but as my eyes gazed at these helpless victims, I thought, *If this isn't hell on earth, I don't know what else would be! This is madness; Hitler really meant what he wrote in 1925.* I felt as if I couldn't stand any longer what my eyes were seeing. The disgusting odor of decomposed and burnt flesh made my head feel light, and I felt sick to my stomach. I threw up what little contents were in me. I could feel the violent rush coming up rapidly, and all I could do was fall on my knees as I began to vomit copiously. However, my mind kept ruminating about the man who had implemented these ghastly places.

After Hitler became the chancellor of Germany in 1933, he systematically gathered and exterminated Jews and minorities—for example: the disabled, homosexuals, and gypsies—that he deemed unfit to be a part of Nietzsche's *master race*.

Between 1939 and 1945, Hitler established about fifteen thousand concentration camps throughout Europe. This was Adolf Hitler's answer for all minorities; it was truly Hitler's Final Solution. Looking at these victims, it was difficult for us to tell the difference between the living and the dead. It was like their eyes had gruesome stories to tell about these camps. In fact, these death camps were in a category all by themselves, because the atrocities were of such magnitude that it was beyond human comprehension. When we first entered the camp, I looked, I saw...but somehow the atrocities were far beyond what my mind could accept. I believe I looked, yet I couldn't see. My mind didn't want to grasp what my eyes were beholding. And as I listened I couldn't hear; my mind refused once again to accept the actual reality of the Holocaust.

However, as lieutenant of my unit, and in spite of my nausea, I refused to allow my body to be controlled by physical symptoms. No one may fully understand why the reality of the Holocaust affected me to such a great degree, but all I could think was, *What if Hitler had conquered the entire world? We would have been—that is, my relatives and I—victims in these ghastly death camps.* Honestly, I didn't know what to feel or think while we assisted these helpless victims. The unpleasant odor in the camp was overpowering, but I didn't want the smell to affect me again.

We tried to communicate with the victims. "We're Americans, and we're here to rescue you!" I told them. "*Ich komme aus...den Vereinigten Staaten.*" (I'm from...the U.S.A.) "*Ich bin...Amerikaner.*" (I... am American.) "*Sprechen Sie Englisch?*" (Do you speak English?)

But they didn't say anything; they didn't talk, cheer, or yell; they were motionless. They simply stood there, looking at us as if they were beyond making a sound. Then I thought, *These tortured souls hardly resemble humans. It's so very sad.* I met a few young men who looked Aryan to me. However, when I spoke to them once again in my father's language, they told me they were German Jews.

One of my GIs, Sam Hill, was next to me. As he began to weep, he said, "God, are you there?" I will never forget what Sam Hill asked that day. However, before I responded, one of the other men asked him, "How can you believe in a God who would allow such terrible things to happen?" I didn't want to get involved in a religious feud, so I kept my opinion to myself.

A few days afterward, some of us had to keep on pushing into the heart of Germany. As we continued with our orders, some of the men remained in the camp. Our journey took us one step closer to Berlin. I started to ruminate about when I was fifteen, in the spring of 1936, and, as I mentioned before, my father had introduced me to that amazing book *Mein Kampf*.

I never thought that, nine years after reading *Mein Kampf*, my eyes would actually witness Hitler's Final Solution. However, with of my philosophy Certainism, I'm not going to judge the Fuhrer. His biography was about a young man's struggle against the ideals of social democracy; hence, the title in English, *My Struggle*.

A republic government may be ideal for some countries, but it wasn't the ideal government for England, and certainly not for Germany. When Hitler was a teenager, he went to Vienna, and while there, his eyes were opened to the fact of the Jews. In the midst of Austria, he noticed that the people had somehow lost their national pride. Then he realized that social democracy was prevalent in his country, and this political system was undermining the dignity of the working class. It was as if the political science behind social democracy was designed to keep his people in check. Hitler saw the repeated social intercourse between the Aryan race and the Jewish people, who were closely connected to the policies of social democracy. The Jews were the instigators of this government.

To Hitler, these people were nothing more than second-class citizens who were polluting the Aryan race. In addition, he saw the Weimar Republic as nothing more than a tool placing the German people in bondage and helpless positions of servitude, as the alien Jews imposed their idealistic form of government on his people. Hitler saw Jews in Deutschland not as Germans, but only interlopers who came to manipulate the Aryan race. The young future leader of Germany sensed that there was a lack of pride among the German people.

Hitler eventually realized that the German people had in fact lost their righteous existence as the *master race*. Consequently, Hitler blamed social democracy for the problems in Germany, and the catalyst behind the loss of the German people's heritage.

Inevitably, Hitler learned it was not difficult to despise the Jews, since they were not members of the Aryan race, nor were they true Germans. He saw them as the architects of social democracy, which had made life extremely miserable for the German masses. He thought if the nation of Germany didn't realize this, it would mean the end of the entire Aryan race. It wasn't long before Hitler started to notice that those who were holding the most prominent positions in republic offices were mainly Jews, the main enemy of the Aryan race.

It wasn't long before he believed this was nothing more than the policies of Marxism (Judeo-Bolshevism.) He saw the deviant plan as directly connecting the social democratic movement in the Weimar Republic to all Jews in the world.

Hitler was convinced that social democracy was the strategic plan of a well-organized Jewish conspiracy, which spread throughout and would eventually take over the entire globe. In time Hitler became convinced that the Jews in Germany were not part of the German nation. He saw them as foreigners whose main goal was to take complete control of the world. Therefore, it didn't matter to him if these people were born in Austria or Germany, and it certainly didn't matter if they were citizens of the Fatherland, because in Hitler's eyes they were intruders.

In *Mein Kampf*, the Fuhrer carefully outlined his most precious and sacred plans, by the methods of Social Darwinism—the fledging scientific idea of eugenics. The Third Reich, by taking a scientific approach, was in fact trying to assist nature by the system of eugenic methods, which simply meant they were trying to improve the human stock by having well-born babies.

The word *eugenics* comes from the Greek *eugenes*, meaning good stock, well born, of good roots. The English scientist Francis Galton first used the term in 1883 as the scientific approach through the epistemological observations of selective breeding, which is applied to humans, for the purpose of aiming to improve the human race. Eugenics is actually the scientific approach of improving mankind's genetic qualities. Abortion is a euphemistic term for eugenics, as medical science seeks to improve the human species by the methodology of controlling the population.

The prime goal of the Nazi regime was to apply the scientific basis of eugenics on a vast mechanistic scale, as it tried to rid the Fatherland of those "vermin" through its mechanism of *delousing*. The main objective of the concentration camps throughout Europe was to suppress the enemies of the Aryan race in Germany, who were considered by the laws of the land, and according to racial purity, to be the political enemies of the Fatherland. What made these people Germany's political enemies in Hitler's mind? The simple idea that they were biologically inferior to Nietzsche's *master race*.

I've realized that the Holocaust was just another front of the war that Hitler was fighting, since the war itself was actually part of the Darwinian struggle; *Mein Kampf, My Struggle*. In fact, it was the struggle for the preservation of the Aryan race. After reading *Mein Kampf* and seeing the realities of the Holocaust, I can now understand what Hitler meant. To Hitler, the extermination of the Jews and all minorities was the only logical solution for safeguarding the purity of the Aryan race. He was honestly convinced that the Holocaust was the best approach for

Germany, and his intentions were honorable—in his eyes, of course—for the reason that his intentions were for the welfare of the Aryan race.

As a Certainist, I'm just trying to be objective, but I know that some of the worst things imaginable are done with the best of intentions.

The Holocaust was, in Hitler's eyes, the racial struggle between the survival of the Aryan race and the "inferior" races, like the Jews and other non-Aryans. It is the struggle between the pure and impure races, the sick and the healthy, the strong and the weak.

The Fuhrer's goal—and the goal of the entire nation, with the exception of only a few Germans—was to fight against the people whose purpose, in conjunction with Hitler's beliefs, was the defilement of all humanity and eventually the destruction of the Aryan race. Hitler said that Germany rightly belonged to the Aryan *master race*: light-skinned Caucasian Europeans. The Aryan people's greatest enemies were the Jews, for, according to the Fuhrer, these people and their religion were responsible for Germany's betrayal in the Great War. They were the Marxists, corrupt politicians, and business leaders, and since they betrayed Germany with their political policy of social democracy, the Fuhrer promised the German people to preserve their culture and expand Germany's borders through his mechanized scheme of expansionism. Also, Hitler assured the masses that by his plans he was in fact executing the will of God, for he was convinced that by fighting the Jews he was defending Deutschland from the machinations of the Jewish race, and by doing this he was working for God.

I'm fully aware that this belief of Adolf Hitler's emerged from the teachings of religion. In Europe, the majority of Christendom held to the notion that if Christians were to kill Jews, they were in fact carrying out the will of God. What I don't understand is that if there is a God, how could this God, who claims to be love, encourage such atrocities and violations of human rights and allow the killing of so many people? My eyes have witnessed the realities of the Holocaust, and it was the most disturbing thing I've ever seen.

As our infantry advanced into Germany, with the hope of reaching Berlin, we stopped in a town, Geilenkirchen. This town, like the rest of other regions in Germany, lay in ruins. It was in Geilenkirchen that I first laid eyes on my future wife, Olga. She was just seventeen, and the most beautiful creature I've even seen. In that moment I knew that Olga Hanna Gildisch was meant to be my wife and soul mate.

I spoke to her in German. *"He! Wie gehts?"* (Hi! How are you?)

She just looked at me. I was nervous, because I had never felt this way before. However, I continued to talk to her.

"Ich heiße David. Wie heißen Sie?" (My name is David. What's your name?)

"Ich heiße Olga." (My name is Olga.)

"Nett Sie kennenzulernen." (It's nice to meet you.)

"Ganz meinerseits." (It's nice to meet you too.)

"Sie sprechen gut Deutsch." (You speak German well.)

"Danke." (Thank you.)

"Bitte." (You're welcome.)

"Woher kommen Sie?" (Where are you from?)

"Ich komme aus...den Vereinigten Staaten." (I'm from...the U.S.A.)

"Sprechen Sie Englisch?" (Do you speak English?)

"Ja." (Yes.)

To my surprise, she spoke English perfectly. Her father was a former professor who had taught philosophy, but in 1939, Professor Bernhard Gildisch was fired from his post because he spoke against the government and its crimes against humanity. On the other hand, Olga's mother, Nurse Gertrude Gildisch, was an ardent Nazi who worked for the Third Reich at Hadamar mental asylum. Because of the Gildischs political difference of opinion about Hitler's policies of eugenics, Olga's parents separated. After the separation she chose to live with her father in Geilenkirchen.

The mental asylum is a psychiatric sanatorium in the town of Hadamar. It is the mental asylum that was used by the Nazi regime when executing its T-4 Euthanasia Program—the mass sterilization of the mentally insane and handicapped. The Nazi regime mainly performed these experiments on those who were physically and mentally disabled. However, when the American infantry first seized the insane asylum of Hadamar, it was discovered via their medical records what these Nazi doctors were doing in the name of the Third Reich.

The medical staff had killed fifteen thousand victims that the Nazi labeled as "useless eaters." Under the orders and supervision of Dr. Gorgass, they had experimented with these "useless eaters" and then killed them. This was done in the name of eugenics, as they hoped to destroy the "undesirable species of humanity." The government of Germany thought, through eugenics, it could interfere with the growth of human population. The medical staff killed from Monday to Friday, putting to death about seventy people a day. After the extermination of those handicapped and mentally insane victims, their bodies were disposed of through the means of Hadamar's two crematoriums. By this method they were trying to produce a society without illnesses or handicapped individuals.

The mother of the woman I fell in love with was one of the nurses who participated in these deaths. Olga shared with me that when her mother left the Hadamar asylum, she was sent to Oswiecim, better known by the German name Auschwitz. There, Olga's mother was assigned to work personally with Dr. Josef Mengele, the "Angel of Death," who performed monstrous scientific experiments on thousands of victims in the name of medical science.

When Olga told me these things, I couldn't believe what she was sharing with me about her own mother. However, she said that even given the inhumane crimes her mother committed against humanity in the name of medical science, she certainly didn't want to begin our relationship by hiding this relevant piece of information from me. Olga told me I would now have to decide if I still wanted to marry her and take her to the United States. She shared this information with me about two weeks into our courtship.

At first it was hard to accept. But somehow, hearing those gruesome tales about her mother caused me to love and respect Olga to a greater degree.

What I experienced for myself, the psychological effect that those concentration camps had upon my mind and body, convinced me that the Fuhrer Adolf Hitler and the members of his Nazi regime were nothing more than fanatical Darwinists.

They wanted to vehemently apply the theory of Darwinism to society, because these people were honestly convinced that they could control evolution by sterilizing the feeble-minded to prohibit these people from procreating. These were just some of the profound thoughts that were going through my mind in the process of ruminating about Olga's mother, who eventually killed herself with a cyanide capsule when Germany lost the war. Olga's father died about nine months before I met her, so this young Aryan girl that I'd fallen in love with was on her own, for she had neither siblings nor living relatives.

We continued traveling east, heading toward Berlin at a fast pace, and I couldn't believe that the east and west had finally met on German soil, in *Torgau*. Here we were, American and Russian soldiers, celebrating, for many of us were eager to reach Berlin. Reaching Germany's capital city would be such a victorious moment for us, since we had been traveling for months to reach Berlin and were one step closer to choking the Germans.

The meeting of east and west was a triumph, but I couldn't believe what our commanding officers were telling us. Their bad news made the joy of that moment truly ephemeral. Orders had come from General Dwight Eisenhower: it appeared that at the last moment, the general decided to halt our troops at the Elbe River, and then ordered that the troops should pursue the rest of the Germans to the southwest.

That meant Berlin was left for the Russians to take. I'm sure the orders came directly from the White House and had some political implication behind them. We were all in shock and disbelief because Berlin has been our main objective for these past few months. Many of our men had died on the way there; now we were being told we couldn't enter the city. However, in spite of how we felt, orders are orders, and we couldn't disobey General Eisenhower.

When the Russians entered Berlin, under the leadership of General Georgi Zhukov, his soldiers raped between ninety-five thousand and one hundred thirty thousand women—even the elderly weren't spared. About ten thousand women committed suicide.

The war in Europe finally came to an end after nearly six long years. May 8, 1945, was declared Victory Day in Europe.

I could have been home within a few months, but I was not leaving Germany without my young wife, Olga. We were married on October 17, 1945, when Olga was just seventeen and I was twenty-four. She was born on December 23, 1927, in Etzelwang.

I really wanted to return home soon after the war, but there were certain complications that we were facing because of Olga's mother. So I contacted my uncles in Massachusetts, and it was particularly because of Uncle Dietrich, who has his own successful corporate law firm, that I was able to bring my wife with me to her new home, America. The senators in our state are Uncle's Dietrich close associates. Therefore, they were able to cut through the bureaucratic red tape so that my wife, Mrs. Olga Hugenberg, could enter the United States legally with me. We returned to America in February 1946.

In the nearly four years that the Unites States fought in World War II, approximately sixteen million Americans served in the armed forces. More than four hundred fifteen thousand servicemen never returned home. The majority of these were killed in combat or were missing in action.

When we stepped out of the plane, there was a lump in my throat as I thought about my brother Georg and my friends included in that number of four hundred fifteen thousand. For those of us who survived, the echoes of the war will linger on in our minds forever. After World War II, historians estimated that about seventy million people were killed, more than half of them civilians.

The Nuremberg War Crimes Trials began on November 20, 1945, and ended on October 1, 1946. I followed the trials to the last detail, but it seems to me that these were nothing more than a political lynching, and a mere diversion from what really happened in the war. The entire nation of Germany, and the world, knew what Hitler was doing to certain minorities, since there were more fifteen thousand concentration camps throughout Europe.

In fact, most people are under the illusion that the world they live in is actually governed by a system of morality. The individuals who presume this couldn't be more wrong, for our society is governed by something called the law. Religion may want to inculcate in its members that society is governed by a system of morality, but in fact it is governed by the law. The law of the land doesn't care if people practice promiscuity or not; what the law is concerned about is the intent of the individual committing a willful crime. The law does not care if something is wrong or right; the law is concerned with whether or not it is legal. And to prove if the act of the crime was illegal, one must prove beyond a reasonable doubt that the person's intent was to willfully commit an unlawful act, and this cannot be judged by the standard of other countries.

Therefore, when Germany's legislative branch of government legalized eugenics, in the guise of the First Nuremberg laws of 1935, these laws inevitably led to mass genocide. And when the *Reichstag* (the former legislative assemble of Germany) legalized mass murder in the name of the *master race*, this was the law of the land. How can this be considered illegal when it was the law, the intent of which was to murder Jews and minorities? An entire nation committed murder by making genocide the legal and lawful procedure of the day.

I know that an example had to be made of those men who committed crimes against humanity. Some people call the Nazi's era an evil regime, and say that the members were indeed monsters. But these people were not monsters; even though their actions epitomized crimes against humanity, they're still not monsters. They're just human beings who were caught up in the moment of their country's affairs. They only tried to obey the laws of the Fatherland at that particular time.

In the war, on the front that dealt with the extermination of certain races, the Fuhrer was trying to preserve the Aryan race, which was in grave danger of becoming extinct. That's precisely why, to me, the Nuremberg Trials were a big joke against the *Reichstag* in Germany. However, the mob, according to Benito Mussolini, "*is fickle, and like a woman.*"

People need to be mindful of Dr. Ishii Shiro and unit 731: the United States made an agreement with this doctor, even though he committed crimes against humanity, in exchange for medical data concerning chemical weapons. The United States government, after its agreement with Dr. Ishii Shiro, covered up the crimes that were committed in unit 731 during Manchuria's occupation by Japan.

Furthermore, it was the legislative branch of government that made slavery legal in America. When the Supreme Court ruled against Dred Scott in 1857, Congress and most Americans were perturbed and shocked by the ruling of the judicial branch of government in the United States. The Supreme Court was in fact endorsing the inhumane act of slavery, for it was lawful at that particular time.

However, was it morally wrong? The answer would be yes, it was. But even though it was a crime against humanity, at that time it was the law of the land. And while the white Southern states were celebrating the Dred Scott decision in 1857, the Northern states were very troubled by the Supreme Court's ruling. The ruling of the Supreme Court simply meant that slavery was legal according to the law of the land. In addition, it also meant that it was legal and binding in all the territories of the United States.

The laws of the land of any country can be changed. The clever answer for the solution for religion is found in my newly invented word *Religenocide*.

Since in the past Congress has repealed certain amendments, it can be done in the future. Our Constitution is not written in stone, nor is any law in the world. The First Amendment should be repealed, just like the Eighteenth Amendment, which was repealed by the Twenty-first Amendment in 1933. The solution for religion is *Religenocide*; however, for this new legal system to be ratified and effective it must be done through the one-world system of "Big Brother is watching you."

The one-world governmental system will have a one-world system code set in place to accomplish this. I firmly believe there will be a one-law system code that controls the entire one-world government that actually implements *Religenocide*. This isn't too difficult to achieve; Alexander the Great did it, and the Third Reich exploited the *Reichstag* in Germany to achieve its main objective.

It is time for the dechristianization, and dereligionization of the entire world. The only thing that religion is good for is the disunity of mankind; Protestants against Catholics, Muslims against Hindus, Christians against Jews, and Jews against Gentiles; it just goes on and on.

From the dawn of humanity, religion has been the biggest liar on the face of the earth. Evangelicals say the Pilgrims came to the New World, America, for freedom of religion. This, however, is a partial lie; the entire truth is that the Pilgrims came to the New World for three main reasons. They were:

1. The people from England came for wealth, to start a new life by becoming rich.

2. There were a few individuals who came for freedom of religion like the Puritans.

3. And there were those individuals who came to have a better life.

Therefore, these evangelicals and Protestants who claim that the Pilgrims came for freedom of religion speak a partial truth, but it's not the whole truth. You have not spoken the whole counsel of the truth unless you have spoken the complete truth.

Most religious institutions are built on a foundation of lies, as their leaders have concocted their religious and deviant tenets for the purpose of substantiating their fabricated doctrines. Their only goal is to gain control of the masses and their minds. People need to be intelligent and ought to question everything, especially when it comes to these ecclesiastical charlatans. Do like the Certainist would. Religion has established the greatest social unrest in the world. If these people can't present substantial epistemological data about their faith, then they must be dismissed or irrevocably silenced once and for all.

My father, the Protestant Pope of Springfield, Massachusetts, was the biggest hypocrite who ever walked the earth, and I can never trust these people, for they are inventors of lies. So I say religion is nothing more than the pestilential whore that has plagued humanity with its pretentious antidote of control and mind games.

For this reason, religion is the courtesan of humanity, for it seeks to enslave men in their ideal of tradition, while it keeps men in bondage and from maturing intellectually. Those who think my hyperbolic statement is too direct need to study Revelation 17:1-5.

Religion is nothing more than a means of stupefying the people and making them victims of guilt, for religion is indeed the eternal pendulum of all fools, those individuals who wish to practice its folly.

The fact of the matter is that religion lied to the masses just before the outbreak of World War I. And at the end of the Great War many felt disillusioned with the church, because religious leaders had lied to the people. As millions of young men marched into the cauldron of World War I, the church was making promises to congregations it couldn't keep. Like that dreamer E. Stanley Jones, others said they were the mouthpiece of God, but in fact they lied to the people in the name of God and religion.

Furthermore, religion does not consider the academic point of view when it comes to science, philosophy, intellectualism, and the theory of progressivism. The unity of religion is purely speculative cosmogony, and with cosmogony comes the concept of man and the declaration of his external plan.

It's okay for the leaders of religious institutions to eat, live, wear, and drive the best, but if others try to achieve this it's a sin of covetousness.

The fact of the matter remains that religion has caused mankind to develop and maintain a static mentality to its social intellectual ability.

In the spectrum of religion and folk psychology, religion is the one that needs to be explained away, not science. So, the fictitious ideals of religion must be intelligently and, with all wits, explained away.

Religion is nothing more than the exercise of storytelling and platonic myths. Hence, the logical reason religion must be explained away is that it will always be the driving force of division among mankind.

They all claim to hold "the absolute truth" of salvation, which is the raison d'être of the religious social unrest in the world. They're all opinionated and deceived disciples of *stultitia*. Religion will one day become an extinct notion in the world, because religion has denied humanity its basic human rights. The principle of free will is synonymous to self-determination, a natural and innate right of human beings. This is decision-making without extraneous force or influence. Thus, in conjunction with the philosophy of Certainism, it embraces the indisputable fact that self-determination is a basic human right and must never be exploited by religious institutions. It was my philosophy of Certainism that brought me my very own *Aufklarung* (enlightenment) from religion, and this was my turning point of emancipation.

Religion forever seeks to deny mankind its self-determination as human beings with inalienable rights. All religious leaders are nothing more than the engineers of lies and deceits, who care only for their coffers. Religion and absurdity go hand in hand. The solution for religion is *Religenocide*.

Chapter Ten

Certainism and Stultitia

The sun was rising and I couldn't believe I had spent all night ruminating about the solution for religion. Then the door of my childhood bedroom opened; it was my beloved, Frau Olga. She told me she was going to start breakfast for us, but I told her I was not hungry. I headed into the master bedroom to wash up. While taking a shower, I couldn't believe all the things that had transpired in just a few years. I'd lost about thirty pounds during the war: my weight was 180 pounds. I was twenty-five, and in a few months I would be twenty-six.

Then I thought, *I need to resume and complete my studies, because I would like to have my PhD as soon as possible. I know there's a lot of work I have to do before I achieve this goal.*

However, as I stood beneath the shower I couldn't help but remember when I started courting Fraulein Olga, before she decided to marry me.

It was in the month of May, and the year was 1945, when I first laid eyes on this beautiful young girl. She looked so attractive to me, in spite of her living conditions. Her hair went to her shoulders and was a bright golden color in the sun. Her bright blue eyes looked deep into my soul, and I knew from that very moment this fraulein was the soul mate I'd been waiting for all those years. Her waist was small, her hips had the perfect shape and match her amazing physique, and her smile reminded me of life, even after all the tragedies I'd encountered, beginning from 1938.

As I continued to admire her I thought to myself, *Gosh, I'd like a smile like that to greet me every morning for the rest of my life. And I'd like to experience carnal knowledge with a body like that. Just look at her ass, those breasts; they're perfect!*

At first, Olga was hesitant to make my acquaintance, so I did my best to woo her. Two weeks after my introduction to her we were on our first date. In spite of the social unrest in Germany, I was certain about Olga.

We would talk for hours about our childhood, for all I wanted was to get to know her. But as we spoke during our dates I realized that she also was intrigued by me, and wanted to know everything about me.

I was very pleased to learn this, since I thought she wasn't going to like me because I'm an American. I had never felt this way about anyone before. In the gang, everyone had someone he admired or a special someone that he kept in his heart. There was never any girl in Springfield, Massachusetts, that I found attractive.

There were many fine-looking girls from my high school and the university I attended. Then again, I'm not the kind of guy who looks to use the female sex for that one thing. I always told my fraternity brothers, "I'm sorry, but I'm not going to have a one-night stand with anyone. It must feel right for me when that time comes." The gang knew I was a virgin, and when I met Fraulein Olga, I still was. Three weeks into our unique courtship I took the opportunity to scout out a remote place with a barn, and that day we had a picnic date there. The day was just right for us. I was certain of what I wanted out of our relationship. Olga wanted to have the picnic outside in the field, and I agreed to whatever my love wanted.

In fact, Mother Nature was on my side, and she knew the era of my virginity would soon come to end that day. The rain started to fall, so we packed up everything and rushed for the barn. As we entered the barn, we started to chuckle, since we were both drenched.

However, the moment of our short-term expression of amusement soon came to an end. As the silence permeated our midst, reminding us that we were alone, I gazed into her gorgeous blue eyes. I wanted to get closer to her, so I took her beautiful face in my hand and guided her lips to mine.

There it was: our first kiss, after all those weeks of wooing. I pulled her close to me in spite of our wet clothes. I wanted to see her naked. I could imagine what her body looked like, since it looked perfect in clothes. I had wondered for weeks about Olga's body, daydreaming of removing the clothes from her voluptuous figure, which provoked me to much excitement.

As we kissed, I could sense that Olga was cold, so I pulled her closer to me. At that moment, my libido was high and my body temperature was very hot. Then, I set the basket down and used both hands to bring her much closer to my burning, aroused body. I knew this was going to be a moment we'd never forget. I was not prepared to undress my beloved, knowing that she was cold. Therefore, I built a secure fire in the center of the barn. As we sat beside the fire, I had already taken off most of my clothes, hoping they would dry by the fire. While Olga's dress was drying, I took the blanket we had sat on for the picnic and wrapped it around her.

She looked at me in my shorts and asked, surprised, "Aren't you cold?"

"No. Most of the time I'm very warm. I'm a hot-blooded American guy."

She looked at me, dazed, trying to understand my phrase. "What are those marks on your chest and thighs?"

"These are from shell fragments. They're actually my marks from battles."

"But your body, David, it's very beautiful."

"I know, thank you. I've been saving myself for you, Olga."

"You mean in your country you never had a girlfriend?"

"That's correct, never!"

"I find that hard to believe, as good-looking as you are, and with your perfect body. You never had a special someone?"

I drew close to her and gazed into her beautiful eyes. At that moment, everything around us was perfect for the consummation of our new relationship.

I whispered in her ear, "Olga, my love, I don't believe in revealing and exposing myself to just anyone."

"You mean I should consider myself special?"

"Olga, from the first moment I laid eyes on you, I knew with all certainty that not only do I want to spend my entire life with you, but that you're my perfect and only soul mate."

With that, we kissed, and she put her arms around me.

I whispered, "I'm really looking forward to giving myself to you completely, Olga."

"You mean this is your first time, really?"

"Yes, Olga, don't you believe me?"

"Of course I believe you, David. It's just I've never met an American GI, particularly a young one, who's a virgin."

Laughing at her innocent comment, I said, "Well, my love, I'm not the kind of young man who allows his emotions to control him. And furthermore, I just couldn't lie about my feelings when it comes to the solemnity of sex."

"You mean at your age, almost twenty-five, you've kept yourself pure all these years?"

"Yes, Olga, don't you believe me?"

"Yes, I do. It's just that you're perfect in looks, and your body is well proportioned and elegant. And I know you're a very intelligent young man."

"Do you find my body appealing, Olga?"

"Yes, David, you're a very good-looking young man. And not only do I find your body appealing, but your face is very handsome also."

"Gee, Olga, no one has ever told me that before."

"Well, I'm telling you now. Don't you look at yourself in the mirror?"

"Yes. I remember the first time I ever masturbated. I was twenty-one, and my fraternity brothers had spoken about it often. I thought maybe something was wrong with me, seeing that as a teenager I had never masturbated. Even though some people believe that masturbation is an important part of human sexual development, I don't like it."

"Why?"

"Because, Olga, to me, solo sexual stimulation is really too oafish. I find it's just not satisfying. Furthermore, my personal opinion of masturbation is that it's for horny teenagers and frustrated old men."

"So, David, I think what you're trying to say is that you wanted to wait for the real thing."

"Yes, Olga. There's a saying that good things take time, but awesome things happen all at once."

"Well, David, something awesome is about to happen all at once right now."

At her statement, I got up from the fire, stood before her, and said, "Well, Olga, my love, what you see now no other woman has ever seen like this."

And with that, I took off my shorts. Olga now saw me naked for the first time. Then I walked to her, knelt before her, undressed her, and began to make passionate love to her.

It was a dream that came true and I loved every moment of my first intimacy with Olga, my prospective wife. It became very quiet; we were no longer talking. I took the blanket and laid it on the floor. I couldn't help but look at her fabulous youthful body. I loved what my eyes were beholding, for she's beautiful, and every aspect of her anatomy is perfect. We rested on the blanket and our lips spoke the language of passionate love. In the midst of our love making my beloved, to my surprise, Olga uttered a deep, but also a loud cry of ecstasy. Then it happened; I felt like a man who had just experienced a new birth, a new dimension, and a new chapter in my life. It was as if all my stress had suddenly been taken away permanently.

"David!" Olga was calling me.

I was still in the shower as I responded to her call. "Yes, honey."

"I thought something was wrong."

"Oh, I'm sorry, honey. I was remembering our first moment of intimacy in the barn. Do you remember?"

"How could I forget, David? You made me a woman."

"And you made me a man."

As Olga gazed at my wet naked body—by now I was fully aroused—I said, "Would you like to join me, Frau Olga?" Then I got the chance to relive my pleasurable memories again, but this time in a totally new dimension.

The following week I had an appointment at Yale University, for the purpose of returning to school. Olga accompanied me on my short trip to New Haven, Connecticut. In the fall of 1946, I officially resumed my studies that I had put off in the summer of 1942. Four full years had lapsed since the day I enlisted in the U.S. Army. It was good to be back at college. Three times a week I would travel to New Haven, and although I had to leave my Olga. I did not like the idea of leaving my wife all alone; therefore, Olga and I decided it would be best for her safety to spend those days with Peggy. Also, I had asked the sheriff to check on them, because I was fearful to leave my precious molecule since she's German.

One evening when I came home early from classes, I picked up my wife from Peggy and asked her if she wouldn't mind going with me to visit the McCrorys. That evening we arrived at their home around six thirty. It was so good to see my best friend's parents, and Daniel's wife Peggy was also there with the twins.

"Oh, David, it's so good to see you and Olga, again."

"The feeling is mutual, Peggy."

After we exchanged greetings, she asked me if, whenever the time was convenient, she could get my approval on a most important matter. Surprised, I thought, *Why would Peggy McCrory need my approval on anything? She's an intelligent young woman, and she lacks nothing except a husband.*

Dr. and Mrs. McCrory were pleased to meet my wife for the first time, and while Mrs. McCrory got acquainted with Olga, Daniel's dad and I left the women to themselves and spent some quality time together in his study.

We talked about many things, particularly Daniel Jr., but as he spoke about his one and only son he began to cry, when he shared the details of Daniel's death in Normandy. He said that when the U.S. Army's 507th Parachute Infantry landed in France, it appeared that Daniel was killed in action by some German officers. Because of the swirling confusion of combat, the army was unable to document the cause of each and every fatality.

Therefore, Peggy never knew what happened in the final moment of her husband's life.

As Dr. McCrory shared this with me, and while he cried, I couldn't help it; I tried not to become emotional, but eventually I broke down and started to cry also. Though, in the midst of the moment, I did my best to comfort him, knowing this kind gentleman had always been there for us, and especially me, when I was younger.

We spent about three hours together, and most of the time, I believe, I supported my best friend's dad in his time of grief. After a while, I told Dr. McCrory about my first combat in North Africa, and what it was like being a second lieutenant in the U.S. Army. And how I dealt with the loss of one of the young men in my unit, for the soldier was only eighteen. He was shot in the head by a German soldier.

As we talked, I realized it had been almost five years since I actually had spoken with Dr. McCrory. From that night, I made a firm decision that for as long as I lived, I was going to maintain a close relationship with Daniel's parents, because Daniel had been my best friend. I had loved him like my own kid brother Georg.

It was really good seeing the McCrorys. Before we left their residence that evening, to my surprise, Dr. McCrory told me about the late Professor Bechstein and the fire that destroyed his house in the summer of 1936. As he spoke to me, I remembered distinctly the words he had used that night. "It's out now, but not before consuming the entire place, which included his house and the stable."

Just then, I realized the relevant contents of his sentence, because the fire actually started in the house and then traveled to the stable. Dr. McCrory informed me that no one was responsible for the fire in the summer of 1936 except Professor Bechstein himself. He explained that Professor Bechstein had fallen asleep in his bed while smoking his pipe.

Throughout the years I thought the fire had started in the stable and then spread to the house. The fact of the matter was that the fire actually began in the professor's bedroom and then spread to the entire property; hence, the reason the old man died from asphyxia that night.

Since the fire started in his bedroom, it took some time before it spread throughout his house and to the stable. I just sat there listening to

Daniel's dad. And to think, we swore each other to secrecy that night because we presumed that the fire started in the stable and spread to the house.

While Olga and I drove home that night, I couldn't believe how bad I had felt for all those years—ten years, to be exact. I muttered to myself, "Then it's really wrong to assume anything. That's why, if I had only followed the principles of my astounding philosophy of Certainism, it would have saved me from those unnecessary moments of guilt. My philosophy gathers the relevant epistemological data and then compels me to make a certain decision."

"David, are you okay?"

"Yes, Olga, I'm sorry if I startled you."

"By the way, David, what's Certainism?"

"Well, Olga, I'm glad you've asked that. What I'm about to share to with you, I've never shared with anyone, not even my fraternity brothers. Certainism is a philosophy of a new theory, which seeks to accommodate the existential views of decisive decisions. In fact, Certainism seeks to overrule the religious tenets of morality, since there's no right or wrong, only what's relevant for that particular moment. It's the active participation of the will; reason over morality."

"But David, my father, before he was fired from the university, was a professor of philosophy for over twenty years, and I never heard him mention that particular branch of philosophy."

"That's because, Olga, I'm the first Certainist, since I'm also the inventor of this new philosophy."

"I know you said that you've never shared your theory with anyone. How do you intend to promulgate you new philosophy if you don't share it with others?"

"That's a good question, Olga, but you need to know that I invented my new philosophy at the age of ten."

"Ten? David, my father never mentioned anything about a philosopher being so young. What I understood from his input is that philosophers are supposed to be old men."

"Yes, that's true, my love, but I actually invented this new philosophy for the reason of escaping my tight-ass religious father and his suffocating religion. However, over the years my philosophy of Certainism evolved to be not just a means of escape, but a dependable lifestyle for me, and my personal *Aufklarung*."

"I'm glad that you asked me to marry you, and I'm even gladder that I consented."

"Why's that, Olga?"

"Because, David, not only are you a healthy, handsome man, you're also very intelligent, so I know our children are going to be intelligent and beautiful individuals."

"Well, that's because you're a very beautiful Aryan woman, my love."

"We're both beautiful Aryan people, David. Can we expect less?"

"No, my sweet, absolutely not."

When we arrived home, I thought that Olga would have wanted to end our philosophical discussion. A few minutes after we got into the house, I learned I was wrong.

"So, David, I'd like to learn more about your new philosophy, since my intentions are to emulate my husband. I'm glad you're not religious, and you're certainly not anything like a pastor's kid."

"Oh, that's mainly because I'm a Certainist, Olga, and being a Certainist, my intentions are to debunk every notion of religion and its *stultitia* teachings."

"What's *stultitia*?"

"It's a Latin noun that means foolishness, and is similar to *insipientia*, which describes the actions of stupid, thoughtless, and unwise people."

"Like those religious people?"

"Yes, Olga."

"David, I've always thought that religious people are the essence of *stultitia*."

"Oh, you're a fast learner, Olga."

"I've no intention of outgrowing my tutelage, David."

"Gee, Olga, you're the ideal cook, an excellent lover, and also a quick learner."

"David, I want to know everything about you, and especially about your philosophy, because, as I said before, my intentions are to emulate my husband and his new philosophy. So I believe like you, David. I'm also a Certainist. You wouldn't believe it, but when we first started to date, and I wanted to know everything about you and your family, I found it a bit strange that you never wanted to talk about your father's career. And then, when you told me later on that he was a Lutheran pastor, I thought, 'Oh, goodness, this guy is too perfect to be true,' but I thought that maybe you were a religious nut! However, I was very pleased when you shared with me that you weren't religious at all."

"Olga, I wanted to be honest with you, but I've been a Certainist for almost sixteen years. Certainism is the ideal philosophy to debunk the very notion of religion, and particularly all religious nuts, who most of the time are trying to change your mind. Certainism holds to the theory of the social development of nations independent of religion. That's why, Olga, Certainism is reason over morality. There's nothing more dangerous in this world than to behold a fool with a purpose."

"So, David, I want to learn everything about Certainism. However, my love, I don't want to keep you from your studies."

"Nonsense, Olga, I've completed my assignments for the week and tomorrow is Friday. I have only one class tomorrow afternoon, around two p.m."

"Okay," she said, "then please continue."

"So, when I discovered my theory of Certainism some years ago, at the age of ten, I became a staunch Certainist. Also, I couldn't stand the better part of religion. My philosophy of Certainism has taught me that people's misinformed opinions must never keep me in bondage, or move me. My revolutionary theory of Certainism has encouraged me to break the status quo, and to define myself as I choose: *Stare Decisis*, which means to stand by my decisions. Religion has the reputation of placing men in bondage, which is precisely why Certainism has taught me it's always better to consider opportunities now, existentially speaking, because in the future, when people are older, life will most definitely limit their choices. Therefore, Olga, when I first laid eyes on you, not only was I sexually drawn to you, but I knew with all certainty, indubitably, that you were meant to be my wife and soul mate. When I first saw you, I thought to myself, 'She's more than human, for I'm certain she's a fairy, or a sylph.'"

Olga blushed.

"Now, for that reason I'm ecstatic that I've discovered this new groundbreaking theory, which I'm certain will one day supplant religion and its superstitious tenets. Certainism will eventually become the centralized philosophical idea that will inevitably transcend into a living reality. Religion hinders mankind's progression of intellectualism, and as a twentieth-century philosopher, I want to prove that philosophy is in fact the love of wisdom, which compels men to search for it as they seek knowledge. Hence, my philosophy of Certainism, which is the reason of science, because I know that philosophy is in fact the ideal ideology for the skeptics."

"What does that mean, David?"

"Good question, Olga. It simply means that humanity should question everything, and never be gullible or quick to believe just about anything."

"But isn't that the way of those religious people, David?"

"Yes, my precious molecule. These *stultus* knob heads will believe just about anything and call it faith."

"But David, that's the way of a simpleton."

"Oh, I'm going to enjoy this, Olga, for you're my first student of Certainism. The most profound quest for all philosophers is the quest for knowledge, and according to the words of Richard Cecil: *"The first step to knowledge is to know that we are ignorant."* But in the quest for knowledge, people must question all theories of learning. Throughout the years I've discovered that the Greek philosopher Pyrrho is indeed the father of skeptics."

"David, when was Pyrrho born?"

"He was born in 365 BCE and died in 275. Out of Pyrrho's school of thought came the theory of *Pyrrhonism*."

"And what's that?"

"That's the teaching of the skeptic of Pyrrho, and his followers."

"So what exactly did he teach humanity?"

"He taught the extreme or absolute theory of skepticism."

"But what does that mean?"

"Well, some individuals, especially in the realm of religion, believe in the dogma of absolute truth. And then there are also those who believe certain knowledge can be attained if an individual diligently goes after it. But Pyrrho believed that certainty of knowledge is impossible and that true happiness must therefore come from suspending judgments; that is, when people make their decisions after gathering relative data. However, since no human being can attain absolute knowledge or certainty of learning, people must question all things, especially when it comes to learning whatever is relevant to that particular period. Therefore, people should always make the best of what they've learned, but must never force their relevant ideals on others. The relevant information they've gathered must also be conveyed to their minds in a practical manner. But the question still stands: can a person possess absolute knowledge?"

"The answer, I guess, would be no?"

"That's correct, Olga. There's always room for questions, and once there are questions there will always be uncertainty, and skeptics. Now, from *Pyrrhonism* came the theory of relativity of knowledge, which advocates that knowledge of what things really are is in fact impossible, because knowledge itself is dependent upon the mind's purely subjective forms of relating to its object and reality. Since the skeptic is one who questions the fundamental doctrines of all things, the philosophical spectrum with the theory of relativity of knowledge and skepticism will compel the masses to question the certainty of knowledge and also the certainty of religion. And since there's no certainty of knowledge, there can never be the certainty of religion in conjunction with a moral law, because how can religion teach that its manuscripts, which may be hundreds or even thousands of years old, are relevant for us today? Hence, the school of Pyrrho of Elis; the father of skepticism. When I read the book *The Stranger* by Albert Camus, it really fascinated me because it's very similar to my theory of Certainism."

"How's that?" asked Olga.

"The character in the book is an extraordinary young man by the name of Meursault. He, as a Frenchman, murders an Arab in Algeria. Albert Camus' character in The Stranger describes a man with the phenomenon ability to live in the present, an amazing individual indeed. His book deals with the fundamental existential crisis of a man and his ability to live under the restrictions that society imposes upon most people. People need to tell religion and society to putain off!"

"I'm not familiar with Albert Camus, David."

"He's a young upcoming author, and I know he's very philosophical. I think that his philosophy will contribute to the views of absurdism, since he advocates individual freedom."

"That's my view exactly, David, for religion sets limits on mankind."

"That's why I agree with his school of thought of absurdism, as he seeks to propagate the theories of humanity, justice, and love."

"What other French philosophers or authors do you admire besides Albert Camus, David?"

"I also enjoy Jean Genet, the controversial French novelist, playwright, and political activist."

"Isn't he a homosexual, David?"

"I think he is, Olga, but why should that stop me from admiring the man and his work?"

"That's true, David. People have a right to be truthful to themselves."

"I agree, Olga. Do you know that in 1938, Jean Genet, while in the army, was examined by a psychiatrist and discharged from the army for being imbalanced, and also an amoral person, because of his attraction to the same sex?"

"Isn't that how society is? They love to tell you how to live and behave, but how can you like yourself if you deny what you are?"

"That's true, Olga. Well, my precious molecule, we should do this again."

"I totally agree, David."

That night after I made sure that the house was secure, my wife and I were in bed. But as Olga and I lay in bed we began to talk about many things, and eventually we ended up on the same topic we had been discussing less than an hour before.

I explained to Olga the way of the sophist, the wise man of philosophical ideas and pursuits, who holds to the pragmatic theory of truth, since the essence of truthful statements may be relevant to a particular era or people, on the condition that people accept the value of what they labeled as their relevant truth.

But what may be considered to be a truthful theory will also remain subjective. There are certain principles that other people may consider to be false, while a percentage of the populace accepts these things as truthful. In the same manner, something that may be truthful may also be very damaging and offensive to others.

Hence, the philosophical pragmatism of the theory of truth: it may be a relevant theory to those who exercise their prerogative of accepting what they call and utilize as their relevant theory of truth. However, the pragmatism of certain things that may be called truth is based primarily on what people have chosen to be their relevant truth for that hour.

Not everyone may hold to this principle, since there are those individuals who will want everyone to see their point of view. But truth and progress go hand in hand, once it's the relevant period of the people who embrace that necessary truth.

Truth, in conjunction with the presupposed doctrine, is applicable by all relevancy to the point of view of people who hold that what they have come to believe is the relevant truth. For example, "*beauty lies in the eye of the beholder*": for the one who's enraptured by whatever or whomever he has taken up with, that's his relevant truth at the moment. However, there are those individuals who will not see what the beholder is seeing, so everything is relative. Now, to take that same famous idiom a bit further, "*beauty lies in the eye of the beholder*" simply means that different people will have different opinions, since the world can never hold to the same beliefs and opinions.

The historical connation behind this idiom goes back to the Greek pastoral philosopher-poet Theocritus. He lived in the third century BCE, and this idiom first came from his wise lips. The philosophical understanding of this relevant idiom of Theocritus is that the perception of beauty is subjective, like all truths, and not everyone will find the same person or things attractive or appealing. To believe that all people can have the same interests is to live in the ideal and deny the actual.

We continued with our discussion, for Olga had many questions, and I loved spending time with her. I never thought that my wife would be so taken with my views on philosophy, and especially my theory of Certainism.

"That's interesting, David. But I still think you're the most beautiful man I've ever seen."

"Thank you, Frau Olga. Remember, I also think you're the most beautiful creature I've seen, my precious sylph, so the feeling is mutual, I guess." With my statement we embraced, as our affection for each other continued to grow each day. "Are you ready to sleep?"

"Somehow I'm not very sleepy, David, and I'd like to hear more of your great ideas."

"Well, in the aspect of pragmatism and the theory of truth, progressivism is needed if the masses are to grasp the theory of truth."

"Yes, my father taught about that philosophy, but what are your ideas on progressivism?"

"Progressivism is in fact a political approach for those individuals who are seeking ways of changing or reforming conservatives' ideologies. This is a relatively new theory. It actually began in the late nineteenth century. It was taken into the twentieth century by those activists who wanted to see not only political but also social reform. But the real change that I'd love to see in my day is the obliteration of all religious institutions. Since progressivism is the principles and practices of the progressive individuals or parties, progressive education is what the world needs as mankind evolves into the ideal intellect, and not individuals who are bound by the rules of men in the form of religious institutions that propagate superstitious tenets. This philosophical methodology seeks to reject the archaic and mundane routine of recitation and strict discipline of the traditional school approach. Oh, I'm sorry, my precious molecule, but I'm sleepy."

"So am I, David."

With that, I kissed my wife and we were soon fast asleep.

The next day Olga and I got up at noon, so all I could do was shower, have something to eat, and be on my way. I arrived exactly on time. That Friday evening I got home around five o'clock, and Olga and I decided to go out on a date for dinner.

We spoke while at dinner and talked about our day, but Olga wanted to learn more about Certainism. Therefore, wanting to please my precious molecule, and since I'd never spoken in public about my theory before, I told her more about my new philosophy.

"Well, Olga, I'm David, and I'm a Certainist. Most people believe that the quintessential elements of life are health, wealth, love, faith, and religion. However, I say to them: keep those superfluous tenets and give me the relevant concept of philosophy. My philosophy of Certainism has taught me for the past sixteen years about the pillars of philosophical truths in the arena of self-truth and the reason of mankind."

"David, what is self-truth?"

"Well, it can be described as the relativity of knowledge, since this is the theory of the certainty of knowledge, which is actually impossible to achieve, as knowledge is dependent upon the individual mind and is subjective to what he has learned or is being taught at that relative moment. Hence, my self-truth is my theory of Certainism, and this self-truth has absolutely nothing to do with the dogmas of religion. Then again, this theory of self-truth, Certainism, is relevant for knowing yourself and accepting yourself, for the main reason of knowing who you are and what you're capable of doing. But that's only after you have accepted your self-truth and have accepted a peace with who you are and what you want out of life."

By that time we had just finished our first course and were about to begin our second. Olga then had a profound question that sort of startled me.

"And what do you want out of life, David?"

"Well, I've never really thought of it, Olga. But since you've asked, I think I should publish my new theory of Certainism, however, at this relevant moment in my life. I'm very happy and contented, because I'm madly in love with you and I'm finishing my PhD in psychology. In less than five years, I hope, I should finish my studies. But honestly, Olga, we don't have a financial care in the world. You asked what I want out of life. Well, I want to grow old with you. And I don't want to be separated from you."

"I'm not going anywhere, David."

"But now that you've asked the question, what do you want out of life, Olga?"

"Nothing."

"What do you mean, nothing?"

"I already have everything, so why should I want anything? I have the man of my dreams."

I was very pleased with her honest response. I knew without a doubt that Olga, my precious molecule, loved me for who I was. By this time we had finished the second course.

I asked her, "When do you think we should begin our family?"

"I want children, and I want to bear yours, but I think we should consider ourselves first, before considering children of our own, David. I think we should get to know each other."

Sometimes I just couldn't fathom Olga; she was perfect. I knew that most women are the ones who are eager to start a family. I love the idea that Olga wants us to wait; jeez, I'm all for that. However, Olga wanted me to continue with my Certainist views.

"And with Certainism and self-truth, when we say one thing and we're not truthful about our statement in conjunction with ourselves, we're in fact diminishing the level of integrity about that particular relevant truth about ourselves. Self-truth can only be defined by what is relevant at that moment for the individual: that which is profound and specific at a moment is only specific for the one who is convinced of his self-truth. Therefore, truth can never be defined in a generalized concept for the entire population."

"Absolute truth doesn't exist, only relevant self-truth does. What may be relevant to someone maybe irrelevant to someone else. Consequently, in the teachings of Certainism and for the Certainist, self-truth is that what applies to you only as an individual, and not as a cooperative theme of generalized absolute truth, like religion teaches. For Certainism holds no grounds for a double-standard mind or opinion. In addition, Certainism teaches you to be certain and know what you want, and what you consider to be self-truth at that relevant moment."

"Furthermore, as a Certainist, I'm determined never to turn to the useless ritualistic regression of religion and its *stultitia*. Certainism is reason over morality. What is reason to one man may be pure *stultitia* to others, for what is reason? Will or morality? All these definitions are in fact conjecture of relative truths, and are related to the theory of self-truth according to the Certainist. Theoretically speaking, reason, not morality, is the only catalyst of living a fulfilled life in the realm of the Certainist, and it's also the ultimate denouement of all decisions."

"Certainism, in the end, will overrule the religious teachings of morality. Desire is the privilege of the human race. To have what one desires is what makes life much more meaningful and challenging, for satisfying one's desire is the final settlement and the purpose of life. Then what is the philosophical meaning of life? The answer is found simply in the decisions that we make, which are inevitably anchored in the theory of Certainism. The *Stare Decisis*, to stand by one's decision, is the true essence of the Certainist."

"Certainism is not a traditional concept of religious tenets. Certainism debunks all notions of religion, because religion is primarily steeped in the confines of the traditions of men. Therefore, religion and tradition are synonymous, like looking in a mirror and seeing the same image. Religion is pure *stultitia* and not philosophy. Certainism is a non-theistic theory. However, Certainism does emphasize the fact that whatever you choose to be or do, according to your ideologies, you must make a decisive decision by allowing your reason to guide you in your choices. At the fruition of your decision, which you have made in conjunction with the philosophy of Certainism, stand by it, and don't apologize to those hypocritical men and religion, for they will try to criticize you for your decisive decision as a Certainist."

"In the realm of intellectualism, Certainism is the cognitive factor that will call mankind to take action. Decisive decision making works in accordance with one's reason, which exercises its sovereign right. The Certainist knows there's no such thing as certainty of knowledge, truth, and religion; however, the Certainist is flexible, for he's not immutable to change. The Certainist will only accept change through verifiable empirical evidence, and if this can't be presented, the Certainist will not endeavor to change because he can only accept change based on the intellectualism of his reason."

"Therefore, David, if forensic data can't be proven to the Certainist, he'll remain in his state until reasonable evidence is presented to him."

"Yes, Olga, because the Certainist bases everything on reason and logic. Without those empirical factors, he's lost. So, the Certainist's prerogative of reason is like the air he breathes. And that's the way of the Certainist. He'll always reject the dogmatic teachings of religion, since religious people have no practical evidence for what they claim to believe."

"That makes sense, David."

By that point, my wife and I had finished our entire three-course meal and there were only four other couples in the restaurant with us. So we decided it was getting late and we headed for home. We arrived at the house about twelve thirty-five. We changed and then headed to the kitchen. We had some warm milk and started on the topic of Certainism once again.

"Religion has fabricated a malevolent fiend, which it calls the devil, for the main objective of breathing superstition into the minds of ignorant men. I like what Fyodor Mikhaylovich Dostoevsky once wrote: *"If the devil doesn't exist, but man has created him, he has created him in his own image and likeness."*

"That's so true, David. These people are so superstitious."

"My sentiments exactly, Olga. There's no devil. He exists only as a figment of one's imagination."

"I wish my father had lived to meet you, David. I'm so proud of you, my husband."

"I'm very proud of you too, Olga. By the way, Olga, Peggy McCrory wants to talk to me, so I was wondering if Tuesday we could stop by to see her."

"That's fine, David."

"And while I'm on the topic of visiting Peggy, my sister, Maria, is living in Alaska."

"Is she married?"

"Yes. She's living in Alaska because her husband is a geologist for the government. It appears she's going to be there for a couple of years. I would like for us to visit her and meet my brother-in-law. And I would like you to meet Jena's baby boy."

"How old is he now?"

"He's about the same age as Peggy's twins. So I'll make the arrangement for us to go to Alaska in two weeks' time. And while we're there, we should see the country."

"Oh, I would love that, David."

"I thought you would. Tomorrow I'll call Peggy and we'll visit her on Tuesday evening."

"Sure, David. Do you know what she wants to talk to you about?"

"Nope, but I've know Peggy for years, since I was six. Gee, I didn't realize—that's almost twenty years. Gosh, I can't believe that in less than five years I'm going to be thirty."

"But you're still young, David."

"That's easy for you to say, my precious molecule, you're eighteen. In five years' time you will be twenty-three, about the age I was when I first laid my lustful eyes on you, Olga."

"When I first saw you, I too felt a strong sexual attraction to you, David."

"Did you, Olga?" Olga laughed. "Why, I thought you didn't even notice me."

"Yes, I did notice you, but I didn't want to be rude. It was the first time I saw you, and I certainly didn't want to stare at you. However, what caught my attention was that I was really impressed by the fluency of your German, and the build of your body and height. You looked so perfect in your uniform, and I loved your eyes, your smile, and I loved especially how your genitals looked in your pants."

"What? You little sneak, and I thought you never noticed me!"

"Oh, I did, David, and I loved what I saw. But it was difficult for me on that day when you first spoke with me. I was embarrassed, because I couldn't help looking at your entire body, and as you continued to talk in German, my eyes couldn't stop looking at your body, especially your private part that I've grown to enjoy so much."

With that, I leaned over and kissed her. "I love you, my precious molecule."

"I love you too, David, my handsome husband. However, I'd like to hear more about your Certainist theory."

"Boy, Olga, aren't you the perfect soul mate. I never thought in my wildest dreams that I would be married, and my wife would have such common interests as me."

"Well, David, my father was a German professor who taught philosophy."

"Okay, Olga, I'd like to share what I know about the *Übermensch*. I'm aware that you're familiar with this word, but what I'd like to do is expound on the philosophical meaning of the word in reference to Certainism."

"Isn't that the theory of Friedrich Nietzsche, his best-know invention?"

"Yes. You're no fool when it comes to philosophy, I can tell."

"Well, I'm not as smart as you, David."

"Smart enough to be my equal, Olga. The theory of the *Übermensch* comes from his book *Thus Spoke Zarathustra*; first published in 1883, and the word appears only in this book. It dealt with the subject that *"Man is something which ought to be overcome."* This encouraged me in the earlier years of my life, when I was boy, because I know that mankind can be overcome by the progression of the intellectual perfection of progressivism. Man can reach the status of the *Übermensch*, but Nietzsche's understanding is somewhat different from the views of the Certainist."

"How's that?" asked Olga.

"This perfect man, however, can reach that ideal stage only if he's willing to channel his passions and become creative, instead of suppressing them, as religion teaches. Christianity puts too much emphasis on the afterlife, and this religious attitude makes its followers the perfect candidates for *stultitia*. This teaching makes them very incompetent. Because of religion, they're less able to deal and cope with the earthly life of excelling intellectually. Religion will never be able to produce the ideal *Übermensch*, only disciples of immense *stultitia* and oafishness. In addition, man would be able to have a true understanding of life, as he grasps the full meaning of his life only if he's willing to seek and advance himself by the method of intellectualism for the purpose of finding meaning through his reason. This will eventually prepare future generations to be perfected as humanity reaches the ultimate goal of the *Übermensch.*"

"So, David, it's just like your terminology for Certainism."

"Exactly, although I never really saw it that way, Olga. It's as if nature ordained for us to be man and wife, because if it wasn't for you, I would have never spoken to anyone about my philosophy. But since I've been sharing my theory with you, it's like I've now shared it with the entire world."

"That's great, David, but why don't you just do that?"

"I need some time to think about this."

"Would you like some more warm milk?"

"No thanks, Olga."

"I'd still like you to continue with your theory, David."

"Okay, but let's go upstairs. I would prefer for us to continue our discussion in bed."

"I'll wash up."

"Fine. I'll just make sure the house is secured, Olga."

Ten minutes later we were in our bed, and I resumed with my theory.

"David, you said that you invented the philosophy of Certainism at the age of ten?"

"Yes, that's true, Olga."

"What really caused your brilliant mind to give birth to this new philosophy?"

"Gee, Olga, that's a very interesting and profound question."

"Why's that, David?"

"Because the things I'm sharing with you, and the questions you're asking me, are things I haven't thought about since the day the theory of Certainism came to me. In the past I've ruminated about many things, but never the catalyst that birthed my philosophy."

"Well, my handsome David, I'm waiting."

"Oh, I'm sorry, it's just you've opened up a thought I hadn't considered for years, not since I was a boy."

"Oh, I'm sorry, did I do something wrong?"

At that moment I couldn't help but gaze at my precious molecule as she looked so disappointed. I knew I had to explain myself to my one and only true love, because I didn't like the tears that welled in her lovely eyes.

"Honey, you can do no wrong on my path. And furthermore, you've done absolutely nothing wrong. I just want to re-emphasize this to you: I'm so in love with you and I'm realizing more every day how much you complete me."

Along with my precious words of love to her, there was a reservoir of tears. She reached for me, cuddling me for some time.

"Hey, what's wrong?"

"As I told you, Olga, when we first made love in this house—do you remember where?"

"How could I forget? It was in the dining room."

"Oh, my love, do you remember that I told you: all you'll hear from my lips are sweet songs of praise. My sweet, you did nothing wrong. All you did was to awaken the essence and the cause of my theory. So allow me to dry your eyes, and let me explain. In the fall of 1930, I was in my father's library, reading about our Constitution and the Bill of Rights."

"What is the Bill of Rights?"

"It's a document that protects the people's rights from the abuse of government."

"Oh, David, I know I'm going to love living in America."

"Yes, I know. But as I studied the Bill of Rights, I came to the Ninth Amendment. The words of the Ninth Amendment caused me to reflect on and think about the meaning of those historic words."

"What does it say, David?"

"The enumeration in the Constitution of certain rights shall not be construed to deny or disparage others retained by the people."

"Okay, I heard you, but what do those words mean?"

"There's a synonym given to the Ninth Amendment. It's called 'everything else.'"

"'*Everything else*'? Why?"

"The brief answer is that the Ninth Amendment states that if there are any additional rights that may be lacking or aren't explicit in the other amendments, it conveys those rights to the people of United States, and most certainly not the U.S. government. There were certain Supreme Court justices who said the Ninth Amendment was a mystery."

"But what are some of those rights?"

"That's an interesting question, Olga. Some are the rights to choose what you want: the right to believe in God or not; the right to choose to have an abortion, even though it's illegal now; the right to give your children up for adoption; the right to dress how you want; the right for boys to have long hair; the right to bring up your children how you wish; the right to have sex with whomever you choose. And here's the one I love the most: the right to have homosexual relationships, and the right to maintain the privacy of that relationship."

"My goodness, all those rights stemmed from that short sentence?"

"Yes, and there are more, but that's enough about the interpretation of the Ninth Amendment."

"You mean it would be a violation of someone's rights, if she chose by her rights of Certainism to have a same-sex relationship, for people to discriminate against her alternative lifestyle?"

"Well, yes and no, Olga."

"What do you mean? But you just said—"

"Yes, my sweet, I know what I told you. However, you must remember that it's the religious community that keeps condemning these people while it hides behind the First Amendment."

"Explain."

"The First Amendment says: *Congress shall make no law respecting an establishment of religion, or prohibiting the free exercise thereof; or abridging the freedom of speech, or of the press, the right of the people peaceably to assemble, and to petition the Government for a redress of grievances.*"

"My goodness, David, I can't believe the rights the people in this country have. In Germany, if you spoke against the government that was the end of your career, or even your life. I remember my father—"

"Yes, but Olga, religious institutions are in fact the biggest hypocrites."

"How?"

"Religious institutions have abused our freedom in this country for their own gain. They have manipulated the Bill of Rights when they claim their rights in the First Amendment, but they are very good when it comes to preaching hatred from their pulpits. When they use such unconstitutional, negative rhetoric about certain people, they're most definitely abusing the rights of others, who're under the protection of the Ninth Amendment, which guarantees certain rights to the citizens of the United States."

"I see, they use the law for their benefit. However, at the same time, religious institutions are denying others their rights while they are accusing others of doing that to them."

"My goodness, Olga, you're so intelligent!"

"Well, I've an excellent teacher. He's my husband and my best friend."

"However, according to my philosophy of Certainism, *Religenocide* must be established. The First Amendment is definitely going to be repealed in the future, just like the Eighteenth Amendment, which was repealed by the Twenty-First Amendment in 1933. Religion has always been a dominant factor in our society, because the centrality of religion was the major source that inadvertently brought about the clash of North and South in the American Civil War. Religion is good for one thing only: it teaches its members how to hate certain people. I know it is pure *stultitia*. Many religious people in this country think that President Abraham Lincoln was a religious man. The fact of the matter is that he had no affiliation to any religious institution."

"David, I've listened to what you've said, but what on earth is *Religenocide*? Are you advocating the annihilation of people who may have religious affiliations?"

"No, my precious molecule. Allow me to explain, allow me to illuminate your intellect, so that you too, Olga, can have your own *Aufklarung. Religenocide* is in fact the first offspring of Certainism, and it seeks to promote and protect the rights of all irreligious people, and also the gay community. *Religenocide* is the theory that will encourage the legislative branch of government to restrict, and control by law, what religious institutions teach about certain people. They will still be allowed to believe in and teach their fatuous tenets, but when they decide to debunk, ridicule, and propagate their hatred against the gay community, and all others, and teach their members to do likewise, then the law of *Religenocide* will be used like the scalpel of Congress to cut out the canker of hatred that's being used against law-abiding citizens."

"My goodness, David, that's very interesting. You've kept these theories to yourself all these years?"

"Yes."

"But David, why don't the people in America just study the Bill of Rights? Don't they read things for themselves?"

"My sweet, you would be surprised. Most religious people are the prime example of *stultitia*. They think if a man quotes from the Bible he automatically has some religious affiliation. Those knob heads don't know anything about their own history. Our sixteenth president, Abraham Lincoln, never made any religion proclamation, so it's right and fitting to say that the late president wasn't a religious man. In fact, he's one of our greatest presidents, but he wasn't religious."

That was the last thing I remembered that night.

The next day was Saturday. By eleven thirty a.m., my wife and I were up. We had an excellent weekend. Monday I left for New Haven, and on Tuesday evening we went to see Peggy McCrory. I was glad that Peggy had taken a keen interest in my wife.

Olga and I stayed for a couple of hours with Peggy. I was always pleased to spend time with Daniel's children. His son, Daniel the third, was growing fast and looking more like his dad. I was very pleased to be a part of the lives of Daniel's children and his parents. We had dinner that evening with Peggy and the twins, and during dinner Peggy said she had two important questions to ask me.

The first question required an explanation. Peggy said that before Daniel was deployed, he had told her that when the war was over he wanted to start a family when he returned. Daniel wasn't aware that Peggy was already pregnant with the twins when he left. He told her that he wanted me to be, not in a religious sense, the godfather of his first child. And because Daniel the third was born first, she wanted to know if it was okay with Olga and me for his son to be my godchild.

I was very pleased, and accepted once Olga had no objections. I thought this was great. Then I recollected that there were *two* important questions, so I asked Peggy what the other question was.

She said that she had to put the children to bed, and was saving the second question for last. Around ten p.m. there was a knock on Peggy's door. I was close to the door so I opened it, and was surprised to see my friend, Jesse Atwood. Surprised or not, I invited him in. We embraced and exchanged greetings, and I introduced Jesse to Olga. After the children were in bed we all went into the sitting room. Soon after, Peggy initiated the conversation.

"Well, David, I'm sure you're probably speculating about the second question."

"Somewhat, Peggy." As we laughed, I sat close to my wife and held her hands.

Jesse looked great; he was always a good-looking guy. He told me that he was back in school and wanted to be an engineer. We continued with our conversation, with much intrigue.

"David, I wanted your consent because you have always been Daniel's best friend. I loved my husband very much, but it is difficult dealing with his loss."

"I'm sure, Peggy."

"Some weeks ago, Jesse and I met in the grocery store. He helped me home with the twins, and during the past few weeks he and I have developed a friendship. However, he said that he has feelings for me. He wants to ask me to marry him. But Jesse told me he's not going to ask me unless you consent first."

"Why, Jesse?" I asked. "You're both adults. You certainly don't need my consent."

"That's true, David. Nevertheless, I've chosen to do it this way out of respect for Daniel and you. Daniel was my friend, but he was also your best friend."

"Jesse, I'm very impressed by the way you have handled this. I know you've always been a man of true integrity. And furthermore, I have the greatest respect for you. I'm very happy for you and Peggy. So please, I give my consent willing. Do what you have to do, Jesse."

With that, Jesse began to cry as he walked over to us and hugged me. Then Olga joined us; Peggy soon came over and we were all in a group hug.

Jesse said, "This reminds me of the summer of 1936, when the gang was in a group hug."

We started to laugh, and although it was a happy moment, I missed my friends, especially Daniel.

Jesse then got on one knee and proposed to Peggy. We spoke for some time and then left for the evening. Jesse informed me that Jack was doing great and was off his medication. He also said that Jack was engaged and would be calling me soon.

I was very happy for them and wished them all the happiness in the world. I thought, *Life can be very unpredictable. Just look: Daniel died, and his widow is getting married to his friend Jesse Atwood.* I couldn't help remembering when we were much younger, and Jesse had told Ryan that looking at Peggy "...*is sheer voyeurism! Man, Ryan, every time I look at Peggy, she always gives me a hard-on!*" To think that Jesse Atwood has always been in love with Peggy, but when Daniel married her in 1942, he was genuinely happy for them. I guess he's really a great guy; all my friends are great guys.

Most people don't know that we're not supposed to live our lives by the rules of the religious world, because it's sheer nonsense, but as a Certainist I have a totally different concept about life. Another guy, I believe, would have been angry and against Peggy and Jesse's engagement. My philosophy of Certainism has taught me not to judge people, because that is the way of the religious-minded.

My wife and I visited my sister Maria and her husband Philip Livermore in Alaska. It was good to see my sister after all those years. Alaska was beautiful, and Jena's baby was a gorgeous little boy. Maria told me that she wanted to speak with me privately before we left. So, while Olga and Philip became better acquainted, I talked with my sister.

To my surprise, Maria had a question about the fall of 1936: she wanted to know why Dad had called Mom "a Jewish whore." I knew I couldn't tell her the whole truth, because I had made a promise to Mom. And furthermore, Olga wasn't going to know the truth about my mother's ancestors. I concocted some alleged reason, to keep the truth from being revealed, and reminded Maria of how Dad usually said derogatory things about people that had no credence.

When we returned home we had two weddings to attend: the first marriage ceremony was Peggy and Jesse's wedding, and two weeks after the Atwoods' wedding, it was time for Jack Eden and Julia Atterton's celebration.

Julia was a nurse and they met during the war. My wife and I were very happy for our friends, and so were the McCrorys, who attended Peggy and Jesse's wedding.

The following week, I told Olga I wanted to visit my parents, who were resting at the Springfield Cemetery. While I was there I also paid my respects to my sister Jena. Her husband's body was buried in South Africa. His parents and Jena, before she died, erected a memorial site for Dr. Andreas Hansel. Now my sister, Jena Hansel, is laid to rest next to it. My grandfather bought two plots many years ago. After I paid my respects to my relatives, I also visited Tobey's grave.

Life was great and I was pursuing my dream of becoming a psychologist. I recognized, with the advice of Olga, that I would prefer to teach psychology rather than to practice it as a medical career. The years went by quickly and I graduated from Yale University with honors in 1951.

I completed my PhD; the topic of my thesis was my new theory Certainism, and how it can be applied to the science of psychology and the reason of man. Some weeks after my graduation I published my first book on Certainism, and eight months afterward, my second book was published, entitled *Certainism and Science*. They soon became phenomenal best-sellers.

Therefore, when Harvard University contacted me, I was very excited because I knew this was the ideal place to promulgate my theory of Certainism, in the academic arena of intellectualism. In the fall of 1953, I began my new career at the age of thirty-two.

I was the father of three wonderful boys: David Ulrich, Jr.; Georg Alfred, named after my brother who died in Iwo Jima; and Hans Brandt. They were four, three, and two. David Jr. is my firstborn, and he looks just like me. We taught them German and other languages as well. My godson, Daniel III, was nine going on ten. I couldn't believe it; I lost my best friend, but it was like having Daniel with me once again, and this time I was watching him grow.

I loved every moment of being a husband, a father, a godfather, and a friend to Jack and Jesse. My first day in class, when I entered the students stood up and greeted me with the warmest applause. I thanked them and asked them to take their seats. Then I introduced myself.

"I'm Dr. David Tolstoy Hugenberg, a Certainist. You may call me Professor Hugenberg, or Dr. Hugenberg."

However, before I could begin with my first lesson at Harvard University, there was an inundation of questions about my theory of Certainism, and my experience in the war.

"Professor Hugenberg, what would you say was the main thing you learned in the war?"

"That's an excellent question. I'm sorry, what's your name?"

"Steve Grissom."

"Well, Steve, I'd like to share with all of you a speech by President Roosevelt. This was his Flag Day Radio Address on June 14, 1942."

Their eager eyes gazed at me with amazement.

"The spirit of man has awakened and the soul of man has gone forth. Grant us the wisdom and the vision to comprehend the greatness of man's spirit that suffers and endures so hugely for a goal beyond his own brief span...We are all of us children of earth—grant us that simple knowledge. If our brothers are oppressed then we are oppressed. If they hunger, we hunger. If their freedom is taken away, our freedom is not secure. Grant us a common fate that man shall know bread and peace. That he shall know justice and righteous, freedom and security, an equal opportunity and an equal chance to do his best, not only in our land, but throughout the world. And in that faith let us march forth to a clean world our hands can make. Amen."

I then said, "Your question is quite profound, Steve, to ask what was the main thing I learned in the war. I'll try my best to answer your question truthfully. It was my brother Georg who first pointed out to me the seriousness of this war. The war, however, was not about me, even though it was a great honor to serve my country. Service and sacrifice are the hallmarks of America's soldiers who fought in it, but the war compelled me to understand that my brothers who fought in the war were my main concern, those sixteen million young servicemen. For this generation is not just the greatest generation, to me they're the modern-day samurai. This generation, like my brother Georg, did not use the pretext of college deferment, but many enlisted. Four hundred fifteen thousand young men never made it home. I lost many relatives and friends in this war. But the one main lesson I learned from this war is the unselfish service to my country and fellowman. The most vital component that is etched in my mind from this war is the fact that the spirit of man has been awakened."

"Professor Hugenberg, I understand a particular segment of your answer, but what do you mean by the spirit of man has been awakened?"

"Well, that's precisely why I've quoted from the Flag Day Radio Address. Allow me to explain, please. In the nineteenth century when the United States almost became the Divided States in the American Civil War, over six hundred thousand men died. After the American

Civil War, the slaves were granted their freedom in 1865. Then fifty-three years later there was World War I and the deaths of almost forty million. This also includes the lives of those killed in the Spanish Flu of 1918."

"So, Professor Hugenberg, what I'm seeing here is the social trend of natural selection and progressivism."

"That's precisely where I'm heading with this. I'm sorry, what's your name, young man?"

"Russ Morris."

"After the events of the Great War in 1918, just twenty-one years later there was World War Two. After World War Two, the death tolls were estimated at over seventy million, half of which were civilians. Certain historians are calling these two events the Thirty Years' War, because World War One began on August 1, 1914, and World War Two began on September 1, 1939. But even thirty-one years is counted from August 1, 1914, to September 2, 1945, when the Japanese delegation stepped aboard the USS *Missouri* to sign the official Japanese surrender. We understand it was the Civil War that liberated the blacks. And after World War One, women were liberated from a misogynist society. It appears to me that society has a natural but negative tendency to put and keep mankind in servitude in the name of religion, and it's somehow okay, or tacitly okay, for religion to place restrictions on mankind by limiting its inalienable rights. But after World War Two, people are going to start casting off the chains of religion."

"What do you mean, that people are going to start casting off the chains of religion? Was not our great nation founded on the ideals of religion?"

"Yes, my friend, that statement has a partial truth to it. Remember that our nation began by denying certain citizens their civil rights. Now, would you like to explain the intricacies of that topic to the class in conjunction with religion?"

"No, sir."

"What's your name?"

"I'm sorry, Professor Hugenberg. My name Kyle Davison."

"Pleased to meet you, Mr. Davison. Correct me if I'm wrong, but you're from a religious home, aren't you?"

"Yes, Professor Hugenberg. My—"

"With the greatest respect to your religious beliefs, Mr. Davison, I think you should keep them to yourself! If you read my book on Certainism, you'll understand my views on religion." "Religion has done nothing more than strangle and stagnate the progression of mankind. After the Great War in 1918, there was the rejection of the rational."

"And after World War Two, it may take some time, but we're about to witness the greatest social revelatory movement in our society. We're going to witness the metaphysics of certain choices as mankind is about to reject the absurdity of religion."

"There's a famous Latin axiom that says, *argumentum ad absurdum*. It describes the absurdity of establishing one's argument based primarily on *stultitia*. Therefore, this is the unsuccessful debate of religion, given that it's only for mindless Neanderthals, because the only hope for humanity is the hope of engaging in the now. It is only by making certain choices based on the philosophy of Certainism that the Certainist will be able to discover the true meaning in this ephemeral life."

"Therefore, the theory of Certainism this is where the logical empiricism will manifest itself in the metaphysical aspect of decisive choices for mankind. Too many restrictions have been placed on the female sex, and this has been done in the name of religion. The roles of women also changed during World War Two, as women were used to build ships, planes, and guns, for the benefit of the war. Don't you see how, according to the words of President Roosevelt, the spirit of man is awakened?"

"We're going to see some seismic social changes, in view of the fact that the end of World War Two has heralded a new era that the world has never seen. Our social religious attitude must change in the realm of abortion and the homosexual lifestyle."

"Yes, but Dr. Hugenberg, aren't you a married man with children?"

"Yes. I gather what you're saying is that once an individual is married, he shouldn't give a damn about other people's happiness? Do you question my sexuality?"

"No!"

"I'm certainly not a promiscuous man, and that's my choice, and I'm not a homosexual, nor am I bisexual. I'm a happily married man with three sons. But Certainism teaches that because that may be my choice, that doesn't mean marriage is for everyone. All of us can't be the same. The fact of the matter about life, we live in changing times and a sure certainty in this world nothing is set in stone; the only certainty in life is change. And we must attune to the vicissitudes of our social milieu, because marriage does not answer everyone's needs. There are alternatives for some."

"So, Dr. Hugenberg, you don't have a problem if someone is a homosexual?"

"What does their lifestyle have to do with me? They can rest assured I'm certainly not going to try to change them, since they were born that way."

"I'd like to share with you, not only what I learned about the war, but what my wife taught me about the Nazis. The war in Europe had ideological objectives, and not just geopolitical objectives, Lebensraum—'living space in the East.' It was the crusade against Judeo-Bolshevism, and indeed the war in the East had already become something of significant meaning to Hitler. In 1920, Hitler's speech about Judeo-Bolshevism was very explicit: 'The goal of rational anti-Semitism must unshakably be the removal of the Jews altogether.' And when SS—Sturmbannfuhrer Alfred Helmut Naujocks 'The Man who Started the War' in Poland in Operation Tannenberg in 1939, it was not only a war of military campaigned, but the war in Europe had evolved into a racial war against the Jews. Therefore, Hitler knew the only way the Third Reich could get its hands on the large population of Jews in Europe; his pretext was the war in the East."

"Soon after when *der Fuhrer*—'the Leader' got in power in 1933, the first system of terror his regime implemented was *Einzelaktionen*—Individuals actions against the Jews in Germany. The Nazis encouraged German citizens to harass and humiliate the Jews, which led to Germany's dismal chapter in history, the Holocaust. The time I spent in Germany I couldn't help but compare the Nazis with the teachings of religion, because the Third Reich not only encouraged its citizens to harass the Jews, but the citizens were led to persecute those of Jewish blood. Now religion has always encouraged its members to act like *Einzelaktionen*, especially when it comes to the gay community. Religion is bent on demonizing the gay community, and it forever seeks to legitimize its bias doctrines, for the purpose of segregation. Listen we can't just sit back and allow religious institutions to marginalize certain people in the name of what religion calls absolute truth."

"The Holocaust is an experience I'll never forget, and this must never happen again. The story of National Socialism was an evil chapter in Germany's history, and its lessens applies to us all. Those of us who live in democratic societies must never sit back and do nothing about particular groups that seek to act like *Einzelaktionen*. Because the Nazis wanted to create a *Volksgemeinschaft*—a people's community of a classless society; however, it was only for those of Aryan blood. This is the same approach with the teachings of religion, as it seeks to teach about a world without sinners; it's like religion and its classless society, only those who are 'saved' are eligible to be members of a *Volksgemeinschaft*. Be vigilant about your rights and the rights of others. Care about the fundamental rights and human dignity of others and that goes especially for the gay community. Religious institutions seek to impose its very own 'Gay Codes' through its discriminatory doctrines of hatred as its members continues to humiliate and harass gays in the guise of the First Amendment. When the rights of any group no matter how small, no matter how marginal are violated your rights, liberty, and freedom are violated also. But the day must never come when we say how did this happen, for there's nothing grotesque or irreligious about the gay lifestyle."

With that comment, the class became more relaxed as they laughed at my last remark. "Please understand that the spirit and the freedom of mankind is exactly what World War Two was all about. Now, in the aspect of marriage and the family, allow me to say that members of the gay community, I believe, in the future should be given the right if they wish to solemnize their relationship. And for those of you who may be religious, before you misunderstand what I'm trying to convey, please allow me to explain. I'm fully aware that some of you may not agree with what I'm about to illustrate on the board, and what I'm going to teach you today. But before I begin, I am going to ask this class a challenging question: what do you understand by the word *family*?"

"My understanding of what my parents taught me is a man and his wife and their offspring."

"Thank you, Mr. Grissom. That's exactly the answer I was hoping to get. Now, Mr. Steve Grissom, why did you give a definition like that?"

"Because that's what my parents and teachers taught me."

"Thank you. But that's a wrong definition of the word *family* describing the family unit."

By now their eyes were fixed on me as they waited eagerly to hear what I had to say next. Just then, Kyle Davison, to my surprise, raised his hand.

"Yes, Mr. Davison."

"So, Professor Hugenberg, what you're actually saying is that there's a proper definition of the word *family*."

"Yes, Mr. Davison. We live in a fettered, Draconian religious society that has molded our thinking process. With the philosophy of Certainism, this theory deals with the *relevant truth* of individuals, and not the *absolute truth* of religious institutions. Certainism calls out to the masses to be truthful to their conscience, and not to be ashamed of what they are, and that they should like themselves. In addition, individuals can never really like themselves if they deny what they are."

"Dr. Hugenberg, I read your first book, *Certainism*, and I found your theories to be very fascinating. I never realized that there's a vast difference from those two schools of thought: *absolute truth* and *relevant truth*."

"Yes, that's correct, Mr. Davison."

Then I began to write on the board so that the class could grasp the profound understanding of the word *family*.

The word *family* appears about 123 times in the Bible; in the Hebrew language it is מִשְׁפָּחָה—*mishpachah,* and it means a circle of relatives, a tribe or people. In the Greek it is πατριά—*patria,* and it means paternal descent: a group of family, a whole race, kindred, and lineage. The definition of family means *family household,* borrowed from Latin *familia,* servants of a household including relatives and servants.

"Now, what do you understand from these ancient definitions?"

"Nothing is mentioned about the male or female sex."

"That's absolutely correct, Mr. Morris, because these three definitions were taken from ancient scripts. But then why has society taught us that family means a male and a female? Because religion has been controlling our social milieu for too long, and that's why our government needs to redefine the meaning of the family unit, because a family does not have to be of the opposite sex, such as man and wife, nor blood-related. The true meaning of the word is those individuals who're willing to give their blood for the ones they love. A family can be people of the same sex. Remember, they don't have to be related by blood. Therefore, by the adoption of those children in a same-sex relationship they're a legitimate family."

"But Professor Hugenberg, why does the Webster's dictionary give such an erroneous definition of the word *family*? As if the family must consist of parents being male and female and the children must be related by blood."

"That's why I wanted this semester to begin by causing the students to question all things in the name of higher learning. Hence, the philosophy of Certainism."

"So, Dr. Hugenberg, is it right to say that religion has in fact imposed its *absolute truth* on a mindless society?"

"Yes, Mr. Grissom, that's exactly what religion has done to humanity. They have brainwashed society and expect us not to question their fabricated tenets. However, the Certainist questions everything and all things, even what he believes. That's why our society is not only going to see a redefinition of the word *family*, but we're also going see a different structure of the phrase *family unit* in the near future. Let me remind you that Hitler also executed many homosexuals in the name of his *master race*. Just give it some time: abortion and homosexuality are going to be decriminalized in some years. With all certainty, my theory of Certainism is more important than the inane teachings of religion, just as abortion is more important than morality, since it solves a self-engendered problem for the moment, existentially speaking, according to pragmatic common sense. We can't limit the rights of others by trying to make them what we think they ought to be."

"Professor Hugenberg, you mentioned your brother Georg."

"Yes."

"Did he ever make it back home?"

"No, he died on Iwo Jima in 1944."

After a pause, I continued. "In 1845, the state of New York was the first state to change its laws about abortion, and it started penalizing women who sought to have abortions. The 1850s saw an unreasonable attempt to outlaw abortion in the United Sates. Then in 1873, the federal government made it illegal for anyone to send information about therapeutic abortions in the mail. But please note, I believe the Supreme Court in the future will legalize abortion. The Ninth Amendment guarantees women the right to have an abortion by making that certain choice, and if the government is going to expect women to be responsible for their children, then they have to give women the freedom to make those choices if they want to keep or abort their children, for this is the reality of the Ninth Amendment, that certain right to choose."

"Professor Hugenberg, the theory of Certainism means the freedom of choosing what you want without fear of reprisal, particularly with the guilt trip of religion."

"My goodness, some of you are actually getting it. Yes, that's precisely what this postwar philosophy is all about. Why should you apologize for the way you are, and what you do? A healthy self-esteem is feeling good about yourself."

With that statement, the young man who previously had asked me, "So Dr. Hugenberg, you don't have a problem if someone is a homosexual?" stood up and said, "Hey, Professor Hugenberg, I know I can't speak for everyone here, but my roommate and I are going to enjoy your class. What you're sharing about your philosophy is amazing!"

"Well, I'm glad to hear that. By the way, what's your name, young man?"

"Sorry, Professor Hugenberg, it's Harley Banks, and my roommate is Zack Clifford. I read in your first book where you wrote that Certainism is the active participation of reason over morality. Man, that's deep, because with your philosophical theory of Certainism, there's a battle that's being waged in the realm of intellectualism and religion. And with the theory of Certainism and the existentialist views, human beings can only define themselves through the metaphysics of their actions, their certain decisive decisions, according to the Ninth Amendment. Therefore, these actions of choice can only be fulfilled in the realm of one's reason."

The eyes of all the students were fixed on him, as if they were amazed by Harley Banks's deep insight on Certainism, and how he interpreted my philosophical theory, which is described in my first book.

"Yes, that's correct, and I'm very impressed by your forensic philosophical observation of Certainism. I can see that you're a true Certainist."

Just then, Harley Banks asked a question I'd never forget.

"Dr. Hugenberg, would say that the abdication of Edward VIII, in 1936, played an integral part in the outcome of the war?"

"That's a very profound question, Mr. Banks, and I'm surprised that someone in this class asked an interesting question like that. I was sixteen when I heard King Edward VIII speak on the radio, and even though I was just a boy, I knew that the world later on would understand the magnitude of this historical event. If the former king had not abdicated, the outcome of the war would have been catastrophic. Britain would have been with the Axis, rather than with the Allies, since the former king, who's now the Duke of Windsor, is in fact a Nazi sympathizer."

"I read an article about the Duke and Duchess of Windsor, and how they visited Hitler, and that many high-ranking Nazi officers were their close friends."

"Yes, that's correct, Mr. Banks. Please bear in mind that for the concentration camps of Nazi Germany, the Nazis got that idea from the Brits and the Boer War of 1899 to 1902. *Die Geschichte der Menschheit ist faszinierend: the history of mankind is fascinating*. Most people aren't aware of the impact of the Boer War and how it influenced the nation of Germany in its policy of ethnic cleansing. When the Boer War began in 1899, between the Dutch colonizers, the Boers, in South Africa, and the British Empire, the Dutch settlers did not want the Brits to rule them. Therefore, the Boer War was the conflict between the British and Dutch. However, the British Empire at first struggled to conquer the Dutch settlers in South Africa, until Field Marshal Lord Kitchener came on the scene in 1902, with his plans of brutal attrition that resulted in his unhygienic concentration camps. Thousands of women and children died as a result Lord Kitchener's plans. The nation of Germany kept a close eye on the events in South Africa. Hence, Lord Kitchener's concentration camps eventually evolved into Germany's mechanized system of destruction for the Jews of Europe."

"But Professor Hugenberg, weren't the concentration camps of Nazi Germany a feint? Did the Holocaust really happen? My dad said it didn't."

"Your dad is entitled to vent his views about the six million Jews who died in these camps. But to deny the Holocaust, Mr. Grissom, is to deny the reality of reason. Remember, I was there. I saw firsthand what Germany did to the Jews of Europe."

"Dr. Hugenberg, I read in your book on Certainism how *Religenocide* is in fact the first offspring of your philosophy. Also, I was impressed about Bill 67, and how this bill can be used to silence religion and its rhetoric of hatred about certain people. Does the number sixty-seven have some special significance?"

"Yes, I chose the number sixty-seven because, as a Certainist, six is the number of man, humanity, and seven is the number of perfection. To the Certainist humanity is ultimate reality, so Bill 67 is a bill I know will protect the rights of many individuals that religion may seek to disparage. Bill 67, I'm hoping, is going to be like the *Verbotsgesetz* Law of 1947, which prohibits the rise of Nazism in Austria. So, just like with the *VerbotsG Act* of 1947, which is the law that prohibits the rhetoric and all neo-Nazi activities in Austria, the theory of *Religenocide* will eventually manifest itself in Bill 67, which is like the *Verbotsgesetz* Law, prohibiting all rhetoric in the religious arena from being spoken against certain citizens."

"Nazism began in the mind of Anton Drexler in Munich in 1919, and the doctrine of the *Final Solution* came to life by the words and the literary content of the Nazi regime. The power of the pen is fascinating. Charles Dickens used his pen to reveal to the middle-class subjects of Great Britain, through his novels, the social unrest reinforced by the Poor Law of 1834, and the Victorian Industrial Revolution. He wrote books like *Bleak House*, *Nicholas Nickleby*, *Little Dorrit*, and *Great Expectations* primarily to make known and speak out on a particular thing about which he had deep concerns: the poverty and injustices ubiquitous in the British Empire."

"The power of the pen is phenomenal. The pen in the literary fiction form can strongly express certain views in reference to the political, social, and ecclesiastical dilemmas in the world. The pen can challenge and stir the people's hearts as it depicts a persuasive animation of relevant issues that have been oversimplified for too long."

"So, students that's why I was compelled to put my ideas of Certainism in the format of my first book, because religion has blinded the minds of many in the name of their superstitious beliefs. I grew up in the Lutheran Church, until I left it at the age of sixteen, but prior to leaving that house of torment, for many years I heard about the diatribes of Martin Luther against the Jews. In his writings, again, the power of the pen influenced the Nazi regime in Germany."

"Dr. Hugenberg, I'm really impressed by your theories. And what you shared today has really opened my eyes! Religion is the first institution that has instigated and propagated all superstitious tenets, and what it teaches, Professor Hugenberg, is in fact against the reason of intellectualism."

I couldn't believe what Kyle Davison, who came from a religious home, was saying. I knew Olga was right: there were those who were eager to receive my philosophy of Certainism.

"That's very kind of you, Mr. Davison. However, it was our eighteenth president, Ulysses S. Grant, who once said: '*I shall have no policy of my own to enforce against the will of the people.*' And the sad fact of this reality is that religions are still forcing their beliefs on others in the name of their God."

I was able to complete my subject as my session came an end, but I was really surprised by the students' response to my theory. More than half the class gathered around me for questions, and there were many words of commendation about my books and lecture. There were about thirty students waiting, but Harley and Zack just waited patiently for their turn. They were the last two to speak with me.

"Dr. Hugenberg, I can't express to you the honor it is to finally meet you! When Zack and I found out that you would be teaching this class, words couldn't express our excitement."

"I'm most pleased to hear this, Harley and Zack."

"We're very pleased to hear your views on the homosexual lifestyle, Dr. Hugenberg."

"Oh, is that why you asked that particular question?"

"Yes, Dr. Hugenberg. Zack and I were wondering about how you felt."

"Yes, I'm listening."

"Do you think you should share this with our professor?" Zack said to Harley.

"Listen, boys, I know where this is going, and as I wrote and said before, the privacy of certain choices is explicitly expressed in the Ninth Amendment. Furthermore, the privacy of your homosexual lifestyle is protected by the Ninth Amendment."

"You mean, you know about Zack and I being more than just friends?"

"I don't know about other people, but it's quite obvious to me. However, don't worry, what you've shared with me is quite safe. And as long as you get good grades in my class, I really don't care what you do in your private life."

"Well, we certainly appreciate your open-mindedness. But what we wanted to ask you: you said that the day is coming when they will decriminalize homosexuality."

"Yes."

"But what should the gay community do until that day? And what about gays in the military?"

"All the religious and biased laws are going to be changed in the future. But until that day comes, I say to you both: make your certain choice based on the philosophy of Certainism, and bear in mind that your rights are grounded in and protected by the Ninth Amendment. Don't allow religious institutions to make you feel guilty about yourselves.

Remember that religious institutions love to talk about their rights in the First Amendment. However, you need to remind those religious institutions of your rights in the Ninth Amendment, as an individual with human rights, which guarantees homosexuals the right to live their existential lifestyle without the fear of harassment from religious groups. Just remember, Harley and Zack, that Certainism and the Ninth Amendment protect you in the privacy of your choice, and your homosexual relationship. But you boys need to know what you want out of your relationship."

"We'd like to continue with our relationship when we graduate from college. Zack and I would like to continue living together as we're doing now, but we know that our parents would never agree to our lifestyle."

"So all of what you said about Certainism, and let me remind you of your words. '*I read in your first book where you wrote that Certainism is the active participation of the will over morality.*" *That's deep, because what you're saying is there's a battle that's going on in the realm of intellectualism and religion. And with the philosophy of Certainism and its existentialist views human beings can only define themselves mainly through their metaphysic thought process of their actions. Therefore, these actions of choice can only be fulfilled in the realm of one's reason.*"

With my verbatim recitation, they gazed at me and then said, "Yes, that's true, we get your point. It's for us not to be ashamed of who we are and what we do, because, as your book stated: '*You cannot like yourself if you deny what you are.*'"

"Yes, but please remember: walk with sound wisdom, because there are those out there, especially the conservative Christians in their religious settings, who will hate you for your stand in Certainism, and your lifestyle, because the Certainist is a revisionist of the religious tenets in conjunction with the Ninth Amendment."

"Thank you, Professor Hugenberg, we really do appreciate your openness and your clever advice."

"You're welcome. Maybe sometime in the future you and Zack can join my family for lunch or perhaps dinner."

"Gee, thanks, Professor Hugenberg, we'll really like that."

I said good-bye to them, but as I watched Harley and Zack walk away I said to myself, "These religious people think that their so-called *spirituality* makes them wise. However, it actually mitigates their intelligence, and most certainly amplifies their oafishness. They think that by condemning and judging others, it will force certain people to change their lifestyle for the purpose of pleasing their rigid religious tenets. But according to Certainism the homosexual lifestyle is only nature's way of keeping natural selection in perfect balance and harmony, and at the same time controlling the population of the earth. However, the only way the gay community can overcome the bigotry of religion, they, like Harley and Zack, will have to be honest with themselves and come out of the closet and '*Into the Streets.*'"

"For I know the day is coming when religion will no longer be viewed as the harmless eccentricity the majority of the masses have considered it to be for many millennia. In fact, Certainism will demonstrate to humanity that religion is actually a dangerous institution to society, and all those individuals who may value the attribute of their very own *Ahura Mazda*, which is mankind's way of wise reasoning, will prove indubitably that relevant truth is much more important than the mundane teachings of absolute truth, which religion has taught for too long. Religion is the vehicle of hatred and people cannot have any confidence or trust in religion, which always seeks to marginalize them. Religion refuses to comprehend the fact that: how can people like themselves when religion teaches them to deny what they really are? Therefore, a healthy and intelligent society must stop at nothing when it comes to cleansing itself of the caitiff, wretched influences of religion. Certainism is a philosophy that will inevitably inspire a new revelatory movement against the bigotry of religion. Religion was in fact the first form of all superstitions, which has blinded the human race to all logical reason, and this is a *nuda verilas* according to historical data. The theory of Certainism will take the earth by storm and be the revelatory movement of the Certainist, for this is the beginning of *Stormy Whether.*"

www.ingramcontent.com/pod-product-compliance
Lightning Source LLC
Chambersburg PA
CBHW052004020726
47501CB00004B/999